What people are

Burn, Beautiful Soul

Some books stay with a reader long after they're read. *Burn, Beautiful Soul* is one of them. Donahue's strong, clever narrative delivers a truly unique and entertaining story. The reader believes Basil, believes *in* Basil, and wants this monstrous demon to succeed as he walks among us. It's *Stranger in a Strange Land* for literary horror enthusiasts.

**Chris Bauer**, author of *Binge Killer*, *Hiding Among the Dead*, *Scars on the Face of God* and *Jane's Baby*

At times unnerving and unsettling, Donahue's prose is as beautiful as it is frightening. ... [He] reminds us that Hell isn't just a place—it's what we make of those places we call home. With enough humor to lighten the mood, and not discount the sensory experiences on the page, Donahue has written a masterful novel that fans of Christopher Moore and Joe Hill are sure to fall in love with.

**H.A. Callum**, author of *Whispers in the Alders*

Basil the demon escapes from Hell, eager to find a better world. The world he finds is ours. But is it better? He finds crass exploitation, abuse, and murder. He finds beauty in nature, and innocence and generosity in the hearts of friends. He finds the troubled and topsy-turvy world we know, a place so deranged that even a demon can fit in—for a while. Basil is not an innocent. He is a demon king, with baggage of his own. He kills the first two people he meets. His clumsy attempts at romance are touching but catastrophic. Eventually, his past and our world's intolerance collide in a violent and shocking climax. *Burn, Beautiful Soul* is *The Wizard of Oz* with a demon Dorothy.

It is Camus's *The Stranger* of late capitalism. It is a loving but unsentimental dissection of America and its people. It is a story you will never forget.

**John Schoffstall**, author of *Half-Witch*

All hell breaks loose when an oversized demon bursts from the bowels of the earth to become an advertising exec in the American Midwest. Such is the ingenuity of William J. Donahue, whose often-unearthly characters manage to reveal much about the human condition. An imaginative farce.

**Don Swaim**, author of *The Assassination of Ambrose Bierce: A Love Story, Man with Two Faces* and *The H.L. Mencken Murder Case*

# Burn, Beautiful Soul

A Novel

# Burn, Beautiful Soul

## A Novel

## William J. Donahue

COSMIC EGG
BOOKS

Winchester, UK
Washington, USA

JOHN HUNT PUBLISHING

First published by Cosmic Egg Books, 2020
Cosmic Egg Books is an imprint of John Hunt Publishing Ltd., 3 East St., Alresford,
Hampshire SO24 9EE, UK
office@jhpbooks.net
www.johnhuntpublishing.com
www.cosmicegg-books.com

For distributor details and how to order please visit the 'Ordering' section on our website.

Text copyright: William J. Donahue 2019

ISBN: 978 1 78904 526 0
978 1 78904 527 7 (ebook)
Library of Congress Control Number: 2019953644

A CIP catalogue record for this book is available from the British Library.

Design: Stuart Davies

UK: Printed and bound by CPI Group (UK) Ltd, Croydon, CR0 4YY
US: Printed and bound by Thomson-Shore, 7300 West Joy Road, Dexter, MI 48130

We operate a distinctive and ethical publishing philosophy in
all areas of our business, from our global network of authors to
production and worldwide distribution.

For Randy G., "only a phone call away"

**Previous Books by William J. Donahue**

*Too Much Poison*
ISBN: 978-1496957856

*Filthy Beast: Fiendish Lullabies*
ISBN: 978-0595337057

*Brain Cradle: Menagerie of the Perverse*
ISBN: 978-0595270293

"We are each our own devil, and we make this world our hell."
*Oscar Wilde*

# Prologue

## Too Far Gone

On the surface, the mortal world feels the subtlest of shifts—a sour scent caught in the wind, a momentary quickening of Earth's rotation, a darkening.

As the month shifts from July to August in the calendar year 1997 A.D., the landscape five hundred miles north and south of the equator roasts in the grip of an oven-like swelter. Shallow streams run dry. Asphalt cracks. Mouths parch. Clouds of biting, stinging, burrowing insects choke the humid sky. The deep-fried human brain inches to the brink of incivility. With the gentlest of nudges, from agents both unseen and inhuman, madness erupts into gleeful acts of chaos, maiming and, naturally, murder.

In Indianapolis, Indiana, the slowly beating heart of the world's greatest nation, a husband strangles his wife of nine years until her face turns purple. An hour later he twines an electrical cord around his own throat and steps off the edge of a folding chair, seeking something he imagines will somehow outshine the place where he has wasted thirty-six years of human life.

Two hours north, in a treeless neighborhood on Chicago's South Side, a twelve-year-old Haitian boy named Claude retrieves a nickel-plated revolver from an unlocked strongbox beneath his parents' bed and wanders from room to room, intent on erasing all traces of his siblings. Within the span of four minutes, his three sisters, including a baby asleep in her wobbly thrift-store crib, and a brother—none of them older than ten—lie dead, leaking precious fluids onto crumb-speckled bed sheets and floor planks sprinkled with dried-up mouse droppings. He decides his parents deserve a similar end, so he slips a fresh bullet into each hungry chamber and waits for their return. As he eases the barrel back into its proper place, he delights at the satisfying

1

*click*. He moves to descend the stairs. The blood-streaked tread of his left sneaker slips on the creaking wood of the second step and he tumbles forward, violently, helplessly, each step rising up to break his brittle bones. The injuries include irreparable harm to several segments of his spinal cord. He settles at the base of the stairs and waits for his final wheezing breaths to leave him, his mind screaming until the moment his body becomes a lifeless rag doll soaked in the gore of his slaughtered kin.

Eight hundred miles east, in Philadelphia's University City neighborhood, a twenty-one-year-old man studying economics at Drexel University diligently grinds his naked genitals against those of an unconscious sophomore who stars on the girls' lacrosse team. Done in by a mostly vodka screwdriver spiked with Rohypnol, the nineteen-year-old victim lies on her back, legs yawning open to expose her downy thatch, her head lolling from one side to the other, as the criminal grinding turns to criminal penetration. Her body protests, yet it fails to reject this alien thing inside her. No doubt the young man's parents, both attorneys whose courtroom victories have earned them shared ownership of an ivy-shagged mansion on the prestigious Main Line and a summer home two blocks from the surf in Avalon, New Jersey, will be very, very proud. He has not yet considered what to do with this mousy little girl once he has finished filling her up, but he knows Mom and Dad will love their perfect little boy no matter what happens next.

It is a fine time in the world's history for bad behavior. Given humans' obsession with outdoing one another, escalation is inevitable.

Out west, on the outskirts of Boise, Idaho, a mob of friends in their early twenties exits a nightclub looking to keep the party going. They find their fun at the expense of a fifty-year-old homeless man originally from Milwaukee, a battle-hardened Marine Corps veteran who survived the hell of Vietnam, no less. Teasing quickly turns to barbarism. They take turns raining blows upon this tattered man, whose sin consists solely of "stinking up" a neighborhood they cherish, even though none of them lives within ten miles of the place that will soon be labeled a crime scene. Instinct urges the vet to cover his head with both arms, leaving his midsection exposed. Two girls drive spiked heels into the victim's ribs, while their boyfriends deliver multiple kicks to the face and back of the head. The assault is "all in good fun," as one of them will tell the police the following morning, but they realize they have taken it too far when one of them caves in the veteran's skull with the curved end of a tire iron.

Horrors of an even more atrocious nature unfold across the oceans, in Russia and North Korea, in India and Pakistan, in Afghanistan and Syria, in Somalia and Nigeria, and in the wildly overcrowded, smog-choked cities of China and Brazil, India and Egypt, Indonesia and Bangladesh.

The only logical explanation: The mortal world somehow senses the looming arrival of a new steward, a beast born and nurtured in a vile, shadowy place. Humans figure they might as well do their worst now so they can prepare themselves to witness misdeeds too repulsive for even the most diabolical mind to imagine.

# Chapter 1

# A Knot Undone

Far beneath the earth's thick skin, a well-tended stew cooks in more than a hundred cauldrons. Oily bubbles pop to foul the air with the sweet stink of rot. The sheen of charred fat caulking each cauldron's rim glimmers in the firelight. Aligned seven rows deep, the cauldrons hold enough parasite-rich slurry to feed an army of unimaginable size.

Starbursts of baked-on blood stain the walls a dark, syrupy brown. Charred roots and used-up bodies—limbless, headless and eviscerated or otherwise undone—pile in every corner as fuel for the eternal furnace. Life should not thrive here, yet creatures slither shyly through the shadows, wary of bigger things that might consume them. Or simply kill them, just because they can, because the opportunity arises, because this is the way it must be.

Humanoid skulls, ribcages and other trophies of torture litter the cavern floor, some hung as decorations on the jagged spires of rock that poke, like teeth, through a low-lying haze. The cavern serves as a graveyard as well as it does an able kitchen. Hand-carved runes decorate the red rock, and a massive metal sign spiked high into the wall serves as a makeshift billboard. Blackened from an age in the fire and smoke, the sign greets newcomers in more than a hundred languages.

*Rahmat. Isibingelelo. Soo dhawoow. Vitejte. Tuaj los. Mwabonwa. Swaagatam. Willkommen. Bienvenue.* Welcome.

Howls carom off bone-smooth arcs of rock to echo in the hollow spaces. The din of suffering drones on, uninterrupted, just as it has for centuries, and as it will, in all likelihood, until the end of time. Spirals of green, stinking-egg smoke seep from cracks in the floor and tunnel through matching cracks in the ceiling, toward the surface far more than a mile overhead.

Each species doomed to live here has steeled itself to the inhospitable environment, though the scaly bipeds lurking in the shadows and climbing the walls are a notable exception. Although their physical bodies have evolved to endure life in the smoke and darkness, their minds conjure dreams in which they live elsewhere—anywhere but here. Each of these ghastly humanoids has a stark choice: Endure the sentence quietly, or grumble to those who will not tolerate such weakness. Those with keener minds keep quiet to mitigate the risk of having their backs whipped, beaten or broken—or, more likely, face an even harsher punishment.

Mercy and understanding have no place here.

Reptilian vampire bats the size of pterodactyls fight for toeholds in high-rise rookeries, resorting to cannibalism when needed—anything for an easier route to the hunting grounds or a better view of the proceedings below. Guano drops to the cavern floor in thunderous globs, in turn providing food for parasites much farther down the food chain. Other gargantuan beasts scuttle across the crater-pocked floor.

A twenty-foot-long millipede gnaws on a heavily tattooed forearm with four clawed fingers. Loose crumbles of rock dance beneath its thousand feathered legs. The mammoth invertebrate senses the approach of something it wants no part of, so it retreats into a tear in the wounded earth.

* * *

"I could vomit, not that I would permit anyone to see," Basil whispers to his companion. His coal-black flesh craves the shadows. His right hoof kicks a loose stone across the cavern floor. The stone strikes a boulder and ricochets like a shot pinball.

"Methinks they would consider your discarded bile a gift," says Kamala, her voice rising from the darkness. "They would sip from the puddle, lap up every drop."

"I'd sooner choke on it or swallow it back down."

"Irritable, I see. What troubles you, sweet prince?"

Basil ticks off the laundry list of offenses deserving of his indignation: the stink of death and feces; the tedious, unchanging terrain; the stale and smoke-dense air he is forced to breathe; his weary mind, tired from lack of sleep; the cruelty of every beast he must keep under hoof, mostly the rabble of soulless villains he must rule; memories of the horrors he has committed in the name of theater, all to maintain his fragile hold on this thing called power.

Discontent consumes him as the pair approach a massive lake of blood, bordered by ancient stalagmites slowly turning to powder. Bubbles burp to the lake's sludge-like surface. He quickly realizes his error—his hooves much too close to the crimson shore—and turns away, eager to keep his distance from the reaches of the clever thing lurking in the depths.

The simple act of existing too long as lord and keeper of this wretched pit has spent his patience. He retreats into the deep shadows, seeing but unseen. For too long he has wished to remain hidden and, more to the point, unbothered.

Across the cavern, two demons bicker over a mostly denuded femur flecked with bits of charred flesh. The smaller demon holds the bone close to his chest, while the taller one attempts to pry the prize away. The smaller one suggests the bone is his and his alone because he found it first, because he earned it. The larger one disagrees and then proves his point by gouging out both of the smaller demon's eyes. The blinded demon screams and drops to his knees, palming the floor, seeking, as if his eyeballs have tumbled from their sockets and he can undo his blindness simply by finding the rogue orbs and then returning each one to its rightful place. The larger demon picks up the dropped femur and, unsatisfied with the lack of sustenance it might afford, tosses the bone aside. The aggressor then decides to replace his trophy with something more generous, so he pins the smaller demon to the floor and removes one of his victim's legs, followed by the other. Tendons pop. Muscles tear. Bones snap. The smaller demon, now legless and eyeless and screaming in agony, begs to wake up from this nightmare.

Basil recognizes the victimized demon, though this one is among the Nameless—those who have done nothing to earn a sobriquet and the freedoms that come with it—and, therefore, insignificant. A demon's will to survive is incredibly strong, Basil knows, yet he foresees the outcome to the episode: The wounded demon will burrow into the nearest crevice, where he will wither, starve and soon enough become prey for beetles and other diminutive critters pleased to consume him in the most efficient manner. He is proven wrong when the taller demon stands over his vanquished brother, raises one of the severed legs and, mercifully, clubs him into oblivion.

Basil knows he should have intervened, for the sake of fairness, of justice, but he stops to consider his inaction. He does not want to lead today. Better put, he is no longer fit to lead. He wants only to close his eyes and sleep. But to sleep here, he knows, is to show weakness. And to show weakness is to welcome death, or at least become an eyeless, legless, pitiful creature, a bludgeoned heap waiting to be reborn as vermin excrement.

"I could vomit," he tells Kamala again. "Kiss my lips and you can taste the puke warming the back of my throat. I just hate it. This damned place."

"Let's walk. Your kingdom has no bounds. I always say you should make a point to see more of it."

"My hatred for this place has no bounds either. I despise it all," he adds, raising an arm in a sweeping motion, with a flourish. "Every stinking, bloody inch."

"Our Fiery Home?"

"Let it be someone else's burden for a time," he says. "These ancient legs need stretching. Time to shake off the ash of this miserable sewer and see something new."

"But this is home, my prince," says Kamala. "And we call you our god."

Bald and thin, with long ghoulish ears, Kamala is a beauty among her fellow she-demons. Her tautly muscled arms contrast the soft flesh of her sagging breasts, the peak of each inch-long nipple made raw from overuse.

"You have no need to go anywhere," she says. "At your command, you have everything you could possibly crave. Name your want and I shall fetch it and lay it at the tips of your hooves."

Basil does not want to argue. He knows he can lie to her and say he simply wants to wander for a while, to acquaint himself with the filthy humans his people have been torturing from afar for as long as he can remember. Yet he has always found honesty to be the quickest cut. He will simply tell her he is bored—so bored, in fact, that if he were able he would have done himself in ages ago.

This terminal indifference has made him weak, exhausted. The weight of his cruelty in staving off one insurrection after another, of serving the penalty for his own sins, has made him a worthless leader.

He misses the comforts his vivid dreams have shown him—things he has never actually seen, tasted or experienced, as far as he knows, yet his unconscious mind feeds him visions so crisp, so stunning, he knows they must exist somewhere. Sun-drenched fields, rivers, trees, starlit skies, birds of every color—he knows these things by name, though he cannot explain how. He misses the up-close odors of an unwashed human woman who has given herself willingly, the magic of his skin against hers, the huff of her hot breath on his bearded neck. He imagines the softness of tilled earth and the raw coldness of snow, the taste of water from an unpolluted stream and the sense of pollen. Oddly, he misses bread and cheese, the simple way they plug his gut.

For too long his diet has been only meat, mostly raw and bloody.

They wander in shadow until Basil decides he is fit to be seen, until he can wait no longer. He steps fully into the firelight—all seven and a half feet of him—and the tongues of flame define his heavily muscled biceps and pectorals, the curve of his round belly, the spiral contours of his oversized ram horns. His smooth, black hooves gleam in the fiery glare, their tips as sharp as cleavers, honed by the red rock. He aches for a reprieve only soft earth can offer.

"I have called this place my prison for too long," he says. "I can abide it no longer. I cannot imagine how you do either, how any of us do."

Kamala says nothing in response, and Basil guesses she remains silent because she knows she has no say in the matter. Besides, she does not dare to insult her lord. Few do, and those who have ...

Thick cloven hooves crack the red rock as Basil observes the kingdom he has built. Our Fiery Home belongs to him, in a way, but every other denizen may claim ownership too—a warzone fit for sharing. Demons skulk in the sanctuary of near darkness and seethe in penance as their lord passes. Each of them wants him dead, he knows, and before long he finds the proof he does not want.

An undersized demon throws a pebble that bounces off one of Basil's horns—marbled and curved like a shofar. Basil turns to eye his cowardly assailant, who flees for the safety of the shadows. He deftly carves a two-ton boulder out of the wall and hurls it. The boulder crushes the Nameless demon into globs of green and red, and rolls to a stop against a stone column. Part of the roof caves in and blankets the antechamber in a fine, red dust. Earth shakes as its underworld settles.

Basil learned early into his reign that the seeds of mutiny cannot be permitted to take root, but he is tired of fighting to sustain a legacy built on malice and brutality. He bristles at the thought of breathing this noxious, stifling air for the rest of eternity—for even another stinking bout of sleeplessness. He despises the thankless demons and imps and ghouls. The idea of taking another meal from a bubbling pot filled with putrescent remains sickens him. He tires of the ever-present stench, so much like the stink of an unwashed anus. But mostly he hates the view, or lack thereof. He longs for peaceful colors and open spaces, for the shade of trees and the chirping of birds and moonlight and the wind whispering secrets into his ear—things he knows cannot be disregarded as myth.

"What about our home?" Kamala asks. "What becomes of it if you step away?"

"There is nothing to break or destroy. No more than I have, at least."

"There will be chaos."

"Isn't there always?"

"It will be different this time. They will try to follow you."

"No. They will try to flee. The Nameless will attempt to take their freedom, which is not theirs to take. Then, when they realize the fruitlessness of their toil, they will try to seize the reins. You will manage, I'm sure. Understand, Kamala: I don't make this move recklessly. I must have a reprieve from this burden. Every moment passes with the urge to paint my hooves with vomit. You will suffer the same curse by the time I return. It's the poison in this place."

"Do you worry for me?"

"You have all the faith I can muster. You are the only one who has earned it, in fact."

Basil stops to lean his forehead against a pane of brimstone. He rears back slowly, like the arm of a trebuchet, and then bangs his head into the soot-smoked rock until it spider-webs, crumbles and collapses into bits. A moment later he steps back to admire the twin indentations matching the outlines of his exquisite horns.

Kamala offers a sadistic smile, her usual countenance.

"What is it you ask of me? To succeed you, my prince?"

"Consider it a temporary promotion."

Her smile deepens.

He knows she has been craving his power, as they all have. And he knows she will not want to relinquish control if he returns—*when* he returns, he reminds himself. Another problem for another day, he decides.

"You face an unpleasant task," he tells her. "They will come for you. They will try to wrest the crown from your head, as if you had a crown to wear. Make the right allies, or have none at all. Seek the wisdom of the Council. Use the warlords to make war, to crush any uprisings. Kill whomever you must. Punish the rest, harshly, joyfully, without restraint."

"All stick and no carrot, you say."

"Precisely. I shall depart at my leisure."

He knows he won't return for some time, so he must make fresh memories of the things he will crave. He approaches a pyramid of wet dung, each of the ten or twelve turds just big enough to fit in the palm of his hand. Likely from one of the outsized vampire bats that linger in the crevices above, he guesses. He picks up the nearest clump of guano and sniffs it to be sure—still moist, reeking of digested carrion. He cups the turd in his hands until it's almost a perfect sphere and then brings it to his lips. He whispers the grammar for animation in *Locuri*, the ancient language of the underworld. He then returns the dung ball to its place on the cavern floor and gives it a gentle nudge. Nothing happens at first, but patience has its rewards. After a moment, the dung ball creeps forward—a cautious inch in one direction, two inches in another—and then rolls away on its own volition, sentient but stupid.

Basil smiles at his munificence for having breathed life into something as simple as a ball of shit. His thoughts then turn to satisfying another urge. He leads Kamala into his chamber, knowing he must make quick work of her. Her eyes grow wide as he takes her by the throat. Digging his talons into the flesh until the tips touch bone, he bends her over a scalding-hot stone. Her skin sizzles against the rock as he penetrates her, from behind—always from behind. He claws at her back and palms her naked skull as he reaches climax. As his semen sprays her scarred back, she reacts as if each drop melts her flesh. He doubts his departure for the briefest of moments, considering how fond he has grown of the glorious pocket between Kamala's legs.

"Do not disappoint me," he growls as he releases her.

"Never, my liege," she squeals. "Any other words of wisdom you offer I will gladly accept."

"None more than I have already shared. Remember: They will seek to end you, because they know no better."

"I expect it. I will crush every uprising."

She does her best to hide her smile of undoing.

He turns and walks out of the chamber, past a legion of imps and demons and other creatures that have no place in a human world, all of which seem to know something strange—something exciting—is about to happen. With Kamala at his side, he passes beneath the outsized welcome sign, past the bubbling cauldrons, doing one final survey of his kingdom.

An imposing young demon, Gideon, emerges from the throngs. He kicks aside a quartet of playful imps and kneels before Basil.

"Your raiders have returned, Lord."

"It's about time."

* * *

"Nothing will change," Basil assures his masses. His booming words will echo through the subterranean realm for a full year. Kamala stands at his shoulder. "Kamala will lead you in my absence. Know this: I will be watching."

The horde cheers at the prospect of the dark shepherd's departure. Some demons have already begun to plot an overthrow. Of this Basil is certain.

He recalls a prior conversation held in the Hall of Ignoble and Prodigious Elders, where he sought the counsel of his closest advisers. The nine members of his Council of Unerring Wisdom were in agreement: Staging the abandonment of his throne and leaving it in the hands of another—a female, no less, meaning Kamala, his crafty administrator—was a poor idea indeed. The dynamics will change in his absence, they said. Chaos and murder will reign, they said. The underworld will forget him, they said. Life in Our Fiery Home will, quite simply, move on.

"The weight of the crown must always be felt, the lash of your whip endured," Calvin, his most trusted adviser, told him. "One does not find himself in such a position because he is kind and forgiving. Your predecessors—"

"I am not interested in the folly of those who fell before me," Basil snapped. "Do not take my exodus as an abdication. A break from here will benefit me—benefit *us*. Every leader must step away for a time to take the temperature of the world around him, to learn from those he considers his betters so he may lead his people more effectively."

"But, sir, who could possibly be your better?" said Lubos, an uninvited guest, lurking in the doorway.

Lubos, the deceitful ghoul Basil had been considering turning to dust for as long as he could remember.

"If I may," Lubos adds, "the title of ruler does not entitle its holder to the treasures of escape, of leisure."

"Watch your tongue, beetle dung," Basil told him. "You forget your place beneath my hoof."

Basil studied the white scar that ran the length of Lubos's lean body, the reminder of the day he was torn in two by a trio of mindless troglodytes. Even Basil could not fathom the depths of such agony, though he had let it happen and, in fact, had encouraged it. Yet Lubos had survived the ordeal, had endured the torture of having his halved body stitched back together, of having each nerve-rich organ stuffed back into its rightful place, however imperfectly, by a troupe of well-meaning imps. After Lubos recovered from the surgery, one of his hips sat higher than the other. As a result, he walked with a noticeable limp, and one arm drooped several inches lower than the other. Regardless, the war wounds seemed to have invigorated him. They somehow made him stronger, meaner, more sadistic.

"Forgive me, my liege. Surely you know what is best." And then Lubos slithered from the chamber.

Basil mulls the idea of putting Lubos to death prior to his departure, and making sure every imp and every demon in every level of the underworld sees it. Lubos's strength and enterprise are matched only by his love for atrocity and the depths of his deceit. Even now, Basil knows Lubos will be Kamala's biggest problem. Kamala deserves a tranquil beginning to her temporary reign, if not relative peace for the duration of his absence. She will contend with mutinies and attempts on her life, but he wonders if she will have the capacity to fend off a revolt led by someone as charismatic as Lubos.

Basil chooses to let Lubos remain for no reason other than apathy. Besides, he considers, perhaps it will be better for Kamala to face a known devil than have a far worse fiend rise up in his place.

He tells his horde he will leave tomorrow, though underground there is no dividing line between days, only a gauzy separation between the moment a demon closes his eyes to sleep, if he sleeps, and the moment his eyes open. "Tomorrow" has no meaning other than "soon". Red and blue fires burn without end, the corners forever alive with shadow.

"So tonight," he says. "Tonight we feast!"

He grasps his sharpened pike by the length of shaft between

two skulls—one human, the other a horned demon. He points the pike toward the back of the cavern, where a band of demons hoists an enormous wooden raft bearing twelve tusked elephants, six giraffes, three striped horses and dozens of naked humans, most of them female. The humans howl as their flesh melts away, dangling in fatty strips from their arms, legs and bellies.

Basil parts the crowd, trampling a few lesser demons in his haste, and strides toward the raft. As the raiding party scatters, the raft falls to the cavern floor and lands with a thunderous *boom*.

An elephant trumpets in horror at Basil's approach, and then breaks free of its bonds. Basil seizes the elephant by its rear leg and slams the beast into the nearest wall. It thrashes pointlessly, and the thrashing soon turns to twitching, then stillness. He lifts the pachyderm's head off the floor and slits the coarse flesh of its throat with his talon-tipped finger. He then slips both hands into the fresh wound and, with one twist, removes the elephant's head. Male demons kneel before him to fill their mouths with the rain of spilled blood, suckling, as if it were milk from a giving teat.

He will not miss this place.

* * *

The cavern descends into frenzy as the horde makes quick work of the elephants, giraffes and zebras, deconstructing living bodies into strips of fatty meat. Demons drag the human females into shadowed corners, where unimaginable horrors await. Basil does not recall authorizing the kidnappings, merely the hunt for exotic game to fill their coffers with fresh flesh, but he knows it's pointless to micromanage, to obsess over every detail. If not the humans, the demons would rape and maim each other. They have learned by following his example, after all. He pities the humans for the carnal nightmares they will suffer before they too become meat.

While the demons feast and sodomize their quarry, he begins the process of his silent escape. He pauses at the front of his chamber and eyes the walls, where he has carved or painted so many of his words with the slurry of ash and black blood. His chest swells with pride at the poetry of his mind, though he's lost track of each poem's meaning. He studies one of his favorites—"The villains come to plunder, the innocent come to bruise and bleed, the beautiful souls come to be set free"—and mutters the tercet twice before backing away.

He has nothing to take with him—no possessions. He has never left the sanctuary of this wicked kingdom, so he does not know how he should feel. Everything will be different above ground, beneath the sun, the moon and the open sky, rich with a million stars, or so he has been told. Fear of what he will find rises in his gut, and he chooses to ignore the emotion because no good can come of it.

Besides, nothing can keep him here for another tomorrow.

His hooves lead him toward the front of the cavern. He weaves between the rows of cauldrons bubbling with shit-meat, reaching out to touch the curved belly of each cauldron, if only to remember the sensation of hot iron on his fingertips. He bends to collect a bowl from the loose pile—a cratered skull, bleached and emptied of its gray matter—and dips it into the simmering slurry.

Though he knows he must leave, doubt weighs on his mind. His eyes wander to the darkened entrance of the Hall of Ignoble and Prodigious Elders, zeroing in on the grayish silhouette of a frail, broken-down demon. Damir.

Damir has never been shy about reminding Basil of his failures, whether or not Basil wanted to be reminded. Basil passes the fuming bowl to Damir, who holds it between two fleshy stumps where his hands had once been.

"So you're actually going to do it," Damir says. He chews on a malignant wart that has eaten away much of his lower lip. "You're going to run away like a coward."

Damir downs the slurry. Bits of meat cling to the stubble on his chin.

"You're mistaken, old one," Basil responds. "I'm embarking on a journey."

"Weak, scared, running away—that's more like it. You think wandering far enough and long enough will enable you to purge whatever poison's muddying your mind. Then, once you're all better, you'll just come back here and walk through the front door like nothing ever happened, every problem solved. Your thinking's all bat shit."

"Tread lightly, Damir," Basil says coolly.

"Why start now? This'll be the last time I see your ugly mug anyway. Wait until you see what's waiting for you topside. Ruthless savages—every last one of them."

"I'll tame that world like I've tamed this one."

Damir cackles. His laughter turns to fitful coughing.

"Even if that were true, even if the humans don't put a cudgel to every inch of your back, you'll find nothing left for you if you come back this way."

"I have faith in Kamala."

"Shit for brains! She'll have you turned inside out. You just had to make a show of your retreat. You just had to announce it to the world like a moron, like a dumb fool. You should've just slipped out the door and come back when you were good and ready. Every demon in this place has already forgotten you."

Damir's ragged laughter stokes Basil's temper.

"Quiet your trap, hoary fuck!"

Basil bends at the waist, his eyes lost in the clouds of Damir's cataracts.

Damir claps his stumps together.

"Pip-pip and cheerio," Damir says. "Be gone with you."

17

"I don't know why I'd expect you to wish me well."

"Basil ..."

"Yes?"

"My gratitude for the soup."

Damir tosses the empty bowl at Basil's hooves.

"Don't forget what you're leaving behind," Damir adds. "The beast in the basement, I mean. Whatever you leave behind will be waiting for you when you return. *If* you return."

Basil turns, intent on thrashing Damir as penance for his loose tongue. Instead, he takes a deep breath and permits this one last jab. Damir knows too much for his own good, but he's smart, cagey—knows which secrets to keep to his ragged, old self. How else would a crippled old demon have survived for so long?

Before anyone else can grab his ear, Basil makes a beeline toward the massive door that will grant him his freedom.

"You would leave this place, and leave me, without giving a proper goodbye?"

*Kamala.*

She leans against the wall of the nursery, the Hardened Womb, where newborn demons coo and howl and draw milk from their mothers.

"You would have noticed my absence eventually," he tells her.

"I thought you would have made our parting of ways a more formal affair."

He places his right hand on her shoulder and then pinches her chin between two fingers. He almost leans in to kiss her, for some reason he can't explain, but kills the urge.

"Do not rule too harshly," he says. "Or, worse, too kindly."

The Nameless, he reminds her, have limited purpose: to submit, to serve, to obey.

"Of course, my liege," she says.

"Be wary of those who wish to help you."

"Travel safely."

"Will you manage without me?"

"Of course, Lord."

"I'm afraid there's no choice anyway," he adds. "Seek the assent of Calvin and the rest of the Council. They can help you."

"I wouldn't dream of taking any other route."

"Stay clear of the Pool of Infinite Perdition," he says, nodding toward the bubbling lake of blood. "Beware Cthaal."

"Always. I'm well aware of his appetite."

"And please make sure no one troubles Damir."

"The old killjoy will fare just fine under me. We await your return."

Basil has been wrestling with whether to share a particularly juicy ort of wisdom with Kamala, and he decides she deserves to know. In fact, she *must* know if she is to lead in his stead.

"One last order of business," he says.

He tips his head and snakes a hand behind her neck. He pulls her close and whispers in her ear. A moment passes between them, then two. As expected, she recoils at his words, her face bearing an expression somewhere between awe and horror. The secret affects her so deeply she can barely move her hooves, so he has to cradle her as they amble.

Of Our Fiery Home's murkiest mysteries, Kamala now knows the most vital. He only hopes she will not need to make use of such privilege.

As they wander, a group of imps follows closely behind, like pigeons eager for dropped crumbs. Basil kneels before them and, extending an index finger, welcomes their approach.

"I have chosen you," he says in *Locuri*. He anoints three imps by brushing his thumb across each one's forehead, blessing them with the halo of his protection. "You are to be my couriers. If I am needed, you are to find me. You have the freedom to roam on the surface, but only to serve me. You are bound to this covenant. Do you understand?"

The imps fidget and jump with nervous excitement. Basil

feels reassured by this action, knowing he will have a lifeline to this place, however tenuous. What the imps lack in intelligence they make up for in loyalty, so they will not disappoint as long as they do not get themselves killed. If conditions deteriorate and Kamala's reign goes horribly, the imps will track him down, and he will then have to return and do something about it. This much he knows. Everything else will be a mystery.

He rises to rejoin Kamala, whose demeanor has shifted to what he would describe as muted joy. She cannot wait for him to leave. He knows he will not be missed. He finds comfort in the fact that the feeling is mutual.

Kamala smiles as they approach a massive door fashioned from fossilized dragon bones, stitched together with wiry roots. She reaches into a stone basin filled with fat-soaked strips of leather. She withdraws a handful of the slippery leathers and drops them one by one into a satchel, which she drapes around Basil's neck. She then motions three oversized beasts— troglodytes, each standing nearly twenty feet tall—to roll back the door. The lizard-like trogs hiss their compliance. Cool, moist air rushes in, and the sensation chills Basil's reptilian flesh.

Basil produces a torch and steps into the darkened tunnel. His hooves tramp a rune-etched sigil buried in the rock. As he rubs his fingers together, a flame appears, and it sparks the torch to life. He places a meaty hand on Kamala's shoulder, and she returns the gesture before rising to kiss him dryly on the lips.

A moment later, he is gone.

* * *

The ghost of an icy wind whispers through the tunnel's mouth, tugging at the carpet of dust coating the cavern floor. The dark hole seems to beg for some sort of attention—to be filled in, plugged up, paned with iron so not one more whiff of air from the outside world can find its way into Our Fiery Home.

A knot of uneasiness tightens in Kamala's gut as she orders the trogs to seal up the demons' lair. The door grates along the cavern floor, overwhelmed by its own weight, and clangs shut. For a moment there is silence, save the ever-present crackling and popping of things afire, and she relishes it—the possibility of things to come. With Basil cast out into the cold, dark beyond, she is alone at the proverbial top of the mountain.

Small groups of demons and imps surround her. Many have dropped to their knees. Lubos stands behind them. Arms crossed and grinning, he does not kneel. Beyond, the ancient Calvin lingers at the entrance to the Hall of Ignoble and Prodigious Elders. His arms hang like ropes from nonexistent shoulders. A limp tail dangles between his legs as if it were a dead snake. She nods toward him. He turns his back to her and retreats into his chamber.

"If Lord Basil returns," she tells the undersized crowd, "destroy him."

"Should we follow?" the demon named Gideon asks. "He is vulnerable now. We can undo him."

"Leave him to the cold," she snarls. "Soon enough he will face a legion of enemies who will stop at nothing to have his head."

## Chapter 2

# Cast Out, Into the Dying Light

Freedom is never free, Basil muses. He wonders how heavy the burden of his escape will feel once he has reached the surface, or for how long the price of his exit will haunt him. For the moment, with Our Fiery Home at his back, he has no reason to care.

*I am different now. I am different forever.*

He wanders, uncertain and cold, through curtains of fire-licked shadow. The tunnel bears teeth of its own, edges of black rock as keen as broken glass, taking small bites of his hooves with each forward step. Out here he is exposed, vulnerable—perilously mortal. He becomes aware of the torch in his right hand, and he wonders if his strength has waned since leaving the womb of his kingdom. He supposes such doubts are acceptable in any act of reinvention.

"I shall emerge from this sac as a beast reborn," he whispers.

The lie slides off his tongue too easily. What horrors and pleasures lie ahead? No one knows, least of all him. He wants only to return to a daydream in which he bathes in the shallows of a freshwater lake, each wave lapping the stink of the ages from his barnacled hide. Alas, the pleasures of exploration in an unknown land will have to wait. He thinks only of assassins crouching silently in the dark—or, worse, the sins of his past.

The catalog of his misdeeds scrolls across the screen inside his skull: battlefield carcasses arranged in an artful, parasite-ridden pile; rivers bearing tongues of flame, riding a crooked seam toward the distant horizon; crudely made knives in the palms of enthusiastic killers, with dullish blades that tear more than cut, poke more than slice, doing their job—bloodletting, maiming, killing; the Pool of Infinite Perdition, the epithet given to the lake of blood where cautious devils come to drink, eyeing dead things, limp and formless in the bubbling syrup, and knowing that Cthaal, the tentacled behemoth roaming the depths, prefers the sport of claiming live prey over filling its beak with carrion bobbing on the surface; sticky brown hoof prints, baked black, leading away from the lake's ragged edge, prowling for trouble.

He grasps at other images as they float in and out of his mind, yet he can only touch the edges before they float away like ashes caught in an updraft. The softest of images from his dreams fight for space in his brain. These vivid scenes, plucked from the storybooks of a human world, visit him when he sleeps, backhanded gifts to remind him, in the cruelest of ways, of his many missteps. He knows they will keep his mind in disarray until he figures out a way to change. For years he has wondered who gave him this maze to solve, and always he comes up short. He never told Kamala of his regrets—another regret tallied—as she is the only one who might have cared to listen.

He seeks a legacy beyond the dubious title he has earned: caretaker of a stinking, murderous cesspool, however well run.

His kinder memories, which he attempts to replay now, date back to his life before he became *someone*. Even as an insignificant brute fresh from the nest, he dwarfed his peers in size and strength, and as he neared adulthood, he grew tall and sturdy, uncomfortably so, yet he had gentleness to his credit. Other demons challenged him, pushed him, sought to hurt him, but he turned the other cheek until he no longer could.

Until circumstances forced his hand.

Even now, Basil cannot fathom his luck. Or lack thereof. He did not crave ascendance or the role of a leader, but power found him amid the bloodiest insurrection of his time. Ten thousand demons died in the chaos if it had been one.

Nothing in particular brought on the so-called "Last Purge" — *last* as in most recent, not as in *final*. A disagreement between two rival bands of demons had escalated into a full-scale war with no discernible sides. Amid the chaos, Basil found himself face to face with an old, one-eyed demon named Byron—his predecessor and, lamentably, his first kill. Without much effort, Basil tore out Byron's throat and watched him die at his hooves. He then removed Byron's head and painted his chest with his predecessor's blood to assume the throne as ruler of Our Fiery Home. It was that simple.

War ravaged his newly inherited kingdom for a short while longer, with Basil eviscerating any creature daring to stand in his shadow.

Or so he was told, for he recalls none of it.

Even now he knows the bloodshed was worthwhile, as the war brought about an era of fragile peace to Our Fiery Home. Apart from the occasional revolt, no wars had erupted since he came to power. Why? He chalks it up to freedom. Whereas Byron had a thousand rules, Basil had next to none.

When Basil assumed the throne, no one was more surprised. To be in charge of something, *anything*, let alone an entire subterranean kingdom with its own ecosystem, its own social structure ... the idea bordered on the absurd, but he made it work. He found a way to lead. If he had ignored his fate and let some other demon take the reins in his stead, Our Fiery Home likely would not have survived—and, by definition, neither would he. No matter how bad things got, and no matter how many horrors he effected, he never wanted his life to end. He never once craved the nothingness of the dreamless sleep.

Now he merely wants to exist, unburdened and alone.

He considers his plight as he follows the seemingly unending tunnel, and he knows he must busy his mind to keep the bad voices silent.

"Failure," they tell him.

"Pathetic."

"Worthless."

Where the tunnel's throat constricts, he squeezes through sideways. He suddenly realizes the folly of his venture, unsure if the tunnel will go up, up, up and out into the world, or farther down, leading him into Earth's heart, the molten core, where not even he will be able to withstand the nuclear blast furnace. The glare of firelight illuminates the ceiling to show three crudely painted circles of increasing circumference — small, medium and large — that serve as guideposts marking his route to the surface.

"Just follow the runes," Lubos told him before he left. "If the light loses you, just follow the air. The smell will tell you the way. Stay right if you want the Americas, left for the Dark Continent."

None of Lubos's verbiage made sense at the time. Still his words do not register.

Basil feels the cool air licking the flesh of his bare stomach. He wishes for a map, a compass, a charred leg of beef — something to motivate him beyond the sole torch whose flame seems to wither with each step. If the fat-soaked leathers burn up and the torch goes out … he doesn't want to think about it, as he has no fondness for the dark. Too many surprises lurking, too many nooks in which hunters can wait patiently for their take. Here, in this tunnel, he sees the perfect setting for a murder — or, better put, an assassination. His ears perk up, listening for hoofbeats, for words whispered from wicked lips, for the sound of an ax blade chewing the air. He winds another leather strip around the head of the torch. It sparks.

More unsettling thoughts creep in, the fact that here, out in the open, beyond the walls of his kingdom, he has no power. "Abandonment bears a heavy debt," one of the Elders remarked. Calvin. True to the codger's word, Basil felt his weaknesses multiply the moment he stepped across Our Fiery Home's rune-etched threshold.

Water drips from tears in the ceiling. It smells metallic, elemental, of the earth. He imagines its origins, seeping through cracks beneath layers of muck at the bottom of a cold, dark lake, trickling through a maze of rock and root and the fossilized bones of ancient beasts before finding an exit to bless the scales of his forehead. The idea of things older than him, beyond him, makes him want to weep. He steps into a puddle, and his hoof slips on the slick rock. He stumbles forward, and the torch goes flying. It falls into a shallow pool, extinguishing the flame on one side.

"Rascal!" he roars. He plucks the torch from the puddle and deftly rewraps the head with a fresh strip of fat-soaked leather. He knows the light will last only so long, and he may be no closer to seeing sun-kissed earth than he was the moment he left Our Fiery Home. He could starve by then. He won't, he assures himself, but he could, and the mere possibility quickens his pace. His breath becomes labored. His calves ache. Soon he reaches an impasse, where the tunnel has collapsed. Lukewarm air leaches through the cracks, and it smells different, somehow fresher, somehow alive, the promise of newness just beyond. Removing the obstacle takes some doing—too much, in fact. His arms struggle against the weight, but soon enough he rolls the last boulder off the side. Pebbles drop from the ceiling and bounce off his hairless head. Panting, he laments the absence of the magic that supposedly blesses each sinewy thread in his body.

He winces at the smell of something else—a stink he has grown used to.

He is not alone.

Others approach. His confidence flagging, his brain convinces him to take cover. He folds his body into a pocket where the rock recedes. As he extinguishes the torch, the darkness pounces. Panic grips him immediately. His throat tightens. He remembers why he slept so restlessly for so long. Whispers bounce off the walls of the tunnel. He cannot be sure as to which direction the attack might come.

An unfamiliar voice: "Smell that maggoty stink."

Another: "Like the inside of your father's pussy."

They cackle in unison.

The moist rock glows with fresh firelight.

Three figures pass, one by one, heading for the surface—minor fiends, hunched as if weighed down. One rakes the wall with a free hand, the talons nearly skimming Basil's distended belly. Their hooves sink into inch-deep puddles, and with each step he hears the telltale clank of iron against rock. They come with spears, he realizes, likely hunting for him. Or they could simply belong to one of Lubos's roving patrols. Should they try to end him, they will fail. He ponders an attack to remove the threat but decides he will act only in defense. The appetite for murder has left him. Instead, he will follow the trio at a distance, using their torchlight as a beacon. He pushes his fear of the inky darkness out of his mind.

By the time he reaches a junction, with as many as a dozen tunnels branching out like the spokes of a wheel, he no longer sees any sign of the fiends' torchlight. He reaches blindly for clues to safe passage. His fingertips brush something unexpected.

*Runes.*

He cannot decipher their meaning, as the runes do not seem to be of demonic origin. He pauses at the entrance to one tunnel and inhales deeply. It smells sour, like demon piss, so he moves to the next, which smells no better.

He thinks of a time, years from now, when some lesser being will find his skeleton down here, stuck between worlds, a victim of indecision.

"Useless," a voice tells him. "Foolish. Pitiful."

Despite its berating tone, the voice in his head makes him feel less alone. The presence comforts him.

"I'm leaving you here to die," he tells the voice in response.

He waits to see if the voice goes silent. A trickle of fresh water adds depth, drop by drop, to shallow puddles at his hooves. *Blip-blip-blip.*

He chooses the third tunnel, despite the fact that it too reeks of a piss pot. Soon he feels the shift. Even in pure darkness he can see signs of light—and, by necessity, terrestrial life—nearby. Doubt paralyzes him as he reaches a fork in the tunnel. A wrong turn will lead him away from the surface and return him to the nothingness below. Finally, something within triggers a decision, and he takes the right branch. All traces of light disappear within a few steps, suggesting he has erred. He retraces his steps and takes a left this time. The path leads up, then down, then up, up, up—toward an alien smell. He slips through a narrow fissure, where he sees it for the first time: a soft light painting a slab of dust-colored rock. He follows the rocky path to the mouth of a cave.

He hurries toward the exit and steps into a purpling dusk.

The sight is almost unbearable. Through watery eyes, he squints into the day's dying light. Tall brown grasses and color-pricked wildflowers sway in a gentle breeze, rolling like waves. Trees linger in the distance, and he can see their leaves flutter in the wind. He reaches, wanting to touch them, to caress the ragged bark of their trunks, to feel the leaves' rubbery texture between his fingers, to repose in their shade, and to ascend their branches into the forever sky.

For the first time in his life he wishes he had wings. He has found a god.

He kneels on the dust-dry rock, overcome by the openness of space. Forgotten images—including, for a fraction of a second, the smile of a human woman with alabaster skin, dark hair and full pink lips—rush to the surface, his brain on the verge of explosion.

He cannot bear it.

*Let me die here, now.*

He has seen this world before. He has, at one time or another, belonged here. Of this he is certain. Tears streak his coal-black cheeks. Sobs wrack his body. A hand hides his face, shielding his wet eyes.

The verse finds him.

*It screams, this lovely parasite*
*Hungry to fill the hollowed husk*
*Plug the pit with hallowed musk*
*To seed, to breathe*
*To fulfill the promise*
*Never given but implied*
*By the architect*
*Unnamed, unseen*
*The tongue tastes lament and deceit and defeat*
*Too much left*
*Untouched*
*Even for the newly hatched mite*
*As the end comes much too soon*

Something snaps behind him, and he turns to see a red, white and blue flag affixed to a silvery pole jutting from the center of a boulder pile. The cloth flaps in the steady breeze, and the movement reminds him of ripples in Cthaal's lake of blood. As above, so below, it seems.

He wanders mindlessly across the meadow. Grasses climb to his waist and tickle the space between his legs. The grasses' straw-like tips graze his palms. Birds of prey soar overhead, calling out. He takes each piercing screech as a welcome.

He has escaped. He is "of the world" again.

In the distance he eyes a seam of black cutting through the sea of brown and green. Every so often he sees movement — big unnatural things, thoughtless and noisy machines, aliens, drones, metal monsters. An unpleasant odor finds his nose, and the burnt smell reminds him of Our Fiery Home. He growls disapprovingly, but he must know its source. He zigzags toward the roadway, wondering how close he can get before conflict finds him, because conflict always finds him.

Moments later he stands at the edge of the black seam as a caravan of cars and tractor-trailers whiz by. Flecks of tire rubber coat the fur of his lower half. A chrome-streaked semi lumbers to a halt next to him. The right turn signal blinks its angry red eye. The passenger-side door creaks open, and a pot-bellied human with dark skin—a shade so rich it's purple more than brown, a shade nearly as dusky as Basil's midnight flesh—nods in encouragement.

"Where you headed, friend?"

"I'm not sure," Basil says warily, realizing he has no idea where he is or where he should go. He also knows he has no reason to trust anyone, especially someone who regards him as "friend".

"Not going too much farther tonight, but you're welcome to the seat."

"As far as you can take me then. Much obliged."

Basil climbs into the compartment, and the cab sinks an inch or two beneath his weight. As with the cramped tunnels that led him out of Our Fiery Home, he finds the cab to be a tighter fit than he would like. His horns scrape the ceiling and carve ruts into the soft fabric. He decides, for the duration of this experiment, to accept being uncomfortable.

The truck lumbers to a start, and they drive in silence for several miles.

"'Bout time you showed up," the human says.

"Beg your pardon?"

"I figured you would have made an appearance a long time ago. I didn't think we'd make it out of the Eighties alive."

Basil lacks understanding, but he senses no malice so he keeps the conversation going.

"I'm here now."

"Makes perfect sense to me, all things considered."

They continue west, toward the sinking sun, and Basil tries to reconcile the distance he has put behind him. The world blurs past so quickly, so indiscriminately, he feels awestruck. He has never seen such magic, can't fathom how the man next to him wields the power over time and space so freely, with this mechanical beast to do his bidding, as if it were nothing.

A moment later the driver eases up on the gas pedal and the world around them comes into sharper focus. The truck slows to a stop at the entrance to a squat, shack-like building with a sole car and three motorcycles in the graveled parking lot.

"This will work for you," the man says. "Listen now: Most people call me Chit, but my right name is Charles Upton, middle initial J, as in James. Born in Franklin, Tennessee. I'm guessing you knew that already, more or less. What else you need to know 'bout yours truly?"

"Nothing at all. I appreciate the ride, Charles Upton of Franklin, Tennessee."

"Remember me. Remember my good deed. Be kind now."

Basil has no idea what the man means.

"Sir," Basil says. "One last thing: Where am I?"

"Fair enough. You just about in the dead center of Nebraska, heartland of the US of A. Maybe a couple hours outside of Lincoln, right on the dividing line between the towns of Beak and Ellicott. Afraid there's not much action in this neck of the woods for someone of your eminence, my friend, but this place right here is probably the closest thing you gonna find to what you're looking for." He pauses before adding, "Head inside and grab a drink. It's your kind of place."

Basil climbs out of Charles Upton's semi and surveys the near-empty lot. It's an unremarkable outpost, even depressing, pale against the grassy plains and infinite sky. He waits for the truck to trundle forward and watches the great metallic beast pull away. A cloud of road dust swallows him as the truck's taillights shrink to crimson pinpricks.

This world, he thinks, is an unexplained treasure. He eyes the darkening sky, thankful for its lack of ceiling, thankful for its dearth of carrion-craving vampire bats or fire-breathing reptiles. Stars sprinkle the night sky, and the moon's ivory crescent hooks in the dead space above a stand of trees so far into the horizon he can't imagine he will ever have the chance to touch them.

He strides toward the box of a building, which bears a hand-painted sign with a cartoon likeness of an eagle. The raptor's painted bill curves around the words "Beak Tavern." He pauses. If for some reason he has to forfeit his life, he would choose to take his last breaths beneath the blessings of clouds and stars, not anywhere cursed by four walls and a ceiling.

He inhales deeply and reaches for the door handle. As he ducks through the entrance, the abhorrent stink of cigarette smoke corkscrews into his nostrils.

* * *

Horns everywhere—the first thing he notices. The cobweb-laced heads of long-dead animals line the walls, each trophy sporting an imposing rack of antlers. White-tailed deer. Caribou. Sable antelope. Moose. Oryx. He imagines the severed heads of his horned minions alongside these decapitated ungulates, their dried blood painting the walls in crude starbursts.

He should feel at home given the commonality, he thinks, but instead he feels unwelcome, an intruder, a potential target. It's the smoke. It's the magic of moving pictures filling the rectangular screen behind the bar. It's the crassness of the music—he supposes that's the right word for it: *music*—spilling like shat sludge from speakers at both ends of the bar. A guitar twangs while a forlorn man whines about his worst day, which includes, near as Basil can tell, a broken-down car, a dead cat and a girlfriend with a gifted tongue and a wandering eye. But mostly it's the four male humans inside who stare at him with a combination of wonder and contempt.

"You lost?" says the man behind the bar.

Basil clops closer because he doesn't want to shout over the caterwauling.

"I'm here to figure a few things out," he says.

"Right-o," says the barkeep. "I figured you would have gotten here years ago, working behind the scenes. You look like you could use a drink."

"Certainly."

"Take a seat."

"I'll stand."

"Whatever you like."

The bartender holds a small, thickset glass to the light so he can look for smudges, of which there are many. He pulls a rag from his shoulder and gives the glass a cursory swipe. He then takes a half-empty bottle from behind the bar and pours amber liquid into the glass.

"Our best scotch, not that it's all that great," he says. "On me."

Basil lifts the tumbler, smells the acrid liquid swimming around inside, and gingerly takes a sip. Liking what he tastes, he gulps down the rest. It stings his palate but he savors the feeling, the way the liquid warms the lining of his throat on the way to his belly. It, too, seems somehow familiar.

"My compliments," he says.

Basil feels a presence behind him. He turns to see three men standing in formation, one behind the other. Hierarchy. Each wears an ensemble of leather and denim. One sports a spiked collar. Two of them don sunglasses, even though it's dark both inside and out. By now the sun has dipped below the horizon.

"What do we have here?" asks the one in front.

Basil nods toward them. He inflates his chest.

"Holy shee-it," says the man wearing the spiked collar. "What mange-ridden jungle cat dragged you into this hellhole?"

"Buy me another drink," Basil says.

"Ha! Listen to this guy. Coming into our fucking bar, telling us to buy him a fucking drink. Motherfucker's got nerve."

Basil senses their character. They have done bad things, as all have, but these humans are unique in their capacity for wrongdoing. Immediately, he can tell they are neither kind people nor particularly good people—a vague sense of knowing, something beyond the gifts of smell, touch or sight.

"That's King Motherfucker to you," Basil says.

The tallest of the three—leather vest, leather skullcap embroidered with an electric-blue snakelike dragon, beard flecked with gray whiskers, scar running the length of his right cheek—takes a step closer and extends a hand toward Basil.

"Name's Cronos," he says. "These sad sacks and me, we're brothers of the Fang and Claw. This is our bar. Consider it yours too."

"Fang and Claw?"

"Fang and Claw Motorcycle Club. Figured you would have had your eye on us. Heard of us, at least. This is home base for the F and C, or one of 'em anyway. There's eighty-two of us—"

"Seventy-nine," another interjects. "Remember what happened last week."

"Right, can't forget what happened last week. There's seventy-nine of us, running from Wyoming to Texas."

"Running from what?" Basil asks.

"Whatever's necessary, chief. A little this, a little that—anything to make sure we're spending one more day above the dirt than the asshole next door. You know how it is."

"Do I?"

Basil picks up his glass, bearing the weight of a fresh pour, and tilts it back. He feels nervous, ill at ease, disadvantaged. These humans know something he doesn't—too many things, in fact—but they seem to think he's clued in. He's smart enough to not tip his hand, knows when to shut up.

Cronos trains his eyes on Basil and asks, "So. Hell finally froze over?"

"I was delivered here, by Charles Upton of Franklin, Tennessee, and his big machine."

"Big machine?"

"An unnatural thing. From outside. Its name eludes me."

"Why here and now? Why lame-as-fuck Nebraska?"

"It seemed like a good place to start," he says, lying. He did not choose to be here. In fact, he chose nowhere specific. He's not even sure what Nebraska is.

"As good a place as any, right? Set the world alight from the inside out. Genius. Pure genius. No one will see it coming."

"Precisely."

"Stick with us, we'll make sure you get where you're going."

The grating song ends and another starts in right behind it. To Basil's ears, the new noise sounds louder, tinnier and more irritating than its predecessor. His agitation grows.

"What should we call you?" Cronos asks.

Basil chooses to not answer, knowing the burden of his identity, the power of names.

"This here's Worm," Cronos says. "And the fella sitting on his ass right behind him—that fat fuck is Hunter. Get off your fat ass and say hello, Hunt. It's not every day Satan comes a-callin'. Praise and hail Satan. All that jazz."

Basil tenses. The coarse hairs of his arms and chest stiffen.

"I don't go by that name. Watch your tongue."

"All right, big boy. I didn't mean anything by it. … So what's the first item on your itinerary? What's the agenda?"

"Agenda?"

"You know, your reign of terror—Hell on Earth and all that business. Maybe burn down a few churches. Deflower a virgin or two. Feed some ugly babies to the meat grinder just 'cause they're ugly babies. Shit like that."

This man is a fool, Basil knows.

Hunter nods toward the TV behind the bar.

Basil marvels at the magic box.

On screen, a voluptuous brunette in a red bikini and ridiculously high heels shimmies along the perimeter of an in-ground pool. Her pendulous breasts bounce in slow motion toward a bespectacled man in a chef's hat and an apron, diligently tending a charcoal grill. As the man hands the buxom brunette a hot dog, she slides most of it, sans bun, into her lipstick-smudged mouth. The screen fades to black, replaced by the red, white and blue logo for Frank's Double-Beef Franks.

"I'd like to fuck her twice with a broken bottle," Hunter says.

"She wouldn't fuck you with your dog's dick," Worm counters.

These men deserve to suffer, Basil decides. Still, he cannot remove his eyes from the talking box tacked to the wall. The corners of his mouth curl because he now has proof: Magic does exist away from Our Fiery Home. He wonders how he can tap into it.

"One request," Cronos says. "If you get the nuke codes, take *all* them commies out—every last one of 'em, the world over, so there's nothing else left to burn, no one but us left standing. I'll be one disappointed SOB if I wake up tomorrow and see the Nebraska plains colored Day-Glo orange, all burnt to shit by waves of radioactive fire."

These words make no sense to Basil.

"He should come with us, Crone," Worm insists.

Worm's name seems appropriate, given the man's rail-thin body. Even so, his wiry mustache and hooked nose give him a birdlike appearance.

"And do what, genius?"

"We got a short run coming up day after next," Worm says. "Out to Oklahoma City, Sweetwater and back."

"Sweetwater?" Basil asks.

"Texas. We call it a fundraiser. Picking up ... let's call them 'supplies' from our friends in Mexico and bringing 'em back here for prompt distribution. Coke, mostly. Some pills. Some heroin.

But mostly coke. Got to pay the piper, you know. It's your kind of racket, I would think. We'll find some respectable trouble for you to stir up on the way out. You know, some tight little minx for you to corrupt with your melted-marshmallow seed, maybe find a church door or two for you to piss on."

"I'm looking for a break from trouble."

"That's a trip," Cronos says with a laugh.

Basil wonders how—rather, if—he will escape this encounter unsullied. Behave, he tells himself. His eyes seek points of egress.

"Look," Cronos insists, "you want in with us or not?"

"I want nothing from no one."

"You'd do all right by us, and we'd return the favor—no shit. Pledge your allegiance to the Fang and Claw, give your word to Ronald, and you're golden."

"Ronald? He's your god?"

"Ronald's the man with the plan, the toucan at the top of the totem pole," Cronos says. "Considering your, ah, track record, I'm sure he'd waive the initiation. He'd treat you real good and nice. Probably make you an officer within five minutes."

"How kind of him."

Basil grows weary of these beastly men. They remind him too much of demons who do not know their place. The reality of the world above—at least the parts that humans touch—cannot compete with his expectations of peace, of paradise. Maybe, he thinks, coming here was a horrible mistake. He wonders if he will ever find the place to which he belongs.

"You're going to have to excuse me," he says. He nods toward the exit.

"Don't be rude," says Worm. "Listen to the man."

"Why?"

"Because he's talking to you."

"I'm done listening." Basil takes a step away from the bar.

"Look," Cronos says. "We don't want trouble from you, and I'm sure you don't want trouble from us. You're an alpha dog by a red cunt hair or two. We get it. But remember: We ain't far behind you."

"Should I take that as a threat?"

"Take it as fact. You ain't better'n anybody."

"Only a child marvels at his penchant for violence and bad behavior. And only a fool brags about it. I wash my hands of you."

Cronos slams his beer onto the bar.

"You're done when we say you're done," he says. "You come in here like some kind of tough guy, like some kind of asshole. I don't give a flying fuck who or what you think you are. You want to leave? You're going to have to beg. You got no power here."

"Consider your next move very carefully," Basil says.

Cronos pulls a revolver from his belt, casually, even sloppily, and aims the barrel at Basil's face.

"I ain't fucking around here," Cronos says. "Know what, big boy? You're going to kneel. Then you're going to unbutton my fly and take every inch I give you."

Basil can only laugh, mostly because he knows doing so will infuriate this lesser being.

Cronos's finger depresses the trigger, and the revolver does its job. The bullet catches Basil just above his left eyebrow, where the scalp meets one of his gnarled horns.

Basil feels a burning sensation at the base of his horn. The unfortunate smell of gun smoke reminds him of Our Fiery Home. The deafening *pop*, however, is the greatest wound. He holds his breath as he considers the weight of this insult. Such an act of disrespect disables Basil's self-control. His lips curl to expose sharpened yellow canines. His body reacts before his mind has time to reconsider.

His fist caves in Cronos's skull. The man's neck snaps, his spinal column collapses. Cronos dies before his body hits the floor, where it settles in a crumpled heap. His toothless mouth yawns open, jaws pulverized. His right eye socket is empty, the eyeball either reduced to liquid or having detached and rolled into a dusty, darkened corner to settle among crumbs and mouse droppings. The left eyeball dangles by its optic nerve, disembodied, the glistening globe resting comfortably on its respective cheekbone.

Hunter falls out of his chair and scrambles toward the door.

"Fucking Christ!" says Worm. The carnage has him in shock.

Cronos's body goes still, save the occasional nervous twitch, the final embers of life going dim.

Basil moves toward Worm, towering over his would-be opponent. He will at least give the weak little man a chance.

"Take the first shot," he says.

Worm takes two steps backward, into the bar rail. His eyes scan the bar for a weapon, and they find it in a half-empty beer bottle. In one deft motion, he cracks the bottle against the bar and rakes the ragged edge across Basil's exposed gut.

Basil barely feels the blow. He smiles, knowing now it is his turn. He wraps a hand around Worm's throat and lifts the man off the ground.

"You've earned the misery that's about to come," he growls.

He stabs the talons of his free hand into Worm's midsection, intent on tearing the man in two. Worm's body proves extraordinarily flimsy. The head rips away from the neck, tendons snapping, leaving the headless body impaled on Basil's left hand. Basil shakes his hand loose, sections of intestine flying, and the body lands with an awkward *thump*.

Basil hears the subtlest of noises behind him, like two glasses clinking together.

"You shouldn't have done that, you know."

It's the bartender, calm as a clam, finishing the chore of wiping down the bar.

"Wrong," Basil says. "They brought this upon themselves."

"Yeah, I guess you could argue that. But try explaining that to Ronald and his merry band of Fang and Claw fuck nuggets. He's a bad dude, sincerely. Even by your standards. A whole lot of hurt is going to come down on you now, my friend."

"What do you mean?"

"You just erased those two pieces of shit, but you let one of them get away. With these sons of bitches, see, they're like the fucking cops. They're brothers, just like they told you. That means you take down one of 'em and whoever's left is going to come back at you hard. They'll have all eyes out for you."

"Let them find me."

"I get it. You're used to making enemies. You're going to do what you're going to do. I mean, you're here for a reason, right?"

"Right." He's beginning to forget what the reason is, if there ever was one.

"Okay, so get to it. Don't let this kind of riffraff stand in your way. They're a footnote."

"Do you have a name?" Basil asks.

"Buddy," he says. "Just Buddy."

"Did you know these men well?"

"Sure did. They were in here just about every day of the week, by my best guess. You sure saw an end to that, didn't you?"

"I apologize for the mess."

"Ah, this ain't the first time I've had to mop up someone else's blood off the floor. Won't be the last either. Unless you got bigger plans, that is. You know, *The End is Nigh* and all that."

"Where do I go now?"

"Depends. What are you looking for?"

"I wish I knew."

"Well, you're halfway between Beak and Ellicott, and there ain't much going on in either direction. My advice? Keep moving. Head east a few hours, you got Des Moines. Chicago's a bit of a ways past that. Head south and there's Kansas City. Damned good barbecue there, if that suits you."

"Chicago," he says, liking how the word feels on his tongue.

"How do I get there?"
"That depends. You know how to ride a motorcycle?"

## Chapter 3

# Fresh Tears and Brittle Bones

Basil's hooves scrape the asphalt. He can practically feel himself getting shorter as the road grinds away at each hoof's outermost layer of keratin. He eyes the speed gauge, sees he is moving at no more than thirty miles per hour, but even this feels too fast. The motorcycle—a Harley-Davidson 1340 Heritage Softail, nothing but muscle, black paint and chrome—wobbles to the edge of the dusty shoulder, so he steadies himself one hoof at a time.

With sufficient horror, Basil realizes Buddy's five-minute riding lesson has not sufficed. He cranks the throttle and the bike speeds to near forty. Basil screams, thinking these will be his final moments. As his weight shifts, the bike veers off the road and plows straight into a wooden fencepost. Basil flips over the handlebars, gets entangled in the teeth of a barbed-wire fence, and crashes into a cornfield.

He settles on his back and waits for his body to inform him of any injuries, of any essential organs in need of mending. He breathes slowly, finding no pain other than the surprise of his stupidity. Involuntary laughter rumbles from within, and for a moment he wishes someone had seen the crash, merely to comment on the spectacle and laugh along with him. He considers the cast of characters.

No one would care.

Maybe Kamala, he guesses, though likely not. He cannot recall her having laughed, ever. Then again, it's been too long since he permitted himself the thrill of laughter.

Something within him—his brain and heart working together, conspiring—conjures an image of the faceless human, a female, who has been at turns blessing and plaguing his dreams for as long as he can remember. He does not have a name for her, nor does he have any pure memories of her, only the vague feeling that she will be forever tied to him, and that he lacks some vital part because of her absence. The curse, he calls it.

He casts the feeling aside, knowing it serves no purpose other than to harass him. Splayed on the dirt, he reassesses his bones for any injuries resulting from the crash. A few bumps and bruises—the barbed wire biting into his left leg—but other than those minor complaints, he feels fine. He will survive.

Enough adventure for today, he supposes. Enough blood spilled.

He studies the dark sky as his body sinks into the pillow of soft earth and broken cornstalks. Glimmering constellations dot the heavens, the sky easing from a soft blue in the west to a deepening purple in the east. He should be happy to be here, in this place called Nebraska, but an unpleasantness stirs. Something deep and primal nags at him as he considers his few interactions with the humans. He laments the incident at the Beak Tavern. Although killing is nothing new to him, this time, after claiming the lives of two human men, he feels … different. Dirty, ashamed, sinister. He wishes the feeling away, tries his best to forget his actions, but the more he tries, the more vibrant and persistent the memory of his misconduct becomes.

To feel the weight of his wickedness—*this* is his punishment to suffer.

The air takes on a chill, and the cooling of his skin reminds him of his ascent out of Our Fiery Home. He wonders how Kamala is faring, so early into her appointed reign, wonders if the walls still stand. He pictures Lubos, smiling sadistically, blood leaking from his mouth, holding the sacred spear designating him ruler. Basil shakes the thought from his skull. Speculation will do him no good if this aboveground experiment is to have any chance of success.

A small brown bat does figure eights in the night sky. Basil traces the frantic yet graceful arcs as the bat tracks down the thousand insects destined to fill its wanting belly. He considers how the insects will give their lives to nourish the bat, how they would likely rather live than die, yet they have no say in the matter—how unfair the world can be to all creatures but a carefully chosen few.

His breath slows, his body sinking deeper into the shallow pocket of earth. He counts the lives he has ended, today and every day before, for no good reason—for anger, for power, for show, for nothing at all. He regrets each murder. The feeling builds within him until it spills out. Tears form at the corner of each eye. Sadness overwhelms him, and the emptiness inside begins to fill, making him cry harder.

A falling star streaks the sky. He follows its tail until it disappears, and even after he can no longer see it, he pretends he can. He imagines the star circling the planet until the end of time, or at least until it chooses to burn up and turn into clouds of stardust. He closes his eyes and expels a heavy breath, followed by another. For the moment, he is thankful that "forever" does not exist, that everything, including each day, has an expiration date.

He, too, will one day be no more.

His last thought, before his body accepts the gift of sleep, concerns the hobbled Harley at the edge of the road. Common sense tells him he should get up and move his newly acquired toy out of plain sight before another thief swoops in to claim it as his own.

* * *

A ball of wet excrement sails through the heavy air and splats against the wall of red rock. The demons cheer, knowing full well such treachery would have resulted in their deaths just a short time ago. Others follow suit, as one after another shits into the palm of his hand and smears the contents of his bowels onto the walls of Basil's chamber, obscuring the gentle words etched into the rock by their former ruler.

A dozen young demons form a ring and link arms. They skip and hop as they sing silly songs of scorn and vilification.

*"Poor old King Basil, his reign here is done. Toothless King Basil, rotting in the sun."*

Chaos possesses Our Fiery Home. Some celebrate the end of a tyrant's reign. Others see the absence of governance as an opportunity to put to good use the cruelty they learned while living under Basil's thumb.

Lubos slithers from his perch atop a blunted stalagmite and, like a carnival barker, beckons the others toward him. Some curious, others obedient, dozens of demons gather around. It's time for a game, he tells them. "Hunting Basil," he calls it. He explains how one demon will play the part of Basil, the outcast, and the others will chase him down "in good fun." Whoever catches the pretender wins the game, he announces, though it's unclear what the prize will be.

"Volunteers?" he asks, as he often does at the outset of his so-called games.

No one steps forward, so he points to a Nameless demon standing off to the side, designating him to play the part of Basil. The demon attempts to flee, but those who stand nearby tackle him and drag him to Lubos's feet. Lubos directs them to smear a B onto the designee's chest. Excrement will do just fine. This young demon has no horns, so Lubos instructs the horde to fashion a crown of root branches and wire. They have no gentility, so the demon bleeds as a result of his newly fitted prosthesis.

Once Basil's Doppelganger is sufficiently done up, Lubos tosses the demon to the ground.

"Get him," he says, dully.

The Doppelganger slips through a web of limbs, breaks from the crowd and snakes along the perimeter. He is surprisingly quick and, as the demons trying to tackle him discover, quite slippery. All of the pursuers laugh and smile, joyous at play, and for a time the Doppelganger laughs along with them. Then the game turns. The Doppelganger's smile disappears. He tires, his lungs struggling to pull enough oxygen from the poisonous air, but the pack continues the pursuit.

As the Doppelganger squirms past, Lubos places a hoof in the runner's path. The young demon stumbles, and this is enough to end the game. A potbellied demon grabs the fallen one around the waist, declaring himself the victor. Others pile on. Then someone strikes the Doppelganger with a closed fist. Then another. And another. Someone produces a rock, another a knotted club. They all move in, taking turns beating the Doppelganger's face and back, stripping the flesh from his thighs and chest.

They hold the maimed Doppelganger aloft and carry him to the edge of the Pool of Infinite Perdition. The body lands with a splash. Then they wait. Soon enough they see movement beneath the surface. A massive tentacle reaches up to snatch the still body. They all cheer.

Lubos steps forward and places his three-fingered hand on the shoulder of the demon first to pounce on the Doppelganger.

"Well done," he growls. "You win."

Lubos hoists the demon over his head and hurls him into the lake of blood. The frantic demon wades toward the nearest shore. The attack comes from below, pulled under just as his outstretched hand reaches for the nearest handhold.

More cheering.

Kamala watches from a distance. She knows she must let this happen. Interfering in their revelry would suggest loyalty to an unwanted king who has abandoned his people.

"This ain't going to end well."

Kamala turns to see the cripple, Damir, using his stumps to drag his inert body toward her.

"Calm will return," she tells him.

"Since when? Basil knew what he was doing when he left. I see your ambition, even if Basil couldn't. Turning this place around is beyond even you."

"I promised Basil I would treat you kindly, old one. Do not give me reason to change my mind."

"You're not going to make it."

"Pardon?"

"They're just playing now, but soon enough the fun and games will end. Lubos has designs on what he thinks you possess, even though you ain't earned the gift Basil dumped in your lap."

"I have no reason to fear Lubos."

"Then you're dumber than Basil's sac of nuts. Even a numbskull like him knew better. He's coming for you, Lubos is. You give him the chance, and he'll undo every part of you."

She backs away from Damir and retreats into the shadows. She knows Lubos craves her power, but she can handle him. To be safe, she will wander for a time, safely away from the fray, and return only after her fellow demons have finished spilling each other's blood. For now she'll let them get drunk on murder and malice. She's smart enough to know the start of her reign will go more smoothly once the hangover has set in.

\* \* \*

The raccoon weaves between the rows of cornstalks, seeking the source of the intoxicating stink. It hugs each stalk like a slalom skier as it zeroes in on the unmoving mound—this incredible, unnamable, hulking *thing*—that reeks of smoked spare ribs and decay. The raccoon darts closer, cautiously, testing boundaries.

The cologne of fresh blood hangs in the air, held aloft by the magic of humidity. The raccoon's usual victuals—garbage and leopard frogs, maybe a few crayfish from the nearest creek—have nothing on this gift of fresh meat. It moves in and, with its almost-human paws, picks at a shallow wound, laps at the crust of dried blood. With all the care of surgery, the raccoon slips a sharpened claw into the tender flesh to restart the flow. Unsatisfied, even greedy, the critter tugs for a stringy morsel.

The reckoning is immediate.

Basil crushes the raccoon in his grip. His fist deconstructs the animal into a ball of fur, organ and broken bone, and then introduces the meal to his soft palate. Three bites later, no evidence remains.

He lays back down, exhausted, yet thankful for a full belly that went ignored for much too long. Even in his grogginess, he notices the light changing as the hint of morning stirs in the east. The light continues its glorious shift, yet he knows he does not have it in him to endure the fireworks display in its entirety. He lingers on the edge of sleep.

The unmistakable grumbling of motorcycle engines roars in the distance. They are searching for him, he figures. The brothers of the Fang and Claw have come to avenge the two simpletons he did away with at the bar.

"They come to break you," the voice tells him.

"Let them try," he whispers. "Let them come," though he does not mean a word. Not now, he knows, in such a compromised state.

He rises from the earth and stands in the cornfield, and only now does he notice the extent of his wounds. The gash on his stomach has begun to heal, and he bends to unwind the snarl of barbed wire that sank its rusty teeth into his left calf, just above the hoof. He winces as he untwines the metal, surprised at the sting as the barbs withdraw from the tender flesh. Physical pain seems new somehow. He wonders if the simple act of being here, so far from Our Fiery Home, will cause his body to deteriorate, wither and collapse into a column of dust waiting to be carried away on the wind.

He stops to study the husks at eye level, each one pregnant with an ear of corn. In the lifting darkness he sees the deep impression his heavy body has left in the soft earth. Odd that a knot of earthworms has gathered beneath him, he thinks, yet he admits he knows nothing of earthworms, only that he and they share a kinship, both borne of the soil.

Each moment above ground conjures a new surprise.

Favoring his sore calf, he limps toward the road to retrieve the motorcycle, hoping the crash has not wrecked his new plaything. His bones feel brittle, muscles useless. He struggles to lift the bike onto his shoulder, but he succeeds. He then hoists it over the fence and begins to roll it up the steep incline, into the safety of the cornfield. Hidden. Safe.

His gut gurgles. The sensation causes a reaction somewhere on the spectrum between curiosity and panic. His anal sphincter suddenly loosens, and for a few seconds he wonders if the sphincter will fail and paint the dirt with the full contents of his bowels. After a moment of intestinal peace, he continues his task of rolling the Harley up the embankment. He then lays back into his earthen nook and closes his eyes. Sleep takes him before the sun creeps over the horizon.

His eyes close, and the dream begins anew.

## Chapter 4

# Lament for the World Left Behind

This strange new world reeks of cat piss and shame.

I stare at the smudge of gray where the moon should be, tucked between two half-finished spires climbing out of the mud. The inky murk of cloud cover has ruined my view yet again. How I pine for the moon, as she has not made time for me in more than a week. She shows only glimpses of herself, podgy and nebulous, so I conjure a poem about a wrestling match between the shy moon and a selfish god who refuses to share the sky.

Another day of rain and gray, giving my face no reason to tack on a smile. When will this horrid trend reverse its course? A lesser man would succumb to his despair, but not me. I can admit my confidence wanes from one day to the next. Memories of recent events—my final moments with my bride at our farmhouse in Berwick—sometimes lead me to the edge of the abyss.

"Please don't go, Emmitt," she told me. "Not yet, at least. She won't last much longer."

"Fortune disfavors a man who does not act, my love," I countered. "And fortune is precisely what I intend to find."

"Mother will be dead inside of a week. You said so yourself. Not being here when the moment comes ... I couldn't bear it. Just the thought of it fills me with dread. Haunt me forever, the old crone would."

"All my love to your mother, dear. Come to me when you're ready to put her behind you. Just follow my trail and put your ear to the ground. What you'll hear is the riot of a man making his mark. All of London will know the name Emmitt Wells."

She did not cry, because she never cried, but I know my

departure hurt her. My hubris made it worse, no doubt. She simply turned and climbed the stairs, likely to wipe her mother's fevered brow.

My last vision of her prior to my escape—an ill-fated flight, it seems.

As the weeks have passed, my story has taken a turn.

I wish our parting of ways could have been avoided, or at least been different. I see no wisdom in dwelling on events I cannot change, but I would be lying only to myself. The niggling thought, our unfortunate goodbye, has done its best to drive me mad. What choice did I have but to make haste for the city, where only lightness and plenty awaited me?

"Strong back, good hands, half a brain for following orders— have those to your credit and you'll own the place." So they said of London's promise. Such a shame everything I had been told of the city was a brilliant lie. Sure, I found an abundance of work for a man willing to break his back in a city rebuilding itself yet again atop the muck of a bloody swamp. I have done my best to break my bones and, with dawn only an hour or two off, will do so again in a few more ticks of the clock.

No one speaks of London's dark side, which shows itself right quick: enough noise to draw the dead out of the tomb, hands against their ears and begging the world to keep the racket down; ever-burning fires, their smoke adding to the gloom of night; packs of glassy-eyed dogs hunting for untaken morsels; roving gangs of pauper children picking pockets from dawn to midnight; plague-ridden whores blessed with certain talents; rats with no manners, also plague ridden, patrolling the gutters of streets they have claimed as theirs; and, if the rumors prove true, at least one supernatural thing, a ravenous hulk with steel blades for teeth and a fondness for the flesh of men, prowling after dark.

Such horrors are alien to Berwick, the pastoral idyll I left behind, a world away. I wish someone had shaken me awake before I dreamed up this nightmare. Not that I would have listened to anyone but my dumb self, with deadened ears, prattling on and on about the virtue of my ambitions.

A man must make his own mistakes.

The newsboys speak of this otherworldy beast roaming the nighttime streets only because every last newsboy likely has a roof over his head. No one else utters a bloody word of it— certainly no one who wanders these streets past dark, scanning the sky for the same elusive moon. It serves no good to think of it, I suppose, because if the end comes, *when* it comes, it will be my time to go. Besides, only a madman would rob himself of the pleasures of stargazing under a clear sky, no matter who or what is out there with him, watching from the coolness of the shadows.

I turn my eyes away from the gauzy spot in the sky where the moon should be, and get moving. I choose to walk the puddled length of Monument Bridge, as I do every night, until my mind is free of verse, my body no longer capable of refusing sleep.

At the far end of the span, I approach the balustrade and listen for the rush of water I cannot see. I inhale deeply, lungs swollen with London's stink, and spit. I wish the moonlight would cut through this godforsaken murk so I could see my product—my whitish pearl of spit—sail through the nothingness and alight on the face of the mighty Thames. Monument's overcrowded twin, London Bridge, looms in the distance. The embers of its torches burn dimly in the fog.

I fear failure might reshape me into something wretched, and therefore I must not fail. The nagging voice inside wants to scream out, "Why bother? Everything your eyes see will turn to bone and dust." Yet I am stout of heart and broad of back, so this darkness will not take hold.

My moment of weakness will pass.

An icy wind scrubs my back. I decide to walk the length of the bridge once more before settling on a dry place to sleep. Likely

I will bed down beneath the eaves of the blacksmith's, the outer wall warmed by the nest of quiet coals glowing within. As I walk, my eyes will search every doorway, every piss-stinking alcove, for any silhouettes eager to make my demise, be it a bloodthirsty beast or a madman with the worst of intentions.

## Chapter 5

# The Curse of Speech

A jag in the gut jolts Basil awake. His hands cradle his distended belly, where the gurgling has evolved into a pain he cannot name. It reminds him of the time he scalded his left hand, courtesy of a magma flow leaking from a seam in Our Fiery Home's floor; the molten rock nearly consumed his smallest finger. This time the lava boils within, taking delight in making a meal of the tender lining of his stomach.

He curls into a ball and whimpers to cast out the pain. The whimpers morph into multisyllabic moans, as if to somehow ward off the ancient evil festering in his ruined gut. His efforts failing, he clamps his eyes shut and simply wishes the pain away. Though he begs for a reprieve from an entity he does not know, the pain goes nowhere. It has made a host of him.

He then resorts to rage. He unleashes a tantrum of screams and screeches, the thrashing of cornstalks and clawing of dirt. Nothing helps. He cares not what his ruckus might attract. Should a proper adversary reveal himself at this very moment and, upon discovering his pathetic self, decide to do him in ... well, it would be an acceptable end. At least the pain would cease.

Finally, with tear ducts flowing, he does what comes naturally.

*Our days together lit me from within*
*Each moment a magic trick revealed, a glimmering jewel*
*A gift worth keeping*
*Everything precious plucked*
*From the cask of my cupped hands*
*Memories linger, night comes swiftly*
*Clouds choke the midnight sky*

*Thick and mute and painted gray*
*Like charred coal*
*Only the moon*
*And its halo of stars to warm me*
*Companions, lovers, brides*
*Nomads*
*I lie awake, drunk with their cold comfort*
*To permit your return, freed from the prison*
*Of my mind*
*If only as a brace against the barbed tongue*
*Of the bitter wind licking the skin*
*Down, down, down*
*To the white bony ridges*
*Of the spine I no longer need*

Cornstalks rustle. Basil opens his eyes and realizes he has company. A small boy in blue-and-white basketball sneakers holds a tortuously bent stick that towers over his head by more than a foot.

"Are you real?" the boy asks.

"Quite," Basil replies. He coughs up a mouthful of crud.

"You look like something from the kinds of movies my mom would never let me watch."

"I can assure you I am as true as the soil upon which my carcass lies, rotting before you."

"Are you hurt? You sound hurt."

The boy raps his stick against Basil's right horn. Basil doesn't stop him, so the boy finds a rhythm: *tap, tap, tap ... tap ... tap, tap, tap ... tap.*

"I do appear to be in some distress," Basil says.

*Tap, tap, tap ... tap ... tap, tap, tap ... tap.*

"Hey, mister," the boy says. "Did you take a bullet to the gut?"

*Tap, tap, tap ... tap ... tap, tap, tap ... tap.*

"If I knew I would tell you."

*Tap, tap, tap … tap … tap, tap, tap … tap.*

"Did you get struck by lightning?"

"Not that I'm aware of, no. Please stop that."

*Tap, tap, tap …*

"Did you fall out of an airplane or something?"

*Tap, tap, tap …*

"Stop that!" Basil roars. "I beg you. Please."

*Tap.*

"Do you have AIDS?"

"Beg your pardon?"

"Daddy says some people have AIDS. The bad people, he says, the soulless and gutless people who put their pee-pees in dark and dirty places. He says it's a disease that makes you go to Heaven sooner than you're supposed to."

"It's only a stomachache, I assure you. A particularly malignant stomachache, but a stomachache nonetheless."

"It could be AIDS."

"Forgive me, boy, but I'm hardly of the mind for pleasantries. Now if you could just run along and—"

"When my tummy hurts, I get to drink ginger ale. Well … I used to. My mom used to give it to me. Sometimes I like to get sick because it reminds me of her, but Daddy's no good at being nice like Mom was. I can go home and get one for you—a ginger ale, I mean. … Well, maybe I'll get two. You're a big son of a bitch."

Basil considers the word: ale. The sole syllable sends a flicker of joy up the internal highway connecting his brain to his ailing gut.

"That's a good boy."

"My name's Elias. I'm seven. …Well, seven-almost-eight."

"Run along now, Elias."

Elias disappears into the maze of cornstalks. Basil hears the boy's young legs rapping against the waxy green stalks. Not far off, perhaps a hundred yards, Basil sees the hint of a structure—a peaked roof bearing a weathervane, the metal mottled green from exposure. Time to make an escape, he thinks. He sits up and leans forward. Immediately, the agony consumes him.

"I'm dying," he tells himself, mostly to see how self-pity feels.

"You get what you deserve," the voice says.

How unfair it would be to succumb to something as pedestrian as an intestinal parasite, having come so close to achieving greatness, right to the cusp. To have come all this way only to die alone because he gorged himself on some dirty little beast whose carrion deserved to rot on the side of the road, tire marks checkering its flattened midsection…

Maybe, he thinks, he just needs to take a shit.

When Elias returns, a can of soda in each hand, Basil is on his knees, still moaning, resting his arms on the motorcycle's front tire. Elias rolls the cool aluminum of a soda can against the back of Basil's neck, and the reaction makes an unmistakable hiss.

"Here you go, mister."

Basil turns to accept the sodas. His oversized mitts struggle to open the dwarfish cans. Lacking patience, he bites into the first one, and the carbonated liquid squirts up his nose, into his eyes. He squeals from the unexpected sting.

"Curse you, cherub!"

He hurls the spurting can, slicing a cornstalk in two.

Elias laughs so hard he bends at the waist. He steps forward and takes the unopened can from Basil's clutch. He pulls back the tab, and the can fizzes open. He hands it back to Basil, who looks pale and sullen—tired.

"Try it this way," Elias says.

Basil empties the can in one gulp. He studies the can's painted-on label so he can commit the vessel of this precious elixir to memory.

"This cornfield belongs to Daddy," Elias says.

Basil burps and adds, "Just your father?"

Elias looks on quizzically.

"It's a fine field," Basil says. "A proper field."

"If you look over there, you can see my house. I live in the attic. Where do you live?"

"A fine question, boy. I'm afraid I'm quite far from where I belong. I suppose you can say I'm a tourist, just visiting."

"I can ask Daddy if you can stay in our guest room. Maybe the barn—that's where the pigs and crickets sleep. He might not say no."

"I appreciate the offer, but—"

"We used to have company all the time, but now Daddy doesn't like most people he doesn't know real good. There was this one fella—Mister Smitty, my mom called him—and he would come over to play with my mom when Daddy had to go out of town sometimes. Mr. Smitty doesn't come over to play anymore. That's because my mom doesn't live there anymore. Daddy says she's a worthless old whore."

Basil purses his lips, unsure of how to respond.

"What do you know about Chicago?" he asks.

"Daddy says there's nothing good in Chicago."

"Of course he does."

"My Uncle Jules went there for vacation one year and never came back."

"Meaning?"

"Sometimes people don't come back. They just go somewhere and stay there, because they like it too much or it likes them and won't let them go. We used to have a kitten-cat—a real pretty one, all orange and white. Her name was Buttons. She got out and stayed out. Daddy says she made friends with the front tire of someone's pickup truck. So now she's gone too. Forever. Just like my mom."

Basil's palms start to sweat.

"Do you have a job?" Elias asks. "Daddy has a job, and it must be a real important one 'cause he spends a whole lot of time doing job stuff. Daddy says you need a job in order to have a happy life, but he doesn't seem very happy to me."

"I'm sorry to hear that, young man."

"He says a job lets you have money, but he says having a good reason to get out of bed in the morning is even more important than having money. Without a job, a man has no value, he says. A job doesn't sound like much fun to me."

"You might be on to something, Elias."

"What kind of job do you have?"

"None at the moment."

"Are you a dirty hippie?"

"You ask a lot of questions."

"Teacher says that's the best way to learn."

"Indeed."

"Does not having a job make you sad?"

"It makes me ... confused."

"There's a place in town that's supposed to help people like you find jobs. Daddy says if all the lazy liberals got off their asses and spent more time trying to find jobs, this GD country would be a lot better off."

Basil's eyes wander, wondering how he will extricate himself from this situation. He escaped the trap of Our Fiery Home. Now if he can only elude the attention of this chatterbox child ...

"Is that your motorcycle?" Elias asks.

"You might say that."

"I hear some people have jobs where they put on leather pants and ride around on motorcycles all day. Maybe I'll do that when I get older."

"I wouldn't recommend it."

As Elias stares all too curiously at the mane of jet-black fur covering Basil's crotch, Basil anticipates more questions he does not want to answer.

"Say, Elias. I much appreciate your hospitality, but I really should be going. Which way did you say town was?"

Elias stands up, puts his finger to his chin, turns himself in a circle and points left—the direction Basil thinks he came from the night before.

Basil gets to his hooves, unsteady, and rolls the motorcycle out of the cornfield. He pats Elias on the head as he passes.

Just before he fires up the Harley, he hears Elias yell, "Why aren't you wearing any pants?"

* * *

The town of Beak grows from nothing—a vast sea of cornfields, pastures and farmsteads, carved up with small stands of oaks, chokecherries and silver maples, and then, *boom*, civilization: one main drag stretching a modest eight blocks, with secondary streets branching east and west. A post office, a diner, a hardware and paint store, a red-and-white CENEX service station, plenty of windowless buildings peddling tractor parts and feed for livestock.

Almost immediately Basil realizes he likes the place, how quaint it seems. Still, he chalks up his good mood to the dry wind and blinding sunshine warming the blood beneath his reptilian skin. A decent night's sleep has him thinking clearly.

The Harley's engine grumbles as Basil rolls through town. His testicles bounce off the bike's leather seat. The spectacle of him catches eyes as he thunders past, and he savors the feeling of exhibition. Partway down the artery of Second Street, he pulls up to the curb and stops in front of a blue mailbox, where a mousy young brunette stands ready to drop a cache of envelopes down the chute. She has a stamp on the tip of her tongue, an envelope in hand, destined for someplace other than here.

"Excuse me," he yells over the Harley's ceaseless chugging. "I'm looking for the place where they help you find jobs."

As if vexed by his impossible appearance, the brunette warily raises her right hand and points over Basil's left shoulder, toward a single-story building. Boxy and battleship gray, the building bears a rectangular sign advertising, "Beak Unemployment Office." A vinyl banner, affixed to the building's façade with a quartet of black bungee cords, flaps in the gentle breeze: "Want to Help Build a Better Beak? Please Come In."

He pulls forward and angles the Harley into a spot between two cars. The front tire rams the curb, but he is able to control it this time. No wipeouts today, so far. He's finding his confidence. This backwards world is starting to make sense.

He steps off the bike and shakes the vibration out of his bones. It feels good to be free of his steed. He takes in the smells of Beak: hope, the promise of simplicity and the pungent punch of cow shit. After three deep inhalations, he swaggers into the unemployment office. He wanders the empty space, peeking over the tops of fabric-lined cubicles, and sees no signs of life other than a lone woman stationed at a solitary desk. An oil painting of a never-ending cornfield—much like the field owned by Daddy, young Elias's father—hangs on the wall behind her. A cigarette smolders in an ashtray next to a silent telephone.

"Oh, you must be joking," she says upon seeing him.

"I'd like a job," he says, exuberant.

"Of course this happens to me today," she says. "Of course it does. Just my luck."

He deflates. Why, he thinks, must everyone go out of his or her way to make him uncomfortable? At least this woman hasn't tried to stab or shoot him—yet. He figures her assaults will come in the form of inquiries and explanations, minutiae. If this is the human condition, he must endure it all. His stomach grumbles. Although the pain in his gut has subsided, his insides feel scoured.

"Well," she says, pausing for effect, "I take it you're here to—"

"Build a better Beak, just like the sign says."

"That would have been my second guess. Have a seat, please. That chair's been cold for more than a week."

"What do I need to do?"

"Run away now, screaming bloody hell," she says, laughing.

He pulls a hand to his face and touches the skin of his forehead. An ache builds in the space behind his eyes.

"I'm kidding you, sweetheart. It's just that ... well, you could say I don't get to meet too many people like you every day, any day. I guess that's one of the good things about the great wide world, the fact that people like you are out there, wandering around, just waiting to be found by someone like me. Maybe not the best thing about living in a place like Beak, but I guess I can't say that on a day like today, now can I?"

She's a broken toy, Basil concludes after just thirty seconds of interaction. He likes her brokenness. He likes *her*, in fact, and he tells her so, simply, "I like you"—he reads the name etched into the dusty placard hanging halfway off the edge of her desk— "Mary Jane Pix."

He introduces himself, offers a mitt of a hand for her to shake. She smiles subtly and drops her head toward the face of a desk strewn with loose papers.

"So, on a gorgeous day like today," she says, "where the two of us are stuck inside looking at each other like a couple of idiots, let's find you a job. Do you have any skills?"

He suddenly realizes he should have given this more thought, *some* thought, *any* thought. He should have practiced his approach. Even so, such unpreparedness feels like an act of liberation. He quickly spins a narrative he thinks she might like.

"I ruled a subterranean kingdom, brutalizing more beings than any mortal human would want to count," he says, his eyes looking upward for words to pluck from the air. He coughs before adding, "If someone challenged me, I dispatched them. If someone disparaged me, they paid the penalty with their limbs, or their lives. If any demons were foolish enough to band together, thinking they might somehow wrest power from my hand, I set my ghouls to butcher them and their families. I took what I wanted, when I wanted it. I gave little, but things ran smoothly in my kingdom—Our Fiery Home, it's called. It wasn't such a terrible place, for a time."

"Uh-huh," she says, looking up from her black-and-white form to peer over the frame of her oversized eyeglasses. "And the reason for leaving?"

"Boredom. Or burnout."

"I can work with that. Don't you worry, hon. Someone like you? You're far from hopeless. Far from it. Okay, so how can we spin this into something ... workable? Well, let's just say you're a bold, assertive leader, with years of experience, in search of a daring new challenge. Up until now you've focused your career in, ah ... let's say workforce management, site planning and organizational dynamics. We can say you have an unblemished record of leading teams well equipped to, ah, execute. How does that sound? It sounds mighty fine to me, if I do say so myself. I think it will resonate."

"Just fine, sure, but all that history is just that—part of a long-dead past. What I want most of all is to roam and observe and write poetry. Put a quill in my hand and an ink bottle on my desk and I will write this world alive."

"Ah," she says, her voice going soft. "You're one of those."

"Those?"

"A romantic! My boyfriend in high school wrote the sweetest, most tender poems you ever did hear. Wrote a new one for me just about every day we were together. He had this *way* about him, this wonderful power over words, a deep love for the world and everything in it—a real gift. The beautiful things he wrote would make me look at the world in a way no one else could, like he saw something just off to the side—something hidden that a simple girl like me just didn't see, at least not without being shown. I always felt like he was trying to open my eyes to something important that everybody else but him was missing. It was an inside joke that just kept on going, only sad more than funny."

She fills the space between them with a heavy sigh.

"That gift of his went to waste, let me tell you, but I guess most of them do, don't they?" she adds. "He died in a farming accident two weeks before he was supposed to leave here to study at Drake. English major. He was out in the fields with his daddy, got his leg caught in that damned machine. All those churning blades got him good. Just chewed him up and spat him out the other side. What a gruesome mess."

She pauses, as if sinking back into the pain of a distant past. Basil indulges her.

"I think he could have done something really neat if he had gotten out of here, away from Beak," she continues. "Instead he wound up as fertilizer, his blood cursed to feed Nebraska soil forever. If you ask me, that's just cruel."

Basil wants to say he's sorry for her loss but chooses not to. By the looks of her—hair graying at the temples, wrinkles at the corner of each eye, the creased skin of her neck starting to sag— her high school years ended decades earlier, and he wonders if she deserves condolences over her lost love so long after the fact.

"In your case, hon, I'm afraid I don't have any fresh listings for 'Demon Poet.'"

"Well, what do you have?"

The chair creaks beneath him.

"Do you mind standing up, dear?" she says. "You'll bust that chair and, knowing these sons of bitches the way I do, they'll try to take the cost of replacing it out of my paycheck even though I had nothing to do with it."

She scrolls through a well-worn printout, maybe fifteen pages long. Her eyes follow her index finger down one page, then another, shaking her head and frowning at each dot-matrix listing. The boxy computer terminal behind her goes unused, the beige exterior cracked, the screen a blank gray sheet.

"Okay, here's something: The *Crete Bee* has an opening at its office in Honey Grove. That's about an hour from here, maybe ninety minutes. Looks like they need an agriculture reporter. Full time, salary is negotiable, based on experience."

"Would I have a seat by the window?"

"You're asking the wrong person."

"What would I be doing?"

"My best guess? Talking to people about corn and millet. Writing news stories about corn and millet, about people who grow or sow or harvest corn and millet."

"That sounds like another prison sentence. Where's the artfulness in a job like that?"

"If you're looking for art, you probably came to the wrong dang place, now didn't you, deary? But let's not give up hope just yet. Let's just see now." She studies each listing with care. "No. ... Definitely not. ... Not for you. ... Not for *anyone*. ... Hmm, this might be something. On second thought, no. ... Okay, here's one: Christian Plattekill's company in Ellicott is looking for a part-time painter."

"Ooh. That sounds wonderful!"

"A house painter."

His shoulders droop.

"All right. Forget that. Now this one here—now *this* one just feels right. It's not poetry or anything, but there's an advertising agency in town looking for a copywriter."

"What does a copywriter do?"

"Use your imagination."

He closes his eyes, trying to picture it.

"I can see the wheels churning up there, but don't hurt yourself, hon," she says. She reaches across the table to pat his ghoulish hand. "In advertising, a copywriter is someone who figures out how to get other people to buy crap they don't need, usually in ten words or less."

"Mind control through verse?"

"That's one way to put it, sure."

"I'll take it!"

"I'm afraid it's not my decision, dear. But someone like you, looking the way you do ... let's just say I don't think you'll have any trouble making friends with the right people. Let me make a call and see if I can set up an interview for you. Is your schedule flexible?"

"I'm not going anywhere."

"Setting down roots in Beak, of all places? Color me surprised."

"This seems like the kind of place where bad things don't happen."

"Just you wait, hon. You got the wrong kind of luck, the Black Hand of Doom's going to track you down no matter how far you run."

## Chapter 6

# In One Hand Poison, the Other a Cure

Basil works his hooves into the plush carpet, and he likes how the ratty fabric fills the cleft of each hoof. Before now, he never realized he was ticklish. The feeling makes him happy but uneasy, somehow fitting as he prepares for the discomfort he assumes will itch his hide soon enough.

His eyes roam the office lobby and settle on the squat end table next to his chair. He riffles a stack of torn and dog-eared magazines and chooses the one he deems the least offensive. Mindlessly thumbing through a weathered issue of *Intrepid Sportsman*, he turns page after page of glossy pictures of heavyset men in camouflage posing next to their fresh kills— first, the captions suggest, a black leopard, a monstrous grizzly bear and a ten-foot-long alligator, followed by a wild boar with its yellowed tusks painted red, a lion with an arrow poking from a wet patch in its black mane and the feathery remains of an obliterated grouse. His eyes move from the red splotches on the page to the same blazing hue in the "Savage Communications" sign tacked to the wall across from him. The chair at the end of the row is askew. Basil wants to bring it to order, align it with the others, but he fights the urge. A deep brown mark in the shape of a lightning bolt streaks the wall behind the sign's middle, likely made by the same source that left a kidney-shaped water stain spanning three panels in the neglected drop ceiling.

So far he is unimpressed. He notices the depth of the office's quietude, thinks too much quiet serves no one. Too much quiet precedes the prowl of death and the infinite nothingness of the dreamless sleep that must follow.

Then, suddenly, the din of voices.

He sits a little straighter in his chair. The wood groans

beneath him.

A man in a short-sleeved white shirt and a fat, too-short necktie enters the office lobby. He looks up from a single piece of paper and stops in his tracks. He steps toward Basil, extends an open hand in salutation, retracts it for a second, and then extends the hand again.

"Mary Jane wasn't so full of shit after all," he says.

Basil introduces himself and accepts the handshake. His clawed mitt dwarfs the man's hand. The pink flesh of his palm feels soft and untested.

"Name's Robert Bulcavage. But I suppose you knew that already. Call me Bob. Come on back."

Basil follows his host through the darkened hallways, the blinds on each window lowered, each nook subdued. The whole suite seems funereal. He passes three offices—lights out in one, doors inched to a close in the other two—as he follows Bulcavage toward the only cheery space in the entire office: the conference room. Floor-to-ceiling windows offer unobstructed views of the cornfields, roadways and pastures carving up sleepy Beak. From his vantage point on the second floor, the landscape seems alive, verdant and starkly different from this cheerless interior. He takes a seat at the far end of the table, opposite Bulcavage—a good twenty feet between them—wanting to hurl something through one of the windows so he can feel and taste the air. He hopes for a quick end to the meeting.

"So you're interested in the job," Bulcavage says. "Why?"

"Why, sir?"

"Standard question."

"I think I'd do well here."

"Of course you would. You would do well anywhere. So why here?"

"I'm not sure I follow, sir."

Bulcavage sighs and lights a cigarette.

"Would you mind not doing that, sir?" Basil asks. "The smell

... it, uh, angers me."

Bulcavage dabs the cigarette's tip into an orange ashtray.

"We'll just save that for later," he says. "Look, I'll tell you something, honest as Abe. I don't think an environment like ours—Savage Communications, I mean—I don't think it would suit you."

"Oh, no?"

"Not by a long shot." Bulcavage softens his booming voice. "This place here, this place is for loners and losers. The people I have working for me? They're here for a reason, and it's not a good one. People don't come to Savage because they're at the top of their game. They come here because they screwed up, because they're afraid or because they ran away and are hiding from something they don't want to find, or someone they don't want to find them. I know that. I'm fine with that. Frankly, I couldn't afford them if they were whole and perfect people. Truth is, I don't care why they're here. They don't get much from me—they don't expect much—but I stay out of their hair, so they enjoy their freedom, more or less. The way I see it, you do what I tell you to, when I tell you to, how I tell you to, and it tends to work out all right. Has so far, anyway."

"Okay."

"So. Based on the bundle of shit I just dropped in your lap, you think you could resign yourself to playing by those rules?"

"I've thrived in harsher climes, under worse conditions, against impossible odds."

Bulcavage smiles and nods his head, fiddles with the cigarette in its ashtray.

Basil is unsure how to proceed, unsure whether he has the job, or whether he wants it at all. The arrangement seems too simple, too straightforward. He waits for clarity.

Bulcavage just sits there, his eyes on the ashtray. The rim scrapes cold ash from the cigarette's tip.

"It's very quiet here," Basil offers.

"Too quiet!"

"That's what I mean."

"They like it quiet. My employees—the ones I have left, I mean. They think if they're quiet they can hide. They're wrong."

"It wouldn't be so quiet with someone like me here."

"I bet it wouldn't, a big boy like you." He laughs, his whole body shaking. "I bet like hell it wouldn't."

"So," Basil says. "Does my office have a window?"

Bulcavage tilts his head, leans into the cushion of his leather chair. Then he gives an approving laugh, softer this time.

"Why? You planning on jumping out of it?"

"I like the light."

Something loosens in Basil's gut. He stiffens to restrain a determined fart.

"Ain't that just the sweetest thing I ever heard," Bulcavage says.

"I've spent too long in the darkness."

"Sure, sure," Bulcavage interjects. "Look, forgive me for being direct, but I think you're someone who appreciates hearing what's on someone's mind. What is it you hope to do here?"

To understand how the world works, Basil thinks. To learn. Maybe to figure out how to stop hating himself so he can return to Our Fiery Home a kinder, more capable leader. He knows he should say anything but the truth.

"I hope to make you happy," he chooses to say. An uneasy feeling builds in his chest, this false subservience, one step removed from begging.

Bulcavage places both hands on his belly.

"And why should I believe you're the person to do that?"

Mary Jane Pix's words echo in Basil's head.

"You won't find anyone with a skill set quite like mine."

"Ain't that the truth."

"I've seen things. I know things. And my words have the power to transform the world."

"Through black magic?"

"Through beauty and grace."

"Okay. You have my attention. Wow me."

Basil recalls a poem he composed not long ago, while making the rounds of Our Fiery Home, wondering if he would ever see anyplace else, if he would ever discover the places he imagined when he closed his eyes. He stands and recites the verse.

*A warning, O wanderer*
*Bore, as a beetle, as a worm*
*To bring down the mossy wall*
*Brick by brick*
*Reach, climb, stretch thy legs*
*Grow wings and seek the wind*
*Walk into the waves and leave a wake*
*The shore a speck of ragged rock*
*Then sink*
*Among skeletons, broken ships, a second sea of lost riches*
*Drown thy self in the depths of memory, then*
*Breathe deep and rise anew*
*Invent a home for the rambling heart*
*Blaze a path on virgin soil, or carve a map of ancient bone*
*So others may follow*
*Bellow, bark, cry the speech of the mad*
*As an explorer, an artist, a child rapt in play*
*Wander*
*Till monster, till beast, till man*
*Taste thy flesh*
*And then say no more*

"Your words, I presume?"

Basil nods.

"And what do you say it means, that little ditty?"

"It means I've come a long way, and I'm here to start over."

"Okay, Walt Whitman. I'll bite. If you think you can put that gentle wit to good use here at Savage, by all means let's do so, but odes and haikus won't do you any good. Here, the kind of work you'll be doing as my copywriter, plain and simple language is your best friend."

Basil rubs his chin, wondering when Bulcavage will shut up, because the man bores him, but mostly because he has to empty his bowels. He assumes it would be impolite to walk away in the middle of a potential boss's diatribe, no matter how pointless.

"Let me put it this way," Bulcavage continues. "As far as I'm concerned, ad copy and poetry don't share too much DNA. Whereas a poem might sit differently with you than it does with me, a good ad will say one thing to all people, even the dumbest of fucks. It's all about clear, precise messaging. An ad can go one of two ways: You either make things better for your client, or you make 'em worse."

"In one hand poison, in the other a cure."

"A more romantic way of putting it, but sure. If you're lucky, an ad campaign will at least help maintain the status quo for the client, and then you can explain away later the fact that even though the campaign did absolutely nothing to grow the client's business, your work helped keep revenues more or less stable in a challenging time, in an already tight market beset by a raft of aggressive new competitors—that sort of BS. My point: In this position you'll be dreaming up the most basic of silver linings about farm equipment, barbecue grills and truck stops—inane shit like that. So let's hope your skills are transferable."

"My pen cannot fail."

"Most of our clients are nothing to write home about," Bulcavage drones on. "Most of them are in obscure sectors of manufacturing you probably had no idea existed, or maybe some sort of service industry, like the occasional plumber or house cleaner or tractor-blade sharpener. Take a deep dive into our book of business and you'll notice that nine out of ten of these enterprises are dinosaurs on the verge of extinction, presided over by stubborn old men with outsized potbellies and zero imagination."

Basil eyes the door, daydreaming of quiet places with holes in the ground into which he can deposit his ample waste. Bulcavage shows no signs of shutting his trap anytime soon, so Basil focuses on preserving the integrity of his body's sphincters.

*Don't break the seal.*

"Each one of these guys—our precious clients, I mean—is wasting too much time, space and money on acquiring more people and stuff to cram into an expressionless brick building, probably no more than a ten-minute drive from our front door, whereas he should be sinking his money into ad programs crafted by skilled professionals like yours truly. Someone who can make a difference, I always like to add. That's our message. That's our pitch."

Bulcavage re-lights his cigarette and picks up where he left off.

"I don't mean to stereotype, but these people can barely string a sentence together, let alone name a book they've read, other than the Bible, though I'd bet ten dollars to a bag of doughnuts not a single one of them has read anything but the kinky parts— the sex, drugs and heavy metal. These people were born here in Beak and, in all likelihood, will happily die here. And most of them wouldn't understand the point of a poem, let alone take the time to crack open a book and actually read one. To them you'll be a big, spicy meatball—a piece of exotic fruit from someplace they think they'll never visit."

Basil just sits there, nodding and clenching.

"Tomorrow's Friday," Bulcavage says, checking his watch. "As good a day as any to get the ball rolling. In fact, we'll be brainstorming on a new campaign, so you'll be jumping right into the fire, so to speak. We'll see what happens from there."

Bulcavage starts talking numbers, vacation days and

employment benefits, mentions something about weekends Basil might need to work every now and again in order to make a deadline, but Basil's mind is hopelessly adrift. He fingers his injured horn as he pretends to consider the job offer, though his predicament—having to shit—dulls his concentration. His fingertips ride the shallow trench left by the biker's burrowing bullet.

As Bulcavage launches into a treatise about a newly acquired client "in need of a swift kick in the ass as desperately as he needs a cogent advertising strategy," Basil interrupts his would-be boss mid-sentence.

"I'm in, sir," he says. "Just one point we need to clear up before I go. About that office window …"

* * *

Kamala kisses the claws of her dearest disciple, Kindness, and leads him along the perimeter, passing the communal rooms of Our Fiery Home. The shadows seem somehow warmer, safer than wandering out in the open—exposed on the offal-stained red rock of the hunting grounds. The air carries the stink of whatever meaty slurry cooks and pops in the cauldrons. The pair slip into the cold, empty hollow once considered the sanctuary of their departed leader, Basil, now a willful outcast.

Kamala knows she must find a safe haven to call hers, but this is no time for retreat. Rather, it is time to tear down and rebuild. First, she needs to settle unsettled business.

"Soon," she says. "Soon the murk will be made clear."

Demons have defaced every word lining the walls of Basil's throne room. Feces drip from the ceiling. Despite the stink, Kamala swears she can detect lingering traces of Basil's scent. She circles Kindness, her gaunt little suitor, studies his sunken eyes and the bent carrot of a nose dangling loosely from the center of his face. Though she has announced nothing of the sort, she has chosen Kindness as her chief adviser. He is among the few she can trust—the few with any sort of intelligence or thoughtfulness, at least.

Her ears listen for hints of insurrection. No whispers, only the same unsettling *scrrrrrrick, scrrrrrrrick, scrrrrrrrick*—she imagines a sturdy bone dragged against a pane of ribbed metal—that has been droning on since Basil left Our Fiery Home, lost to the world. The way sound travels down here, she cannot know from which direction the disturbance comes, how near or far its source. A call to battle, she thinks, or perhaps an alert for a clan of assassins to remove her from the seat of power. As Basil said, they will come for her, in time. She knows she will not sleep well anytime soon, at least not until she exerts the will to stand up and say, "This is how it's going to be." She imagines an army of hungry demons scraping flinty blades against nearby rocks: always sharpening their weaponry, craving the nectar of freshly spilled blood.

Then she notices an eerie quiet. The chorus of *scrrrrrrricks* has come to an abrupt end. Only the ever-present snap of overcooked coals exercises its voice. In the distance, a demon squeals, acquiescing to another, no doubt losing pieces of itself or, quite possibly, offering up the gift of its life.

"We will meet with Basil's precious Council," she says.

"And then?" Kindness quivers. His narrow eyes remain fixed on the doorway. He seems to expect the ax to fall at any moment.

"The Council will soon be no more," she says. "Should they resist, each of the nine will be made into a corpse. And you, dear Kindness, will take their place."

Kindness has no words for her. He pales.

She ceases her pacing to face him, her eyes finding his. She bends to brush his lips with hers, and then places a hand on his slight shoulder. He sinks beneath the weight of it.

"Understand, my dear," she says. "We must erase Basil's footprint, undo everything he has put in place. As of now, this morass has no use for the gentle or the thoughtful—us. It benefits only those who consider suffering a form of currency. This must change, and it shall. Before long, the memories of Basil's reign will fade. He might as well never have existed."

"I know what you must do," he says. "It's just ... I am concerned."

"You cannot let fear consume you."

"I have no say in the matter."

"Now is our time—yours and mine. Trust me, my love. Even before Basil put this place behind him, his mind was miles away. He hadn't been with us, hadn't led us, for far too long. You might say I did his job for him, piece by miserable piece. Who do you think did the work of keeping the ceiling from caving in? Who do you think kept the mutinies at bay? You think he knew how to make this machine hum or that he even cared to keep it from the verge of collapse? Hardly. He was too concerned with feeling doleful or otherwise consumed by his failures. He was a dumb little boy lost in his mind. Now he is gone forever. Soon my name will grace the door."

"You have my confidence, of course. My concern has little to do with your abilities. I fear for your safety."

"And, more to the point, for your own."

"Yes, my queen," he chokes out, as he releases a wracking sob. A line of spit spills from the emptiness between his fangs. He raises a clawed hand to hide his tears. "Forgive me. I am a lamb. A weak little lamb."

"Is that what you want, little lamb? To be sacrificed and served as meat for those with an appetite?"

"Of course not!"

"You must find a way to be strong. We deserve the world we have been seeking, but it will not reveal itself willingly. To survive what's to come will require great courage from both of us. I need your courage. Your sacrifice will come, but it will not be of the flesh. I don't intend to create this world without you, my love."

"Your faith in me is a gift, but—"

"Revolutions do not come peacefully, dearest, but I can assure your protection. The safest place will be at my side."

"I'm … I'm not so sure."

She opens her arms and welcomes Kindness to her. His rail of a body folds into hers, and she holds him against her sagging breasts. She strokes the strands of thinning black hair hanging limply from his scalp.

"There, there, dearest Kindness, my pathetic little beetle of a boy. It will all be over soon—all this plotting and unpleasantness. I don't favor this duplicity any more than you do, but fixing what's broken sometimes requires tossing out all the dirty old pieces and starting fresh. Just burn everything down and build anew over the ash."

"Murder sickens me."

"My dear, it's a miracle you've lasted as long as you have."

She knows her words hurt, as proven by the sharp prickling in her back, as Kindness's claws sink into one of the few unspoiled parts of her scarred body. She responds by digging two of her own claws, ever so slightly, into the base of his skull. He recoils immediately.

"Remember your place, dear," she whispers into his ear. "Don't pick this tender moment as the one you decide to grow some hair on those little marbles of yours. No offense, dear, but any number of ghouls your better would gladly step forward to enjoy the fruits of our arrangement. Blame the creator for his error in placing those little bits between your legs. We both know it is I who should have you bent at the waist, heaving and filling you with a sticky mess, not the other way around. I'll bet sometimes you even dream of it. I would hate to cast you aside because you did something foolish. I would miss our talks."

"Forgive me, my queen. Sometimes … my emotions … all these changes, so sudden."

"Tell me, dearest: What is it you fear?"

She knows the answer. Her question has less to do with *what* but with *whom*.

"I dare not speak his name," Kindness says.

"Let me handle Lubos. He too will soon be a memory."

"We have been hiding in the shadows since Basil left. You have shown yourself to *no one* since the moment you took power. What must they think?"

"Do you consider me a fool? Or worse, a coward?"

"I would never suggest such a thing, my queen. It's just ..."

"What good is an adviser who cannot speak his mind?"

"Lubos has only venom in his heart. I will sleep better once his head has been parted from his body."

Although she cannot admit such a thing to a creature as timid as Kindness, she feels the same. Among demons, Lubos stands on his own—famous for his cruelty, cunning, tough as a piece of cooled iron. And he will not give his life easily.

# Chapter 7

# Cold, Wet and Damning the Maker

Basil's cool hand rests on the doorknob, palms moist, hooves shifting on the carpeted floor. Nervousness stays his hand, his eyes boring a hole through the gold-tinted plaque on the office's front door. In his core he knows nothing bad can happen— nothing terrible—yet his heart races, made worse by his tired mind and empty stomach.

A shit show of a night has led to a wreck of a morning.

His coal-black skin glistens with sweat and rainwater. Worse, his mind has lost its sharpness, the result of a sleepless night he thought would be his last. Perhaps he should just turn around and lope down the stairs, and then head east to start over somewhere else far from here; this, at least, would spare him the embarrassment of a public tongue lashing courtesy of a lesser being, a human no less. All the omens seem to point him in this direction. He knows his sorry appearance and his obscene tardiness will make a less than glowing impression for his first day on the job. To make matters worse, he smells like a sewer— an aromatic blend of mud, fear and caked-on cow shit.

And everything had been going so well until now.

He recalls the precise moment his fortunes shifted, the previous afternoon, when he shook hands with Bulcavage and agreed to take the job as Savage Communications' chief copywriter.

It all went downhill from there.

\* \* \*

By the time Basil left the Savage interview and descended the stairs to exit the building, the day had turned old and gray. He hurried out the door, impelled by the demon in his gut, knowing he might not make it outside in time. He stopped just beyond the exit door and squatted behind an overgrown shrub. There, in the mix of mulch and spent cigarette butts, he unleashed the mostly liquid contents of his bowels. The expulsion burned so intensely he half-expected tongues of fire to spring from his anus and set the shrub ablaze. The smell choked him—atrocious, even by his standards.

As he finished, he inhaled deeply, because he couldn't help himself, and stretched his arms wide. The bones in his back cracked in reply. Beyond the stink of his feces, the air smelled different—electric, almost alive. He eyed the western horizon, where the haze-shrouded ball of the late-afternoon sun had dipped perilously close to the crown of a modest hillside.

Although his brain waves had flat lined after listening to so many of Bulcavage's hollow words—the phrases "retirement plan" and "graft" and "vacation days" had no meaning—Basil felt remarkably light in the hoof. Just two days above ground and he had started to find his way, with a real job and everything. Sure, two humans had forfeited their lives to him—the collateral damage of his arrival, a necessary write-off—but he knew he would forgive and forget those transgressions in time.

Besides, those wretched pig-men had deserved his wrath.

He studied his open palm, where a strange sensation lingered. A prickling of sorts, he might have called it. The coarse skin felt the same as it had an hour ago, yet it seemed somehow different after shaking hands with Bulcavage, a symbol of their agreement: Basil had consented to showing up the following morning, promptly at nine a.m., and every weekday thereafter, "ready to set the world on fire"—Bulcavage's words. Basil felt infallible yet also indebted, loving and loathing in the same body. He saw Bulcavage for what he was: a direct, untrustworthy and single-minded authoritarian who liked to hear himself talk, a ruthless fool in blind pursuit of the possessions and titles and accomplishments he thought were important.

Even so, Basil had a soft spot for his new boss, the man who had handed him an opportunity others had not. And he assured himself he would not disappoint, chaotic bowels be damned.

Basil's first day among the willfully employed would begin in a few mere winks, so he knew he must rest well if he were to awaken with a nimble mind, ready to produce his best words. He climbed onto the motorcycle and fired up the engine. The smell of fuel exhaust seared the stink of his own feces from his nostrils. He backed out of the parking spot and pulled forward. The bike wobbled beneath him. At the stop sign near the far end of the lot, he glanced over his shoulder to survey the four-story building in which he would make his mark—an eyesore of brown brick and reflective glass, to be sure, but *his* eyesore—and gave an approving nod.

His stomach rumbled in time with the bike's engine, knowing he needed to sate his appetite. Otherwise, his mind would not ease. As the landscape zipped past, his eyes darted from one new scene to another. Hay rolls and cornfields and wandering streams where cows drank. He urged his brain to remember the route—right after left after right—but before long all semblance of civilization had faded from view. With a newfound terror, he found himself alone on a barren stretch of road that seemed to stretch toward the edge of the earth.

His skin chilled as he registered the approach of an entity his brain could not explain. The monstrous-looking thing churned toward him, and he slowed the bike as the yellow-and-green beast skulked to within striking distance. Unnatural smells crept into the tunnels of his nose. He had grown used to the presence of these mechanical beasts, all metal and rubber, but he could not yet fathom the hows and whys of their existence.

*Magic abounds in the mortal world.*

This particular beast dragged its prize in a crudely made wagon. The pungent odor of organic material saturated the air.

Decaying prey, perhaps. A human imprisoned in an all-glass vestibule seemed to control the beast, or worked in tandem to accomplish a shared goal—symbiosis. The man waved toward Basil as the two vehicles passed one another, and Basil waved back. Basil took note of the treads of the oversized tires and the name "John Deere" etched into the beast's metal skin.

The precise etching reminded him of Our Fiery Home, of the imaginative klatch of demons who carved designs into their flesh using rudimentary blades and a tarry mash of blood and charred bone. Most of the symbols suggested ownership or privilege, while others were simplistic mutilations to depict an affiliation with a certain tribe or faction. No symbols marred his flesh, though he saw value in the ritual—an act of creation, turning the body into art.

Basil eased the Harley to a stop, at which point he decided to turn around and follow the tractor back toward town. John Deere would know the way. He followed slowly, less than three lengths from the wagon's rear. The bike sputtered and nearly tipped over more than once. The poison of diesel fumes, and the moist-earth smell drifting from John Deere's wagon, filled his lungs. In another hundred feet, the tractor veered off the macadam and onto a muddy two-track cutting through a field. Grasses undulated like waves in a storm-stoked lake. He stopped at the two-track entrance and watched the tractor stop beneath the roof of a rusty Quonset hut nearly a quarter-mile into the field.

A familiar uneasiness consumed him. He recognized the feeling as the seeds of panic, about to germinate. Beak, the town he had come to know, had disappeared. In its place: nothing but flat desolation, save thin stands of cottonwoods and a few weathered structures of manmade origin.

He had lost his way.

The light shifted, and the air changed sharply—a smell and a feeling. A chill wind cooled the flesh of his back. As he looked behind him, he saw a massive bank of purple and gray clouds creeping across the sky. Slowly, the horizon swallowed the last embers of daylight. The temperature dropped ten degrees in seconds.

Something bad was about to happen.

Basil leaned into the handlebars and opened the throttle. The bike took off. The sudden acceleration jerked him backward, nearly pitching him off the seat. After steadying himself, he crouched forward and became one with his steed. He squinted into the rising wind.

Darkness ahead of him, darkness behind. Instinct told him to seek shelter.

He crested a slight hill and spotted a path to salvation: a sole ash tree, in the middle of a freshly shorn field. He eased off the throttle and pulled off the roadway. The bike shuddered, battling one trench after another. Before long he came beneath the aegis of the tree. Nearly forty feet tall from the base of its trunk to its highest branch, the tree swayed in the ripping wind. Groaning and creaking, each leaf-swollen branch seemed to sound some sort of alarm. He parked the bike next to the tree and waited.

Roiling clouds stretched east to west, south to north. Only then, in the final seconds of ambient light, did Basil get a sense of the infiniteness of the sky, now violent and furious. No ceiling here, so unlike Our Fiery Home. He found this both comforting and unsettling, because everything must reach its end eventually. Lightning electrified the belly of a storm cloud, and the mere sight of it knocked Basil on his rear end. He scrambled to the tree trunk, his flesh meeting the bark. His mind filled with thoughts of murk and doom. What kinds of malevolent creatures prowled the clouds above? He envisioned a winged and tentacled beast, feathers scraping the barren plains with each flap of its mighty wings, while a great cyclopean eye scoured the earth in search of easy prey to fill the cavities between its mountain-peak teeth.

The rains came a moment later.

Basil shivered beneath the tree, his rear end soaking in an inch-deep puddle. He cursed the creator. He cursed himself. He cursed the rain. And the wind. And the lightning. And the tree. And the unseen beast roaming the sky. And all of humankind. And himself again, for thinking he could survive away from the womb of Our Fiery Home, a place he both loved and hated, but also a place free of the misery that came from being caught in a windswept downpour.

As a thunderclap cracked overhead, a bolt of lightning shot from the clouds. A splintered branch slammed to the earth, all twelve hundred pounds of wood and leaf landing less than ten feet from where Basil cowered in a tight little ball. He fought every urge to flee, to run headlong into the field, but he stayed put, screaming into his armpit. He could not best an invisible monster that hurled its weapons from above.

He wondered if he would ever see the sun again. He retreated into his mind.

The hours passed slowly, unmercifully.

*Her* image—rather, pieces of her, parts of her—came in fractions. Despite his efforts, he failed to connect the threads, and her image faded from his mind. His failure gave him something to mull other than his sure demise.

Instead he ruminated on the familiar: the forceful taking of Kamala, or any other she-demon he wanted; his choicest poems; the quiet corners of Our Fiery Home; and, of course, Lubos. First, Lubos's imposing silhouette, then snapshots of his foe's many war wounds: the milky-white left eye, lolling like a spun marble; the discolored scar running the length of his torso; the yellow canine jutting from a hole in his lower lip; the crooked sneer that came from the joy of watching another creature suffer.

Basil whipped his head against the trunk to shake the images from his skull.

The rains eased over the next several hours, the winds calmed.

As the first fingers of dawn reached above the eastern horizon, Basil lost his fight to keep his eyes open.

He came to a short time later, unsure of who or where he was. All evidence of his horrible night had disappeared. The sky had turned a light gray—the violence over, the monster having moved on.

He craved the sun, to dry him out, but it chose to hide. As he tried to stand, his body felt the depth of its weakness. Water dripped from the fur coating his lower half. Shivers owned him, and the lack of control horrified him. His stomach ached with pangs of hunger. Then he remembered: the job.

"Aw, *fuck*," he hissed.

He climbed aboard the Harley, brought it to life and cranked the throttle. Mud kicked up from the rear wheel, but the motorcycle foundered in the dense slop. By the time the front tire touched asphalt, mud that smelled like cow shit—because most of it was, in fact, cow shit—caked most of his body. He followed the roadway, trying to recognize something familiar, something that suggested he was on his way back to Beak proper. He turned down an unmarked road, which showed him familiar sights. Homes and office buildings loomed in the distance—hallmarks of civilization. He smiled at his luck. A moment later the engine sputtered, and the bike died a slow death in the middle of the road.

"Go," he commanded it.

Nothing happened.

"I said *go*, you wicked thing!"

Again, nothing.

Rage consumed him. He leapt off the bike and raised both balled fists over his head, happy to smash the infernal machine to bits, but he had the presence of mind to stop himself. Instead, he rubbed his temples to ward off a blooming headache. He would need this steed in the days to come, he knew, so he rolled it to the side of the road and eased it into a ditch filled with rainwater and pollywogs. Having no other choice, he took a deep breath and galloped toward Beak.

He arrived in downtown Beak within ten minutes. Men and women with places to go and appointments to keep crowded the sidewalks. Not a single face looked familiar, but he recognized the building façades. A woman in a yellow sundress hissed at him as he passed, but he had no time to make friends. Not today.

The sound of hooves clopping on asphalt echoed in the dead spaces between storefronts. A man in a short-sleeved shirt, overalls and a blue USA hat called out.

"Hey, big boy. Strap on an applecart and a feedbag and we'll make a million bucks."

Basil tensed the fingers of both hands into fists. He imagined the man's disembodied head—USA cap and all—skewered on a spear. He could practically see it, the dried blood staining the corners of the man's gaping mouth, clotting his ear canals. The vision inspired him to quicken his pace.

He had no idea what time it was when he approached the office building housing the Savage Communications' HQ. As he galloped, he detected movement to his left. A well-dressed woman with long brown hair strode purposely toward the building's entrance. She seemed to be racing him to the door. Oversized sunglasses with brown lenses obscured her eyes, but a subtle change in her gait suggested she was giving him a wide berth. He reached the door before her and held it open.

"Good morning," he said.

"It's ten thirty, ding-dong," she said. "Only an ape says 'good morning' after nine."

She stepped through the doorway without making eye contact, made a left and kept walking, never looking back.

Basil closed his eyes and committed her perfume to memory. He studied the way her rear end moved in her tight skirt, how her hair bobbed in time with her confident stride. This vision in high heels made him curious, hungry.

Then: *Oh, right … work.*

He ascended the stairs to the second floor and arrived at the door to Savage Communications. He rested his hand on the knob and watched drops of manure-speckled water darken the carpet beneath him. He took three deep breaths and then turned the knob, wondering just how poorly this day would go.

* * *

"I thought we agreed on nine," says Bulcavage, clearly annoyed. "You missed that mark by more than an hour. I just about gave up on you."

"Quite sorry, sir," Basil says. "Let's just say I had a long night. A bad night, you might say."

"Don't make it a habit."

"It won't happen again."

"You look like dog shit, friend. Smell like it, too, if I'm telling the truth."

"Like I said, it was a long night."

"Shit happens. I get it. But let's not get in the practice of disappointing each other. Agreed?"

Basil nods furiously.

"Come on back."

Basil follows Bulcavage into the conference room, where red and black balloons float in the corner. Two trays of bagels wrapped in plastic sit on the table, undisturbed, and behind them stand three unopened bottles of pop—one Coca-Cola, one Diet Coke, one Sprite—and twin columns of red Solo cups. Bulcavage claps and then plucks a lighter from the table. He lights a sparkler, and the thermite tip catches. He hands over the lit sparkler. Basil accepts it, reluctantly, and holds it between his thumb and forefinger. Sparks of white light bounce off his mud-caked claws.

Basil eyes a shoddy sign taped to the wall in the quiet space above a dry-erase board. The glittery blood-red letters—W-E-L-C-O-M-E—pop against the pane of dingy white. It reminds him of the torched metal sign adorning the cavern wall in Our Fiery Home. An odd feeling builds within him: a combination of anger, sadness and nostalgia, akin to homesickness.

Basil feels a presence behind him, and he turns to see two people standing in the doorway. A tall, skinny man with thin-rimmed glasses offers an unenthusiastic wave before turning and wandering out of the conference room, presumably to go back to his office. The other, a short woman in a ruffled dress buttoned up to the neck, takes a long look at Basil. She wrinkles her nose and then huffs as loudly as she can. She storms off, stomping her feet as she goes.

"Don't mind them," Bulcavage says. "They're just excited."

"Obviously."

"So ... today. We'll get your paperwork settled and then brainstorm about the new campaign for one of our longest-tenured clients. They're undergoing a bit of a change in their approach to the business, so we could use a fresh perspective."

"Can't wait."

"Some backstory: The owner died and now the son is taking over. Dreadful little shit who probably wants nothing to do with us. So, we want to come up with something that's going to bowl him over, really knock him out of his loafers. Something to assure their current customers that things will be just fine going forward, even though the heart and soul of the business is now six feet into the dirt."

"It's nice that the kid wants to take over where his father left off."

"Here's the kick in the ass: The damned kid doesn't want any of it. Not a bit. Truly, that little devil is going to put the screws to every last customer. We just want to get something in front of him so he knows we give a shit, so we can bill them for something tangible before the son of a bitch decides he wants no part of us and pulls the plug because we're an unnecessary expense."

"Are we? Unnecessary?"

Bulcavage seems unsure how to answer.

"Anyway, the paperwork," Bulcavage says as he takes a seat. "For starters, I'll need a driver's license and a Social Security card."

"Uh."

"And you have neither, right?"

"Not that I'm aware of."

"Right. Why would you?"

"Is that a bad thing?"

"Fuck it," Bulcavage says. He tears up an employment form and lets the pieces fly like tossed confetti. "We'll just do it the old-fashioned way."

The woman in the ruffled dress reappears in the doorway, her feet an inch or two shy of the conference-room carpet's worn edge.

"I'm here for my bagel, Bob," she says.

"Come get it. Last I checked we don't have a butler."

"I am *not* coming in there. I don't know how you could bring him here."

She storms off again. Her perfume—dead flowers, by Basil's best guess—lingers like a fart in a closet.

Basil turns to Bulcavage, asking, "Is there a problem, sir?"

"Don't mind her," Bulcavage whispers. "That's Karen. She's just a little—"

Karen slaps both palms against the glass pane behind Basil.

"This is the worst thing you've ever done, Bob," she yells, though the glass dulls the sharpness of her words. "It's criminal is what it is! It's a GD assault! I don't want to have to stare at his demon dick every day. Tell him to put on some GD pants!"

Basil imagines a fireball in his hand big enough to incinerate Karen.

Bulcavage turns back to Basil and says, brightly, "Okay. Let's go meet Herbert."

# Chapter 8

# Transcending Death

"So what do we have today, Bob?"

The nameplate on the desk reads "Herbert Teak". The man in the chair behind it looks kind enough: tall, thin and bespectacled, salt-and-pepper hair brushed tidily to one side, dressed in pressed khakis and a short-sleeved madras shirt. He looks put out by the big, black demon taking up the entire corner of his cramped office.

"Hey," Basil says. "Herbert Teak from Beak!"

"I'm from Des Moines," Herbert says dryly, without turning to Basil.

"Before we talk about what happens next, let's catch up on some existing business," Bulcavage says. "The douchebag from Omaha HVAC was, shall we say, less than impressed with the first proof of the direct mailer you put together."

"Are we talking tweaks," Herbert asks, "or a tear down and rebuild?"

"Blow it all up. Frankly, the client said the design sucks. The ad copy too. I'm just telling you because this is what he told me, but he said using it to line the pan of a birdcage would only increase its value. You know, so a bird could shit on it."

"A little harsh."

"Don't get bent out of shape, Herb. What do we do about this?"

"Smash the client's spine," Basil offers. "He'll never walk again. It will humble him."

"Uh ... let's call that Plan B," Bulcavage says. "In the meantime, let's consider a less lethal form of response. Herbert, have three new mockups on my desk by first thing Monday morning."

Herbert nods, his lips pursed, jaw clenched.

"On to Big Bair Agriculture and Machinery," Bulcavage says. "You remember Alan Keller was sick ..."

"Do I?" Herbert says.

"Christ, he was half-dead the last time he was in here. You must remember. Old, decrepit, sickly guy who brought in the rhubarb crisp that stayed in the conference room for two weeks? I think the dish sprouted limbs and crawled out of here on its own."

"That horrid thing? Guy deserves to cook in the chair for that atrocity."

"For chrissakes, Herbert. He died, you know. He's dead. Kaput."

"Oh. Shit. Sorry."

"So, with the kid taking the reins from the old man, we've got our hands full. Stupid know-nothing kid hasn't learned a damned thing. Has no clue what the hell he's doing. You can guess where we're going to fall on his list of priorities. Too busy fucking up everything the old man put into place. Likely steer the whole kit and caboodle into a nosedive. But that's not the story we're going to tell. No one's writing any epitaphs here."

"I mean it, Bob. I'm really sorry. I'm sure Mister Keller was a very nice man. I didn't mean to disrespect—"

"Herbert. He's dead, and he'll still be dead no matter what you say about him. No big deal. Just shut up about it now."

Basil does his best to listen, but the weight of his sleeplessness— from his nightmarish experience in the lightning storm, from a lifetime of vigilance underground—drags him to the brink of exhaustion. His eyelids want to close. Talons dig into his palms. Teeth sink into his bottom lip, anything to keep from losing consciousness and dropping to the floor like a felled redwood.

"Time's a wastin'," Bulcavage says. "I'd like to get something together by day's end. And, now that we're fully staffed"—he gestures to Basil—"I'd like to give them live copy. What do you think?"

"Paint by numbers," Herbert says. "Easy enough: black background, light on copy, shot of a father and a son on a Big Bair combine at the end of a long shift, the day about thirty minutes shy of sunset, the leftover daylight on their faces and the golden wheat field that spreads out before them. Pair the image with some BS about relationships, about making memories, because they're all we have. Then mention some garbage about Old Man Keller, about how things will stay the same even though he's no longer with us. You can practically hear the voiceover: 'Even though the old coot is gone, his spirit will guide us forever.' Not that we'll have voiceover."

Herbert and Bulcavage bandy back and forth, the conversation going off on far-flung tangents, until Basil is thoroughly confused. He nods off, and time passes. He jolts awake at the sound of his name.

"Yes, sir," he says, louder than he should have.

"What do you think of what Herbert just said?" Bulcavage asks.

"I think it's good," Basil says—again, louder than he should have, and having no idea what Herbert just said.

"And?"

"And well done, well put."

"I'm sure a guy like you will come up with infinitely better garbage than the garbage I just gave you," Herbert says. "What I gave you was nonsense."

"Agreed," says Bulcavage. "We need a hook—something to build a campaign around. Our 'Just Do It.' Our 'Plop, Plop, Fizz, Fizz.' Basil?"

"I like what Herbert said. Someone should write it down before we forget it."

"Herbert's not our chief copywriter."

"But ... we're a team."

"Exactly. Herbert's job is to take your brilliance and turn it into full-fledged creative. Consider it your job to inspire him. In this case it looks like the cart's preceding the horse. I'd love to hear an original thought from your end of the table—aside from inventive ways to paralyze our clients."

"I guess I do have one idea."

They wait.

"Transcending death," Basil says.

Herbert laughs out loud. He moves his hand to his mouth, trying to hide a smirk.

"'Transcending death'?" Bulcavage repeats. "'Transcending death.' What the Christ is 'Transcending death'?"

"My idea. You know, for the campaign hook. Isn't that what we all want, to live forever in some way? For our memories—or the memories others have of us—to endure?"

"We're selling threshers and augers here, not salvation."

Basil keeps going, further fleshing out his idea. At one point he's describing a scene in which a young boy sails a mile above the earth, in the wisps of clouds, the wind tousling his hair. In the scene, as he sees it, a flock of gulls surrounds the boy, then suddenly, the boy becomes an eagle. Only then does Basil realize he has stopped making sense. His tongue seems to have gone on autopilot, his mind somewhere else entirely—lost in a fog, miles from here. His body wants to curl up in a ball by the side of the road and wait for the fog to burn off, for this problem he has created to melt away.

Bulcavage turns to Herbert and says, "Is he shitting me?"

Herbert leans back in his chair, eyes scanning the barren walls. His head turns to hide a mischievous smile.

"You're shitting me, right?" Bulcavage says, this time directly to Basil.

"I think it works," Basil replies.

"Apparently."

"No good?"

"No. No good."

"I guess I am a little tired."

"I should hope so. My second grader could do better."

"There's no need to be nasty, sir."

"You think this is nasty? This is civil. This is pattycake. You want to see nasty? Say 'Transcending death' again."

"I've said it only once, sir. You're the one who keeps repeating it."

Bulcavage jots a note on the sole piece of white paper on the table. He mumbles something under his breath.

"Beg your pardon," Basil says. "Was your babble meant for my ears?"

Bulcavage looks up, his eyes finding Basil's, and says, "If I wanted you to hear it, you'd hear it."

"Says the coward ..."

"I'd watch myself if I were you."

"You think I have reason to fear *you*?" Basil says. He stands, his whole body as tense as strung piano wire, and flips over the empty chair next to Bulcavage. "You'd squirm beneath my thumb like a halved slug. I'd leave you nothing but a sticky puddle."

"Well, this certainly took an unexpected turn," Herbert says.

Basil realizes his gaffe, how horribly he has overstepped.

"Look, Basil," Bulcavage says. "I don't think—"

"Excuse me," Basil interrupts. He takes a deep breath and adds, "Forgive my outburst. It's been a tough couple of days, and I'm not too dense to realize my insolence has no excuse. I'm happy to work up a few other ideas. Give me the afternoon. Please. That's all I ask. I tend to work better alone anyway, when my mind can wander."

Bulcavage raises a hand and wishes Basil away.

Basil clops sideways out of Herbert's constricted office. He lingers behind Bulcavage and spies the bald spot at the back of his boss's head. A few flakes of dandruff dot the perimeter where the hair has retreated from the shiny scalp.

He considers how easily he could dispose of this insignificant human. With one swipe he could remove the head from its place between the man's shoulders, then core out the skull, artfully plucking any lingering gray matter from its cradle, and burnish the bone in fire. The finished product would make a lovely serving dish for whatever tasty snack he desired.

He exhales and exits the room, knowing he has words to write and make precious.

* * *

Basil sits at his desk, head supported by both clawed hands. Fingers drum against his bare forehead. Exhaustion overwhelms him. He yawns to expose yellowed canines.

*So much for* that *grand experiment.*

But who could blame him for his outburst, or even for falling asleep on the job? No meeting should take more than an hour. Even he knows this. Still, he should have behaved better. He gazes out the window to study the sunlit landscape. A rap at the door robs his mind of the chance to ramble.

"A minute?"

It's Bulcavage.

Basil waves him in.

"Let me be frank," Bulcavage says. "That stunt wasn't what I was hoping for."

"Me neither. An inauspicious beginning indeed."

"Did we make a mistake here, you and me?"

"It's too soon to tell."

"Realistic optimism. I love it," Bulcavage says, smiling and pointing a finger in Basil's face. "Tomorrow's a new day and all that."

"I had a long night. I—"

Bulcavage holds up a hand, not wanting to hear it.

"Listen, everyone has days they want to wipe clean. I have my share too. Nothing a good night's sleep can't cure. Speaking of, where are you staying?"

"Staying, sir?"

"You'll leave here tonight. You'll go somewhere and lay your head down on something soft—a pillow, a pile of dirt, a whore's ass. Where will that somewhere be?"

"I'll find someplace dry. Someplace quiet."

"So you're homeless."

"I'm a wanderer."

"A wanderer, sure, but that's not working too well for you right now, is it? You need a little stability. Listen: After work, you're going to follow Herbert. He's going to introduce you to a guy, a friend of mine. His name is Anton Zhuk. Good ol' Anton will fix you up. Considering where you came from, what you've been through, I think you'll appreciate having a roof over your head again."

"I appreciate this kindness."

"Kindness has nothing to do with it. We can't afford another performance like the one you gave today." Bulcavage pauses. "You can't speak to me like that, especially in front of Herbert—in front of anyone, in fact. Understood?"

Basil wants to reach across his desk and crush Bulcavage's windpipe. Instead, he nods in agreement and chalks up his inaction to personal growth.

"It's late on a Friday, meaning the workweek is just about done," Bulcavage adds. "Get some rest. Use the next two days to get your head straight."

"Yes, sir. You think Herbert would mind stopping somewhere before taking me to my new residence?"

"Yeah, I suppose you'll be needing a few things to make yourself comfortable—a toothbrush, a towel, some pornography. Maybe a Duraflame so you feel right at home."

"I need to fetch my motorcycle, sir."

"Whatever you need."

Bulcavage sighs and backs away from the door, leaving Basil to dream up ideas for making the name Big Bair Agriculture and

Machinery linger in people's memories.

* * *

Basil hunts and pecks his way around the keyboard. The words are just beginning to come when Herbert appears in the doorway.

"Chop, chop," he says.

"Pardon?" Basil replies.

"Bob says I'm taking you to Anton's. It's Friday at five. Let's go."

Tomorrow is a new day, Basil thinks, just like the boss says. He turns off his computer and follows Herbert out the door. As they descend the stairs, Basil recalls the brunette he encountered that morning. He exits the stairwell to the first floor and peers down the hallway, hoping to catch another glimpse of her. No signs of life other than a phone chirping faintly in the distance.

As he leaves the building, he steps past the shrub he recently desecrated with his volcanic feces. Herbert ducks into a small silver sedan. One thought fills Basil's mind: *This is going to be a tight fit.*

"You'll have to cram," Herbert tells him. "I just got this thing detailed, so try not to get any demon schmutz on the seat."

It takes some doing, but Basil succeeds in pretzeling himself into the passenger seat. His face pressed against the glass of the windshield, knees at his chest, he hopes for a quick ride. Then, he remembers.

"My bike!"

"What?"

"Mister Bulcavage said you would take me to my bike."

Herbert makes a point of checking his watch, even though it would be just as easy to eye the neon-green numbers of the digital clock recessed into the car's dashboard.

"Well, where is it?"

"I don't know exactly."

"Then I can't exactly take you to it, now can I?"

"If you drive around, I'll let you know if I see anything familiar."

Herbert sighs and backs up quickly, jerkily.

Basil's cheek becomes one with the windshield. His oily skin smudges the glass.

"So," he says, attempting small talk. "Herbert Teak from Beak."

"Des Moines."

"Oh, right-o. What brought you here?"

"To Savage?"

"To Beak."

"The same automobile you're presently fouling up."

"Ah, good thing I'm fluent in smartass. What's Des Moines like?"

"It's fine."

"Just fine? It couldn't have been *that* fine if you left."

"I said it was fine."

Basil tries a few more times to unlock the mystery of his co-worker, but Herbert scuttles every attempt. He directs Herbert to "turn here" and "make a left here," adding, "This looks familiar" before deciding a moment later that the surroundings, in fact, do not look familiar at all. Finally, Herbert says he has had enough.

"Listen, man. I don't have time for this. It's the weekend, and I have shit to do. We've been driving in a circle for twenty freaking minutes and you have no idea where you're going. At this pace Anton will be a freaking *corpse* by the time we get there!"

An uneasy silence stands between them before Basil points an elbow up the road and says, "There it is."

"What?" Herbert throws up his arms, incredulous.

"My bike. It's in the ditch over there. I can see the handlebar sticking up."

Herbert pulls forward and slams on the brake pedal. The

sedan squeals to a stop next to the toppled Harley. Basil uncoils himself from the front seat and clops to the edge of the road. In one smooth motion he hoists the bike from the ditch and straddles the saddle.

"See? Right where I left it. I guess I'll follow you."

He tries the starter, but nothing happens.

"Shit," he says.

"What now?" Herbert calls from his car.

"It's not working."

Herbert storms from the driver's side, moving in short, stuttered steps, mumbling one curse word after another. The only ones Basil can make out are "shit licker" and "badger fucker." Herbert brushes against Basil and looks for what he expects to find.

"You're out of gas, genius!"

"Gas?"

"It's what makes the damned motorcycle go boom-boom, shit for brains!"

Herbert seems to realize the insult that slipped from his tongue. By the look on his suddenly pale face, he half-expects to have his belly sliced open by one of Basil's raptor-like talons.

Basil gives a slight smile and says, "We have a saying where I come from: Some days you eat steak, and others you eat shit. I guess both of us are eating shit today."

\* \* \*

Basil trails Herbert's sedan, his newly refueled motorcycle rumbling beneath him. By the time they pull up to a drab single-story building, its stucco walls colored green with some sort of fungus, the sun is about to dip below the horizon.

Herbert parks his car and hurries to an apartment at the front of the building. He reaches through a screenless storm door and knocks on the brittle wood until the door creaks open.

Basil takes extra time getting settled, double-checking the placement of the kickstand and the tightness of the gas cap. He's happy to have learned that motorcycles and other "go-go machines" — Herbert's words — need fuel in order to function, but having to pay for the fuel to make the bike useful presents another worry. He makes a mental note to repay Herbert for having lent him the money, however grudgingly, needed to fill the tank.

As Basil looks up, he sees Herbert standing next to a short, fat, unsmiling man in ill-fitting pants, leather sandals and a button-down dress shirt, the fabric all white other than the cocoa-colored stain above the breast pocket.

"This is Anton," Herbert says. "He'll make sure you have a place to sleep tonight."

As Herbert hurries off, Basil offers his appreciations for all of the help. Herbert either doesn't hear or doesn't acknowledge it. Basil watches his co-worker drive away. Tires screech as the car rounds a sharp corner.

Anton stands in front of Basil, mute as he takes in the sight.

Basil introduces himself, but Anton remains as still as a garden gnome.

"Mister Bulcavage tells me you have a room."

"I have room, yes," Anton says, his accent as thick as a milkshake. "Bulcavage, yes. You bet. You bet."

"One thing, though: I don't have any money. I *can* pay you, just not today."

"Is okay. Is okay. You good for. You good for."

"Another thing: I like windows."

"Sure, sure. No meltdown. No meltdown. Same team, same team," Anton says, slapping his chest. "You follow."

Anton leads Basil to the back of the building, stopping in front of a maroon door bearing two figures — one of them brass — representing the number thirteen. In actuality, the first digit is missing, the ghost of the number one where the brass number should be. Anton turns the knob and puts his shoulder to the door. The door groans open.

"Bulcavage say you need apartment. Is yours, he tell me."

Basil steps through the door and stands in the middle of a mostly empty room. It has a plaid couch with worn seat cushions and, in the far corner, a small television with an octopus of wires and cables dangling from its rear, coiling on the floor and snaking their way into holes in the nearest wall. He looks to his right and sees an all-glass back door. He smiles, knowing he will have daylight. The back door leads to a small patio, which amounts to little more than a concrete slab. A man lies motionless on the slab.

"Uh ... is he okay?" Basil asks.

"Is Chester," Anton says. "He live next door. Is neighbor."

Basil slides open the screen door and steps onto the slab. He lifts a hoof and nudges Chester's ample belly. The man's gut feels harder than expected.

The attention rouses Chester, and he sits up with a snort. He runs a hand through the shock of wavy gray hair above his age-spotted forehead and introduces himself, though the word comes out more like *Chesser*.

Anton begins, "Chester is—"

"I'm a monster and a madman, a saint and a whore," Chester says. "I'm a maker, an artist, a minstrel, a conquering hero, a poet of the heart—"

"A poet!" Basil beams. "I, too, am a man of verse. We should gather together and regale each other with odes to our shared love of letters."

Chester crinkles his nose, contorts his face into a sneer and utters a word from his dry mouth that sounds remotely like *nah*.

"Wan' go to the bar?"

Basil recalls his introduction to bars—Beak Tavern—and the encounter that ended with blood on his claws and a bullet lodged in one of his horns. He declines the invitation.

"I'm not so well equipped for exploring anyway," Chester says.

The crotch of Chester's pants darkens. A moment later Basil smells the sharp, sobering trace of warm urine.

"Oh god, oh god, oh god," Chester stutters.

"Make yourself comfortable," Basil says. He slides the screen door back into place. Then he closes the sliding glass door and pulls the blinds tight, blocking out any signs of Chester. The room darkens. Through the glass he can hear Chester's sobs. The sobs turn to laughter and then to silence.

Basil turns and looks at Anton, who offers a blank stare in return.

"No keys. Don't lock door," Anton says. "See you around." Then he heads for the front door and closes it behind him, leaving Basil to himself.

Basil walks through the room, his hooves leaving shallow impressions in the dirty carpet. He knows he will adore the light pouring in through the glass of the back door, assuming Chester finds his way home. He perks his ears and registers only the drone of Chester's snoring and a gentle hum emanating from something mechanical hiding in the walls. For the moment he has peace. He smiles at his good fortune.

He steps toward the TV and stares at the blank screen. His distorted reflection stares back. After a minute he presses the ON button.

He realizes, in those first precious seconds, his world has forever changed.

## Chapter 9

# So Many Sins, So Few Regrets

My bride must know of my failure. More to the point, I must tell her. But as I sit here in this mildewed tavern, writing these words by the light of a dim candle, my hand has ideas of its own.

*London has been brought to its knees*, I write, and the lies flow from there. I go on to explain how I have made my name in industry: building canals to start the limitless parade of coal from the mines west and north so London can burn brightly. This is only partly true. I say I have come into a most respectable position: a commander of pickmen, leading the whole lot beyond the walls of this great city, and into the wilderness of the unknown, toward Marlborough in the west, Nottinghamshire in the north. I cannot possibly know for how long I will be gone. Not until the canals are complete and you can see the fires of London from the hills of Berwick.

*But know this*, I write: *Through shed sweat and spilled blood, I am remaking this world.*

I tell her the work is tiresome to most, but it is fine to me. I barely have a free moment to rest my weary head, to give my abraded hands the briefest respite. I am learning, teaching and making my mark, both on the landscape and in the minds of men who matter in a civilized world. My time in the wind and rain, knee deep in muck, will have its dividends. My work will draw eyes, and soon the men who decide matters of wins and losses will whisk me from this hole in the mud, away from the stink of oxen and the fog of dead, brown air. My pockets will fill, and then all my days hence will pass in a proper office on the blessed span of London Bridge, warmed by the comforts of gin and a well-fed hearth.

I can imagine, can I not?

The letter I know I should write: I have erred, horribly so. I walked away from a land of plenty to be a lowly pickman, digging holes in the wet, stinking earth. I break my back twelve hours a day, all for a few shillings per week. Despite the breaking, the men above me have no intention of admitting me into their circle. They see me as a beast of burden, nothing more.

I am an animal, a servant willing to eat dirt for a handful of coins.

A wiser man would have learned something from Roger Roberts, the woodenheaded heir to Roberts Farm, down the road from the farmhouse in Berwick whose door I never should have abandoned. Like me, young Roger departed Berwick for London, only to return eighteen months later, thin and gray and blinded, one eye as useless as a dead bird. "London changed me," he told me, though he neglected to say precisely how. Or perhaps I neglected to ask. He implied city life had made him better. His sightless eye proved otherwise.

London changed him all right, just as it changes me. He left before it killed him. I, too, have the sense to know my stubbornness, and to not allow my stubbornness to lead me to the brink of death. Sacrifice has helped me save quite a bit, at least. This I can tell her in truth. Night in and night out, my body finds rest on the cold ground, my lips parched and stomach empty, all to sock away every penny so I might one day afford a proper place to call home. How much will be enough? No one has been able to say.

Brooding aside, my faith in my abilities remains strong, as does my faith in the random hand of good fortune. But even I, a stubborn fool, can admit this experiment must end soon. I have another month in these bones, two at most. By then I should have enough saved to afford *something*. By then I at least can say I came to this city, worked my back down to its bones and earned enough to stay here until I am an old and tired man, though I shall not stay. By then, I will be able to say without a lie on my tongue that I had succeeded here but *chose* to return to Berwick.

Life reaches its end all too easily in London—a slaughterhouse, a gallows, a maker of widows. Villains with blades and clubs prowl about for gentle souls to slay. Gaol fever chokes the air, eager to burn me up. A godless beast stalks the midnight streets, hungry for meat. The worst: the gnarled rope of the Tyburn Tree. If I let my imagination roam, I can hear the rope groaning as my body swings, purely because my pauper's hands slipped into some fellow's untended pockets. My remains would rot in a coffin shaft, pockets picked clean and shoes peeled from my feet.

My bride would never forgive me for leaving her without a body to bury.

Berwick calls to me. I miss the smell of the sea, if not its salty skin. I miss the clear skies. I miss the cows chewing their cud, tails swaying. And I miss her—my bride.

Yet these secrets will remain as such, unspoken.

I wonder how she is. Wonder is all I can do for now. In these darkest hours of mine, I fear I may never see her face again, at least not in this life.

# Chapter 10

# The End of Hope and Prayer

The pastor nods toward the first pew as the organ hums the last cheerful bar of "Jesus, Joy of Our Desiring."

A thin woman rises from her seat and creeps toward the pulpit. Her foot slips on the carpet of an unnoticed step. As she regains her balance, she reaches the lectern and places her Bible off to the side. She twists the microphone down and then up, back to where it had been—perfect. The Bible falls off the edge of the lectern, and the book lands with a boom just as the organ music ends. Her arthritic knees crackle as she bends to pick up the weathered book. When she stands, her cheeks blaze red. She clears her throat.

"What you're about to hear will be unlike anything else you've heard here at Crows Gorge United Methodist Church," she begins. "We all know the saying about desperate times, right? Well, those times are upon us."

She pauses to take a breath and steady her trembling hands.

"I was in the market just the other day, in the produce aisle. Across the aisle I saw a child—a boy, no more than four, five at the most—standing with his young mother, perhaps twenty-five, blessed and pregnant. The boy was doing as boys do, putting their chubby little hands where they don't belong. I saw him pick up an apple from the display case. You know how they stack those apples, almost like they're in a pyramid straight out of the Egyptian desert. Well, I swear that apple must have been a puzzle piece, a key of sorts, because every other apple in the pyramid-shaped display came crashing down, cascading down to the floor. Apples, apples everywhere."

She takes another pause, this one purely for effect.

"I've never seen such rage," she says. Her voice becomes soft, almost sinister. "Not from the mother, mind you, because none of us would have faulted her for taking a rod to the child for letting his hands wander. No, it was the little boy, throwing a terrible fit! He picked up one of those apples and hurled it clear across the market. *Splat!* Then he did the same with another, and another one after that. One of them almost hit me, if you want to hear the truth. And when that boy's mother went to discipline him like he deserved, what do you think happened?"

She waits for a response that doesn't come.

"That little boy just started swatting his mother, swinging at her—lashing out at his own flesh and blood, at the very woman who made him. Kicked her in the shins. Even punched her right in the belly, right in the space where his little baby brother or sister was doing nothing more than trying to take shape. Mom doubled over, nearly fell right to the floor, and that little boy just kept up his not-so-little fit, raising Cain right in the middle of the public grocery."

She doesn't need to finish the story.

"What do you think caused that outburst? I know what I think."

She inspects the puzzled faces of the Sunday morning congregation.

"Demonic influence," she says. She repeats the phrase, smacking her Bible against the lectern to emphasize each word. "I've seen this influence at work, not only inside that little boy in the grocery, but everywhere I turn in these troubled times. Have any of you seen what's happening over in Beak, right in our backyard? The beast is among us, spreading his poison like a rain soaks the ground, and we're lapping it right up."

The pastor hurries to the lectern so he can whisper in Edna's ear. She nods insistently and waits for him to walk away.

"I want to thank Pastor Greg for being gracious enough to let me speak with you today," she says. "I think he thinks if he gives me five minutes to say what I have to say, I'll take that as a gift and then keep my mouth shut, as quiet as a mouse in an open pantry. 'Wait and see,' he likes to say. That's what he thinks we should do about what's happening over in Beak. He is wrong."

The pastor forces an audible sigh.

"The time for waiting is over," Edna seethes. "It's already too late, in fact, but most of us just don't know it yet. The devil has been made flesh, here to defile and deface and destroy us all. The time for hope and prayer has reached its end."

She bends toward the microphone.

"Now is the time for war!"

The microphone squeals.

"We are under … attack. Our way of life is under … attack. The Lord Jesus Christ is under … attack."

The pastor returns to her side and remains there, pursing his lips.

Heads turn in the congregation, chattering, trying to make sense of what's happening.

"I can imagine how you must be feeling," she says. "Some of you may be confused, scared, or maybe you just don't want to admit what's lurking just outside our door—standing on the seam between worlds, between darkness and light, between the good in us all and the evil that has worked to consume us since we first set foot in the garden. I know. I've seen it. And let me tell you, the hour of decision has arrived."

She closes her eyes and inhales deeply. The microphone picks up the sound—like the hiss of a bull snake—and broadcasts it throughout the church.

"I believe I have been called here for a reason. The enemy has awakened from its slumber and now walks among us, right here in Beak, intent on luring us into eternal darkness. I'm here to tell you we must steel ourselves. We must prepare for the battle ahead. And we must be willing to fight and die and ki—"

The pastor steps in to separate her from the lectern and, more importantly, from the microphone.

"Thank you, Edna," he says. He bends toward the mike, hands grasping both sides of the lectern and his elbows pointed up, as if to box her out. "Let us pray to the Lord."

# Chapter 11

# Revisions

"Well, look who decided to show the fuck up."

The scowl on Bulcavage's face suggests he is, in a word, unenthused.

Basil, by his best guess, has blown past the start time for his second day of work—a Monday, no less—by more than an hour. The boss has every right to be furious, but Basil is too giddy to care. The knowledge he has acquired in the past forty-eight hours has made him, in a way, bulletproof.

The secret: The humans consider him a god, or at least a demigod. Of course, they cannot possibly be expected to know the truth, but he will do nothing to correct their false assumptions.

"We're done here," Bulcavage insists. "Take whatever shit you have at your desk and get the fuck out. This is the last time I ever take Mary Jane Pix at her word."

"I had an unbelievable weekend—"

"Spare me. I don't give two shits for any more of your sob stories."

"Don't you want to hear the reason for my lateness?"

"There's no excuse. Out. Now."

"I get it now. I understand the world."

"Yeah? How the fuck did you manage that feat?"

"Television. I've been watching television since Friday night. Nonstop, give or take a ten- or twenty-minute catnap."

"So now you're an Einstein?"

"The world outside my door terrifies me," Basil says. "I don't know how you stand it."

"Welcome to the club."

"I feel like I know so much, but at the same time I feel ..."

"Yeah?"

"Slightly dumber."

"What was the bug that bit you?"

"World news. Fables about doomed love. Cartoons starring anthropomorphic ducks and rabbits. Shows about Nazis. Humans seem to have a strange fascination with these Nazis."

"We do love our monsters."

"And the advertising! So much wonderful advertising!"

"Wait until you get to the daytime soaps. You'll have plenty of time to watch 'em too, because you don't work here anymore."

"Don't be silly," Basil says, buoyed by his newfound confidence. Humans fear him, he knows. They're terrified of him, in fact, or someone much like him. Their fear of him, of the evil they think he has come to sow—this is the best weapon he could ask for.

"Go fuck yourself," Bulcavage says. He slaps a hand on the clammy flesh of Basil's left pectoral and tries to push him away, yet Basil does not budge.

"I understand how you must feel," Basil says. "You're angry. You're embarrassed because you think you made a mistake hiring me, but I can assure you of this: You chose well. Grant me an audience so I can share my idea for the Big Bair campaign and I'll prove it. If you like what I've come up with, take it and use it however you see fit. If not, I'll walk out the door and you'll never see me again. At least not for a while, if you catch my drift."

Bulcavage's expression softens, his anger yielding to an even more primal emotion.

"My brain brims with ideas to inform my work," Basil adds. "Give me thirty minutes to prepare."

"Take an hour."

"Half that is all I'll require. Round up Herbert and let me present to both of you while it's still fresh." He knows he can dispense with the pleases and thank yous.

Bulcavage pretends to mull over the idea, but Basil knows his boss believes he has no other choice.

\* \* \*

"Legacy," Basil begins. He pauses for dramatic effect.

"Alan Keller was nineteen years old when he put the building blocks of his business in place with nothing to his credit but callused hands, a strong back and an unbreakable will. He loved what he did, and he cared about the people who bought the things he made with those callused hands—their struggles, their triumphs, their *stories*. It's what he did with every breath, down to his very last one. Although Alan Keller has moved on from this world, his spirit endures. It inspires us, it lifts us up, and it leads us boldly into the future.

"Guided by the next generation of the Keller family, we're building upon Alan's legacy with this simple promise: We're going to keep the story going—ours, and yours. It's what Alan would have wanted, and that's what we're going to do." Basil's voice drops to a whisper, adding, "Big Bair Agriculture and Machinery—reaping the harvest since 1959."

Basil tips his head and awaits a reaction, expecting applause. None comes.

"What do you think?"

"It's ... not bad," Bulcavage says. "'Transcending death'."

"In so many words."

Basil puts more flesh on the bones of his campaign, suggesting interviews of real-life Big Bair customers, grizzled farmers in ball caps talking not about the quality of Big Bair's wheat threshers and grain augers—"The quality of the product is a given," Basil explains—but about their fears and hopes for the future: bad harvests, the lack of suitable heirs to lead the family business, shrinking subsidies making it harder to earn a living wage from one year to the next, etcetera.

"And how does that soft-boiled stuff help?" Bulcavage asks.

"Because in a horribly uncertain world, we are their rock. The world doesn't give a shit about their troubles or their worries or their pain, but we do. Or, Big Bair Agriculture and Machinery does."

Bulcavage nods.

"We'd use the campaign to just let people talk about their lives and tell their stories, whether good, bad or ugly," Basil says. "No ad-speak, no sales angles—just the truth."

"We're not journalists."

"Just the truth, sir. We can do a whole series of radio ads, a print campaign, maybe some TV spots. Imagine."

"Imagine? Try impossible."

"Nothing is impossible. Look at me."

"It'd be way too expensive. I'm talking about one full-page ad with a good hook—just one measly ad. You're talking about telling stories."

"I'm talking about telling a *new* story, and letting other people share their stories. I'm talking about connecting. Isn't that what we're trying to do here? Build a strong connection between Big Bair and its customers? Isn't that the story you would try to sell to Alan Keller's shit stain of a son?"

"We'd have to hire all these photographers, do all these sugary interviews ..."

"That's where I come in. Besides, you'd be able to charge more. A lot more, by my best guess. Thousands more, I would think, all of it flowing right into your back pocket. Pitch it and see what happens. What do you have to lose?"

Herbert clears his throat, adding, "He's got a point, Bob."

\* \* \*

Basil clops down the stairs to the first floor, wearing a smile from ear to ear, his yellowed canines on full display. He knows he nailed it. He just *knows* it. Even though Bulcavage gave him a lukewarm "maybe"—green lighting the campaign, and hopefully affirming his employment—he feels invigorated by his usefulness, by having done something worthwhile, by having thought of something that could do some good for someone somewhere. He swings open the fire door and steps fully into the hallway.

"Jesus fuck!"

It's her, the brunette from the parking lot.

"You scared me half to death," she says.

"I'm ... sorry. Excuse me. I didn't mean to alarm you."

"You didn't," she says, stepping around him. "It's fine."

"I'm Basil," he says to her back.

She stops and turns halfway around, eyeing him from top to bottom and back again.

"Melody," she says over her shoulder. She keeps walking.

He watches her until she disappears into her office.

"Melody," he repeats, liking how the name sounds on his tongue. The smile returns, and he proceeds to the exit so he can find his motorcycle and go exploring.

He cracks open the glass door to the outside world, and he stops in his tracks.

The sheer size of the gathering in the lot surprises him, even shocks him. The jeering begins—boo, hiss, boo.

"Go home!" shouts a masculine voice enflamed with anger.

Basil's brain registers the blur of an incoming projectile. He winces as the object smacks his forehead where the flesh meets the base of his injured horn. A purple sphere rolls on the concrete, mimicking the curling arc of a C. The unmistakable tang of chopped onion finds his flaring nostrils.

## Chapter 12

# Slightly Crushing Pain

The Harley rumbles to a stop in the shade of a Kentucky coffee tree. A veil of road dust follows close behind. Basil kills the engine and brings the motorcycle to rest. "My little noisemaker," he says as he pats the rounded fuselage, which reminds him of the curve of Kamala's belly. He puts a hoof to the kickstand and parks the bike, nudging a crumpled-up Budweiser can out of the way.

The parking lot is strewn with red-and-white empties, as well as an ashtray's worth of spent cigarette butts, a used condom and a few dirty diapers, all balled up and waiting—just waiting—to be unfurled, like left-behind landmines. Dried loaves of dog shit skirt a rusted metal trashcan with an affixed canister offering complimentary trash bags for responsible dog owners. The lip of a green trash bag flaps in the gentle breeze. He dismounts and lets his body wander, to catch up with his roving mind. The cooled remains of a small campfire include half-burnt logs and more empty Bud cans, the aluminum charred black.

He feels uneasy, moody, as he ponders the day's mixed blessings. He's thrilled at having nailed his presentation for the Big Bair campaign. Even better, he finally had a meaningful encounter with the elegant brunette from the office building's first floor. Best of all, he learned her name: Melody. *Melody*, his mind repeats.

He sneers at the lingering stink of onion juice. The whole left side of his face feels sticky, reeks of an unwashed armpit.

The memory of the scene in the office parking lot—his first truly hostile welcome—has him vexed, even disturbed. Even the bikers at the Beak Tavern extended good tidings at first; sure, the conversation went irretrievably south and he had to destroy them, but the interaction started out with such potential, such promise.

The small mob in the office parking lot hadn't afforded him the courtesy of speaking his mind—nothing but open hostility, without so much as a hello. He had to tiptoe through a gauntlet of more than twenty people, each of them shaking a fist, wagging fingers in his face, yelling hurtful epithets. Some of them waved signs bearing needlessly cruel tidings such as "To Hell With You," "Keep the Devil Out of Beak" and "Jesus Hates You." The most memorable sign read, simply, "Go Off and Die, Anywhere But Here." One of the protestors, a sixty-year-old fuddy-duddy in an orange trucker cap, blood-red suspenders and a gray T-shirt with a sweat stain running from the neckline to the protruding nib of his belly button, spat at Basil's hooves. Basil fought the instinct to slit the man's distended belly east to west and let the grayish snakes of intestine wriggle onto the asphalt. Instead he backed away, climbed onto his noisemaker and thundered away, toward the safety of isolation.

He has found solace here, though his skull throbs with the nut of a headache he knows could turn into a crusher. He craves the consolation of cool water to wash the pain away, and maybe to wipe clean the memory of the sign-waving, finger-pointing mob seemingly intent on spoiling his sacred space: the workplace.

A thin ribbon of dirt draws him beneath the umbrella of a lush, green canopy. After a half-mile, he hears the first suggestion of the prize he has been seeking: the burbling of water. His pace quickens. The trail widens and brings him to the edge of a stream, perhaps fifty feet wide from one bank to the other. As he exhales, his lips curl into a smile.

The softness of wind, the rustling of tree leaves, the rush of water over split rock—together they push any ills from his mind. All evidence of mankind recedes. Birdsong fills his ears. He abandons the trail and steps into the pastern-deep water. He looks in both directions, upstream and down, and sees no movement other than flitting birds, the lilting of chokecherry branches and the poetry of water.

A plane roars overhead, a mile above, but he smiles knowing the machine will come no closer.

He cannot escape the sound of human movement. He imagines a long, slinky dragon, made entirely of metal, scrabbling across the plains—iron skin, well-greased gears propelling every joint, its fuselage-like torso dragging a chain-link tail. As squat as a badger, the dragon belches lava-hot coals and farts contrails of black smoke, its claws carving up the soil and mowing down acres of wheat quills. Black ooze seeps from every metallic pore and fills the ruts in its clamoring wake, the ooze turning to asphalt as it cools. The dragon then sprouts blade-like wings from grooves in its back and takes to the sky, painting cottony clouds with the filthy soot of industry.

Basil clops downstream. The water deepens, rising to his fur-covered calves. His tail dips into the water and swims like an eel. The coolness travels up his spine to his brain, and for some reason the sensation makes him want to cry.

He leans forward and cups his hands into the water so he can splash the oniony stink from his face. The fraction of an image flashes into his mind, followed by the feeling of falling through blackness, of floating, and then burning in the cold, the knowledge of sure death. It's a snapshot plucked from one of his dreams, however brief, though this is the first time he has experienced it while awake. He gasps to steady the drumbeat in his chest, and his panic slowly subsides.

"What in Cthaal's name was that?" he asks. He then answers: "I wish I knew."

He straightens, calf-deep in the stream, waiting for some other surprise to wallop him. When it doesn't come, he refocuses on his surroundings: wind, water and sunlight, the roving clouds of ragweed pollen. Still, he frets over a possibility that seems to be more and more certain: Something incendiary lurks within him, practicing great patience, and one day it will do its job of exploding.

"A problem for another day," he utters, yet he knows the task of pushing this far-off threat from his mind is not as simple as he wants it to be.

For now he has chosen to immerse himself in this place, and here—in this sylvan sanctuary on the edge of the Sand Hills—he can make a home, however temporary: away from humans, from demons, from responsibility, from evil of any sort, just him in the midst of the natural world and the perfect circle of death and rebirth.

The thought returns him to his own creation, wondering if he is doing what is intended of him, according to a maker—or, respectfully, a Maker—with intentions. With everything that has happened in recent days, everything he has become, he wonders if he is following the proper path or simply making a grand mistake worse with each passing day. Either way, he knows it does not matter, because it seems no one will show up to undo any of the deeds he has done.

A raptor soars noiselessly overhead. What a glorious place. How sad that so few of his kind will ever have the opportunity to see such beauty. How unfair that, barring a handful of the named Chosen, his people will spend their lives staring at the same boulders of blackened rock and tongues of eternal flame. Guilt tugs at him, but he knows one thing: Demons belong where they belong. The few beautiful souls wandering among them deserve better, but they cannot be helped.

He eases his body into the stream and lets the water flow around him. Organisms live and die around him: silvery minnows pecking at microscopic mites, a thick-bodied water snake struggling to swallow a crayfish that refuses to go without a fight, flies buzzing in tightly knit swarms. He leans forward and dips his face fully into the water, this time without incident. His mouth opens, and the creek flows into him, down his gullet, becoming part of him, even for just a short time.

Despite all the horrors he has seen, despite the suffering he has brought to so many, he feels privileged, fortunate, loved — godlike.

His thoughts turn to Kamala. Jealousy stirs in the hollow of his chest as he wonders how she is faring in his rightful place. He pictures her ample bottom nestled in the crook of an imaginary throne of bleached bones. All must be going fine below, he concludes, given the fact that none of the three imps he anointed as messengers has found him, no dire warnings of an insurrection or any other looming tragedy.

A bank of dark clouds creeps in to blot out the sun, and shadow consumes him.

Basil alternately rues and craves a return to Our Fiery Home. He knows he will have to go back someday. When he does, a foe will be waiting.

His thoughts shift to Lubos and his appetite for havoc.

A sense of unease builds in his gut. Something tells him the world is about to be turned on its ear.

# Chapter 13

# Sunlight for a Stale Dungeon

The fire knows all. It has yet to steer Kamala astray. The tongues of flame tell her the time has come, and she agrees.

She strides across the cavern, making sure every demon bears witness to her procession. Her loving acolyte, Kindness, trails her by a pace. He scampers like an underweight ape, knuckles scraping at her hooves. Others fall in line behind them, so they move as a pack.

"We will transform this place," she tells Kindness. "We must."

"They will want a plan," he whispers, his voice shaky. "You must address the needs of the many and the few."

"I know what I must do. To remake this place we must have the Council's blessing. Without it, we will have no order, no progress. The shift will fail."

"Shift, my queen?"

"The awakening I intend to bring to life. Only through peace can we secure our future."

"They crave their precious violence. They cling to it like an infant to its mother's throbbing teat."

"To what end?" she asks. "What purpose does their hunger for destruction serve?"

"It's what they know. It's all they understand."

"Only because a better option has not been handed to them."

"I'm not the one who needs convincing, dearest," he adds. "These brutes trust in the old ways."

"Change has come. Basil saw to that. Not everyone will survive what's to come. Not everyone should."

Kamala and Kindness share a look, an understanding. Many will be left behind—some banished, others destined to be broken and fed to the furnace.

"Those who wish to share in our vision will be welcome," she says. "They will have a place at our communal table. Those who oppose ..."

Kamala wields Basil's spear as proof of her authority. A modest horde falls in line behind her. Dozens of imps scramble underfoot, chirping excitedly. Two troglodytes, all muscle and bone and plate-like scales, not a single complex thought in the spongy space between their ears, serve as imposing bookends—fitting accompaniment for her first act as the master of Our Fiery Home.

Though paltry, her band of rebels will gather ranks. It must.

Together they skulk toward the Council's chamber, the Hall of Ignoble and Prodigious Elders, where Basil's long-serving bureaucrats congregate—to eat, sleep, shit, fuck—the ancient ones, the storytellers, the keepers of Our Fiery Home's history.

Throughout her life they have shared their knowledge selectively, keeping secrets, lying. Still, they have value. They have more worth alive than dead. If she has their confidence, she can rule without war. If not, the mass murder that follows will be her one and only act of bloodshed. The Council will offer no sane alternative to her plan. They watched the ceaseless parade of horrors under the rule of Basil and his predecessors, but even they must see Lubos and his warlords as a collective threat. Warlords lack the sensitivity to govern, after all, having no interest in preventing their brittle society from unraveling.

Yes, each member of the all-male Council of Unerring Wisdom will have a choice: The Hall of Ignoble and Prodigious Elders will either remain a tidy workplace or become a tomb. Killing is not her first choice, but she can accept selective murder as a path to peace. Root out the villains and leave the decent to breathe life into this stale dungeon.

She stops short of the entrance to the Hall of Ignoble and Prodigious Elders, ready to shape this world into something better. The handle of Basil's well-worn spear sweats in her grip.

She smiles, because she knows her fate is about to turn.

As she steps through the darkened doorway, a foul smell tingles her nostrils. Her hoof slips on something wet and spongy. In the firelight she sees unmoving shapes dotting the slick chamber floor. As her eyes adjust, she recognizes lifeless bodies— hollowed out, emptied of their precious organs—mingled with amputated limbs and disembodied heads. A severed hand drags itself across the floor, like a dying spider clinging to the last fibers of life. The hand trails a clutch of noodle-like veins and tendons, shiny in the firelight, in a fruitless bid to escape.

"Kamala, dear," says a voice, like a door with rusty hinges. "Do come in."

Lubos steps into the center of the chamber. He licks blood from two of the three remaining fingers on his ragged hand. A septet of brawny demons shadows him, each bearing weapons of iron and bone. One slithers in to snatch the spear from Kamala's grip.

"I've been expecting you," Lubos adds. He places a hoof atop the severed head of Calvin, the elderly demon who once headed Basil's inner circle. The strands of Calvin's long beard, once gray, are stained red and black. "The Council of Unerring Wisdom had been expecting you too, as I understand it."

"I am rightful ruler, Lubos," she insists. "Basil saw to it—"

"Basil's will matters not," he snaps. "You'll never see him again, nor will any of us. His reign might as well have never existed. He's irrelevant. By definition, so are you, I'm afraid."

Kamala knows not to speak. She realizes her ambitions no longer matter. Her gaze catches a new piece of art: Basil's pet, the crippled Damir, tacked to the wall in the shape of a Y; two spikes pin each of his clawless stumps to the pane of rock, two more through his shoulders, one driven through his mouth. Damir blinks at her, still wanting to live. She considers this horror her punishment for not heeding Damir's warning.

"Let's assume, for one playful moment," Lubos continues,

"that Basil has any influence over anything. Considering his uninspired governance, I do believe the Council of Unerring Wisdom would have let you have your way. If you had heard any of the drivel they had been spouting since Basil stepped into the wilderness, I do think Calvin and the others would have agreed to whatever silly ideas you put forth. Such a pity we'll never know."

Lubos pads toward her and warms to her sleek body. He folds into her, their genitals nearly in alignment. He brings a bloody hand to her head and cradles her naked skull. His snakelike erection stabs her, the tip moist and sticky against the soft skin of her belly.

Kindness whimpers, looking nervously from one side of the cavern to the other. He crawls closer to Kamala, perhaps to protect but more likely to seek her protection.

Kamala exhales and shuts her eyes tightly, because she knows what's about to come. She will endure pain. She will bleed. She will be broken and reduced to nothing. But she will survive, because this is the way of their world. She will make a good pawn, even a trophy. The same cannot be said of her love, the meek Kindness. He is unnecessary, and no one but her will miss him. Tears wet her eyes. She should have left him behind, to hide in the shadows until all was safe.

His blood will be on her hands.

"You will enjoy your time beneath me," Lubos whispers into her ear. "I will enjoy hurting you, and watching others do the same."

He turns sharply and rakes Kindness's face with the claws of his free hand. Kindness's lower lip sails across the room and drops to the floor with the weight of a wet sponge. Kindness collapses, sobbing the broken syllables of Kamala's name.

"Shut him up," Lubos says to Kamala.

"Get up, Kindness," she says, doing her best to soothe. "Kindness, dear …"

Curled into a tight ball, Kindness murmurs and sobs.

"He seems to lack the proper motivation," Lubos says.

Kamala watches as Lubos pounces, straddling Kindness. Lubos's claws slash, left to right and back again. After a moment, a heaving Lubos retracts and studies his attempt at art: Kindness's wretched face, now a slab of bloody meat—lip absent, cheeks ragged, one eyelid sliced down its middle, an ear hanging by a morsel of cartilage. Lubos waves his henchmen over and makes a crude motion with his hands, moving his palms together and then apart.

Four ogre-like demons step forward, and each clasps one of Kindness's limbs. It happens slowly—the tearing, the popping of tendon and bone, the horrid screaming of unimaginable pain. One of Kindness's arms tears free, followed by the other. Warm blood wets the walls. Two of the oversized demons play tug-of-war—a leg in each meaty grip. The left leg pulls free, the game of wishbone won. Kindness's torso falls to the gore-soaked floor. The screaming stops abruptly, leaving a gentle gurgling to fill the void.

Lubos presses his tongue into Kamala's ear and then drags the forked tip across her cheek until it swipes her bottom lip.

"Your end will come in the Room of Contrition," he tells her. "Every wretch will take a piece."

"No!" screams Kindness, showing courage despite his dismemberment.

"Drag that waste of a thing off and drown him in the stew," Lubos says. "His flesh will become tomorrow's gruel."

The winner of the tug-of-war hauls Kindness off by his one remaining leg. With each passing second, Kindness's screams grow softer, farther off.

Dear, sweet Kindness. His cries echo in Kamala's ears. She will mourn him at a better time. She studies the chamber floor, committing these horrors to memory.

Lubos pinches her chin between two fingers.

"You weren't made for this place," he tells her. "You want something different than what our world can offer. So do I, of course, but our views differ. You seek peace in Our Fiery Home, and this is where our paths diverge. Such a small-minded perspective doesn't surprise me, considering your time in Basil's shadow. He knew the limits of his power, and he left because he knew he was capable of so little. His weakness kept him from fulfilling the needs of our people."

"You know nothing," she seethes.

"For an age our people have languished in the dark, smothering in this stinking, smoking dungeon," he counters. "We must bring down the walls, and let the sun shine on this place. Our children must wander the earth as they wish. Let us have freedom. Let humankind taste our suffering for a turn."

"The rules!" she cries. "The agreement!"

"The lie," he hisses. "'The Great Lie.' Basil knew it. You know it too."

Lubos drags Kamala out of the chamber, into the main hall. His three-fingered hand grips the column of Kamala's neck. He throws her to the ground, and her face bounces off the pane of red rock. As she lifts her eyes, she sees it, but she refuses to believe. Hundreds, even thousands, of well-armed demons tremble before her, each one rabid with ambition, eager to feel the sun on his back and fill his heaving lungs with air that has not gone stale.

"Open the damned door," Lubos commands.

Twin troglodytes guard the massive door separating Our Fiery Home from the rest of the world. As the trogs stare blankly, Lubos leaps up and grabs one by the lower lip, pulling him downward. "Are you daft? Open the damned door!"

A moment later, the door creaks open. Cool air flows into the main chamber. The fires flicker.

"Nameless—come to me," he commands. "Any of you. Any of the Nameless."

A scrawny demon sprawls at Lubos's hooves, pushed to the ground by a demon named Gideon. "Take him," Gideon offers.

Lubos lifts the Nameless demon by the bud of a horn and tells him, "Go ahead. Lead our procession into the great unknown."

"Leave Our Fiery Home?"

Lubos nods and adds, "Step across the seal."

"I'll turn to dust!"

"A myth! An invention! Basil lied to you. Everyone has lied to you. Nothing will happen if you leave. No harm will befall any of you, in fact, whether Chosen or Nameless. Step across the seal and you'll see."

The demon hesitates.

"Step across that *fucking* seal or I'll have these trogs pound you into paste," Lubos says. "Your choice."

The Nameless demon takes a tentative step toward the open door and stares into the abyss. The tips of his hooves linger at the rounded edge of the sigil—the one bearing primitive runes no demon has been taught to decipher. As the Nameless demon prepares to step across the seal, Lubos thrusts a fist into the demon's back, and he tumbles forward. The demon scrambles to his hooves and struggles to reenter Our Fiery Home before his body withers, but Lubos prevents him.

After a moment, the Nameless demon stops his thrashing. He stands still, absorbing his alien surroundings, feeling the air cool his pimpled flesh.

"I told you," a jubilant Lubos screams to those around him. "This Nameless one has not turned to ash! None who follow will! Basil tried to control you with lies, wanted to keep you as slaves, to keep you compliant and powerless. Take comfort in knowing each of you can come and go as you please—north, south, east and west. But hear me: We will go north. We will claw our way to the surface."

Scores of Nameless demons trample Kamala as they rush to exit Our Fiery Home for the first time. She balls herself to shield her most tender parts from carelessly placed hooves. She winces, knowing Lubos has already won.

The pillars of Our Fiery Home will crumble.

# Chapter 14

# A Foot for the Serpent's Tail

"It's bigger today," Herbert says. "The crowd, I mean."

"Oh," Basil says. He checks over his shoulder and sees Herbert's lanky frame filling the doorway. "Hey."

"These damned people just keep two-by-two-ing, like a brood of rabbits. You should be flattered by how much they hate you."

Basil peeks out the window and surveys the parking lot. He sees forty people, maybe fifty, each of them holding a cardboard sign, each of them chanting the string of words Basil can hear plainly, despite the half-inch barrier of tempered glass: "Demon, addict, rapist, queer, evil isn't welcome here!"

Over and over, just like that.

*Sigh.*

"It's been almost a week since that nut-job pelted me with the onion," Basil says. "They just keep getting louder and meaner. Only a few protestors are milling around the lot when I get here in the morning, but the place is rotten with them by the time I leave. And, like you said, more of them keep coming day after day. It's like they've learned how to spontaneously reproduce. Maybe they're pod people."

"Imagine that," Herbert says.

"What do they expect me to do? Just pick up and leave?"

"At the very least, yeah."

"Where's Bulcavage?"

"Pounding the pavement, most likely, trying to drum up new business. First time I've seen him do that in years. I think the response to the Big Bair campaign has invigorated him. You get his notes on the Hooke Cookers project? He wants us to come up with something mind blowing—he actually used those words, *mind blowing*—even though he gave us zero direction. He always

129

does this. So. Grills. Meat smokers. How do you blow someone's mind with a freakin' charcoal grill?"

Basil presses his face to the window, wondering how to make a fissure crack open the earth's crust just outside the office door and have it swallow up all of those hateful pricks—a nice, big hole to send them tumbling through the smoky updraft, into the heat of the underworld. Wishful thinking, he knows, because his ancient magic has left him. Up here, his *Locuri* spells have no power. Only cruelty, brute strength and the wiles of persuasion serve as his weapons. Any one of those traits should carry him through most situations, though he can't imagine how they might help him solve the mess unfolding outside. Not without taking a bullet to the brain, at least.

"I can tell you're distracted," Herbert says. "Bulcavage won't be back until tomorrow, so we technically don't *have* to do anything with the Hooke campaign today."

Basil hears the words, but he keeps staring out the window, into the sea of people who dislike him—despise him, it seems—for no good reason other than he faintly resembles the antihero of a myth they don't fully understand.

Herbert goes to leave Basil's office and lingers at the door.

"I should tell you," he begins, "I've sort of been talking about you—you know, with your friends outside. They're having meetings."

Basil turns.

"Meetings?"

"It's sort of a series now, at the Methodist church over in Crows Gorge. They even gave it a name: 'A Snake in the Garden.' They talk about what to do about you—or, in some cases, *to* you. They think you've risen from some mystical lake of fire to breed impurity into the bloodline and spread your wickedness. I don't remember the verbiage word for word, but that's the kind of stuff you hear. Not that it matters. I'm persona non grata there now."

"Why's that?"

"Beak's a small town. Like any small town, everyone knows every damned thing about everybody else. They know we work together, you and I, so naturally they asked me what I thought of you."

"And?"

"They hate you more than herpes. They're obsessed."

"What did you tell them about me?"

"I said you're all right, seem like a good enough guy, and that I didn't think you were up to anything nefarious. I told them they should see for themselves, suggested they talk to you and try to understand who you are and why you're here before they decide to drive you out in a parade of oil torches and pitchforks. That suggestion went over like a rock off a cliff. They told me not to come back if I didn't have anything constructive to offer."

Basil nods and kneads the stubbly flesh of his chin.

"You're all they talk about," Herbert continues. "How you're going to ruin the crops, pollute the air, impregnate their teenaged daughters with your demon seed. It's almost comical. Twisted, for sure, but comical. One of them insists his son is possessed, his dog is dying and the field behind his house is plagued with some sort of demonic fungus and beginning to sink into the marshes of Hades, all thanks to you. It's ridiculous. But I guess it's not all that ridiculous, judging by the looks of you."

Basil notices an inconsistency in Herbert's voice, a strange affect he can't quite put his finger on—something he hasn't noticed until now.

"I am ridiculous in this world," he says. "Spend a few hours beneath the surface meeting some of my people and you'll see I'm a pussycat by comparison."

"They're making plans, you know. Battle plans."

"Who is 'they,' exactly?"

"Edna and her band of merry idiots."

Edna Babych, Herbert goes on to explain. She's the one who's been leading the protests. Herbert describes her: a graying brunette in her late forties, maybe early fifties, rail thin with sunken cheeks and thin, berry-red lips. Oh, and she always wears the same denim jacket, embroidered with sparkling red sequins that spell out a rather eerie idiom: "Three Nails in Flesh and Bone. Three Days in Darkness. One Path to Eternity in the Arms of the Lord." He's been attending services at Crows Gorge United Methodist Church for a year or so, he explains, and he remembers having seen her once or twice before all this nonsense started—mostly he remembers the jacket—but the few chatty members of the congregation advised him to keep his distance. "A zealot," they called her. "A nutcase." Her becoming an outspoken leader in the church came out of nowhere, he adds, more or less coinciding with Basil's arrival.

"You two have already met, sort of," Herbert says. "She's the onion tosser."

"Oh, her. She's got a good arm."

Herbert steps to the window and scans the crowd. He points to a woman in the middle of the pack, standing deathly still, her eyes boring holes into the building.

"That's Edna right there, in her glory," he says.

Basil doesn't know if she can see inside or not, doesn't remember if the windows are mirrored on the outside, but he can feel the sting of her marble-cold eyes wishing on him a fate much ghastlier than death. Her austere appearance suggests she would make a disappointing foe, yet her hatred for him implies otherwise: She seems willing to burn down the building, and reduce to ash any heathens inside, if it means she can get to him.

Basil wonders where Edna calls home. Finding out a detail as mundane as someone's street address should be easy in a town the size of Beak. Put another way, the problem of Edna Babych can swiftly disappear if he so chooses.

"Most of them are pretty normal, actually," Herbert says of the protestors. "They just want to make sure you're not a threat to their homes, families and house pets, that you don't want to deflower anyone's goat. But when a nut like Edna shows up, the reasonable folks find a way to lose their voices. Under her direction, they've discussed a scenario in which they call in the Feds to have you removed. She was throwing around all kinds of good ideas, like firebombing your apartment and stringing up Anton and Bulcavage until their feet stop kicking."

"Why them?"

"For harboring you, I suppose. Bulcavage probably does deserve jail time for the things he's done and the people he's screwed over, but not for the reasons Edna's suggesting. No, Edna says he should hang for welcoming you into the community in the first place, for aiding and abetting a—what did she call you? … Oh, right: 'a pox upon our way of life.' She says you're an infidel polluting God's holy land. She actually used that word: infidel."

"What are the Feds?"

"The G-men. The dark underbelly of the federal government or at least the side that would deal with the otherworldly likes of you. Edna probably thinks a quick phone call to Washington would excite a legion of Men in Black to descend on Beak and drag you off to some top-secret subterranean hideout for gassing and prompt dissection."

"My doors do not lock. Let them come."

"Trust me. The G-men probably already know you're here. They know everything. Part of me wants to believe you're the property of the military-industrial complex—like, you escaped from a research lab in some remote government facility a mile beneath the surface, and the people in charge just haven't yet realized you've gone missing."

Basil's eyes return to the chaotic scene in the parking lot, where a man climbs onto the hood of the brown sedan next to the lot's sole motorcycle. The man unzips his fly and douses the length of Basil's precious noisemaker, from the fringed lever covers to the curve of the leather saddle, with a stream of lemon-yellow urine.

"Well," Basil says, "this is unfortunate."

Herbert winces at the sight.

"Don't get me wrong," he offers. "To some people around here, you're sort of a local treasure. There's this weird sense of pride because you chose Beak, of all places, to spend some time. It's along the lines of 'George Washington slept here', I think. For better or for worse, you're our problem and no one else's, and we're going to come up with the solution."

"Is that how you see me? A problem to solve?"

"Not me, but I'm not a fanatic. I can't say the same for Edna Babych. To her, you're Public Enemy Number One."

As if on cue, Edna raises both hands in Basil's direction and crosses her arms in the form of a crucifix. The gesture seems almost profane. She then belts out a banshee-like scream intent on rattling the windows.

All Basil wanted was an office with a window overlooking the trees and the grassy plains. Now that he has one, he can't bear the view. He reaches over and yanks on the cord, drawing down the blinds to block out the light.

## Chapter 15

# The Bat Beneath the Bridge

Tyburn. A body dangles from the gallows, its shadow twirling in the twilight. Timbers creak. Fibers groan, stretched by the pull of lifeless freight. I wonder what terrible sin this luckless reprobate committed. Theft, most likely—an undignified crime, or so say the men who mete out such punishment. Given my own circumstances, I could forgive a man for taking what he needs, even if it does not belong to him.

Better to die at the gallows than to starve like a mongrel, especially while surrounded by so many fortunate souls blessed with plenty.

As if on cue, my empty stomach lets me know it has not been fed in some time. I have grown used to its complaints. A different feeling has displaced the pain—a cousin, of sorts: not quite pain, just a *there*-ness.

I drift among other soot-faced laborers. Their stink engulfs me, ties me to them. My feet cold and wet, my hands bleeding, the muscles in my lower back just one task from giving in. I shake off the cold, as the chill air withers the sweat from my hair and the back of my aching neck.

The hidden sun sinks behind gauzy clouds. Yet another gray day will end without me feeling the warmth of the sun on my whiskered face.

God has abandoned this place, and me along with it.

Shop owners and workers who earn their keep without breaking their backs depart from the bridge's middle, leaving the shops shuttered and churches barren. When a man or woman catches my eye, my gaze lingers. I imagine the soft, warm bed this blessed individual crawled out of early that morning, wondering if the bedclothes are still warm. I follow close behind, trying to will a handful of pence out of their pockets and into mine.

If only I could master such deceit.

My first order of business is to fill my belly, and then find somewhere warm to rest my tired body. I can afford a hot meal. I can afford a warm bed. Yet my predicament requires me to hoard. I must have "enough" to acquire a proper home rich with the fineries my bride deserves—or, more likely, to fund my journey back to Berwick and lessen the magnitude of my failure. I wonder: Do kindness and splendor exist within London's bounds? Foulness plagues every block. Can't walk for a moment without stepping in some porridge-thick slurry of mud and excrement. Can't go a length of rope without stirring up a literal rat's nest.

Perhaps when I have enough, a hidden world will avail itself to me and the sun will shine on the spot where I will build my new life.

For now, I see only this shadow world.

Nightfall will arrive shortly. I ponder the pains of suffering yet another sleepless night evading "Old Billy, the Beast of London Bridge", as the newsboys have dubbed him—a devilish thing as strong as an ape and as cunning as a stoat, a slippery bugger. Old Billy's supposed origin chills the blood. They say the creature made its London debut the day after a wealthy haberdasher named William Diggle got put to the gallows. As the story goes, the constabulary fingered Diggle for choking the life from some unwilling toms—a dozen perhaps—though he swore his innocence until the moment the rope snapped his neck. The newsboys insist Diggle used his last breath, right after they looped the noose over his head, to curse all of London.

So goes the legend.

Fresh rumors about Old Billy's murders circulate with each passing day, the details of his handiwork more gruesome with each telling. Some swear the beast is a malevolent fool in a stovepipe hat and a blade in each hand, while others characterize him as a monstrosity with the claws of a jungle cat and shark's teeth where human teeth should be. One shopkeeper suggested Old Billy is not of this world, a creature powerful enough to punch a hole through the veils of space and time to make a home among hapless earthlings. Most seem to think an angry God has opened the Gates of Hell and unleashed our doom-maker.

I believe the beast may be the last of a dying species, driven to rage by the stink, noise and other ills of the encroaching English.

Most days I would not blame the poor chap for acting up.

I have seen Old Billy. Thrice I have seen him — once, leaping from one rooftop to another, backlit by the smudge of the moon; a second time, crouched in an alley, greedily feasting on fistfuls of meat, the entrails of a freshly killed cur, no doubt; and a third, the night before last, the beast passing right by me as I worked to pry a rock from the wall of the blacksmith's, where I have chosen to hide away my modest cache of coins. Old Billy stood so close I could have reached out and touched the scales of his lizard-like legs, his swaying black tail, before he disappeared into the night.

This sort of thing simply does not happen in sleepy Berwick.

Of course I cannot be certain of what my eyes have shown me, given the fact that my sustenance-starved brain fails me more than it serves. Yet part of me believes I share a bond with this creature — man and beast somehow coupled. For I have watched Old Billy, and he has permitted me to watch him: he the actor and I his audience.

I am hardly the only one, of course. The newspaper stories gleefully quote hysterical Londoners claiming to have faced Old Billy, or to have survived confrontations with the randy old boy: a bread maker who arrived at his shop well before dawn to stoke the coals in his oven, to see Old Billy's gleaming eyes staring down from the rooftop; a weary laborer, like me, who saw the beast leap from the edge of the bridge and into the gloom above the Thames; and, in one case, a banker who witnessed Old Billy lurking in an open second-story window, leering at the banker's wife as she emerged from her weekly bath.

Not all have been so fortunate in their encounters, if one puts his faith in the stories the newsboys have to share. By my count, seven have been murdered, absurdly so—a night watchman, among them—with certain body parts consumed or otherwise unrecovered, the stories say.

"The work of a maniac and nothing more." So said a constable quoted in the daily news, though the same constable seemed either unable or unwilling to assure the public anything could be done to stop the supposed maniac from claiming more victims.

Most see Old Billy as a villain, as an evil presence to be cast out. But me, given my situation, I see enterprise.

Old Billy owns the darkened corners of night and fades with the rising sun, likely resting somewhere warm and quiet by the time the first rays of daylight creep over the horizon. I imagine the old boy stuffing his body into a fissure beneath the chapel at Saint Stephen's, lounging atop a pile of cleanly picked bones, or dangling by his feet, bat-like, from the underside of London Bridge, his claws sunk into the hollow spaces between stone slabs. No matter where he beds, he is vulnerable.

One needs only to engage the imagination to know where to look.

If I could find a gentle way to stop Old Billy's heart, my pockets would fill and, in turn, my troubles end. I would then call for my bride and have her find me so she could see that my promise to conquer London's wilds rings true.

*Tomorrow.*

Tomorrow I will put my fevered brain to work. Once I have the quiet time to work up a plan of attack, I will hunt down Old Billy. And when I find him, asleep in his lair, I will peel the hide from his scaly old back.

My feet lead me back to Monument Bridge. My mind wanders. I think of home, of Berwick's quiet hills, its rugged coast, its starry skies. And of course I think of her. A cold gust drives the tears from my eyes.

Chapter 16

# Stoked Embers

"Take the weekend to think about it," Bulcavage tells his team. "I'm not asking you boys to walk on water here. Just do the job I'm paying you to do."

Herbert slaps the table with his doodled-up sketchpad.

"We wouldn't need the weekend if we knew what the hell we're supposed to do, Bob. At least give us a nudge in the right direction. In *any* direction, for that matter."

Basil's eyes jump from Herbert to Bulcavage, expecting fireworks, expecting to have to intervene, or perhaps to pile on. He has grown fond of Herbert, or at least he knows not to count his co-worker among his enemies. Bulcavage is a different story. For the moment, Bulcavage is a question mark.

"I only know what you know: Hooke's people want to try something different," Bulcavage says. "They have a new line of cookers they're all hot and bothered about, and they want us to pimp it. I'm thinking of a splashy print campaign—the national hunting and fishing magazines—and maybe some outdoor signage, if the stingy bastards agree to the budget."

"*Outdoor* means billboards," Herbert tells Basil.

"We can't afford to lose this one," Bulcavage continues. "Sales of their existing cookers have gone stale, they say, so they need to punch up the branding for the new line. What else do you need from me? Everyone likes barbecue, for chrissakes."

He takes a breath—more of an annoyed sigh.

"Tell you what: They gave me a prototype, so take the damned thing home, fire it up and throw on a few drumsticks for dinner. That should inspire you."

"I got shit to do, Bob," Herbert says.

"You got work to do, Herb," Bulcavage says. "Don't make

140

this awkward. I need you two" — his index finger draws a line between Herbert and Basil — "to collaborate on this little science project. Spend some quality time together. It'll be good for both of you. Consider it a team-building exercise."

"I'm free this weekend," Basil says.

"Of course you are," Herbert says. "No one likes you."

Bulcavage laughs, adding, "Check with Anton. He's always got something dead in his freezer. I'm sure he'd be happy to let you roast some hunk of meat on a spit."

"Barbecue, sir," Basil interjects. "It's barbecue, not rotisserie."

"Whatever. Just have something fleshed out and ready for me on Monday morning. We'll want to do the storyboards and have whatever you come up with ready for the client by Tuesday. And another thing — "

A ruckus interrupts Bulcavage, and all three lift their eyes toward the door. Two female voices bicker from somewhere in the office. Determined footsteps follow.

"Where is he?" says a familiar voice.

She hurries past the conference-room door and then, course correcting, backs up to block the doorway.

Basil's stomach drops. It's her: Melody.

"By all means, Mel," Bulcavage says flatly. "Do make yourself at home."

"I've had it up to here with this shit, Bob," she says. "Those loudmouths in the parking lot are driving me up a goddamned tree. I had a flat tire last night — a fucking flat tire — probably from all the goddamned broken bottles those fuckers have been leaving all over the goddamned place. Hell, I wouldn't be surprised if someone slashed my tire on purpose. Because of *him*." She stabs the air, pointing to Basil. "You ever try to change a tire in heels and a skirt? It's not fun."

"We're all making sacrifices, Mel."

"The whole place smells like a goddamned sewer — all those fuckers pissing and shitting in the bushes. And they just won't shut the hell up with that goddamned chanting. All because of *him*," she adds, circling Basil's face with her index finger.

"What do you want me to do about it?" Bulcavage says. "They'll go away eventually."

"He's your employee, Bob. You're responsible."

As if noticing Herbert's presence for the first time, she pauses in her assault. She gives a wave and a knowing wink.

"Mel," Bulcavage says. "Everything in life is temporary."

"Bullshit," she says. She crosses her arms and tilts her head. "You," she says, pointing emphatically to Basil. "Come with me."

Basil rises from his seat and follows Melody down the hall. They file past a scowling Karen, her right cheek brushed with a wisp of powdered sugar. Basil scowls back and sticks out his tongue for childish emphasis. Melody flings open the office door and makes a beeline for the stairwell, Basil failing to keep up with the echo of her footsteps. By the time he makes it to the first floor, Melody is halfway down the hall. She disappears into a door he presumes to be her office.

Basil approaches the pane of frosted glass, which bears a collection of letters rimmed with gold foil: MELODY K. MULRONEY, ESQ. He pushes the door open to see Melody leaning over a wide oak desk, where a petite, well-dressed blonde nods her head, popping her gum and diligently taking down notes.

"Tell him to be here ASAP," Melody demands. "Tell him he owes me a favor."

Melody stomps into an adjacent office, all glass from floor to ceiling. She dons a checkered blue blazer and leans down to check her face in a desktop mirror.

Basil smiles at the blonde. She squints and returns the smile, though it somehow seems less than sincere. With the phone's beige receiver crooked between her cheek and shoulder, she points to the mouthpiece and mimes two words: *It's ringing.*

Half-listening to the blonde's conversation with someone named Brandon, Basil lets his eyes rove, hoping Melody returns quickly. With the certainty of a hound on a scent trail, Melody strides back to the reception area. The two lock eyes. Something tells him to maintain the stare.

"We're going to put an end to this bullshit right now," she says. "I don't know who in Hell you pissed off or why, but even *you* have rights here. ... You've met Audrey," she adds, nodding toward the distracted blonde.

Melody moves to the window. She bends at the waist, and Basil's jaw involuntarily drops as he takes in the view. He pats down the patch of black fur struggling to cover his budding erection.

Basil begins, "I think we—"

"Don't say anything," she says, her voice soft, quiet. Her eyes scan the parking lot. "Just shut your trap and be still."

He stands in silence and wills his erection to fade.

"Okay, he's here," she says. "Follow me. Try to look solemn."

Seconds later Basil finds himself outside, the sun warming his skin, facing the full wrath of the crowd. The hostility deafens him.

He takes his post behind Melody. The knob of his erection jabs the small of her back.

"Not so close," she says through the side of her mouth.

She stands with her back to the door, legs shoulder width apart, hands on her hips, a model of cool composure, fully in control. Basil admires the curve of her hips, the back of her head, the way the russet-colored hair cascades over her shoulders.

A broad-shouldered man dressed in dark blue parts the crowd and nods to Melody. He sidles up to Basil and tips the brim of his hat. Sunlight bounces off the silver badge pinned to his left breast. Basil squints from the glare.

"You and me going to have a problem?" the officer asks.

"No, sir."

"Good man. Now be quiet and let Melody do her thing."

The officer hands Melody a worn white bullhorn and then turns to face the crowd.

Edna Babych stands by herself, away from the chaos. Even from a distance Basil can see the determination in her thin lips. Her eyes glint with fury.

"My name is Melody Mulroney," Melody barks. Her voice booms through the bullhorn. "I'm an attorney who works in this building. You should know that each of you is trespassing. This is an act of unlawful protest."

She takes a breath. "Furthermore ..."

Her legalese flows, the words authoritative, convincing, even poetic.

Basil leans forward and inhales the sweet scent rising from Melody's scalp, her perfume and other odors drifting from the hidden parts of her body. His erection pokes through the thatch of fur between his legs, looking for fires to put out.

"Each one of you is interfering with my client's right to work unmolested," she continues. "That's a violation of his rights and the rights of every individual working on this property. Officer Pierce will see to it that you disperse and leave the property peacefully. Consider this your only warning. If you persist with this unlawful behavior, I will take appropriate action on behalf of my client, and see to it that you are dealt with to the fullest extent of the law."

She lowers the bullhorn and retreats into the building, while Officer Pierce steps forward with arms extended. Basil watches as the sea of signs recedes, the grumbling protestors amble off. Officer Pierce accompanies two men to their pickup trucks, and one of them hands Pierce a canned beer. All three of them laugh like old friends.

The crowd dissolves within two minutes. Everyone returns to his or her vehicle, with one exception. A defiant Edna Babych remains, standing less than ten feet from Basil's hooves. He can see hatred etched into the lines of her face.

"Have a good day," he chirps, not sure what else to say.

Just as he turns to head back into the building, Edna spits on the ground. He feels her eyes on him, expecting a blade to the back.

He steps inside, eager to banter with Melody. Instead, he finds himself alone, eyeing the rust-colored stain on the carpet beneath the water fountain. His smile fades. He wonders how to proceed with her, whether he should trot down to her office and offer to pay a few bucks for services rendered, or whether he should wait for her to bill him. Eventually he skulks into the stairwell and clops up the stairs toward his office. He meets Herbert on the windowless landing, and the two mince words.

"So ... I guess I'll see you over the weekend," Herbert says. He struggles to maintain his loose grip on the oblong Hooke-branded cooker. The large, gray cylinder trails a pencil-thin wire.

"Company barbecue, we'll call it," Basil says.

"More like forced fun," Herbert responds.

"Should I come over your place or—"

"I'll come to your place on Sunday. Let's say eleven. I'd like to be home by two."

* * *

Edna Babych sits at the library desk and dutifully turns page after page. Her stomach grumbles. She looks up from the black-and-white drawing of a pointy-eared humanoid with bloody fangs, slits for eyes and needle-like spines jutting from its scaly back. The figure crouches above a helpless baby in the middle of a field, crescent moon overhead. Edna sighs in disgust. The page turns with an audible snap.

She lifts her gaze to study the men and women—more women than men, mostly mothers reading to their sons and daughters— at the surrounding tables. Much too crowded for a Saturday morning, she thinks. She guesses at the basest acts each sinner has committed in the past twenty-four hours. Some doozies for sure, by the looks of 'em. Each one of these heathens deserves the electric chair. She's certain of it. Drop a bomb in the middle of the Beak Public Library and the world would be a better place, no doubt about it.

She eyes the sign for the women's restroom. She'll have to pay a visit soon enough, though she decides to wait for one or two more of the nearby desks to clear out so as few people as possible see her enter, so as few people as possible can trace the source of the noises she'll undoubtedly make in the process of soothing her uncooperative gut. She then returns her attention to the book, so she can take her mind off the daily battle with her intestines and focus on a more important task: uncovering the secrets to besting her enemy.

A moment later, halfway into a passage about demons roaming the English countryside, she closes the book. She detects a subtle change. She feels the shift in her bones, especially in her rump, the sensation vibrating in her tailbone. Then she hears the approach: the sound of one hard surface clacking against another—the telltale clopping of horse hooves ... or the cloven hooves of a goat.

*No*, she thinks. *Not here.*

At first she refuses to believe it. Then she has visual confirmation.

The enemy approaches.

Basil, the demon, strides down the aisle. The creature offers friendly nods to some of the folks reading their newspapers or magazines or, more likely, pornography cleverly disguised as art.

She locks eyes with the enemy. He—*it*—stops in its tracks. Then it proceeds, heading straight toward her.

"Good day," it says.

"Every day is a good day in the eyes of the Lord," she replies.

It leans across her table and, incredulously, plucks the book from her hands.

"*A Seeker's Guide to Slaying Warlocks, Werewolves and Wyverns,*" it says, reciting the book's title. It drops the book onto the table in front of her, and the sound booms in the cavernous library. It shrugs its reptilian shoulders, seemingly out of embarrassment. "Good luck with your endeavor," it adds.

"Have a seat," she tells the demon.

It hesitates. Sitting across from her is the last thing it wants to do, she knows, which is why she extends the invitation.

"Go ahead," she adds. "We're on neutral turf."

The demon pulls the chair out from beneath the desk, making a noise like stone being dragged across a sheet of metal, and flops a stack of books onto the desk. In turn, Edna reaches across the table and pokes the stack with her wiry finger until she can read the spines of all three books. The one at the bottom of the pile: *Fanaticism, Zealotry and the Erosion of Western Civilization.* The middle: *Blood and Treasure: A History of Killing to Win, from Pangaea to the Persian Gulf.* And the one on top, the thinnest of all three: *Into the Inferno: Man's Place in Hell.*

"Fact checking, are we?" she asks.

"Enough with the pleasantries, Edna," it tells her. "What do you want from me?"

*It knows my name,* she thinks. *I must be doing something right. I must be doing a lot of somethings right, dadgummit!*

"My distaste for you has nothing to do with what *I* want," she says. "It's nothing personal, you see. It's about what the Good Lord God wants."

"And what do you pretend to know that might be?"

"To destroy you. To see you writhing on the ground, to hear you scream his name in contrition, to see your skin burning off in your own accursed fire."

"Pity," it says. "This skin doesn't burn, lady—as fireproof as asbestos, I'm afraid. You're going to need a more colorful imagination."

She has no response.

"In all seriousness, I wish you would just leave me alone," it says. "Every other human has."

"And therein lies the problem. Too many people in this miserable pit of a town have turned a blind eye to you. Believe me, I wish I could go on living my life like an ostrich bird with its head in the sand, pretending you don't exist. But I see you, demon. I see you clear as day."

"You seem to think the two of us are engaged in some sort of battle to the death. I'll put my hand on any book you want and swear that you don't factor into my thoughts—except maybe twice a day, when I see the trouble you're stirring up outside my place of employment. I'll wonder: *What kind of craziness does Edna have in store for me today?* All I want is peace. If I sought something else, you'd know by now. If I really wanted to, I could make it so no one ever sees you again."

She bristles.

"I beg you," it continues. "Just leave me to my business, and I'll gladly leave you to yours."

"That's exactly what you want the world to think. But I know better. Every word out of your mouth is a bald lie."

"Would you like to know what I *really* want, Edna?"

She grips her blouse and holds it tight to her chest.

"I know exactly what you want, beast! It's written plain as anything in the Good Book. John, chapter ten, I think: 'to steal and kill and destroy'."

The demon wags its horned head.

"I've seen too much death and destruction in my days," it says. "Conflict and chaos have no place in my itinerary. No, I'm here to learn and to absorb all things beautiful. And Edna, I want you to hear what I'm about to say: I'm not leaving this place until I've had my fill, and nothing or no one will stand in my way. Least of all you."

"Just go on thinking that," she says calmly.

She eyes the tables around her, imagining someone somewhere will see her speaking with the enemy and misinterpret her intentions. Even the smallest misstep could break her tenuous hold on the mantle of power in the church she fought so hard to win.

"Go crawl back into whatever slime-slathered hole spat you out," she says, waving the demon away. "I'll see you soon enough."

"Unless I see you first."

The demon rises from its chair, collects its books and clops off. Heavy hoof steps crack against the marble-hard floor. It stops for a moment, as if wanting to say something further, but keeps on going. Its horns disappear around the edge of a pea-colored bookcase, but the clacking of hooves echoes. Her gut voices its displeasure with another urgent gurgle. She gets up and heads not to the restroom but to the checkout desk, flagging down the first attendant she sees: a redheaded woman, maybe mid-thirties, thick in the hips, large breasted. Edna wrinkles her nose.

"Why is he here?" Edna hisses. "*It!* Why is *it* here?"

"I'm sorry, ma'am," the redhead whispers. "I don't understand."

"Of course you don't, deary. The demon. Why is the demon here? You know, the big, tall, devil-looking brute that's been stinking up the aisles with his brimstone B.O.? The Antichrist?"

She slams her books onto the counter in front of the redhead.

"It's a public library, Miss Bab—"

"Free for people! For humans! Not him! He belongs at the bottom of a ditch!"

Edna pushes her stack of books off the edge of the counter. The falling books topple five columns of Dewey Decimal cards that had been stacked neatly on the desktop. The cards scatter like thrown confetti—under the copy machine, beneath the redhead's slippers, into the office of the library manager—as Edna marches off to find a suitable restroom so she can move her nervous bowels.

# Chapter 17

# One Lock, Many Keys

Herbert slams the car door.

He moves to the rear of the vehicle, fretting over the discolored paint of the trunk and roof. The trunk yawns open, exposing the assorted pieces of the all-gray Hooke cooker. Reassembling the contraption takes some doing. Sweat drips from the tip of his nose.

Nothing ever goes as planned, he thinks. Not today, not this week, not this life.

The cooker must weigh fifty pounds if it weighs an ounce. He struggles as he hurries up the path toward Basil's door. The squat L-shaped building wears a coat of paint he might describe as mustard brown—drab, carelessly chosen, sad. Orange shutters frame each picture window. He stumbles on a patch of broken concrete, and the egg-shaped cooker slips from his hands. Metal clangs against pavement. A rectangular panel tumbles onto the grass and he's forced to retrieve. He clenches his fists and holds them to his forehead.

Only then does he realize he does not know which apartment is Basil's. He curses under his breath.

He sees Basil's accursed Harley in a spot by the curb and decides to knock on the door directly in front of the motorcycle. After his knuckles rap on the paint-flecked wood, he waits ten seconds, then twenty. No response. A dying rosebush withers in the dirt patch to his right, nothing but twigs, thorns and shriveled leaves. An orange shutter dangles by one hinge, and spiders have spun their feathery webs in the space between the shutter and the window frame. He knocks a second time and the door creaks open.

"What?" the hardened voice demands.

"Excuse me. I'm looking for Basil."

"The demon?"

"I suppose so. Yes."

"Go fuck yourself."

The door slams. Displaced air caresses Herbert's cheeks.

He knocks on four more doors, earning a similar response from each surly tenant.

"Just one more," he whispers. "Bulcavage can go to Hell if he thinks I'm wasting another minute chasing down this goat-footed dildo."

At the next door, number thirteen—the first digit is gone entirely, and one of the nails that should be holding the three in place has gone missing, so the digit hangs on its side, looking like a lower-case W in cursive—he puts the dented cooker down and raps gently, almost too gently. He turns his body so he faces the parking lot. He can see his car.

The door opens so swiftly he can feel the air being pulled past him.

"Yeah?"

"I'm looking for Basil."

"Yeah?"

The smell of whiskey seeps through the pores of the screen.

"I'm guessing I've got the wrong place. Sorry for—"

"What's a guy like you want with a piece of work like Basil? If you're looking for trouble ..."

Herbert takes a step backward. He knows by now that it's better to run than to stay and fight.

"Shut up and let him in, Chester."

It's Basil's familiar baritone, far off.

"Ah, I'm just fucking with you," the man at the door tells Herbert. "Come on in, buddy."

Herbert genuflects to collect the cooker. As he takes a reluctant step across the threshold, he sees Basil reposing on the couch, beer in hand. The demon climbs off the couch to make the requisite introductions.

"Chester's an English professor who got canned because he's a drunk who likes to screw around with undergrads," Basil says.

"He's a lying son of a bitch," Chester says. "Don't listen to a word out of his mouth. I'm on sabbatical, voluntarily."

As the door closes behind him, Herbert thinks he will call in sick tomorrow to make up for the perfectly good afternoon he is about to sacrifice.

\* \* \*

The smell of charred flesh fills the living room, wafting in from the patio. Herbert watches through the screen as Basil stands on the concrete slab. The sun highlights the veins bulging from each of the demon's absurd muscles—bowling balls for arms, calves as sculpted as carved granite. Dutifully manning the cooker, Basil nudges the rack of ribs with his right finger. He then slips the finger into his mouth and deems the ribs almost done.

"Another hour, maybe," he says. "I offer a blessing for this beast. Its life has ended so ours may endure. Tomorrow could be our turn, the fates dictating our flesh becomes sustenance for the bellies of our betters."

"Speak for yourself," says Chester. He punctuates the sentence with a resonant belch.

"Can we speed things up?" Herbert asks. He sucks the last slosh of foam from a Miller Lite bottle.

"All things take time to achieve greatness," Basil says. "Chewing on raw meat means nothing, but to prepare it, to care for it, to make it tender—this is where the art comes in."

"I'm ready for the art to fill my belly now," Chester replies.

"Food is more than load for the gut," Basil replies. "It's a celebration, an offering of peace, or a seed of sacrifice on the eve of war."

Basil goes on to explain how demons celebrate in Our Fiery

Home. He describes a septet of brainless troglodytes cranking massive spits, each wooden spike bearing the gift of a gargantuan beast abducted from the surface—the head of a tusked elephant, the armored carapace of a rhinoceros, the charred spindles of a giraffe.

The account is so vivid, Herbert can practically hear the pockets of mammalian fat bursting and hissing in the open fire.

"You smell that?" Basil asks. "Flesh over flame is a joy, but flesh over flame seasoned with the right blend of spices? Cumin, paprika, granulated onion, maybe a little cayenne—you'll never have anything better."

"I don't want to know how you know this stuff," Chester says.

"Books. I spend my Saturdays at the library, leafing through piles of cookbooks, memoirs, novels. Oh, and rather than sleep, I watch TV. A lot of it."

"So does everyone else," Herbert says. "It's the national pastime."

"Sure. Only I pay attention."

"I don't sleep either," Chester says as he raises a half-empty rocks glass. "I pass out."

"Because of your excessive alcohol consumption," Basil says.

"Yes, Basil, that *is* the joke."

Herbert ignores the exchange and turns to Basil. "Why don't you sleep?"

"There's just too much to do," he responds. "My time here is short. Plus, I'm not fond of the things I see when I close my eyes."

"Nightmares?"

"Not exactly. My dreams are mostly unpleasant, but ... well, they also cause me considerable pain."

"How so?" Chester asks.

"Each night I dream a different chapter of the same story: the same characters, the same places, just different parts of the same, drawn-out fairy tale. Sort of like I'm being forced to relive an experience I suffered through but can't quite remember. It's plagued me my whole life, as far as I know."

"Sounds like a punishment to me," Chester slurs.

Herbert asks, "What happens in these dreams?"

"It's a simple story. When I sleep, I see the world through the eyes of a man—a human man. His name is Emmitt Wells. He's English, though he lives in a London unlike today, a London from long ago. There's a woman, and even if she's not in a particular episode of the dream, she always has a presence. The whole dream revolves around her. Don't ask me her name. Don't ask me what she looks like, because I can't quite make out the details of her face—always a smudge, nothing more than a smudge. But I can hear her voice. I can see the silhouette of her body, smell her, feel the warmth of her body against mine."

"That doesn't sound so bad," Chester says. Another belch.

"Things happen, as they often do, and the story never ends well," Basil says. "Every time I part ways with her, I do so with the knowledge that she will suffer, and I know I have played a part in her suffering. The worst part of it all: I know there's nothing I can do to prevent any of it. I fail. I try to help, but I fail. In the end, everything goes dark and cold, and then the story starts all over again from the beginning."

"You must have fucked up something royal," Chester says.

"Pardon?"

"Yeah, you fucked up right well and good in a past life. That's why you look the way you do now. Blame the Dungeon Master, the String Puller, the Maker and Undoer of All Things."

"That's assuming he believes in reincarnation," Herbert says.

"It doesn't matter what he believes," Chester says. "The only thing that matters is whether or not it's true."

"I don't follow," Basil says.

"If literature teaches us anything, it's that the necks of those who stray from the straight and narrow path are doomed to bear a heavy yoke. There's a reckoning at some point. In other words, there's no such thing as a free sin. Look at Adam and Eve. Look at Shakespeare's Macbeth. Look at the works of Tolstoy. Christ, look at every big-titted bimbo who ever felt the cold steel of the madman's blade in any campy slasher flick from the past twenty years. You're Prometheus. You're Sisyphus. Only instead of having your liver pecked out by scavengers or being forced to shoulder a half-ton boulder up a mountain for all eternity, your punishment comes to you in the form of those rotten dreams you're forced to relive over and over and over again. To be cast out of Eden *and* be forced to relive your mistakes every time you close your eyes? That's a particularly creative brand of cruelty."

"Unless," Herbert interjects, "all demons' brains are hardwired that way—like, maybe you all share the same dream."

"I wouldn't know," Basil says. "One demon does not speak to another about the frailties of his unconscious mind."

"Like I said, you fucked up," Chester says, "and because of your fucked-up-ness you died and came back, reborn in the fires of Hell and cursed for the rest of your days. At least, that's the kind of nonsense someone with a King James Bible on his nightstand might have you believe."

"Our Fiery Home," Basil says.

"Say what?" says Chester.

"It's not Hell. It's Our Fiery Home."

"Whatever. You're a case study in rebirth and retribution."

The room goes quiet. They sit there and sip, Basil and Herbert from their brown bottles, Chester from his crystal glass. The ribs continue their transformation on the slats of the cooker.

"I don't know what Bulcavage wants from us," Herbert says finally.

"You mean the Hooke campaign?" Basil says. "Simple. He wants us to find an artful way to sell an artless hunk of metal."

"No poems this time. No 'Transcending Death' soliloquies."

"Of course not. There's nothing to this thing—just a big metal box."

"More like a cylinder."

"It's not about the *thing*," Basil says as he raps the cooker's metal shell. "We're selling the story."

"Which is?"

"The best things in life take time."

"Like?"

"I don't know. Making a fine wine or a good cheese. Baking a soufflé. Or human germination—the product of nine months in the womb after sperm meets ovum."

"Naturally."

"We're selling indulgence. We're selling hedonism—that's what this is all about."

Herbert tosses an empty bottle into the trashcan and grabs another from the fridge, the shelves barren save a few bottles of Miller Lite, a jar of honey mustard and an open package of butcher paper bearing something pink and bloody.

"Where did you get the ribs?" Herbert asks. "I can't imagine you standing at the butcher counter, waving your paper ticket and saying, 'Ooh, ooh. I'm next!'"

"From Anton, just like Bulcavage said. I asked and he delivered. *'Nothing but best for you,'*"Basil says in his best Russian accent. "What's Anton's story?"

"You'll have to ask Bulcavage."

"I'm asking you."

"The less you know about Anton—and about Bulcavage, for that matter—the better off you'll be. Even I don't ask too many questions."

Basil holds up his hands, palms facing up. He wants more.

"From what I gather, Anton is Bulcavage's brother-in-law," Herbert says. "Bulcavage married Anton's sister."

"Where is she?" Basil asks. "I've seen neither hide nor hair of her. In fact, I haven't heard a word about her until now. I had assumed Bulcavage was a serial bachelor."

"Nobody knows, really. Just rumors. Most people say he's a bad man, our boss."

"How so?"

"The agency—just pocket change, something to legitimize him. He's got his hands in everything. Drugs, most likely, and ... well, I don't want to call it human trafficking, but I don't know what else to call it. He owns this place, too, this whole apartment complex. Just look at the degenerates who live here. He must rent rooms by the hour."

A few seconds pass before Herbert realizes his gaffe.

"When I say *degenerates*, I mean present company excluded, of course," he adds, much too late.

All three share a laugh.

Herbert hoists the bottle to his lips and takes a long swig. He checks his watch and doesn't care that it's nearly five o'clock.

* * *

A spread-eagled Chester snores on the chaise lounge. A dangling hand flicks his toppled rocks glass, sending it rolling in a half circle across the concrete slab.

"Five bucks says he pisses himself," Basil says.

"Is that a common occurrence?" Herbert replies.

"More common than you might think."

"He's a colorful character."

"Chester? He's brilliant. He's an alcoholic and a lothario, but he's brilliant. And he's a real mess. If you're around him long enough, he's liable to puke in your lap or try to slice your jugular in a drunken fit. He means well. You won't find a better neighbor."

"You said he's a college professor?"

"Technically. I don't know the whole story, but he's got tenure over at the university in Lincoln. He's on sabbatical for doing something stupid. I'm sure there was alcohol involved, and undergrads in less clothing than they should be around a college professor more than twice their age. He screwed some big-shot alum's daughter, probably."

"And what about you? We've been working together for almost a month now, and I still know nothing about you, other than the fact that you're a demon with a fondness for the written word."

"Ask me a question and I'll answer as best I can."

"Where'd you come from?"

"From below. Imagine the place you might think of as Hell, only it's not quite as bad as you might think."

"Well, that's something."

"It's worse."

Basil explains why he left Our Fiery Home, how he crawled his way to the surface, describes the short list of characters with whom he mingled: Kamala, the bastard Lubos, Calvin and the other Elders in the Council of Unerring Wisdom, the ghosts of those who ruled the underworld prior to his rise.

"Oh," Herbert says, wrinkling his brow. "Do you have a family?"

"I had a mother. She's gone now. I never knew my father. He could have been one of a thousand demons, or he could have been a thousand and one demons. Mating works much differently in Our Fiery Home. Here, humans pair off—one to one, more or less, for as long as they can stomach each other. Down there, you see only the most temporary of couplings. One lock, many keys."

"And why do you call yourself Basil?"

"That's the name I was given."

"By who?"

"I don't remember exactly. The name came to me so long ago, and I'm fortunate to have it. My mother never had one. In truth, very few demons are blessed to have a name, and the Nameless have next to no rights."

"Why?"

Basil twists the cap off another beer and drains half of the bottle in one pull. The tinny notes of blues guitar spill onto the patio from speakers in the living room. When Albert Collins's "I Ain't Drunk" comes on, Basil taps the concrete with his right hoof in time with the thump of the bass drum.

"Couldn't say. To have a name is to have power, to have privilege, to have the freedom to roam. The Nameless? They are told they may never leave Our Fiery Home, not that most would ever want to. Most are too frightened to go anywhere, even though they will never find a worse place."

"You mean there may be others up here, like you?"

"There is no one else like me."

"But other demons, I mean."

"Of course."

"I've never seen one. Not ones that don't look like regular people, anyway."

"They're here, among you. They know how to hide. Call it camouflage. Most humans have no patience to just sit and observe. A demon, though—a demon will stay put for a week, frozen in place, if he knows it's his only way of staying unseen. Eventually he will act. Just turn on the eleven o'clock news and half the stories you see bear the fingerprints of demonic influence, if not their outright involvement."

Basil goes on to list events in which demons likely had a hand, ranging from high-profile missing persons and the goriest of murders to wartime genocide and the poaching of endangered wildlife. If demons have a fondness for anything, he explains, it's exploiting the weak and vulnerable, eager to push any living thing to the brink of extinction.

"If you looked close enough at photographs taken at Auschwitz or Bergen-Belsen or the so-called Killing Fields of the Khmer Rouge, you would likely see the faces of non-humans, directing traffic."

Herbert looks on, horrified.

"You probably won't see another demon in Beak, though," Basil continues. "I haven't sensed any. Most demons up here tend to stick to the major population centers, as I understand it — more targets. Plus, they like the warmer climes, so they stick as close to the Equator as they can. A demon is neutral blooded, meaning his body temperature depends largely on the temperature of his surroundings. Airdrop a demon into the middle of a Nebraskan winter, and he's likely to make a beeline for the nearest working fireplace and stay put for five straight months — and no one will even notice he's there."

"But I can see *you*. In fact, everyone can see you."

"I choose not to hide. That's the point of my being here. By staying in a quiet, do-nothing place like Beak, I've essentially chosen who can see me. Why risk hauling ass to Manhattan or Chicago or L.A. and proclaiming, 'I'm here!' That's a death wish. I'm not fool enough to think I'm infallible, that I'm immortal."

"Aren't you?"

"Of course not. By my best guess, I'm barely a hundred years old, but it's difficult to know. Time passes much differently below ground. We have no sunrises or sunsets to measure the day, no clocks to dole out the hours. No one celebrates birthdays in Our Fiery Home."

"Yeah, I guess candlewax is an endangered species down there. All that fire."

Basil reaches over to clink bottles with Herbert.

"So, I've been wondering," says Herbert. "What happens if you ... you know? What happens if you die?"

"The earth will consume my remains, and my dust will return to the sea and the sky, the soil. I assume my memories will become one with the ether."

"That's the end of you? Nothing after?"

"I have no reason to believe a Great Beyond awaits me. The Elders said nothing of it, and only they would know. The day my heart drums its last beat, I will be no longer."

"If you're in Hell, I suppose that seems about right. Unless you make amends for the things you've done before you kick the can, there's nowhere else to go. Terminus."

"Not Hell," Basil corrects. "Our Fiery Home."

"For the record, I don't think you have anything to worry about. No one's screwing with you. Except God, maybe. You must hate him."

"How can I hate something I have no knowledge of?"

"I figured you two would be at each other's throats."

"If he does exist, and I suspect he does, I hope he does reach out to say hello someday. For now, I'm content interacting with humans like you. A few exceptions, perhaps. Edna Babych and her tribe of acolytes come to mind. I don't much care for her."

"The feeling is mutual, believe me. But she'd slit her own mother's throat if she thought it would bring her two steps closer to salvation."

"I wish she'd leave me alone."

"Hasn't she? The mob's dispersed. Your girlfriend Melody saw to that."

"She's not my girlfriend."

"Yeah, but you'd like her to be."

"Who wouldn't? Present company excluded, of course."

"What's that supposed to mean?"

Basil doesn't respond, and Herbert doesn't push the matter.

"You two are close, it seems," Basil says.

"She's a good listener."

The roar of a souped-up muscle car or pickup truck mars the quiet. Herbert imagines the cornstalks rattling in the glare of taillights as the vehicle rips past.

"I simply cannot understand why humans have to make such a bone-breaking racket every hour of the day," Basil says.

"Probably because they don't know any better. Or maybe just because they can."

"A flagrant abuse of freedom."

Basil leans back and eyes the heavens, as if counting celestial bodies.

"You should have seen me down below, Herbert. I'm a shadow of myself up here. I feel small."

"I can't imagine why. Based on the way you throw around that Harley, I'm guessing you could bench press a Sherman tank."

"You speak of strength, whereas I'm talking about power. I am blessed with other talents besides my physicality. My gifts are diminished here."

"Like what?"

"How about you, Herbert Teak from Des Moines?" Basil says, redirecting. "I know nothing about you."

"No, no, no. You said to ask you anything. You said you had other gifts. Like what?"

Basil shakes his head no.

"Can you spit fire? Part the ocean? Melt a nickel with nothing more than a hard stare?"

"None of that. But I can control energy. Oh, and I can reanimate the lifeless."

"You're saying you can bring the dead back to life?"

"Most times, yes. Some are beyond help."

"This is some bullshit," Herbert says. He turns to Chester, unconscious in his lounge chair. "You hear this nonsense, Professor? Go peel some flattened road kill off the asphalt for Victor Frankenstein here to resurrect."

"Like I said, I can't do it up here," Basil adds. "It's just the way things work."

"How, pray tell, do you make this happen?"

"Let's just call it magic. That seems to be the best word for it. My people have a language for it, spoken only in whispers. Each word has its own weight, its own dominion over the forces that govern Earth's core."

"Magic?"

"Magic."

"I'm afraid not, Merlin. There's no such thing."

"How do you explain me?"

Herbert pauses and then says, "I guess I can't."

"Precisely. And what is magic but something no one has quite figured out how to explain?"

Herbert has no response. He tilts back in his chair. The sky opens up—a sheet of purple and soft blue, pocked with the flickering pinpricks of far-off stars.

"You need magic in your life," Basil says. "You need mystery. Otherwise, what's the point? It's hard to stumble upon magic if you believe it doesn't exist."

"Right-o. Save that gem for your next ad campaign."

Herbert chokes on a swill of beer. As he recovers, he asks, "So you're not Satan then?"

"No."

"Does Satan exist?"

"You mean is there an all-powerful demigod responsible for all of the world's evils?"

"You said it."

"You ask good questions."

"So is there?"

"To answer that would spoil the surprise."

"You're such an asshole sometimes. Most times, in fact."

"Your turn, Herbert. From what I can figure out, you're here in Beak for the same reason I am, more or less. Bulcavage says you're trying to escape or outrun something that's eventually going to catch up with you."

Herbert's head turns sharply. His fuzzy gaze settles on Basil for a moment, and then his eyes dart elsewhere.

"There's nothing to know," he says. "I'm boring. I'm wallpaper."

"That's what you want people to think. You live alone?"

"Mostly."

"I'm not sure what that means."

Demon alcohol has worked its witchcraft, and Herbert knows it—but he doesn't care. Any internal governor that would have prevented him from sharing the most guarded details of his personal life has taken a hiatus. Now, several beers into the night, he knows he will spill every secret with only the gentlest of nudges.

"I live with my father, or what's left of him, anyway," he says. "The dementia has pretty much taken over, so he doesn't much resemble the man I used to know. Some might consider that a blessing, though."

"Why did you choose to live in Beak?"

"Why did you?"

"I didn't choose anywhere," Basil says. "Ending up here was a complete accident. Or maybe it was fate."

"I guess I could say the same thing."

"No girlfriend?"

"No time. No interest. But mostly no time."

"I know loneliness. I see it in you."

"Isn't everybody lonely?"

Basil nods in agreement.

"Believe me," Herbert says. "What we did today is probably the most excitement I've seen all year."

"How sad," Basil says, smiling.

"I'm serious," Herbert adds. "I've been dreading this afternoon since the moment I left the office on Friday. But I've enjoyed this get-together."

"I'm glad something good came of it."

"Probably not enough, though. We haven't spent more than a minute talking about Bulcavage's bullshit cooker campaign."

"We'll be fine. I have an idea."

Herbert takes another swig.

"Truth is essential," Basil says. "I might not be the best judge, but those ribs were a religious experience. Bless that cooker! We don't even have to lie about it."

"I'm sure the pig had something to do with it."

"What time is it?"

Herbert checks his wristwatch. "Eight thirty, more or less."

"Listen, we both need our beauty sleep, and you're drunk as fuck and need to sober up. Can you get to the office a little early tomorrow? Maybe an hour or so?"

"I could. What kind of scheme are you cooking up now?"

"Those ribs tasted so damned good, it felt almost wrong eating them," he says. He nabs a moist napkin from the edge of the table and scours the area until he finds a pen. He scrawls furiously. "And what's the best representation of wrongness? Of sinfulness? Of indulgence?"

Herbert shrugs his shoulders.

Basil smiles as he holds up the napkin.

Herbert eyes the crudely drawn stick figure. Despite its primitive design, the figure seems remarkably familiar.

"You're looking at him," Basil says.

# Chapter 18

# Mercy

I wake with my back to the damp stone pylon, a sharp pain in the sole of my foot. A shadow looms before me. A blackened oak truncheon sways in the mist.

"Get on then," the constable yaps.

Both my legs have fallen asleep, so I struggle to find my feet. I stumble for a few steps, ambling into the ochre murk of early morning.

"Break a neck, filthy sot," the constable says to my back.

My mouth parched, lips cracked, I wish for the luxury of drunkenness. I haven't sipped from a mug of ale in weeks. My stomach pleads for a proper meal, mostly barren for too many days on end, save the crusts of bread and the uncooked stalks of root vegetables that end up as rubbish behind the nearest public house.

What a wretch I have let myself become.

Though the contents of my troubled mind have no place in the most recent post to my dearest back home, I have cautioned her to stay put until summer. By then, I admit to her, I will have either secured my full fortune or applied my savings to the cost of hauling my arse back to Berwick.

The feeling returns to my legs by the time I reach the end of Monument Bridge, so I lean over the balustrade to eye the Thames rushing by. How I love the presence of moving water. How I grieve for the cataracts of the countryside, the waves cleaving the fossil-riddled rock of the northern coast. Thought it's not the same here, in kinder weather I imagine wandering to the water's edge to wash my face, underarms and, most urgently, the grimy cleft of my arse.

The Thames is no trickle, though, and I have yet to master

the strokes needed to swim from shore to shore. Certainly no one has offered to teach me. With my luck of late, I would lose my footing and become one with the Thames, the current grabbing me, forcing itself down my throat. I would sink like a fieldstone, my corpse reduced to grub for catfish and any other bugger craving a nibble. Some fisherman would find my bloated remains washed up on a pebbled shore somewhere across the English Channel.

At times like now, such an end seems acceptable.

I turn away from the river and find something to lean against so I can eye the handful of stragglers, like me, who wander the bridge all hours of the night. Drunkards, mostly, roused awake by the suggestion of daylight or kicked out of their stupors by passing constables, or heavy-breasted harlots retreating to their flats after a sticky night's work.

Speak of the devil, and he finds you just fine.

A tom in a bright blue dress steps toward me. Her bone-white bustier catches my eye, all scooped out to reveal a chasm of soft flesh. No more than twenty, by my guess, she gives a curt smile before returning her eyes to the stone walkway, likely to avoid the craters that might crack her ankle. I suppose any tom worth her trade could still earn her keep with a cracked ankle, as she does her best work on her back anyway.

I search for any hints of weakness I might exploit.

"Shilling to spare," I say to her behind.

She turns, eyes me from boot to cap, and pads toward me. Her heels clack against wet stone. She is beautiful—brilliant, in fact. Her eyes, despite their icy blueness, seem warm.

"And why should I?" she says.

"I'm quite hungry. Tired. I could use the help, miss."

Lies come easily to me now. I am all right with playing the role of taker.

"I'm hungry and tired too," she says. "You don't see me begging for other people's pocket coins."

*Just brain her,* the voice tells me. *Brain her and pry your mitts into whatever darkened fold she keeps her stash, remove what you find and move along like the whole business never happened.*

I would never, could never. It strikes me that such thoughts fill my brain so freely. Desperation does that to a man.

"Come with me," she tells me.

I hesitate, because I have seen little kindness in all my weeks in London.

"I ain't going to bite you," she says. "That'll cost you. You coming with me or you just going to prop up that beam until the sun pops up?"

I step toward her and thank her profusely.

"I ain't done nothing yet," she says. "I'm Alice. What do I call you?"

I stutter, as some time has passed since I have told my name to anyone. We walk silently in the mist. As dawn approaches, figures materialize out of the gloom. Men wearing well-kempt mustaches, long coats and proper hats, shoes without holes in their bottoms. Women in velvet dresses, boots laced to the knee. Newsboys staking out their corners, eager to announce the triumphs and tragedies of another spent day.

A low fog clings to the streets, keeping the stone damp. Alice leads me down a close alley, and I realize she could very well be escorting me to my doom. The streets waver. If my belly does not fill soon, I will succumb to my failures.

She does not know it yet, but her kindness is saving me.

"Come on then," Alice says.

She stops at a darkened tenement and opens the paint-peeled door. I follow her up three flights to another door, which has no lock. The wood creaks open and reveals a small, one-bedroom flat, clothes strewn everywhere. She lights a candle.

"Find a seat and rest a bit," she tells me.

I collapse onto what I presume to be a mattress, though so many dresses and nightshirts blanket the surface I cannot be sure.

She goes to the pantry and shuffles some packages. She returns with a block of pale cheese. My eyes move from the cheese to her shadowed face and back to the cheese. The kindly whore's mercy makes me want to weep.

"Go on then," she insists. "Have your fill."

I take the whole block and gnaw away as if it were a cob of Indian corn, feeling each bite in my sore gums. When I finish, she hands me a cup of lukewarm tea. She offers no lumps.

"I don't recall seeing you before," she says. "Gentle souls don't belong."

I wonder what she sees in me as I explain my predicament, how I came to London with dreams of conquest, to reap the riches of city life. Things have not gone quite as planned, I add, but I feel as though my luck is about to turn. Her generosity, I tell her, is a sure sign of the upending.

I cannot explain why, exactly, but I omit any mention of my bride.

Of course, I dare not speak of my looming hunt for Old Billy.

I sip my tea and ask her to return the favor, to share the story of how she came to London.

"I'm from Cotgrave," she says. "You know it?"

My head wags no.

"Dreadful li'l mining town. I had enough of that early on. Came here first chance I got. I ain't regretted it yet. A roof over my head. A warm bed all my own. Bread and cheese in the cupboard. The work is steady."

"You're a whore." I take another sip.

"Right good at it too. Most women of my means, they have to share a room with three, four, even five or six of their lot—that is, if they ain't dumb enough to have shacked up with a plain thief."

"You mentioned bread?"

She retrieves half a loaf and slips it into my hands. I happily tuck into the brittle crust.

"Do you like the work?" I ask. Far too many days have passed since I last traded stories with someone who cares, or pretends to care, which is just as good.

"You do what comes natural," she says. "Work is work. I've saved a bit, hoping it leads to something better. Don't ask me what something better looks like. Ain't got a clue, in fact."

The lifting light chases shadows from the room. For the first time, I see her unblemished face, free of wrinkles or any signs of wear.

"Pardon my prying, miss, but how old might you be?"

"I'll be sixteen in a just a bit," she says. Her eyes look up, and she mouths words I cannot quite make out. "Four more months. In four more months I'll be sixteen."

My heart sinks. Here I am, thirty years old and the fire in my belly reduced to embers, a wretched beggar seeking sanctuary in the flat of a fifteen-year-old tom.

Perhaps today is the day to admit defeat and return to Berwick, resume the life Father had set out for me: a fisherman who cannot fish, a waterman who fears the water. Or perhaps I can beg Alice for the money I might need to nab a place like hers: warm, dry and safe enough. For all she knows, my pockets are bare.

*Bollocks.* If she can make it on her own wiles, I can do the same. I will track down Old Billy yet, clobber him to death and make a fortune on his knotted head.

"I should be getting on," I tell her. "I won't forget your kindness."

"Don't be shy if you need to come back," she says. "I know how dreary the nights can get."

I hurry out the door, belly full for the first time in weeks. My stomach does not know quite how to handle such fortuity. An odd sensation fills me. The edges of my vision go white. I stumble down the stairs, using the walls of the second-story landing as a brace.

Minutes later my feet touch cobblestone. The sun does its best to eat away at the stubborn fog. The skeletons of London Bridge and its smaller sibling, Monument, loom in the near distance.

Soon, I tell myself. Soon I will have the life I deserve.

# Chapter 19

# Crude Self-portrait

Bulcavage pulls a ceramic mug to his lips and takes an audible gulp. He taps his foot impatiently.

"Enough with the suspense," he says. "Are you going to open your goddamned mouth and say something, or should I do a few laps around the building and then track down a fresh cup of mud?"

"He's getting to it, sir," Herbert says. He lowers his voice and turns to Basil. "Get to it, buddy."

Basil stands at the far end of the conference-room table, motionless, mountainous, beside an easel draped in a black sheet.

"Well?" Bulcavage says.

"Sin," Basil says finally.

"What about it?" Bulcavage says.

"That's the campaign."

"Just get to it," Herbert says, nervously.

"I will, but only because I know Herbert probably has to throw up again," Basil says. "I'm afraid at least one of us had a little too much fun yesterday."

Basil takes a deep breath and yanks the sheet from the easel. The sheet catches the edge of the poster board, and the whole thing topples to the ground. The wooded legs of the easel clack together, and the poster board smacks the conference-room floor, ruining the board's upper right corner. Basil fumbles to correct the easel and places the poster board back into position, using his body to shield Herbert's skilled etchings. A moment later, he steps to the side to reveal their creation.

The room is silent as all three stare at the cartoonish image: a cloven-hoofed demon, with a pitchfork and oversized horns, leaning against a barbecue grill with its lid lifted, heat lines rising from the rack of ribs smoldering on the slats. In the quiet space to the left of the grill, two words jump out in a bold script worthy of a logo for a caped superhero: *Devil Smoke*. A jagged, fiery flourish makes each word pop off the page. Beneath the logo sits a three-word phrase in an unremarkable sans serif that could use some TLC: Too Damned Good.

"Viola," Basil says.

Herbert shakes his head and mouths a correction to his copywriter.

"Voilà," Basil says.

"What's this?" Bulcavage asks.

The boss looks unimpressed. Even a little annoyed.

"A rebranding," Basil says. "What do the words 'Hooke Patio Cookers' say about anything? What does 'Model Number X-Three-Five' communicate to anyone who might consider buying it? Nothing. It says nothing. It says shit, in fact. Less than shit, really. Why would anyone remember it? Why would anyone care? Now *this*?" He points to the caricature of himself, more or less. "*This* says something."

"I told you to write up an ad, not tear everything down and start over."

"I know, sir, but this is better."

"How is defiance better than giving me what I asked for?"

"Hooke's old identify was pointless. Stale. Useless. It said nothing about what they were trying to sell—and what we, as their marketing arm, were failing to help them sell. What is delicately smoked meat, after all, but an indulgence in a conquered land where man has earned the power to say, 'I will run no more!' Man has tamed the world around him, and he should enjoy the fruits of his conquests. The war against nature has ended, and man has secured the right to call himself a god. He should enjoy the privilege of taking the time to cook a dead animal on his patio if he so chooses, because there's nothing left to come and take it from him."

"You do know Marvin Hooke is a devout Christian, right?" Bulcavage says. "His wife is a goddamned pastor, for chrissakes."

"Christians will love this more than anyone," Basil assures. "Imagine the appliances section of every department store, or wherever else people buy grills and smokers, each one with a big, red inflatable of this mischievous fella"—again, he points to the caricature—"practically daring them to buy something that looks just a little wrong but also a heck of a lot of fun."

"It's the fucking devil."

"It's not *really* the devil," Basil says. "It's a cartoonish interpretation of the devil. Now if we changed the name to ... I don't know—Satan's Meat Smokers, let's say—now *that* could pose a problem. I'll grant you that. Call this an interpretation. Call it folksy."

"It's you."

"No, sir. I am not the devil. And my skin is black, not blood red."

"It sure looks like you."

Herbert interjects.

"Sir, what I think Basil is trying to say—"

"I don't want to hear it, Herb."

Basil's shoulders drop.

"It's brilliant," Bulcavage says. "Fucking brilliant."

\* \* \*

Basil slows his heartbeat, his trembling knuckles poised inches from the inch-thick frosted glass of the door bearing Melody's name.

"Are you coming in or not?" It's Melody, from the other side of the door.

*Shit.*

He steps inside and sees Melody standing at the reception

desk, rifling through piles of loose paper.

"What do you want?" she demands.

"I was just—"

*Shit.* He should have rehearsed.

"You were just what?"

"Where's your secretary?"

"Audrey saw it in her infinite wisdom to have a migraine today—and a slight case of food poisoning. 'A slight case,' she said in her message. How can you have a slight case of food poisoning, and how the fuck do you know it's a slight case?"

"She's lying."

"Of course she's lying. Am I an idiot? Are you?"

"Sorry to hear about your troubles," he says. A brown rectangular placard on the secretary's desk reads: AUDREY PERNIE, GATEKEEPER. Two makeshift signs—sheets of bleached-white paper with printed type, bold and imperfectly centered—read: "Do I Look Impressed?" and "Go Ahead and Ask. I Dare You."

"She must be important," he says.

"Audrey? She's feckless, but she takes care of the paperwork, which I abhor. Normally I wouldn't care if she weren't here. It's just that today was a ... never mind. Are you here to pile on?"

He sighs sharply and reminds himself he has nothing to lose. Nothing, that is, but abject failure and the indignity he will never live down.

"Would you like to have dinner tonight?"

"With you?"

"Well ... yes."

She takes two deep, drawn-out breaths. Her tight smile grows wider and wider, and she laughs until she is practically in tears. He has never seen her look happier.

"Christ. Why the hell not? I can't imagine today getting much worse, so if there ever was a day to break bread with the Prince of Darkness, this would be it."

"I'm not the Prince of Dark—"

"Do you have someplace particular in mind?"

"Wherever you like. I could pick you up at sev—"

"Let's say Carlo's, right at the corner of Second and Barberry. I'll meet you there."

She turns and disappears into another room. The door eases shut.

Only then does he realize they didn't confirm a time, but he's not about to follow her around the corner and ask.

\* \* \*

Basil raps lightly on the door to Bulcavage's office.

"A minute, boss?"

Bulcavage waves Basil in and directs him to have a seat.

"Listen," Basil begins, "I've been meaning to mention it, but it hasn't really mattered until now."

"Is it Karen? Is she trying to put the screws to you again?"

"No, sir. Karen's fine, though I do wish she would stop hissing at me every time she passes my desk. Still, at least she notices. I prefer scorn to snubbing. It's just …"

"Just say it, my boy."

"I appreciate you giving me a place to live—I honestly do—but I thought you should know that I have yet to receive a dime for my work."

Bulcavage feigns surprise.

"Must be a problem with payroll," he insists. "I'll sort it out in the morning."

"Mighty kind of you to look into it, sir, but I need money tonight."

"Hot date?"

"Melody and I will be dining out."

Bulcavage leans back into the cushion of his oversized chair and clasps his hands behind his head. Darkened spots color the fabric beneath Bulcavage's armpits.

"*Mano a mano* with the Ice Queen, eh?"

"Pardon?"

"Nasty old bitch. I bet her nipples could cut glass, not that I've ever had the pleasure."

Basil has no idea what he means.

"She wasn't always such a cold fish, so maybe you can warm her up—bring her back from the tundra, as it were," Bulcavage continues. "Where are you two lovebirds going?"

"Carlo's? I think that's what she said. I don't know the place."

"Just tell those oily wops you're a friend of mine. Better yet, I'll call ahead and let them know you're coming. It'll be on the house."

"I'd rather pay with my own money, sir. Money you owe me."

"Sure, sure. I understand. I'm glad you said something."

Bulcavage bends at the waist and unlocks the bottom drawer of his desk. He retrieves a dinged metal lockbox and fishes in his front pocket for the key.

"How much you need?"

"I don't know. How much do I need?"

Bulcavage pulls a stack of bills from the belly of the lockbox and counts out five hundred dollars in twenties and fifties. He places the cash on the desk in front of Basil.

"Need anything else, Romeo?"

"Such as?"

"Party favors. Blow, pills, something to get her in the mood— even if she's not in the mood, if you catch my drift."

Bulcavage dangles a plastic bag dotted with small white pills, each one bisected by a thick slash. He opens the bag and plucks out half a dozen pills. Each shock-white orb pops against the mottled pink of his meaty palm.

"One or two of these and a glass of red, she'll be yours for the taking."

Basil dabs each pill with the talon of his index finger, counting one by one.

"The money is all I require," he says. He pushes Bulcavage's hand away, and the pills drop onto the glass-covered desk. Each pill shoots off in a different direction—one skittering onto the floor, another spinning to a stop at the base of a paperweight—as if trying to escape.

"Right," Bulcavage says. "You got it all figured out. Now what are you going to carry your cash in, numb nuts?"

## Chapter 20

# The Big Night

It's a few minutes shy of seven o'clock when Basil opens the door to Carlo's. He passes through a black wrought-iron gate and approaches the host at reception: a rail of a man with a pocket of dark, sagging skin beneath each eye.

"Table for two," Basil says. "Away from the kitchen, if you —"

"She's already seated," the host says in a crater-deep voice that belies his insignificant frame. The man's nametag reads *Paolo*. "We *do* have a dress code in the dining room, sir."

Basil looks down to consider his nakedness.

"Might you have a blazer my size?"

"Not likely, sir," Paolo says. "A moment." He turns and whispers into the ear of a dark-skinned teenager in a crisp white shirt, the makings of a mustache riding his upper lip. The teenager disappears and returns a moment later with a red-and-white checkered tablecloth, folded neatly. Paolo takes the tablecloth and unfurls it with a firm snap. He then hands it to Basil. "Don this table drape if you please, sir."

After the briefest hesitation, Basil accepts the tablecloth-cum-blazer. He holds it to his nose, smelling dust and fryer grease. He sighs and wraps the tablecloth around his back, as if it were a shawl.

"Perfect fit," Paolo says. "You can follow me."

The dining room smells fishy, as in sole or salmon. He sees Melody from across the restaurant, her head down, reading something propped on the table. The part in her dark hair shines like a beacon. His heart thumps in his chest.

"You didn't have to dress up on account of me," she says without looking up. "Nice fanny pack."

He shifts the fanny pack Bulcavage gave him as if to imply,

"This old thing?" The vinyl yellow-and-red pouch bears the garish logo of Just Dandy Corndogs, a purveyor of frozen foot-long corndogs that, according to Bulcavage, had been a Savage Communications client for a brief moment in time. Basil's muscled gut tests the limits of the buckle adjoining both ends of the adjustable waistband.

"I was starting to think you wouldn't show," she says. "Have a seat before someone finds another way to make you look silly."

He mouths a thank you to the host and turns back to her.

"I was running late, apparently," he says as he eases into the chair. "Frankly, I'm a little surprised to see *you* here."

"You don't strike me as someone who would be surprised easily," she says. "I thought you would have asked me out sooner, the way you've been sniffing after me."

"I hope I didn't frighten you."

"Not in this lifetime. So why did you?"

"Why did I what?"

"What synapse fired in that watermelon-sized noggin of yours that finally gave you the nerve to ask me out?"

"I guess today was one of those days where everything went right. I haven't enjoyed too many of those, especially up here, so the timing seemed appropriate."

A young lady in a white button-down shirt and black slacks creeps toward their table. Her trembling hand places a menu on the edge of the table in front of Basil. The menu catches on a bread plate and slides off the table, falling flatly to the crumb-specked floor.

"It's okay, honey," Melody says to her. "He won't bite. I'll make sure of it."

The waitress smiles and hurries away.

"You really should be nicer to people," Melody tells him.

"I didn't do anything. I even smiled at her, if she had bothered to look me in the eye."

"Yeah, about that. I'd refrain from showing any teeth, if you can help it. When you smile, you look like a rabid dog hungry for a bone to chew on."

"I'll keep that in mind," he says. He purses his lips in an attempt to hide his fangs.

"So. Why is it you decided to come here?"

"You picked the place."

"Not the restaurant, dumdum," she says. "I mean here in a broader sense."

"To Beak?"

"To Beak. To Nebraska. To the United States. To Earth, for that matter."

"You've got to start somewhere."

"So this is just the opening salvo?"

"Something told me this is where I needed to be. Call it instinct."

"So you just walked through the Gates of Hell and just … arrived here? There's a portal to Hell beneath our feet—that's what you're telling me?"

"We call it Our Fiery Home, and it will be beneath your feet no matter where you are in the world. There are corners of my kingdom that my hooves have never touched, and will never touch, inhabited by creatures I will never meet. I'm here because my nose led me here."

"I'm a big believer in going where you're called. Frankly, I'm confounded that I'm sitting here, sharing a meal with the devil, at a nice-enough restaurant in downtown Beak. I wonder what that says about me."

This devil business again, he thinks. He decides not to correct her.

"You seem like a nice person," he says.

"I find it hard to believe 'nice' is the quality you're looking for in a woman."

"Then why did you say yes?"

"A girl's got to eat, and I believe some opportunities you just have to explore. Besides, you don't seem like the kind of person who takes no for an answer. Wait—is *person* even the right word? Clarification: You don't seem like the kind of *being* who takes no for an answer."

"I'm getting a little tired of those kinds of remarks. You know nothing about me."

"You're the freaking devil."

"Sticks and stones. I prefer Basil."

He will no longer deny the implication, guessing her opinion of him as some sort of ancient, all-powerful demigod might somehow work in his favor.

"So why don't I just possess your body and do whatever sadistic things you imagine I might do to a female under my control?" he asks. "Why should I even bother going through the trouble of manufacturing all this pretense if I could just swoop in and take what I want, whenever I please?"

"I don't know. Sport?"

"I suppose that would be crueler."

"You don't know a thing about women at all. You ever hear the phrase 'Keep your friends close and your enemies closer'? That's why I'm here."

He raises his water glass and toasts, "To enemies."

Their glasses clink.

"Is this really what you want to talk about?" he asks.

His frankness seems to disarm her. He watches the tension leave her body.

"I suppose not. But first I want to know who I'm dealing with."

"If something horrible were going to happen, it would have happened by now."

He is tired of having to prove himself. At least in Our Fiery Home his word meant something.

The tall, gaunt host appears tableside and explains in his rich baritone that their waitress seems to have taken ill. He asks for their orders. Melody opts for the crab cake. Basil, who hasn't consulted the menu, says, simply, "Something rare, please. And a glass of something red."

"So," Melody says as the host departs for the kitchen. "Tell me about Hell."

"Please. We don't call it that. It's just home to me."

"Right. Sorry. Tell me about home."

"There's not much to tell. It's always dark, save the glow of the firelight. Lots of shadowy nooks, lots of places for killers to lurk and their victims to hide—*try* to hide, anyway. If you were to pay a visit, you would see sights your eyes would not believe—nightmarish beasts that astonish even me from time to time. So many hunters of every size and shape, with plenty of doomed prey from which to choose."

"Sounds familiar. Give me an example."

"Troglodytes. Pterodactyl-like vampire bats. Venomous centipedes, each one's armored trunk longer than a school bus. Dragon-like salamanders that belch acid."

"Interesting pets," she says. She tears a piece of bread into small pieces and pops a sliver of crust into her mouth. She nods as her jaw does its work, one eyebrow raised, lips firmly together. He struggles to translate her expression. She's unimpressed, perhaps. Or maybe she thinks he's lying.

"We have a kraken," he says, sounding almost boastful. "Cthaal, we call it. The creature lurks at the bottom of a blood-filled lake, the Pool of Infinite Perdition. No one really knows how big the beast is, or how many tentacles it uses to rove the depths, but it's monstrous. Mean son of a bitch too."

"A kraken, you say," she says flatly. "Now *that's* something."

His shoulders droop, dejected. What does he have to do or say to impress this woman? He wags his head, thinking he should just call this date a bust, head somewhere else and find someone who appreciates his company. She seems to notice the darkening of his demeanor.

"What?" she asks. "Did someone get his fragile little ego bruised? The poor little Prince of Darkness gets his feelings hurt because the big, mean girl isn't paying him enough attention? I mean ... come on, man."

Basil sighs heavily.

"Seriously?" she says. "I mean, seriously? Did I actually *injure* you?"

"It would be nice if you were at least civil."

Her arms fall to her sides. She looks to the ceiling so Basil sees only the whites of her eyes.

"Now you're making me feel bad," she says. She plants her elbows on the table, and her palms prop up her chin in mock enthusiasm. "Okay, tell me about your kraken."

"It's quite remarkable that the beast even exists," he says, newly buoyant. "This thing must have twenty, maybe twenty-five tentacled arms, each one as hard as iron and lined with rows of suckers, and in the center of each sucker is a venomous spine. It's the perfect killer. Let's say some fool splashed down into the Pool of Infinite Perdition and ended up in Cthaal's tentacles. Even if he somehow managed to escape Cthaal's crushing grip, the venom does its work all too well. The doomed fool's heart would likely stop before he reached shore. How such a thing comes to be, I simply cannot fathom. Lucky for me, Cthaal is about as brainless as a paperweight—clever but brainless. If it had the slightest thirst for power or aspirations of any kind, it would dominate every one of us, with no one to oppose its rule. Even I don't mess with it."

"Brainless kraken aside, your home must have *some* positives going for it."

"Imagine the worst place in your country, and then subtract the guns and the consumerism and the culture and the thin veil of civility that seems to keep everything from falling to pieces," he says. "Then add all these fantastic beasts looking to fill their gullets and claw their species one ladder rung closer to the pinnacle of the food chain. On top of those, add the humanoid creatures like me, most of them intent on killing each other for reasons other than sustenance—power, mostly, though some kill simply to pass the time. Death pervades, much like your warzones here, but our sins are committed face to face, never from a distance. It's much more personal that way. It's more honest, I think. So that's something."

"If you're going to kill someone, at least have the decency to do it to his face."

"Precisely."

"I was being sarcastic," she says. "Why would anyone choose to live in such a horrid place?"

"For most, it's not a choice. But my home does have its charms."

"Charming, indeed. You must be happy as a crab in a sandbox."

"It's a love-hate scenario. I carry Our Fiery Home with me wherever I go."

As he talks, his mind feeds him images of the over-warm, over-dark place he once ruled—or *still* rules, technically. He misses home, or at least parts of it, to be precise. The world made sense down there: simple, straightforward and all too comfortable in its many shortcomings. Despite the beautiful things he has seen above ground—the gorgeous human female sitting across from him, as one example—he has felt a profound sense of unease each day among the humans. But he reminds himself he's not supposed to fit in here. It's a vacation, a respite, and nothing more. This whole experience, at its heart, can be only one thing: a temporary escape.

Melody works her jaw on another piece of bread, and Basil follows suit. He butters a roll, tears it in two, and pops both halves into his mouth.

"You have fine table manners," she says.

"Why shouldn't I?"

"Because you come from a land of savages. You said so yourself."

"That's no excuse for acting like a savage. Everyone should have the brains to know what a salad fork is for."

"I suppose."

Basil's glass of wine arrives. Ever so gently, he brings the stemmed glass to his lips and draws a long, quiet sip. Melody does the same, and for the first time all evening they share a meaningful silence. They lock eyes every few seconds before one or the other turns away, before the stare becomes awkward—before it means something.

"You mentioned the whole hunter-and-prey situation," she says, killing the quiet. "I can't imagine you ever having to worry about death, about dying."

"On the contrary. Thoughts of my demise consume me. Every day in Our Fiery Home I wear a target, so it's only a matter of time before my life reaches its end. I would live on only in memory, but even memories have a shelf life."

"How do you know the end is truly the end?"

"I know some humans believe in some sort of afterlife—a Heaven, a Hell, maybe something in between—but my people never learned such things. To us, the end is the end. Stay in power to stay alive, the teachings say. One day my brain will deteriorate and my limbs will fail, but the end comes only when the heart says it's time."

"So you're *not* immortal."

"Far from it," he says. "You could slit my throat with those candy-apple claws of yours right now, and I would meet my end by the time the dessert menu makes its way to the table."

Of course, doing him in would never be so effortless, not that he would tell her such a thing. He doesn't need to brag, at least not yet.

\* \* \*

Two oafish demons drag Kamala into the Room of Contrition. They move to the center of the room and await instruction from Lubos, who lingers at the entrance.

"Lash her to the slab," he tells them. "Face down."

The demons know the routine all too well: bind the left wrist first; force the offender onto the slab, a heavy palm on the skull and an elbow in the center of the back to hold the offender firmly in place; snake the leather through the cylindrical channel bored through the slab's base; bind the other wrist; bind each pastern to its respective hook, anchored deep into the floor, one on either side of the slab.

"It's a shame you won't have a hand in our victory," Lubos tells her. "You're going to miss out on so much of what's to come."

Her chin burs into the rock, so she can only grunt.

"We're a lot alike, you and me," he says. "We want the same things: liberty, prosperity, the freedom to roam. And we shall have them. The human world is ours to take, and take it we shall. We've been quietly infiltrating their world for ages, and what good has it done us? We're still down here, breathing this poisoned air, begging for scraps. No longer. Now is the time to make some noise. Now is the time to take what belongs."

Kamala arcs her neck. She can feel the vertebrae straining until she's able to tilt her head to one side.

"What will you do?" she asks.

"Simple. We invade."

"There are far too few of us to become conquerors of anything. Basil estimated fifty thousand demons in Our Fiery Home, no more. The humans must have millions."

"Precisely. Hand-to-hand combat is the second wave. A band of demons—a few hundred—has already ascended. They aim to bend the will of those who control the levers of power, to weaken the humans' resistance. Then we attack, and the battle will not be fought by demons alone. Every imp will brandish a blade, and every creature that shares our home will be enlisted with a singular purpose: the spilling of human blood."

"Enlisted? More like enslaved."

"The ends justify the means, my dear. Fear not: We will have our peace. First, we must destroy those who wish to keep it from us."

"This is our home. Why do you wish to abandon it?"

"You've never been to the surface," he tells her. "You can't imagine the promise it holds. Here, the walls constrain us. Up there, you see only horizon. When Basil chose me to lead his hunting sorties to the human world, his motives were clear as glass. It had little to do with merit or praise. Rather, he wanted me gone from here, to have me out of the way, because he saw me as a threat. But I'm so glad he did, because it opened my eyes to the possibility. Basil felt the pull. You must feel it, too, as we all do. We were meant to ascend."

"We have endless room to expand here, below."

"Not expansion. Destruction."

"Mass suicide—that's what you're talking about. Any demon who follows you deserves the fate that will greet him. If you wish to leave, no one or nothing will stop you, but leave this place intact. Leave the world to do its own work."

"You must know the legends as well as I do—of how Our Fiery Home came to be. The Eternal One cast out of paradise, only to make his home beneath the surface in the warmth of the firelight. He was meant to return, to feel the sun on his face. As are we. Call Our Fiery Home what it is: a broken society on the verge of death. I will bring about its demise. The fires will go out, and every creature that shares our home will ascend or forfeit its life. And one will lead the way."

Lubos unfurls a three-fingered hand, gesturing beyond the walls.

"Look to the Pool of Infinite Perdition," he says. "An army with Cthaal before it cannot fail."

"Failure is inevitable."

"All, including our tentacled friend, must follow me. My reign has come."

"Basil remains king, and I his alternate. You know this."

"Basil rots in a ditch."

"Even if you had earned the throne rightfully, Cthaal obeys no one. A rancorous beast like that won't abide your attempts to tame it."

"Dearest Kamala, don't heavy your head with such worries. I have arranged other busywork to engage your mind and body."

As Lubos steps to the side, more than a dozen demons spill through the ragged entrance to the Room of Contrition. Lubos extends an open palm, as if offering Kamala as an unopened gift. The demons descend on her, jostling for position. Pushing and shoving turns to the clawing of eyes and throats, the demons brawling over which of them will have her first.

\* \* \*

The gaunt host returns to Basil and Melody's table, this time bearing their entrées. The aroma of freshly cooked meat makes Basil drool in his lap. Melody pretends not to notice.

"Compliments of the house," the host says as he sets a beautifully garnished crab cake before Melody. The puck-shaped patty has an artful drizzle of a beige-colored sauce and a pink-and-white radish carved to look like the bloom of a flower. For contrast, Basil's scratched-metal plate has no accompaniment, no gilding of the lily. It's nothing more than a cut of brown meat with blackened edges, sizzling in a broth of reddish juice. A dollop of Béarnaise butter melts into every meaty crevice. An oversized steak knife juts from the filet's center.

As Melody readies to fork a piece of crab cake into her mouth, she says, "So tell me more about where you live."

"My boss, Mister Bulcavage, he put me up in a nice place. I

have my own patio, my own TV, my own bed, which I almost never use."

"Not up here, dummy. I mean down below."

"Oh, the underworld? I tend to roam, but I do have a chamber—a nice chamber, by most demons' standards. It's got a throne, made from the bones of those who have fallen before me. My poems line the walls. I have a reasonably soft spot to lie down, when it's needed."

"And what happens there?"

"I sleep, fitfully."

"Is that all? It must get lonely down there."

He thinks of the company he keeps in Our Fiery Home: Kamala, a few tolerant imps, the cast of characters in his dreams, the voices in his head he now knows by the names Conscience and Ego. He guesses she's referring to something else.

"Oh, copulation?" he asks. "If you want, you take."

"Pardon me?"

"You want sex, you take it from the nearest she-demon. You crave fellatio, you command her to please you: 'Use your mouth until your tongue tastes my seed.'"

"That's abhorrent."

"I can assure you, it's all rooted in fairness. Whether it's sex or territory or food, the strong prevail—like your consumerism and capitalism. If you have the means to acquire something, you do so. If whomever you're trying to take it from cannot stop you, then the spoils are yours to keep."

"That's not capitalism. That's rape."

"It's not rape. It's just the way things are."

"Do you ask their permission before you stick your monstrous penis inside them?"

"Well ... no."

"So, rape."

"No. I—"

"Rape while the raping's good, is that it? 'What do you want to do tonight, Basil?' 'I don't know, Beelzebub. Let's go rape that hot bitch over there.' Rape, rape, rape—raping all the time."

*"Please!"* He slaps the table with his heavy palm. Silverware clatters against the wood. A water glass tips over. He changes his tone and whispers, "Please stop saying rape."

Melody's eyes scan the restaurant, and he wonders if she's looking for the exit.

"Let me back up," he insists. "If I see a she-demon, I simply take her by the back of her neck, bend her over the nearest rock. There isn't any force involved, no violence. Usually."

She dabs the corners of her mouth with a napkin.

"How's the crab cake?" he asks.

"Disgusting."

"Send it back."

"I'm not talking about the crab cake."

She looks anywhere but directly at him. Her tongue glides across the edges of her eggshell-colored teeth.

"Look," he pleads, "it's just the way it is down there."

"Aren't you in charge? Aren't you the one who makes the rules?"

He does not answer. Of course he is in charge, but he cannot turn the world upside down, cannot upset the natural order. Other demons—most of them, anyway—have no humanity in them. They respect only one thing: power. Yes, he has committed horrible crimes, but only because he had to, because not committing them would have invited more death, more pain, more chaos. Yes, he would rather live peacefully, quietly, but so few others of his kind share his desire. He would rather wander, free from the fear of taking a blade to the throat, decapitated and dismembered, his limbs hung at every outpost as proof of the king's demise. But how can he lead a life of peace in such a rotten place? How can he possibly undo a system that has thrived for as long as it has solely because of its abject brutality?

"You're the chairman and CEO of Sex Assault Central," she

adds. "You should have that printed on your business cards, you're so damned proud of the fact."

"Catchy," he says.

"Consider it my gift to you."

Based on the hardness of her stare, she wants nothing more than to gouge out his eyes, maybe castrate him for good measure.

"I've been doing all the talking—to my peril, apparently," he says. "Tell me about you."

She sighs and says, "I'm an open book."

"Hardly."

"Herbert must have told you everything you need to know."

"Herbert's locked up even tighter than you are."

"Aw, poor Herbert. I feel bad for him."

"He'll find his way." Basil pauses before blurting, "He's different, you know."

"Of course I know," she whispers. "I'm surprised he told you."

"He didn't tell me anything. I just know he's not like me. Gay, possibly, or maybe asexual."

"Does it matter?"

"Not to me, but it sure does to him. I don't think he wants to admit whatever he is. He should. He would live more happily."

"I think he's waiting for his father to die."

"Do you two know each other just from workplace proximity?"

"If you want to get technical, I guess he's a client."

"Good thing for client-attorney privilege."

"Maybe we should talk about something else." She waits a beat. "So you're a copywriter?"

"I prefer to think of myself as a poet who has been relegated to writing ad copy."

"We're all relegated to doing something we don't love. Otherwise we'd all be artists or entertainers or animal cuddlers of some sort."

"Yes! And the world would be better because of it. Let's say you're an artist. What is your medium of choice?"

"Me? I don't have an artistic bone in my body. My *art*, if you want to call it that, is my business. In my little world of helping corporate douchebags negotiate salaries and retirement benefits, I'm Monet, Hopper and Botticelli all wrapped into one."

"Bah. You just haven't found your calling yet."

He slathers his filet with Béarnaise butter and consumes the steak in three swift bites.

"Honestly, I don't have much of an interest in that kind of stuff, other than the most basic sense," she says. "Music, I like a good beat. Art, I can appreciate a Cezanne or a Renoir. Sculpture, I'm a sucker for Rodin. But I would rather work than put pen to paper or try to paint another pointless still life, and I'm fine with that."

Basil's lower jaw hangs, his mouth agape. He hears her words, but he can't fathom a life without the joys she so callously disregards as ephemera, as throwaways.

"Even in Our Fiery Home we have music, in a sense," he says. "It's mostly guttural sounds and bone-on-rock percussion, but art flourishes even in the shadows of the underworld. We sing. We tattoo our flesh. We write, or I do, at least. My words line the walls of my chamber. Without them I wouldn't have lasted as long as I have."

"So let's hear it, Yeats. Blow me away with one of your heart-rending poems."

"I couldn't. I shouldn't."

"You're not leaving this table without sharing."

He wants to, and he knows he will, but he must show modesty, however false. He contorts his face, pretending to struggle with the idea of sharing his precious words. In truth, he already knows exactly which poem he will have her hear — one of his most recent. He stands and, shielding his crotch with a napkin, breathes deeply.

"What are you doing?" she asks.

"Reciting a poem, like you asked."
"Well, *sit down* and do it, numbskull," she says, laughing.
He complies and clears his throat.

*I will go*
*As the daylight goes*
*The stars at dawn, the receding tide*
*I will go*
*As the soft breeze blows*
*Impermanent, impertinent, irrelevant*
*I will go as Earth's moon goes*
*A chalk-white marble in a puddle of tar*
*Sinking, stinking, suffocating*
*A speck of dust*
*A grain of sand*
*A mote of a mite on the corpse of Colossus*
*We will go*
*As the seasons go*
*One by one till only one remains*
*Till all things go gray and still*
*Till only the architecture of time remembers*
*Till that too comes crashing down*

She brings her hands together and mock claps, adding, "I liked it."

Her reaction leaves Basil feeling as though his precious words have made no impression. So he retreats somewhere safer.

"How well do you know Bulcavage?"

"Well enough to know he's a prick," she says. "Honestly, I've had only a handful of interactions with him—maybe a dozen in the three years I've had an office in that building—but not one of those interactions has been pleasant. My office is right beneath his, so usually it's me banging on my ceiling—his floor—begging him to stop stamping around up there. It seems like every week he's having another one of his hissy fits. Such a prick."

"He insinuated you two used to be close, so to speak."

"He wishes. Isn't he married to some breed of Siberian beauty queen?"

"Allegedly."

"He doesn't like me because I'm the enemy. Herbert came to me the day he got the job offer, asking me if it was a good deal. It wasn't. So I drew up a contract, filled it with all kinds of perks, bonuses, term clauses, and basically forced Bulcavage to sign it. Now Herbert's practically bulletproof. If he were a spiteful person, Herbert could walk out the door with every client in the Savage bullpen and there's nothing Bulcavage could do about it."

"How'd you manage that?"

"Willpower. I've never trusted Bulcavage, like I don't trust most men, so when Herbert came to me, I was thrilled to make sure Bulcavage knew exactly what I was doing and why. I wanted him to see me fuck him in the ass right to his face. Let's just say it's my little way of giving back. I imagine you negotiated a nice package for yourself."

"I just got my first paycheck today, actually."

She cringes.

"Well, then," she says. "We'll just have to see Mister Bulcavage around campus and let him know that's not acceptable."

Basil waves a clawed hand, dismissing the idea. He turns toward the window and notices the setting sun, about halfway through its nightly chore of sinking into the western horizon. The colors still amaze him—reds, purples and blues, giving life to the clouds.

"As a woman, as a human being, I would never waste my time with an asshole like Bulcavage," she continues. "Like I said, I don't have time for anything but my business, so I can't afford to get emotional. I like it that way."

"Tell me about it." He leans forward, his chin cupped in one of his palms.

"I always wanted to be a lawyer, even when I was young. All through high school and college, and then law school, my plans didn't change. Of course things never turn out exactly as you expect. Once I passed the bar, I started with a firm in Lincoln that practiced almost exclusively in family law—divorce after divorce after divorce—so every day I counseled hurt and miserable people fighting over dollars and cents and real estate and custody of the family dog."

"How bloody."

"Right. It was nothing but bloodlust and pettiness all the time, all to prove a goddamned point, all to punish someone your client used to care about. And nobody was whole afterward, so nobody got whatever it was they thought they wanted at the outset. It was pointless. And *I* was pointless. I stopped practicing family law a few years ago—five, maybe six at this point. Now I mostly help business owners and executives stay out of trouble and plan for the future. Succession planning, some business transactions—that kind of stuff."

"Making the rich richer?"

"How else can you make an honest buck these days? I used to have an office in Lincoln, but after I got out of the divorce racket, I guess you could say I retreated here, back to where my parents raised me. I retained a fair number of clients from my time in Lincoln, and it's all either phone work or filling in the blanks on contracts, so I rarely have to see people face to face. I can't remember the last time I stepped foot in a courtroom."

"I think that's the first thing of substance I've learned about you," he tells her. "It's nice to see you're flesh and blood after all. If you don't mind me saying so."

He half-expects her to douse him with her drink and stab him in the forehead with the business end of a shrimp-laden cocktail fork. Instead, she laughs.

"Fair enough." She smiles, letting him in a little. "What else do you want to know?"

"Anything about you—not your business, not your clients, not how much of a prick you think I am or my boss is. Tell me something about you."

"I have two cats, Jackson and Jefferson—Jack and Jeff, when they're not in trouble for something. I have a sister who lives in Rhode Island with her husband and their twenty-seven kids. I like loud, fast cars—red, preferably—expensive shoes—again, red—and polar bears. And I'm a sucker for black-and-white horror films from the Fifties."

"Your sister has twenty-seven kids?"

"Hyperbole. I think she has three now. Maybe four, actually."

"You two must be close."

She cocks her head and smiles.

"That wasn't so hard," he says.

"I sort of want to crawl under the table right now."

"I'm not going to hurt you, you know."

"No kidding."

He tamps down the beast within, the one that wants to utter the warning: *You have no say in the matter.*

"Tell me something about you I don't know," she says.

"I've already told you so much."

"Actually, you've told me almost nothing. I know you have a pet kraken. I know you'd make a shitty Boy Scout."

"I don't like the dark," he says.

"What?"

He dips his head and smiles in return.

"It's true. Until I came here, darkness was foreign to me. I can't stand it, the way it feels on my skin."

"But you live underground. As far as I know, the sun doesn't shine there."

"Yes, but the fires always burn. Dark places, dark corners—I veer from them both, because of what lurks there, waiting. Tongues of fire follow me at my command. If the flames were to burn out, my end would soon follow."

She says nothing, offering a break in the conversation. He quickly steps in to fill the silence with a thought he had misplaced.

"It hurts to get hurt, I know," he says. "I haven't forgotten the feeling. Down there, in Our Fiery Home, I'm constantly wandering, mumbling to myself, having conversations in my head that I know I will never have. Trust me, I'm a train wreck too."

"Not me," she says. "I'm always in control. I'm not giving anyone any ammunition—no information that someone else can use against me."

"Where's the fun in that? No one likes a robot."

"No one fucks with a robot either."

"What's life without the pleasures of another's company?"

"You would know. All that rape."

As quickly as she let him enter the garden, she expels him.

"I didn't mean anything by it," he says.

"Look, Basil. I've had a nice time tonight. Honestly, I have. But you've got to know that this—whatever *this* is here, between us—this is going absolutely nowhere. I can promise you that much. You want someone to talk to? Maybe I can be a friend. Maybe. But other than a cup of coffee, there's nothing here for you. Nothing."

"You have more to offer me than you can imagine. You remind me of someone."

He envisions the faceless woman from his dream. A dull pain flowers in his chest.

"This world is a better place because of you," he tells her.

"I've been hearing hollow gestures like that all my life. Maybe not *exactly* like that, but close enough. You hear them from just about every guy who wants something from you and then disappears once he's gotten it."

"I do wish humans were more honest. Their behavior confuses me."

"Hunters and prey," she says. "That's the difference between your world and mine. Where you come from, you know the hunters. Up here, they're all chameleons. I wish I'd learned that lesson sooner. I'd be a different person today."

Basil nods.

"Can we get out of here?" she says.

His eyes turn away from hers—suddenly watery, hinting at some hidden-away grief the conversation has unwrapped—and scour the restaurant for someone who can fetch the check.

# Chapter 21

# The Reptile's Quest for Love and Meaning

Melody's curious perfume lingers. Basil remembers their awkward goodbye in the restaurant parking lot, the electricity of their bodies pressing gently together. He replays her parting words to him—"You're a sweetheart"—before she stood on her tiptoes, him bending to meet her, her moist lips leaving their cherry-hued imprint on his left cheek.

He straddles his noisemaker, the Harley, taking the ghost of Melody's perfume with him. He considers his options for how to spend the rest of his night. It's barely nine thirty. Chester will likely be expecting him, as they have spent just about every evening together since Basil moved in, discussing the ways of the world and knocking back obscene amounts of alcohol.

Not tonight, Basil decides. He craves a companion of a different sort.

He fires up the motorcycle and departs into the night. The bike's sole headlight illuminates the barren strip of asphalt, his mind consumed with the sights, smells and essence of Melody K. Mulroney, Esquire. Pinpricks of light twinkle on the horizon— hints of civilization amid the nothingness—matched by pinpricks of light twinkling overhead. He briefly considers the possibility of other civilizations out there, above, light-years away.

He pores over every aspect of their dinner, the way she challenged him, and, more than anything, the way she looked at him, like she hated him but couldn't help but like him just a little. Maybe more than a little. She shared so much with just the briefest glimpse of those icy blue eyes.

"There's something between us," he hollers over the rumble of the engine, just to hear the words aloud, "no matter what you say."

On the horizon, a blare of neon eats away at the black night. A long, squat building appears out of the darkness. The sign out front—Cheeky's Midnight Roadhouse—suggests this is the sort of destination his body craves. A shabby road sign advertises "$2 Buds, $1 Hotdogs, free T&A" in black lettering, though a blood-red S stands in for the second dollar sign.

*This particular den of iniquity will have to do.*

As he guides the Harley into the lot, tire treads bite into the wet gravel. He makes a wide berth around a phalanx of pickup trucks, tractors and at least one mud-spattered ATV. Instinct leads him toward the building's rear, away from the melee. The noisemaker comes to a dead stop at the edge of the lot, where the gravel meets an unkempt patch of grass and, beyond that, a modest stand of woods. The swollen gland between his legs leads him across the parking lot, a hound sniffing out a dying rabbit. He opens the building's fiberboard door and, with a deep sigh, steps inside. A haze of cigarette smoke greets him, followed by a curtain of acid-strong perfume that instantly spikes his libido.

The animal within him takes over. His lower lip trembles with unease.

The low lights reveal silhouettes of men in ball caps, maybe a woman or two, seated around a two-foot-tall stage with five fire poles that stretch from floor to ceiling and a raised, rounded platform at its center. A thick redhead dances atop the platform, her hands cupping her heavy breasts—shiny, cherry-red fingernails against alabaster flesh—as her hips sway to Foreigner's "Urgent."

Skirting a row of chairs beyond the blare of the spotlights, Basil studies the dancer—the slow rotation of her ample hips, the roundness of her over-full breasts, the rubberlike muscle of her thighs—as she leaves the platform and steps onto the greenback-littered stage. He settles into an undisturbed corner where he can let his imagination do its job. His hand grips the pulsing thing between his legs. The dancer drops to her knees and leans forward. Her pendulous breasts sweep the dollar bills into a loose pile.

He's too busy dreaming of the acts he would command her to do to certain parts of him to notice them approach. A cloud of perfume fogs his mind.

"Hey there, tall, dark and satanic," says a thin brunette with a raspy voice. She weaves her hand into the slot between his arm and his side, and palms the indent at the small of his back where scales and fur comingle.

A second dancer—a blonde, also thin, with smallish breasts obscured by the netting of a white brassiere—takes the other side, trapping him. The blonde smiles, showing crooked teeth and well-pocked cheeks marred by too much or too little of some essential thing, or perhaps just the horrors of age. She says in more than a whisper, "Want to get off? Fifty for both of us. Whatever you want, wherever you want it. Ten minutes or until you blow your top, whichever comes first."

A female hand fondles his fanny pack and creeps south. Panic overtakes him. He recoils, sloppily trying to undo himself from the pair. He stumbles backward and feels the ridges of his spine against the wall. They take a step closer.

Television has taught him all about these kinds of places. Even so, the women's aggression unsettles him.

"I have no money," he tells them and squeezes past.

His hooves clamor against the sticky floor, and he nearly trips over an untended barstool. He plants himself in a leather chair away from the strobes' glare and immediately has to reposition himself because of his tail. He pushes the fanny pack to the side and sinks into the cushion. "Assimilate," the voice tells him, but he knows even his best efforts to blend in will bear no fruit. Still, he hopes for a moment to still his raging mind so he can figure out how to achieve his goal.

"Hey, stranger."

The soft, confident voice both soothes and arouses. He looks to his left and sees her, the redhead from the stage, standing before him. Her breasts are conveniently at eye level, nipples poking through the diamond-shaped holes of a mesh tank top.

"Saw you come in," she says. "Want some company?"

"You're very talented," he tells her. He nods toward the stage. "You have no idea. Mind if I sit?"

He motions to the empty chair next to him, but she parts his legs with hers and drops her weight onto his left leg.

"I've heard about you," she says. "I mean, who hasn't heard of you? But I mean I heard you were over in Beak. I didn't believe it. Lucky me."

She reaches up and uses two fingers to trace the arc of his injured horn.

"Are you here for anyone particular?" she asks. "Any*thing* particular?"

"Just visiting."

"Will you remember me?"

"I don't see how I won't," he says.

The erection in his lap pokes through the tuft of black fur. Her eyes widen.

"We'll just have to make sure you don't forget anytime soon." She circles her index finger over his cock. "Let's say we go do something about *that*."

"I don't have much money."

"Sure, honey. I'll take what you can give me. I scratch your back and you scratch mine. Deal? Like I said, remember me when you see me next."

He wrinkles his forehead.

"I've done things," she says. "But I'm guessing you already knew that, sugar. I hope you'll be kind when the time comes."

She slides off his leg and takes his hand, leading him by the talons.

His eyes home in on the thong cleaving her dimpled ass cheeks, the flesh glowing red, blue and yellow beneath the strobes. She turns and beckons him toward her. As he bends down, she yells above the din, "My name's Divinity."

They arrive at a red door guarded by a bald man with no waist, no neck—his body shaped more like a refrigerator than a man. Divinity leans into the bouncer, and the two have a conversation that goes on for longer than it seems it should. The bouncer raises his arms at one point, yelling, but Basil can't decipher the words over the chorus of Poison's "Nothin' but a Good Time." Finally, the bouncer steps aside, and he gives Basil a dirty look as he passes.

The Kiss-N-Tell Room has eight cubicles, each one fronted by an opaque lace curtain. The curtain is pulled across in only three of the cubicles, but Basil can see into each of the occupied areas—a faceless woman either on top of or kneeling in front of a faceless man. Divinity leads him into the unused cubicle at the end of the row on the right and tells him to have a seat as she pulls the curtain across.

"What was that all about?" Basil asks. "With the bald guy."

"Oh, that's just Steve being Steve," she says, prying off her mesh top. "He thinks he's doing us a favor by being such a hardass all the time."

She wastes no time. She straddles him and places both palms on his naked pectorals, inhaling sharply through pursed lips to suggest she's impressed. She then kneels in front of him and caresses his thighs, combing the fur with her fingernails, inches shy of where he wants her hands to be. She then turns her back to him and sits in his lap. She moves her hips in a clockwise motion, her ass cheeks massaging the head of his cock, now fully exposed.

"Yeah, baby. Yeah, baby. Yeah, baby."

She reaches down and takes hold of his wrists, and slaps his claws onto her breasts, which he deftly cups. They're softer than he would have imagined, softer than other breasts he has felt. Softer than Kamala's.

She continues to grind away, sliding side to side, up and down.

Basil detects a change in her scent.

She turns around to face him. One of her hands snakes down the curve of her belly and finds the top of her thong. She pulls it back to reveal the dark patch of fur lurking beneath, and then bunches this slimmest of garments to one side so flesh can meet flesh—hers against his.

"See that?" she asks. "My pussy will make you do somersaults."

He merely grunts, the animal inside him finding its way out. His gaze moves to her breasts, targeting two precise spots—one on each breast—the slightly darker flesh of the areolae. His claws slide down to her hips and draw her closer. The moistening patch beneath her legs glides along the underside of his exposed prick.

She throws her head back and gasps.

"Enough," the voice tells him. "Get inside of her."

His eyes zero in on the flesh of her exposed neck—a bone-white column begging to be choked or slit. Her outrageous smell, all her undulating parts and the smooth-as-wet-glass tactility of her pubis all work together to undo something within him. Sense abandons his better self, and the reptile within takes control.

"Do it," the voice growls. "Fuck this creature until it no longer moves."

He stands up, and she falls backward into the curtain. As she grabs hold of the fabric, the curtain tears away from the ceiling—rod and all. Her screams do not deter him. He grabs her and tosses her onto the loveseat. Despite her flailing and kicking, he turns her onto her stomach and tears off her thong. As he prepares to enter her, a thick wand of spittle drips from the space between his exposed fangs.

Then comes the blow to his broad back. He turns to see Steve, the bald bouncer, holding the leg of a wooden chair. The rest of the chair lies scattered across the floor, demolished. Steve's face beams with amazement. He seems stunned that the blow had no effect. After a second's hesitation, he whacks Basil across the neck with the chair leg.

The reptile turns back to Divinity.

Steve drops the chair leg and swings wildly, fists pounding. One blow connects with Basil's ear, stunning him. Basil grabs the man by the throat and tosses him into the wall — in fact, through the wall. He can smell blood.

Twice he crouches: once toward Steve, intent on stopping the man's heart; and once toward Divinity, eager to bend her over a chair and tar her insides with his seed. But he halts. Each time a quiet but convincing voice, unlike the one that encouraged him to fuck Destiny into oblivion, tells him to stop.

"Retreat," it says.

His arms tremble, his conflicted mind being pulled in opposite directions by two distinct governors. He clenches his fists and looks to the ceiling. His roar shakes the walls.

He departs swiftly, hoof steps drowned out by the thump of the bass drum droning through the overhead speakers.

* * *

The music jags to an abrupt stop inside Cheeky's Midnight Roadhouse, as bouncers, bartenders and a few topless dancers realize what has happened. Several rush to the dancer, Divinity, and the bouncer, Steve. None of their injuries seems to be emergent. Blood dribbles from Steve's busted nose, oozes from the pin-sized holes in his neck. Divinity tests the rotation of her wrist, swears it's not broken.

A moment later, the music starts back up. "Here I Go Again" by Whitesnake. A curvy silhouette slinks beneath the strobes. Dollar bills float to the stage like thrown paper airplanes.

One figure stands as still as a statue.

The ponytailed bartender with a handlebar mustache and a protuberant mole on his left cheek drops his jaw in disbelief.

He utters the words *Holy shit,* and the act of moving his lips rouses the rest of him. The world looks different than it did five minutes earlier, when he walked into Cheeky's nearly an hour late for the start of his shift, dreading another night of slinging beers to know-nothing rednecks.

He forgets any worries over the pocket change he may have forfeited as a result of his lateness. He now knows he'll have no trouble making up the difference—and right quick. He hurries to a small chalkboard behind the bar and drags his index finger north to south and north again until he IDs the correct number, conveniently listed beneath the word *Bounty.*

His heart pumping wildly, the bartender fumbles for the receiver of a liquor-glazed phone in perilous proximity to the speed rack. He dials the ten digits and gulps as he listens to the rings tick off. When someone picks up the other end of the line, the bartender gives his name and location, followed by two more words.

"Found him."

# Chapter 22

# An Unfamiliar Hand

Only a fool would abandon paradise for a pit. But this is exactly what I have done. Sometimes a man does not realize his folly until his mistakes have had their way with him. Now I know, for I have unwrapped the gift of regret.

I want to scale the balustrade of Monument Bridge and step into the air, fall like a brick and shatter against the Thames. But what I want most of all, what I crave, is to hitch a ride on a wagon and roll back to Berwick. Upon my arrival, I would indulge in everything I quit: a warm bed of my own; the cool salt air blowing in from the sea and, when the winds go still, the stink of manure wafting in from the tilled fields; and, most of all, my bride's warm body against mine as the first hint of sun colors the eastern sky.

I cannot win. London has bested me.

I wander, sullen and shaken, soggy from the dreadful mist that haunts this place, knowing full well my plan to track down Old Billy will be yet another folly—nothing more than tough talk from someone who cannot finish the task he set out to do. A cough rattles in my chest. My body craves warmth, comfort, something soft to fall into, even for a short time, to ease my mind of its burden.

My feet know the way, even if the rest of me does not.

I leave Monument Bridge and step into the borough of Southwark. Brick gives way to the softness of mud. Always this wretched mud. My feet sink with each step. As the mouths of side streets pass, I study the sad faces of others wrestling with regrets of their own. To end up in such a miserable place, how could they not rue their blunders? My nose wrinkles at the stench of emptied chamber pots. Boots soaked through, my feet swim in a shallow soup of urine and liquefied feces.

My mood darkens further.

I stand at the paint-peeled door, which looks different in the day's fading light. A hand grasps the handle and pushes the door open, but I cannot imagine this hand is my own. Feet climb the stairs, but they cannot be my feet. Knuckles rap another door, three floors up, but they must be someone else's knuckles, scabbed and bleeding.

The door creaks open. Ruddy-cheeked Alice, the fifteen-year-old whore, stares back at me.

Do I choke her or kiss her?

"Well?" she says.

My body sways. To a teenaged girl, a broken man like me must look a fright.

Her eyes soften, and the corners of her mouth produce the slightest smile. She pulls her nightshirt over her head and lets it fall to the floor.

"Come on in then," she insists.

The floorboards creak beneath my wet, mud-ruined boots as I step across the threshold. The door closes behind me.

## Chapter 23

# Some Kind of Idiot

Basil jolts awake, his pulse racing. The fog of sleep lifts in an instant, his mind a sharpened blade.

*Something's wrong.*

He closes his eyes to lend strength to his other senses, smelling, listening for the telltale din. A faint jingling, a cousin to the sound of running water, trickles in from the living room. He slips out of bed and moves with the shadow into the lightless living room. A silhouette darkens the space by the backdoor. He glides across the carpet, soundlessly, and flicks open the back door. He reaches into the darkness and grabs a fistful of collar, and hurls the intruder clear across the living room, into the far wall. The wall buckles.

Basil flicks the switch on the near wall. Harsh yellow light floods the living room. A blond male—young, maybe eighteen or nineteen—tries to gain his bearings. He struggles to liberate his shoulders, still embedded in the buckled drywall.

"Christ, Jesus!" the intruder yips.

As Basil steps forward, the kid draws a small knife. Basil kicks it away.

"You broke my hand!" the young man cries.

"Whose fault is that?"

The kid tries to back away, but he has nowhere to go, so he skitters sideways into the kitchen.

Basil pulls a chair from the kitchen table. He turns the chair and straddles it so he can face his attacker.

"What's your name, son?" he asks.

The kid hesitates and then stutters, "C-C-C-Carl."

"It's almost three a.m., C-C-C-Carl. Why are you here?"

"The Lord sent me."

"Come on, Carl. We both know that's not true. So let's try that again. Why are you here?"

"Edna sent me."

"Edna sent you. Of course she did."

"She told me I had to volunteer, that it was my duty. I didn't want to argue with her."

"Listen, Carl. First things first: I assume you're here to try to kill me, but you're woefully unprepared for the job. Nothing but a lousy pocketknife. A pocketknife, Carl. To assassinate a demigod. You should know that human weapons cannot kill me." A lie. "On top of that, you're out there on the patio trying to pick a lock, but I never lock my doors. Why would I? Please don't take this the wrong way, but are you some kind of an idiot?"

"No, sir." It's all Carl can manage.

"How old are you, son?"

"Seventeen."

"On a suicide mission at seventeen. She sends a seventeen-year-old armed with nothing but a pocketknife."

"I brought other stuff," Carl says, seeming to want to impress.

"Great! Let's see it."

"It's in the bag," Carl says. "Out on your patio."

"Well, go get it. But Carl … be careful."

Carl gets up and sidles past Basil, trailing bits of drywall. He tiptoes onto the patio and retrieves an olive-colored canvas bag, which he drags across the floor and places at Basil's hooves.

"Tricks and treats," Basil says. "Let's do an inventory."

Basil rummages. He fishes out a dull machete, three butcher knives and a framing hammer, and then a pistol—an ancient Ruger Single-Six. A small and heavy object rolls around the bag's bottom. Basil plucks the oblong shell and holds it up, studying the waffled pattern in the glow of the kitchen light.

"A grenade," he says. "A fucking grenade. Where did you come across this little bundle of joy?"

"I don't think it's live. Everyone threw a bunch of stuff into the bag. They said I could take my pick."

"How democratic. What were you going to use?"

"Pardon?"

"To kill me. What were you planning to use to do the deed?"

"The hammer, I guess. Maybe the pistol."

Basil rises from his chair and leans on the kitchen counter. He fishes a slice of pumpernickel from an open cellophane bag and drags the bread across the basin of a frying pan on the cold stovetop, wiping up jellied bacon grease. He pops the grease-sopped bread into his mouth and gives his jaw a workout.

"Listen, Carl," he says. A few loose crumbs spill from his mouth. "You seem like a nice kid. No matter what Edna tells you, I'm not here to lay waste to anything or to destroy your institutions or in any way insult your precious god."

"Then why *are* you here?"

Basil doesn't have the opportunity to answer. A blur moves through the open back door. Booted feet fall heavily on the carpet. The man carries a baseball bat above his head, in attack position, his mouth open and screaming.

"Paul!" Carl yells. "Wait!"

Basil grabs the frying pan by the handle and wings it across the room. The pan catches Paul on the chin, and he drops like a sack of flour—out cold before he hits the ground. The bat windmills to a clattering stop on the kitchen linoleum.

"Who do we have here?" Basil says, nudging the man's feet.

"That's Paul," Carl says. "He's with our church."

"What's he doing in my living room?"

"He was my ride. My getaway, better put."

"I see. Well, time for you to go home, Carl. But thanks for stopping by."

"What about Paul?"

"I'll make sure he gets home safely."

"But he's my ride."

"I don't know what to tell you, Carl. Maybe the keys are still in the ignition. If not, that's your problem to solve. Now get out of here."

"Yes, sir."

"And, Carl?"

"Yes, sir?"

"Make sure we never see each other again."

Carl drops his head and slinks out the back door. He slides the door closed behind him, sealing in Basil and the unconscious Paul.

Basil wanders his apartment, looking for a length of rope or cord or something else with which to immobilize his comatose houseguest. The best he can find is the octopus of cables connecting his television to the port in the wall, but he's not about to part with the conduit for his beloved TV programming just to string up a would-be assassin. He decides to call Anton.

Anton, to Basil's surprise, answers on the second ring. Basil explains the situation, and Anton appears at Basil's front door less than five minutes later, armed to the teeth. First he hands Basil a length of rope, followed by a roll of electrical tape and, finally, a used plastic drop cloth. The remnants of a six-pack, two lonely cans of beer, dangle from his fingers by a plastic ring.

Anton nods toward the unconscious man on Basil's floor.

"Where you bury body?" he asks.

"He's still alive, near as I can tell," Basil replies. "I just want to make sure he's secure when he comes to."

"You want beer?"

"No, thank you. I'm surprised you like that swill."

"When in Rome," he says. "In Leningrad, I drink Stoli. In U.S., I drink Anheuser-Busch. I blend. Who is man on floor?"

"Someone who wants me dead."

"He lose."

"Yes. He lose indeed."

Basil twines the rope around the man's wrists and ankles, and then winds the electrical tape around each knot. Once he's confident the man cannot escape, he slaps the man's cheeks—gently at first, then roughly. He sits Paul upright, though the man refuses to stir. Perhaps he put too much spin on the frying pan. The guy could have a broken jaw. Or a grievous brain injury. Or a severed spine.

"Piss on him," Anton says.

"I think I'll just use water. Thanks for stopping by, Anton. You probably shouldn't be here when he wakes up. You don't need the aggravation."

Anton rubs his hands together, as if absolving himself of any responsibility. He points toward the far wall, newly caved in, and says, "Tomorrow I bring spackle." He and his two cans of beer take their leave.

Basil goes to the sink and fills a bowl with cold water. He then stands over the unconscious man, Paul, and drips the water onto his forehead. When that doesn't elicit a response, he dumps the rest of the bowl across Paul's face and chest. Paul seems confused when he opens his eyes, finally.

"Hey," Basil says. He snaps his fingers to get Paul to focus. "Do you know where you are?" When the man doesn't respond, he asks, "Do you know *who* you are?"

Paul takes a moment to study his surroundings, and then he focuses on Basil. His expression shifts from confusion to contempt.

"Your end is near," the man says.

"Clearly," Basil replies. "It's Paul, right? I sent your pal Carl on his way. I'll make this brief: Please tell Edna that if she'd like to have a civilized conversation, I'm all for it. But please tell her to call first, rather than having her idiot cronies drop by at such an impolite hour."

Basil can feel Paul's hatred for him.

"Isaiah," Paul says. "Chapter fifty-nine, verse three: 'Your hands are stained with blood, and your fingers with guilt. Your lips speak lies, your tongues mutter malice.'"

"So sweet of you to say, Paul. Look, it's getting late and I need my beauty sleep. Make yourself comfortable."

He peels off a length of electrical tape and goes to place it over Paul's mouth, but Paul does not cooperate. He lashes out and bites Basil's palm, sinking in his teeth.

Basil doesn't flinch, though Paul's teeth hit bone. Instead, he lifts his hand until Paul comes entirely off the floor. The man's jaw muscles cannot take the strain, and he falls to the floor in a heap. This time Basil forgets his tenderness, and roughly slaps the tape over his captive's mouth.

"It's a damned shame, Paul," Basil says, studying the blood dripping from his wounded hand. "You know nothing about me, but you assume I'm here to do harm simply because of the way I look. I hope you realize you're the invader here. You're the aggressor. You're the one who's spilled blood tonight—all in the name of a supposedly civilized god."

He places Paul in a chair and winds the tape around his arms, legs and waist.

"You'll be safe here until morning. Now if you'll please shut up for the next few hours, I need my shuteye."

# Chapter 24

# Consumed

Hours later my feet descend the stairs and lead me into the light of day. I can still taste Alice on my overworked lips. I can still smell her, her sharp musk lingering in my whiskers, on the tips of my fingers.

The yellow-gray gloom stings my eyes. The sun hangs low in the sky, the perfect white orb cutting through the haze of cloud cover and coal smoke. The sun's return brings a smile to my face.

Alice has slain me, and part of me is thankful for this death, for now I can have my resurrection. In this state I have no strength, the slot between Alice's loins having sapped all the might from my body. Now I must satisfy yet another appetite, by filling my gut.

The bakery in Owlsditch bustles in late morning. I ask the woman behind the counter for half a loaf of bread. She, the baker's wife, squints at me and shows a toothless grin. She must smell Alice on me too.

"Two more gone missing just last night," the baker's wife says. "Two more, just up and gone, as if God came down and plucked 'em right up. It's the monster, I'd bet, sent here by God himself, 'cause he don't like what we been showing him."

"All things take care of themselves in time," I say.

I dare not share my intent to fell Old Billy.

I collect my bread and weave out into the street, renewed by my solitary purpose. I have my bread, I have my will, and I have a clear mind, thanks to a proper night's sleep beside a randy young tom who knows how to warm a man's blood.

The only necessity I lack is the means to stop Old Billy's black heart.

A wagon passes, hauling hay for ponies and sheep,

presumably. The wheels dig for traction against buried stone. The muleskinner whips the arse of his sickly draught ox, and the wagon lurches forward. Long-handled farm tools clatter against the boxboard.

Barring a pistol, a spear will do just fine. I smile at my good fortune.

With all the stealth I can muster, I cross the street and follow the confetti of straw. As the wagon stops at Owlsditch Mews, the muleskinner slides from his perch and limps into the stables.

Ankle-deep mud tugs at my boots as I creep to the rear of the wagon. As I pull on a long wooden handle, out comes a thatch of hay woven into the four iron prongs of a pitchfork. I toss the fork back into the wagon and yank on the second handle, knowing the muleskinner will be returning at any moment. The wooded handle ends in a splintered point. It will make a fine spear. The shovel's broken-off spade sits on a patch of loose hay. I take my spear and slip away.

My belly full and weapon secure, my thoughts turn to the task ahead. If I were Old Billy, where would I be? Close to my hunting grounds, but not too close. I imagine the scaly bugger balled up like a sleeping cat, tail curled over its nose, its body waiting for some unspoken signal that the sun has retreated, the world of shadow begging its return.

As I head toward London Bridge, memories of Alice consume my mind.

The fingers of my right hand find their way to the space beneath my nose. Alice's ripeness takes me back to the previous night. My trousers tighten.

"Focus on Old Billy," I whisper.

The beast would be nimble and unafraid of heights. Perhaps the beast has coiled itself in a belfry or a church steeple. No, in my mind it is a creature of the earth, borne of the soil, so it will want to be encased, as if in a tomb. It will favor someplace quiet, damp and cool, far from the fuss of humans, until it is time to feed. Clever Old Billy would have chosen somewhere with multiple points of ingress and egress.

London's streets bustle with industry. On every unoccupied plot, workmen piece together structures of brick and timber, bone and blood. They carve up the earth with glee, adding to London's blight. Already the city booms with constructions of every sort, from the medieval palace to paupers' shacks. Why must they add to the congestion? To lure in fools like me, I suppose.

Old Billy could be anywhere. I will know the place when I see it.

I consider my connection to this *thing*, this stranger in a strange land. Perhaps the fabric of our bond stems from the fact that neither of us is welcome here.

A dark cloudbank moves in, and the light shifts. The dross and din of enlightened London fall away, and I tramp lonely streets abandoned by all but rats and curs and orphaned beggars. At least the mud has thinned, as my boots find purchase on bare brick.

I roll the cold from my shoulders as I approach a massive stone edifice. Its three crumbling stories have done their best to find a way back to the ground, but the bones still stand. Shaggy brown vines snake up the walls. Glass crunches beneath my boots. Absent their panes, the windows are open sores, invitations to pigeons and vagrants—and perhaps the accursed creature that will make meals of them all.

"As good a place as any to begin," I declare, though no one listens.

I skirt the building, looking for a proper way in, and I find it in a boarded-up doorway with a few planks dangling from rusted nail heads. Perhaps the doorway had once been well capped, but someone or something went to the trouble of breaking the seal. I duck beneath a horizontal beam and nudge open the door with my elbow. Shedding old paint in long strips, the door yawns open to reveal an empty space—perhaps an old factory floor where important widgets were once made, or a storehouse where munitions for war were once kept at the ready for swift shipment to foreign lands in need of taming.

Footprints checker the dusty floor. They seem of human origin. Most of them, anyway.

I hold my spear before me. When I find Old Billy, lost in his murderous dreams, I shall drive the spear through his brain, then his heart, until his limbs cease their thrashing. The dirty work done, I will retrieve the nearest constable to prove the deed has been done and collect my twenty pounds in reward. Then this peasant life will fall behind me.

My eyes seek signs of life, signs of movement, yet they find nothing notable on the empty first floor save a broken chair and a clutch of dirty bed sheets drawn up into a pile. An able nest, perhaps. Chains dangle eerily from the ceiling. I am thankful for the light from the knocked-out windows, yet I know I will have to enter darker places if Old Billy and I are to find each other again.

A moment later I arrive at another doorway, pressed open with a gentle palm. A stairway leads to a windowless cellar. The light goes only so far. I take the steps two at a time, going as quietly as I can, but the weight of each footfall announces my approach. Twelve steps later I enter the cellar's mouth— dimly lit, cold, heavy with the odor of a caged animal. My boot clips something on the floor and sends it sailing. The ribcage of a small animal ricochets off the wall and breaks into a dozen discrete bones.

If only my bride could see me now, hunting monsters with nothing but a broken spade in hopes of sending the bugger home to the inferno. How ridiculous.

This is all for her. Or is it? If it were, I would have stayed home in Berwick, built a life with her there. Instead I escaped to a loveless place that holds nothing for me. If she had been my sole concern, I would not have propelled myself into Alice's arms—or, more to the point, between her legs.

Shame darkens my mood.

I look up from the filthy floor, eyes wide in the dim light, and shudder at an alarming sight: a silhouette at the edge of the shadows. I crouch to my knees, spear ready to do its job, and wait for the attack. Instead, the silhouette stays put, still as a mannequin. Slowly it sways. Then, it lurches forward, and I fall onto my arse. My spear traces a violent arc across the dusty floor.

The fumes of gin, the tang of sweat.

As the old man clamors past me, he tramples my right foot. He trips as he gets to the staircase, his face smacking the wall. He climbs one stair at a time, hand gripping the banister, struggling with each step, gasping for breath. The vapors of gin trail him. He gets to the top of the stairs and roams the floorboards.

Columns of dust cascade from the ceiling.

My heart stutters in the aftermath. I fumble for my spear, and my hand grips something soft and somehow familiar. The smell hits me first. I squint to see, but the stink tells me I have thrust my hand into a smear of human feces. I yell in disgust and wipe the foulness from my palm. After feeling around for the handle of my spear, I scout for any signs of Old Billy. Finding none, I climb the stairs and find my way out to the street.

Thick, gray clouds have moved in. The sun has gone into hiding yet again.

I am man enough to admit my ineptitude. Scared stiff by an old sot, with the stink of yesterday's breakfast marring my hand—annulling Alice's lovely musk, most regrettably.

I must press forward.

Three more burned-out tenements, an old church and an abandoned factory black with soot produce no more clues in my search for Old Billy. In all, I have found nothing but a growling street cur tending to her puppies, desiccated turds and piles of time-bleached bones from four-legged beasts.

Then I find the entrance to the tunnel by the edge of the Thames. Where it leads, I cannot know, but I must explore. I wander in near darkness for an hour, maybe two, my feet soaked and stinking of sludge. Panic fills me, but I tamp it down by telling myself, "No one else can do what I must." I turn back only when I realize the foolishness of my endeavor: wading through an inky tunnel filled with other people's waste, searching for some *thing* that could kill me before I have the chance to smell it coming.

Some time later I find myself within range of the tunnel's exit. My belly swells with fear, figuring now, my feet a mere Gunter's chain from the care of sunlight, Old Billy will take me in his claws and relieve me of the burden of my viscera. But as I step into the light, I realize I am safe. Soggy to the bone, but safe.

My feet know the way home, wherever home is—back to a random dry spot on Monument Bridge, I suppose. My mind wrestles with thoughts of my bride, of Alice, of Old Billy, as I put Owlsditch behind me.

An old man with soot on his face runs past. Then another. The commotion builds with every forward step. Then the telltale smell of burning wood fills my nose. Ashes ride the air. Even in the gray sky, I see the column of smoke rising. I follow the ink-black tendril, seeming to lead me toward to the base of Monument Bridge.

Scores of Londoners stand at the span's entrance. Smoke stings my eyes. I push my way through the crowd. Two constables sprint toward the scene. I follow, curious.

About halfway onto the bridge, the constables stop well short of the blaze. Even from here I can feel the heat on my face, but I cannot tear my eyes away. The inferno consumes the blacksmith's. The roof of the building where I had stored nearly every penny—the fruits of my backbreaking as a canal pickman—collapses before me.

I sink to my knees, mouth agape. For I realize I am seeing my future alight, melting into the earth.

## Chapter 25

# All Eyes on the Grim Horizon

Basil stands over Herbert's left shoulder, arms crossed, as the graphic designer taps away at the ivory keyboard.

Through the magic of software, Herbert wraps words around images on a digital canvas that only a few minutes earlier had been a featureless white sheet.

Basil's amazement with man's technology has not dulled. Even now, more than a month into his adventure, he finds a new reason each day to believe the universe has no boundaries.

"You're too good for this place, Herbert. Just look at that masterpiece."

A blood-red devil with googly eyes, fangs and a pointy van dyke, stares back from the screen. A cloud-shaped word bubble hooks into the space between the tips of two shiny black horns jutting from the cartoon devil's forehead, each one perched above a thick, well-tended eyebrow. The Devil Smoke logo—the L capped with the prongs of a pitchfork, the viper-like S complete with slits for eyes and a slinky, bifurcated tongue—looms in the upper-right corner. Herbert adds a textbox in the center of the word bubble and fills in the space with seven random lowercase letters, not a single vowel among them.

"What do you want it to say?" he asks.

"Go with this: 'Sinfully good'."

"Good enough for now. You'll fix it later."

"I'm not used to seeing you so excitable."

"Working here, I rarely have reason to get excited about much of anything. You should know better than anyone. Stimulation doesn't just waltz through the door of Savage Communications every day. But *this*—this is fun."

"Precisely. That's why you should look elsewhere when I

leave here."

Basil eases Herbert's office door to a close until the lock clicks into place. Bulcavage is nowhere to be found—out pounding the pavement for new business, apparently—but they're hardly alone. From her over-perfumed office just two doors away, Karen is surely plotting Basil's demise, her ear pressed to the wall as she admires the army of Persian cat figurines crowding her desk.

"There's not much else in Beak, at least not in this line of work," Herbert says. "I'll be here for at least another year or two. After that, who knows?"

Although subtle, the tint of disappointment colors Herbert's words. Basil sees an opportunity to intervene.

"I don't know why you feel indebted to stay here. Someone like you should have no problem finding good work wherever you wish to call home."

"You could say the same. You've got a real knack for this stuff. Hell, we should branch out and do our own thing, start our own agency. Why take a piece when we can have the whole pie? We could call it Teak Demon Communications."

"Demon Teak would be better—you know, alphabetical," Basil says with a smile. "Hey, I like the idea. I'm just glad to see you've discovered your confidence."

"So? Let's do it. Let's build something together, you and me."

"I can't."

"Why the hell not?"

"I can't stay here much longer. Clock's ticking."

"By 'here', you mean Beak? Or 'here,' meaning above the ground?"

"Both, most likely."

"But you hate it down below. It's all you talk about."

"Love. Hate. Two sides of the same coin. I belong beneath the earth, Herbert. Besides, I believe I've begun to wear out my welcome."

Basil's thoughts return to the prior night. He thinks of Edna's two buffoons, Carl and Paul, showing up at his back door with murder on their minds. If the men had had a full brain between them, the situation might have ended in tragedy. Instead, Carl left in peace, and Paul wound up spending the night as an unwilling houseguest. Basil delivered Paul to the doorstep of Crows Gorge United Methodist Church—Edna's church—early this morning. As his noisemaker pulled away, he saw Paul thrashing on the church's front lawn, bound, gagged and furious.

Basil can laugh about the late-night incursion now, but the incident at the strip club he nearly destroyed is a different story. He half-expected to see Officer Pierce waiting for him at the office first thing this morning, ready to haul him off to a windowless cell. Steve, the bouncer, must have survived his injuries. Basil had to give the man credit for taking his lumps. Then there's Divinity, the big-bottomed, redheaded stripper. He hopes she's all right, too, having recovered from what he did— or *almost* did. He'll have to drop by Cheeky's later and apologize for his overenthusiasm, and for almost doing something very, very stupid. He easily could have killed them both, after all. Maybe he'll stop somewhere on the way home and pick up a box of cookies or some other gesture of his regret and hand-deliver the goods along with an apologetic note.

"Forget people like Edna Babych," Herbert says. "There's always going to be an asshole eager to make your life difficult. You should stay. You seem happy here."

"Happy as anyone can be in a world ruled by human men."

"So stay. Screw Edna. Screw Bulcavage and his shitty agency." He drops his voice. "We'll go off and do our own thing. You and me."

"That's a good dream, Herbert."

"'Do what you want, where you want.' That's the advice you gave me."

"And it's still fine advice. You should follow it."

*This is as good a time as any to uncork this bottle.*

"You don't belong here," he tells Herbert. "There's nothing wrong with a place like Beak—I'm thrilled to have come here, in all honesty, and to have met you—but you can't be yourself here. You stay here, you'll die having pretended your whole life away."

Herbert's spine stiffens.

"Answer me this," Basil says. "Why do you live alone?"

"I live with my father."

"By choice?"

"Mostly. Dementia has taken most of him by now. He's from Beak originally. A few years ago, early into the decline, he kept talking about his childhood, about growing up here. I thought maybe being here would help him."

"Did he live with you in Des Moines?"

"Back then he was still living in the house where I grew up. With my mom."

"Mom's gone?"

Herbert nods.

"So you lived alone there too."

Herbert nods again.

"It's tough," Basil adds.

"What is?"

"Sharing your life with someone."

"I wouldn't know. Haven't quite figured out the formula yet."

"Hopefully when your father dies you'll start living your life the way you should."

Herbert says nothing, seeming to hope the conversation will sprout wings and turn into something else, leading them elsewhere.

"I've seen glimmers of the man who lives within you," Basil says. "Anyone can hide from the truth for a time, but they can't keep it down forever. You're no different. Secrets have a way of crawling out of whatever box they've been locked inside.

You should love the person you want to love. You wouldn't be hurting anyone."

"Depends on who you ask."

"You're a good man, Herbert, a good person. You'll never tell me, but I know something happened to you. You can let the bad things destroy you, or you can turn them into something else. It's your choice. But I'll tell you this: You're a kind, gentle man who deserves to be happy."

"You can see that in me?"

"Anyone who's paying attention can. From the minute I met you, I knew something had broken you somewhere along the way. If you're not broken, you're not living. You'll be fine. Mourn whatever you lost, but don't take the blame. Remember, but move forward. Move on."

Herbert seems shaken.

"You look like you want to punch me," Basil says.

"Let's just finish this blasted campaign and call it a day. I'm suddenly exhausted."

They stare at the screen, studying each of the design's elements, looking for loops they haven't yet connected.

"I like it," Basil says. "Let's print it and leave it down on Bulcavage's desk. Let him tell us everything we screwed up so we can start over from scratch tomorrow. He can choke on his own advice, for all I care." In a ridiculously high-pitched tone, he mocks, "'Even if the client hates what you give them, at least they know you're putting in billable hours.'"

"I don't know," Herbert says. He studies the screen and points to a quiet space in the northwest corner of the screen. "I like what we have, but I still think we're missing an important piece."

"No shit. Isn't everyone?"

* * *

Edna Babych brings both palms to her forehead, trying to soothe the pain splitting her skull. Her hands creep into her hairline and grab as much hair as they can gather. Her whole body shakes with rage. She eyes the crucifix on her desk, which she has not kissed in days, and wants to say something dirty.

She simply cannot understand why her god has suddenly gone silent.

"Why have you forsaken me, Lord?" she begs. "Tell me what I must do to drive this damned thing back to the darkness."

The demon—*Basil*, they call it. Her archenemy. She cannot fathom how others don't see its presence here as anything but the gravest of threats, one that will surely kill them all, if not in a rolling ball of ash and flame then slowly, like bone cancer, taking one piece after the next until nothing remains but a hollow, useless shell.

When the demon first slithered through a crack in the earth, fully prepared to reduce everything in its path to rubble, Beak fell silent—and this she cannot forgive. Instead of the townsfolk voicing their outrage and dissent, they met the demon's arrival with indifference, even open-armed acceptance. Not her. From the moment she heard the news, she committed herself to driving the SOB back to the world of lust and shadow, in accordance with the Lord's will.

She still remembers the feeling of vomit rising in her throat, the taste of it on her tongue. She was working as a cashier at the Bag 'N Save in nearby Pasturelands when one of her co-workers mentioned, so casually, "Have you heard about what's going on over in Beak?" That's when Jesus whispered in her ear, told her to devote all of her energy—every breath—to using her church as the Lord's machine gun. Holy bullets, the voice told her, hungry for the taste of demon flesh. When she walked into her pastor's office, reciting parts of verses from the Book of Revelation and offering to take the fight directly to "The Beast," she hadn't even changed out of her work clothes. She was still wearing her Bag

'N Save apron and slightly wrinkled collared shirt with a milky stain on the front, the result of a miscue while spooning the remnants of her seven a.m. strawberry yogurt into her mouth.

"Let's just wait and see," Pastor Greg told her. "We don't even know if it's true."

"Jesus told me we have no time to 'wait and see,'" she said, her spindly fingers making annoyed quote marks in the air. "We have to organize *now*."

"Funny. I must not have gotten the message."

"Big surprise. We can't let the enemy establish a nest and leave his poison puddles for any of God's children dumb enough to lap them up."

"Now, Edna—"

"Don't 'Now, Edna' me. We must do something about this unholy brute right flipping now, before it's too late. Before there's nothing left to save. Now do your job and let's assemble a group of the willing to ship this goat-headed villain out of town on a rail."

Her words to Pastor Greg took on increasing virulence. "You're a worthless, toothless weakling of a man—a phony-baloney prophet with no spine for the Lord's work," she told him on Day Two of her tirade, and the hectoring worsened from there. "War!" she cried on Day Three. At one point she not so subtly suggested she saw him ogling the rear ends of some of Beak's most athletic middle school boys, though she admitted he couldn't take all of the blame for his sin because the demon probably had its mitts in him by now, pulling the strings.

It took Edna only five days to convince do-nothing Pastor Greg to put Beak in his rearview. She quickly stepped in to assume the pulpit.

Things went well for a short while. The protests. The electricity, the excitement coursing through the congregation during her fiery sermons. Everyone rallying around a common cause, rallying around her, galvanized by her divinely inspired words. Then that loud-mouthed attorney who works in the same building as the demon started sticking her big Jew nose where it didn't belong—like they always did—and dragged the spineless crumb bum of a cop, Pierce, into the mix along with her.

As far as she's concerned, those two traitors to Christ both deserve to burn in a soup of hot lava. Now everyone's all worried about getting in trouble, about hurting someone's feelings, about spending a night in jail. She knows better. Better to suffer now, in this world, than to burn forever as retribution for not taking a stand against some evil thing casting a shadow on the church's doorstep. She's noticed too many empty seats during her sermons the past few days. She feels her power slipping.

"Help me understand, Lord, if you understand." She takes a breath and screams at the ceiling. "Are you seeing what's happening here? This is your battle to lose, so tell me what the flippity-flap I need to do!"

Her stomach groans. She hasn't eaten a morsel in days, and she won't until she figures out how to solve the problem the Lord has placed in front of her.

"God's love is my bread," she reminds herself. "God's love is my bread."

The door cracks open. It's Ned Lavender, the church's mealy-mouthed music director.

"Everything okay in here, Miss Babych?"

"Just fine, Neddy. Now leave the minister to do God's work."

He opens his mouth as if to say something else but says nothing and retreats from the doorway. The lock clicks behind him.

Maybe the Lord is testing her, she thinks. She admits this would make perfect sense, considering the many tests he's asked her to endure over the course of her nearly fifty years: lost parents, lost siblings, lost jobs, Crohn's, the curse of men. It's a miracle she still has love in her heart for him, if for no one else.

Finally, she reaches the decision she's been dancing around

for days. If Beak has given up on the cause, to rid the town of this scourge, she'll take matters into her own hands, because she can't let this *thing* subsist any longer on the blessed soil God created for the children he loves so dearly. Any method for achieving her goal is acceptable, regardless of the consequences. The line between right and wrong no longer exists. Arson, mob violence, murder—all seem perfectly suitable paths to the same place: salvation. The only question is which path to choose, as she's not even sure if this damned abomination—she refuses to call it by name—can be killed.

Carl and Paul certainly couldn't get the job done. Carl hasn't answered his phone, so there's no telling what horrors he had to suffer in the demon's lair. Either that, or he's a victim of the demon's brainwashing. And Paul, what an indignity, being hogtied and left on the church's front stoop, with a handwritten sign, "Free to a Good Home," stapled to his forehead.

"Another thumb in God's all-seeing eye," she whispers.

If the demon cannot be killed, she's confident she can at least maim it enough to send it limping off to someplace other than here.

She imagines digging a pit just outside the door of the office building where the abomination works and filling the pit with holy water, borrowed from the Catholics—much like her trusty crucifix. The beast would trip into the blessed hole, and she would just sit back and watch the water melt its flesh like a hot blade on butter. Then she considers the logistics of having to acquire so much holy water—a hundred gallons easy, she figures, maybe two hundred—and that could turn some heads, meaning someone in charge might catch wind of how she took the helm of Crows Gorge United Methodist Church. She couldn't let that happen.

Maybe hydrofluoric acid or gasoline would work better, she thinks. Either would be easy enough to procure.

Other options spring to mind. Cutting the brakes on the

SOB's motorcycle. Taking a torch to the office building where it works or the leper colony of an apartment complex where it sleeps, *if* it sleeps. Hiring a sniper to take roost atop one of the buildings along Second Street and waiting until its loud-mouthed motorcycle rumbles past, and then pulling the trigger once the bastard's horny-toad skull fills the crosshairs.

God willing.

Voices fill the hallway just beyond the office's flimsy door, pulling her from her reverie. As the voices grow louder and more animated, she rises from her seat to remind whoever the heck is out there that they're in God's house, so if it's not too much trouble, please keep the flipping volume down to a dull flipping roar. She yanks open the door and sees Ned talking with a bald-headed bear of a man with two black eyes, wearing a neck brace and using crutches to support his weight. Beside him stands a tall, buxom redhead who looks like she's been crying.

Ned turns to Edna and says, smiling, "You're going to want to hear this."

* * *

Kamala's eyes home in on a spot in the ink-black corner, the same darkened space on the far wall that has held her gaze for the duration of this ordeal. It's the only view she has, bent at the waist over the stone slab, arms extended and held taut to the floor, wrists bound with leathers slick with her own sweat. Her chin bleeds from the ceaseless friction, the skin worn away, bone against rock.

How many, she wonders. How many goons so far have worked to ruin her with their worst? Ancient history, she tells herself. The more important question: How much more of this will she have to endure?

*Again and again, the stabbing ...*

*The unbroken rhythm ...*

*An oversaturated sponge ...*

The warm flesh of her belly and breasts has thawed the cool rock beneath her, and the ragged bonds have sunk their teeth into the tender flesh of her wrists and pasterns. The wounds on her back have scabbed over. Her lower half has gone numb, though she imagines the backs of her thighs glazed, her hooves in sticky puddles, glued to the floor. Her stomach feels poisoned, wondering if the semen has somehow leached into her gut.

How many more can there possibly be?

A flood of warmth fills her as another finishes his task with a pitiful whimper. She prays for this one to have been the last, but then another steps up and enters here, thrusting even more violently than the last.

"Forgive the barnacles, deary," says the demon as he mounts her. His pelvis bounces off the cushion of her rear end. "Can't scrub them off. Here's hoping your cunny can do the job for me."

She recognizes the old demon's cackle—the father of her dearly departed Kindness, the gentle demon she witnessed being pulled limb from limb by Lubos's heavies—but doesn't dare conjure the image of a face: neither her ill-fated lover's, nor that of his progenitor, now joyfully defiling her.

*Kill me.*

"Kill me," she whispers.

"Oh, it's not so bad," he says. He's huffing now, digging his claws into the meat of her bleeding hips. "I'm almost done."

The thrusting slows—another gush of warmth—and the old demon pulls out, then slips wordlessly out of the chamber.

Another steps up to fill her.

Moments later, another.

And yet another behind him.

To each one she repeats her plea.

"Kill me."

The realist in her knows her words have no effect, as none will show mercy. And even if one does, she knows those in line behind him will gladly abuse her corpse.

Lubos calls to her from the entrance to the Room of Contrition. "Save some energy for the troglodytes," he tells her.

She hears movement. Her bald chin grinds against the stone as she struggles to turn her head. A thick-bodied demon with a milky eye—one of the Nameless—approaches Lubos and begs for an audience.

"Kneel," Lubos tells him.

The demon does as he is told.

"An update on the excavation, liege. At your instruction, we've widened the mouths of three tunnels to the surface. Two have collapsed. We may need an additional route to accommodate the girth of your war party."

"Do as you see fit," Lubos says. "However many you think we'll need."

The demon with the milky eye drops his head toward the floor and offers an upturned palm. Lubos drags two of his talons lightly across the demon's callused skin, from the wrist to the fingertips, adding, "Praise, praise."

Kamala credits Lubos for his ambition, his knack for manufacturing fantasies her imagination fails to show her. He aims to unleash every brute and then lead his army to the surface, all to spill blood and sate his lust for war. Such a force would cause endless havoc in the world of men, especially with the kraken Cthaal at the fore, though she cannot fathom how he plans to tame such a vicious beast.

Kamala's gaze returns to the darkened corner. She gasps as Basil's face stares back. Her vision becomes hazy, as if a veil covers her eyes, and she struggles to blink the image away. As her vision sharpens, the mirage evaporates.

*Basil. His failings caused this. He is responsible. He should pay the price.*

She curses him for having left, for having created the vacuum that permitted Lubos's ascendance, and, it seems, the sure death of Our Fiery Home. She curses him for causing the savagery she's had to endure. She curses him for his silence now, for not bursting into the Room of Contrition to end her so-called atonement. She curses him because, if he were here right now, he would surely step to the front of the line and inject her with his own venomous seed, just like all the others.

She corrects herself: He would find crueler ways to mistreat her. Or he would break her bonds and carry her off in his arms. His mercurial mood would determine his course of action.

Another burst of stinging warmth.

Her insides absorb the gluey muck. She closes her eyes and imagines her limp body falling into a cushion of warm, dark nothingness.

# Chapter 26

# Ashes

Thunder rumbles in the distance as the first drops of rain lick my face. Let the rains come, so I can rinse the stink and smoke from my body, wash the misfortune from my life. As I observe the wreckage of the blacksmith's on Monument Bridge, doubt riddles every choice I have made.

My right foot throbs, likely broken, a casualty of either my carelessness or my stubborn luck—likely both. My stomach stirs, having done away with the bread from this morning. My savings, swallowed up by the fire. The rains soak me to the bone. I wander, pitiful. Broken. Failed.

London has beaten me.

I retreat to a dry place beneath an awning. A pool of rainwater drenches my feet. I swear, just one more quandary, no matter how slight, and I will leap from the balustrade to become one with the Thames. A figure approaches, and I recognize the same constable who had kicked me—in the same foot that now likely bears the calamity of a broken bone. I step out from beneath the awning and walk as hurriedly as I can.

The constable does not follow.

"I am alone," I whisper, as if to remind myself of my plight.

Even if I wish to return home to Berwick, I can no longer afford the trip.

Hours pass, my mind swimming in regret.

Darkness has sunk its teeth into London by the time my feet return to the brick of the bridge. The blacksmith's smolders, now little more than a ruined shell. The rains have extinguished the fire, though plumes of white smoke rise from the pile. I pick through charred timber and warm stone, to see if I can salvage something—anything. I step into the thick of it, pushing aside timbers, toppling stone. My skin turns black with wet ash, but I find nothing. Other miscreants have already picked the site clean, I suppose, or the fire burned hot enough to melt metal, my coins having rejoined the earth as liquid copper and silver.

The cool dusk air seeps through my wet clothes. I hug myself, trying to stay warm, but I cannot drive off these damned shivers. My body begs me for a few hours of shuteye in a dry and quiet place. Perhaps my prospects will look brighter in the light of a new day.

The steeple of Saint Botolph's Church at Owlsditch appears through the murk. Candles burn yellow in a second-floor window.

I follow the street and turn left at the corner.

Away from the light, I skulk toward the church. My hand caresses the stone of the gable wall, moist and grainy beneath my touch. Three small windows line the bottom floor, where the foundation meets moss and cobblestone. Iron bars bisect two of the three windows, but the third is unguarded—the iron bars pried back. As my fingertips glance the rain-slicked glass, the window creaks open. It will be a tight fit, but I can squeeze. The street has no witnesses who might betray me. I slide my feet through the opening. As I lower the rest of me, I lose my grip on the slippery jamb and tumble to the cellar floor. The window slams shut behind me.

My knee aches from the fall—yet another insult to my weary frame. I crouch on the floor and wait for a response to my clamor. None comes. I am safe, someplace dry. I waste no time stripping the clothes and stockings from my chilled skin.

The air has its own weight, its own scent—nothing like what I'd expect of a church cellar. It smells like the surety of all things turning to dust. Standing naked in darkness, all my bits exposed, I imagine malevolent crawlers as bunkmates: colossal rats, bats clutching the walls, weevils making tracks on the grubby floor.

Lightning illuminates the rain-streaked windows. Only then

do I see my surroundings. Several wooden tables. A slab, carved from marble or some other heavy stone. Chairs stacked from floor to ceiling. A pile of neatly folded linens.

I place a makeshift bed sheet on top of a wooden table and heave myself onto its surface. My feet peel away from the clammy floor, and I curl into a ball, pulling the linens atop me. I know my sleep will be fitful, but at least it will be sleep.

* * *

My eyes open at the first suggestion of daylight—almost dawn. I have slept, dreamlessly, all night.

Something is wrong. My skin prickles, my body alerting me to unseen danger. First the smell, a combination of sweat and dead meat. Then the sounds of scraping, slithering. The flash of movement in the lifting dark. The impossible weight atop me. Coarse hairs and cool scales stroking my skin. Knife blades against my throat.

*Old Billy has found me.*

"I watch," says the gravelly voice. "I find."

Old Billy speaks! He speaks the language of the King!

His claw traces patterns on the skin of my throat, my naked belly, and points farther south, and then teases back up again.

"Let me go," I beg him. "Please."

"What you seek?"

"Nothing. I seek nothing." The words spill from my mouth in yelps.

"No hunt me," Old Billy says. "No stalk me."

His use of the word *me* chills the marrow in my bones.

"Anything! Anything you say!"

Old Billy slips off the table, pulling me along with him. Before I can protest, I am dangling, Old Billy holding me aloft by an ankle. Instinct does its work, and urine wets my chest and face, puddles on the floor.

A heavy reptilian tail makes S-curves in the air. Old Billy takes his free hand and grabs me by the throat. The upside-down world goes right side up.

"Home," Old Billy says, beating his chest.

"I ... I don't understand," I gasp, choking.

"Leave."

"As soon as you release me, I am gone."

"Go far. No Lundy. Lundy mine."

My brain waits to respond, trying to understand.

"Leave London?" I ask. "I will! I will!"

"You stay. Next time you burn," he tells me. "Like blacksmith-y."

His words puzzle me. Seconds pass before his meaning penetrates the mucus of my crippled brain: The creature started the fire. The creature burned the blacksmith's to the ground. The creature destroyed my savings, admittedly meager, dooming me.

I strike Old Billy across the face. My hand bones break.

Old Billy's fingers tighten around my throat, and he tosses me backward as if I were an empty sack. I smack the wall and drop to the floor, my skull taking the brunt of my fall. Bones crack and crunch. In the dim light I see Old Billy in full for the first time. His face is almost human. Horns spike toward the ceiling, and immense fangs fill his hideous mouth. He has hooves where feet should be. He stands taller than any man I have ever met. Such a thing should not exist beneath God's Heaven, yet here it is, made flesh.

"Stay here, you burn good," he tells me. "Stay here, you burn forever."

Old Billy retreats into a darkened corner and then crouches beneath one of the tables. I wait there, sprawled on the floor, expecting him to advance and tear out my throat. But I see nothing, hear nothing but pebbles falling, though the carnivore's stench lingers like a patch of London fog. As sunlight paints the windows, I see what I could not have noticed the night before: a gaping tear in the wall, just big enough for Old Billy to slither through and sleep off a night of murder and mayhem. Outside I hear wagon traffic, and I realize I have survived an encounter with a flesh-and-blood devil.

I spent a full day looking for Old Billy, every instinct wrong. Only dumb luck led me into his lair: the cellar of a church at the foot of Monument Bridge.

My eyes remain fixed on the hole in the wall as I fumble for my clothes, still as wet as they were when I removed them. My hand struggles to close, the bones having shattered against Old Billy's stony jaw. I could exit the way I came in, through the window, but I will not risk disturbing Old Billy. Instead I wander the room in search of a proper route. I find my escape in the form of a door, blocked by a heavy oak bookcase. With all the care I can muster, I slide the bookcase away from the door and slip out, then ease the door closed behind me.

"Breathe," I tell myself.

My legs tremble as I ascend a small staircase, only four to five steps, leading into the belly of the church. I am too numb from the run-in with Old Billy to consider a way out. As I slip through the back room, a gray-haired priest startles me, and I him. He wastes no time arming himself with a bronze staff, intent on braining me.

"We have nothing for you here," he says. "Back to the street, cadger!"

"Forgive me," I try to explain, suddenly aware of my dishevelment. "I've lost my way."

I hold up my empty hands to show him I mean no harm.

"You mean to rob us again," the priest insists. He waves his staff like a weapon. "You'll hang!"

I should explain I have no intention of robbing him. Instead I back up and spill through another door. Imagine my surprise when I slip on the stone at the foot of the altar, the whole church opening up in front of me. I get to my feet, fall off the riser and sprint down the empty aisle toward the exit. A jolt of pain stings my foot with each step. I slam into the heavy oak door and tumble down a stone staircase, into the mud-drenched street.

The sun hangs low in the bright sky, not a cloud on the horizon. I nearly cry at the sight of so much blue. I stand on the church steps, half-naked, and weave my limbs into cold, wet, mud-caked clothes. As I turn to eye the church at my back, I fully expect to see Old Billy clawing at one of the cellar windows. For a moment I wonder if I dreamt it all. I know better.

Monsters do exist.

I wander from the bridge, away from Saint Botolph's, back toward the baker's. Perhaps I will return to the church in an hour, take the constable with me, and venture into the cellar to show him where Old Billy sleeps. That alone should be good for something—if not the full twenty pounds, then at least half. Old Billy's last words to me—"You burn forever"—chill my plans.

My belly voices its concern, again. My organ's cavity is as empty as my pockets, as barren as my hopes for the future. I have only one option.

I limp back to Alice's apartment, only to find the exterior door locked. She gave me a soft place to land—so soft—and I crave the touch of her youthful bosom against mine. I wait outside an hour, two hours, as I have no place else to go. The only thing I have left to offer is my time.

Perhaps I should make a life with Alice and her ambition, her resourcefulness, her magic tongue. My bride in Berwick is a world away, and I am a new man here. I can become someone else entirely, simply start over and let London's coarse hairs harden me. If I can convince Alice to admit me, I would have a place to rest my weary head. I would have a roof, protection from the elements and shelter from Old Billy. By way of a compromise, I would never again leave the house once the sun has set.

For now I will do what I have done, simply wander, my belly

empty and head free of the ridiculous idea to subdue a demon that even the lawmen cannot deter.

For now I must stay in London, no matter my promise to Old Billy. Just one riddle to solve: Do I stay the same man or become someone my bride would not recognize?

My feet guide me back to Monument Bridge, past the burnt shell of the blacksmith's, past the bakery and the public house, within sight of Saint Botolph's at Owlsditch. My mind feeds me memories of Alice's warmth beside me, her sour breath on my neck.

"Emmitt!"

I know the voice, that of my love from Berwick. My polluted mind plays its tricks.

"Emmitt!"

Closer now.

I turn to the sight of her walking toward me.

My bride.

From Berwick.

From a world away.

Another illusion, I know. I rub my eyes, to cure me of their lies. London's poison has infected every part of me.

Her face is a blur.

Then, she is upon me, her arms around my neck.

"You're real," I say.

Somehow, she has found me. I melt into her. Her nails find sore spots on my back. I sink until my knees buckle and take me to the cobblestone. She joins me, and her tears flow into mine. She must think this reunion has overwhelmed me. What she cannot know, will never know, is that each tear of mine represents a sin against her, the salt of my guilt. At once I am mourning two deaths: that of the man I once was, and that of the one I know I will never be.

"Emmitt," she says, cradling me. "What's … what's become of you?"

Her glee regresses to worry, as it should, because I wish to end my life at this moment, right in the middle of Monument Bridge. No merciful god will come to take me away, I realize, so my thoughts naturally turn to a baser concern: *Can she smell the day-old sweetness of Alice's honeypot on my breath, in the whiskers of my beard, or have the rains cleansed me of her fragrance?*

"Is there somewhere we can go?" she asks.

I manage only tears.

"I knew I shouldn't have come!" she squeals. "I have traveled all this way only to find ... *this*? Say something! Emmitt!"

"It's just," I tell her calmly, quietly, "I'm so delighted to see you, my dear."

"Have you gone mad?"

"I have never seen a better day, darling."

"Oh, Emmitt. Are you well?"

"It's been so long, and ..."

"Emmitt, I'm weary. I didn't expect my journey to take quite so long, to be quite so difficult. Is there somewhere we can go? Somewhere away from this ... this noise and stink?" She waves the air away from her nose.

"How did you find me?"

"Your posts, dear. I followed your posts. Though I aimed for London Bridge, the coachman dropped me here. Monument. Call it fate."

My mind races.

"You've come all this way," I remind her. "You have much to see."

"We'll have plenty of time for that. I'd rather rest. Where can we go?"

Where indeed.

"Emmitt, I have some news."

"Your mum. Yes, dearest, a pity. I regret you had to send her off without me."

"No. Not that. I didn't come here alone."

Her hands move to her belly.

"You're ...?"

I cannot bear to finish the sentence.

Apparently neither can she, because she only nods.

Only then do I register the fullness of her face, the swell of her belly against the fabric of her gray Brunswick gown.

"How far along are you?"

"When did you leave Berwick? Nearly seven months have passed between us, by my best guess."

Her assessment astounds me, as it seems a year or more of my life has withered away since I saw her last. My mind replays my final night in Berwick, when I led my bride out of bed by the hand and pressed her against the wardrobe so I could enter her. As I stabbed away, I thought not of what I would be leaving behind but of the riches I would surely find once my boots touched London's hallowed soil. She begged me in whispers to "be quick with it" while her dying mother groaned for a swift end to her misery from the other side of the wall. I obliged by spilling my seed as quickly as I could, not that I had much say in the matter. Now, seven months later ...

"I'd like to remove myself from this filthy street," she says. "Where can we go, dear? Where is home?"

I am caught.

I get to my feet, wondering how many coins rattle around in my pockets. I have none, I remember, my savings destroyed by Old Billy and his spiteful fire.

*Alice.* She has that place all to herself. I can sneak back, choke the life from her and dump her body into the Thames. Everything of hers then becomes mine. Becomes ours.

*No.*

But if not that, then what? Give up Old Billy in hopes of reclaiming a small fortune? Memories of my encounter with him — his rancid breath, his claws around my throat, the bitterness of my own urine — expose the folly of my plan. I imagine leading a pair of constables into the church cellar to wake up Old Billy, the episode ending with the hairy bastard ripping us all to pieces.

No constable would believe me anyway.

"Let's get you something to tuck into," I tell my bride.

"Emmitt, I'd like to lie down."

"In time, my dear. First a bite, and then …"

Again, I do not finish the sentence, only because I have no clue how to end it. I walk her to the door of the pub and fish for any coins that might have fallen into my pockets. She places a gloved hand on my chest.

"I have money, Emmitt," she says. "A little, anyway."

"I'll be back soon," I tell her.

"But we've just found each other."

"I must … I must arrange for transportation home. You must be exhausted. I wouldn't dare ask you to take another step."

She smiles, her tension easing. I check the sky, figuring I have five hours until nightfall. I bend toward her and peck her on the cheek.

"Have a bite, dear. I'll return before you have a chance to miss me."

I limp away from my bride and the child budding inside her, holding her gaze until the sea of Londoners consumes her.

## Chapter 27

# Let the Walls Close in, or Let Them Come Down

Basil steers his noisemaker off State Street, left onto Broadway, beneath the rows of elms and cedars he has grown to love. He's an hour late, probably more, not that anyone will care. Bulcavage is hardly in the office at all anymore, off doing whatever he's doing. Says he's scouring the sidewalks for prospective clients, herding new accounts. More likely he's tending to other interests: poaching elephants for ivory, hooking thirteen-year-old girls on crack, trafficking Russian women to serve as sex slaves-slash-brides for wealthy American men, and who knows what else. At least that's what Herbert says.

Basil eases onto Crescent Avenue, the road that leads to the office parking lot, and the view shocks him—as does the rush of sound.

Nearly a hundred people mill in the parking lot. Edna Babych stands on a makeshift stage, barking into a megaphone, riling the crowd. The spangles of her hideous denim jacket catch the sun.

"Fuck," Basil mouths, and he rolls the noisemaker into a spot at the end of the far row, maybe ten yards from the lot's edge.

"There!" Edna cries.

Basil looks up to see Edna with her arm outstretched, pointing directly at him.

"Stone him!" she screams.

As Basil steps away from the motorcycle, a pebble skids along the asphalt and bounces off his hoof. Protestors swarm him. He can smell their anger, their hatred, their cravings for his death.

"Rapist!" yells one, inches from his face.

"Unholy!" screams another.

"Pig!" barks another. This one douses Basil's cheek with lukewarm liquid—coffee, he's happy to discover, not freshly brewed urine.

"Go home, Satan," yips a child of no older than eight.

"That's not my name," Basil screams back. He gallops toward the building entrance and sees a man with a familiar face standing motionless by the door: Officer Pierce.

More than a dozen protestors block Basil's path. He tries to be gentle, tries to sidestep as many as he can, but they do their best to obstruct him. In his efforts to evade them, he knees a young woman in the gut. As she doubles over, he bloodies her nose with his elbow. He checks over his shoulder to see Edna on her stage, wild eyed and trembling and smiling like a madwoman. Behind her, he notices for the first time, an oversized T fashioned from planks of pine comes alive with the morning sun. The cross stands more than twelve feet tall from top to bottom, by his best guess.

"Crucify! Crucify! Crucify!"

He reaches the door and says to Pierce, "Aren't you going to do anything?"

Pierce responds dully, "Nope."

Basil enters the building, and he's thankful to see Pierce step in front of the glass door, blocking any of Edna's murderous lot from coming inside. Small favors, he thinks.

He clops down the hall and cracks open the door to Melody's office. Melody's assistant, Audrey Pernie, gabs away on the phone, cracking her gum. She shields the handset with her palm and whispers to Basil, "She's not in, sweetheart."

A lie, he knows. He turns toward the well-lit conference room and sees Melody through the glass panel, working her way through a pile of papers.

Basil waves off Audrey and enters the conference room.

Melody colors a paragraph of text with a yellow highlighter. She doesn't look up.

*Uh-oh.*

"Do you see what's going on out there?" he says.

"Yup."

"Can you do something about it, please? You know, like last time?"

"I've done more than enough for you already, Basil."

"But you have such a gift for crowd control."

"Tell me about Rebecca Devine."

He pauses to consider each syllable. He can't place the name.

"Oh, come on," she says. "Your ancient brain can't be *that* feeble."

"You'll have to enlighten me. I've never heard of her."

"You might know her as Divinity. Takes regular shifts at a charming little titty bar called Cheeky's. You were there recently, as I understand it—right after our dinner the other night, in fact. Ring a bell?"

*Fuck.*

"I don't know what she told you—"

"She didn't tell me a damned thing," Melody says. "Looks like she's chummy with your friend Edna Babych, though. Those two are thick with each other now. You couldn't help yourself, could you? You just had to go and do something stupid. Just like every other idiot with a piece of meat between his legs."

"Listen—"

"You're on your own. That poor girl is likely to press charges."

"For what? I didn't do anything."

"Oh no? Seems to me you went to a strip club and roughed up a stripper when things didn't go your way. You should think about getting a lawyer."

"I didn't rough up anyone but the bouncer, and that's because he hit me with a chair."

"Because you tried to rape that poor girl."

"No."

"Yes."

He hesitates. Then, by way of a defense, he says, "I was lonely."

"No," she says, locking eyes. "You were just being you. Rapists rape."

"I got confused."

"Go get confused somewhere else. You don't belong here. That should be crystal clear to you by now."

There's nothing else for him to say. He could apologize, but he knows she won't accept it. He could give her some time to cool down, not that someone like her needs time to make up her mind. He doesn't blame her. She might be right about him after all.

He exits the conference room, clops past Audrey Pernie, and steps into the hallway. As the door closes behind him, Audrey chirps, "Catch you later, dolly-doll."

* * *

Basil and Herbert stand at the second-floor window, watching the crowd rock Basil's noisemaker back and forth until the motorcycle topples over with an alarming crunch. Members of the mob cheer and raise their flexed arms as if they're part of an oppressed tribe that has removed a dictator from power.

Herbert says, "You don't have to tell me, but—"

"I got carried away," Basil replies. "There was a girl, at a strip club just outside of town, Cheeky's ..."

He hopes Herbert will use his imagination to fill in the rest.

"What happened?"

*Shit.*

"I made a mess." He explains how a nice young woman, the redhead, was kind enough to give him a lap dance. Then things took an unfortunate turn. "I got a little overenthusiastic. A couple of folks got hurt, maybe. Melody would tell you I did 'something stupid,' to use her words."

It feels good to admit, freeing.

"You're a lot dumber than you look," Herbert says. "You know everyone's watching so they can catch you doing something that proves you're the monster they think you are. You know they're just waiting for you to screw up so they can run you out of town."

"I leave at the time of my choosing, no sooner."

"Yeah, you're in control. Clearly. You asshole!"

"If you have something to say, I want to hear it."

"I'll leave the chastisement to Edna, but I do have to tell you something." Herbert draws a breath. "A reporter from the *Crete Bee* came by this morning, asking questions about you. Crete's at least an hour from here, probably closer to two. It seems word about you is getting out. I don't think that's a good thing for you. It was just a matter of time, I guess."

"What do you mean?"

"You were the town's dirty little secret before, but you were *our* secret, and everyone wanted to keep it that way. So if what you're telling me is true, about the stripper—"

"How could I deny it?"

"Well, I think this is the straw that's going to break the camel's back, as they say."

They watch Edna on her stage. She stands next to a tall, buxom woman with a mane of red hair collected into a tight ponytail. She looks different than the woman Basil met the other night, but it's her. It's Divinity. Regret sours in his chest.

"This poor, lost little love bug," Edna says through her megaphone, though the window glass dulls her words. "She was doing her best, trying to earn money doing things no woman should have to do, and in walks this *thing,* this *devil,* this *beast.* It debases her. It degrades her. It abuses her. It tries to steal life from her. Yet here she stands, proof of her strength to do what every one of us must: resist. We must drive this *thing* from our sight. For decency. For our church. For our Lord in Heaven above. And for our dear Rebecca here, this precious little love bug who strayed from the path but has found her way back into the loving arms of our Lord."

Herbert turns to Basil.

"Pure venom," he says. "Even by Edna's standards."

"I detest that woman," Basil responds.

"She loves you too."

"I fear the time of my departure draws near."

"Maybe if you apologized ..."

"I've done what I've come here to do. More or less."

He's not so sure.

"You can fight this," Herbert insists. "All you have to do is show them you're not some bloodthirsty, sex-crazed goatfucker."

"I'd love to hear your prescription for starting such a conversation."

"We're in advertising, for Christ's sake. We spin bullshit all day long."

"No, my goodbye tour begins now. I'll help you hit whatever deadlines we have to hit. I'll get to the Sand Hills one last time. I'll do whatever I can to mend the rift with Melody."

"Knowing her as well as I do, that's one Humpty Dumpty you're not likely to put back together."

"What else do we have to do for the Devil Smoke campaign?"

The overhead panels groan, a fluorescent tube sparks, and the ceiling splinters. A round and reddish-black mass falls to the floor. The stunned creature finds its feet, on spindly legs, and spins in circles, chirping nervously. Herbert leaps onto the nearest desk.

Basil can't believe his eyes. Neither can Herbert, understandably.

"It's an imp," Basil says, to himself as much as to Herbert.

The small, horned creature dives behind the base of a swivel chair.

Basil bends down and whispers gently, "Come to me, little one."

He extends an open palm, and the filthy little thing—covered in cobwebs and the white chalk of chipped plaster—steps into the harsh light. The imp makes a cradle of Basil's palm, and the master brings his child near to his face. He recognizes this Nameless imp as one of the three he chose as scouts just prior to his ascent, as one who could alert him to any disturbance afflicting Our Fiery Home in his absence.

This cannot be good.

Basil takes a deep breath and exhales.

"What news do you bring?"

The imp chirps to Basil in *Locuri,* the primitive dialect native to the tongues of all demons and imps. Basil gives a long sigh.

"When?"

The imp responds with a series of clicks and pings.

"And what of Kamala?"

The imp chirps excitedly, then sadly.

Basil sets the imp down.

"You have earned your freedom, little one," he says. "I name you, Boothe."

"Uh ... Basil," says Herbert, still crouched atop the desk. "Can you fill me in here?"

"Forgive me," he says. His eyes alternate between the gaping hole above and the pieces of wrecked ceiling scattered across the floor. "This is an imp, a breed of creature native to the underworld. To a demon, an imp is a cross between a slave, a pet and a playmate. Think of it as an aphid to an ant colony—symbiotic, to a large degree. Before I left Our Fiery Home, I tasked this little one and two others with seeking me out if conditions down below took a turn for the worse. It appears they have, to put it lightly."

"What is it?"

"Kamala has lost control and Lubos has swooped in to take her place," he says. "He intends to follow in my footsteps, you might say."

"How so?"

"He's making plans to come to the surface, and he's bringing a few friends along with him."

"Why?"

"Simple, really. He wants to right a perceived wrong. He aims to bring war and death to your people."

"What exactly does that mean?"

"It means the end."

"For your world or mine?"

"Both."

"I see."

"It is, in a word, regrettable."

"That's one way of putting it."

Herbert doesn't seem to believe what he's just heard. Or he doesn't want to. Basil can't blame him.

"Why did you call him 'Boothe'?" Herbert asks.

"It suits him, don't you think? Every demon and imp lacks a name at birth, and remains one of the Nameless until assigned such by his better. Without the gift of a name, a demon or imp lacks freedom of movement. At least that's what they are told, as a way to restrain them, to protect against revolt. They're prisoners, fearful. It's why so many stay in Our Fiery Home. It seems Lubos has undone that protection."

"So what becomes of Boothe now?"

"If he's like the others, he'll likely roam up here for a bit. He'll tire of the landscape in time. Chances are he'll find his way back to the underworld. For most of our kind, Our Fiery Home is the only place that makes sense."

"What are you going to do now?"

"I'm afraid my timeline has changed. I must stop Lubos."

An hour later, Basil ventures out into the parking lot, with Boothe perched on his shoulder. The crowd envelops him, and he swings his beefy arms, thorn-tipped elbows out, enough to enjoy a wide berth. He pushes through the crowd and heads toward the last row in the parking lot, where he finds his toppled noisemaker, shiny with bodily fluids. He runs a smooth palm over the chassis to wipe away the sheen of mucous and urine. The words DIE DEVIL DIE have been etched white into the black paint. He clenches his teeth, revs the engine and then speeds away, leaving the jeering crowd at his back.

\* \* \*

At the mouth of a side street, two whiskered men dressed in leather, chainmail and denim, each astride a motorcycle—all black paint and polished chrome—wait in the shade of a towering elm. One of the motorcycles has a sidecar bearing the weight of a silent passenger: a life-size model of a human skeleton outfitted in chaps and a patched-up denim vest, its skull protected by a strapped-on German *Stahlhelm* with a sharpened silver spike on its crown.

After watching the demon speed away on a Harley that looks all too familiar, the two bikers bark over their grumbling engines and nod in agreement. One of them points to the four-story stucco building and drags his finger across his throat. The other smiles and nods in assent.

The two Harleys roar to life. A second later, only the fumes of cooked fuel linger in their place.

## Chapter 28

# The Quiet Chorus of Smashed Redbirds

Peace. The first suggestion of daylight creeps across the horizon and kisses the smudged glass of the east-facing windows. As the darkness recedes, the sun paints the living-room wall a soft orange.

Basil smiles to welcome his last day on the surface, above ground, among humans.

He stares at the trench his hooves have made in the living-room carpet, the result of nearly nine hours of incessant pacing. He hasn't slept all night. No time for sleep, only for reflecting on earth-bound delights. Boothe, the imp, has curled up in a tight ball beneath the television. Basil shakes away the flower of jealousy, wishing for a mind settled enough to indulge in sleep.

He has reached his decision. His time on the surface, with only the sky overhead, has reached its inevitable end. He will return to the realm of rock and fire. Given Boothe's revelation, he hopes to find something left to rule when he gets there.

Boothe stirs as Basil clicks on the TV. A talking head from the local news station extols the joys of another sunny day: high of eighty-three, on the cooler side for late August, a few clouds and a steady wind blowing in from the southeast. He checks the clock, which tells him it's almost seven a.m.

The plan: First, fry up a dozen eggs and however much bacon he has left in the freezer, fill his belly, then ride his noisemaker out to the Sand Hills for one last quiet stroll through the woods and meadows, and end the day with a bath in the creek, only the minnows and pollywogs to keep him company.

He envisions the scene: plopping down in the middle of the creek to wash every limb and scrub the rim of every orifice; lying in the pebbled streambed and staring at the cloudless blue sky, framed by branches whose leaves have begun to yellow; and letting the cool water plug his ears, invade his pores, so he can absorb each drop as a way to take at least part of the creek with him.

Eventually he will dry off and head to the office so he can resign. The goodbyes will be difficult. Only Herbert will listen. Only Herbert will care. Basil will do what he can to mend fences with Melody, though he imagines a best-case scenario in which she tells him to go fuck himself, which would suggest she actually gives a lick. He'd choose revulsion over indifference any day.

He turns off the TV and sits in the middle of the living-room floor, facing the open window and the flowering dawn. He closes his eyes, his lips curling into a smile as the sun warms his face and naked chest.

* * *

Three middle-aged men in white short-sleeve shirts, bright-blue neckties and wrinkled khakis struggle to raise the twelve-foot-tall wooden cross. As they ease the base into a hastily dug hole, two of them steady the cross while the third fills the hole with dirt and loose gravel.

Edna Babych steps forward to test the cross's stability. It wobbles at her slight touch. She squints from the sunlight reflecting off the glass of the four-story building in which the beast does its earthly business.

"Shoddy," she says. "A stiff wind will blow it over. Do better."

"I don't even know why you want this thing here," says Ned Lavender, the church's music director. Sweat beads his brow. "It's purely for show."

"Not if I have anything to say about it," she whispers. "I hope that damned devil vomits when he sees this, boy."

She steps back to admire her handiwork, the horizontal beam blocking out the morning sun. The sight makes her smile, but it's not quite good enough. Not yet.

"Anything worth doing is worth doing to the Lord's satisfaction," she says. "This"—she waves at the unsteady cross—"this will not please the Lord."

Officer Pierce, who has been patrolling the parking lot since dawn, steps toward Edna's group. Keys jangle at his belt.

"Do you have a permit for this?" he asks.

"This isn't hurting anyone," Edna tells him. "Now move along, Barney Fife. What you should be doing is marching right inside that building to arrest that flipping brute. Raping that poor girl and all. Did you ask him if he had a permit to do that? He's not even American, you know."

"No one said anything about rape, Edna."

"Oh, what in the blazes do you know about anything?"

Edna wears a new accessory: a figurine of Christ liberated from a foot-tall crucifix that she yanked from the wall of her home. The Christ figurine dangles from her neck by a thick nylon cord, an eyebolt bored into the center of the Nazarene's thorn-pricked head. She massages the wooden Christ with the fingers of her right hand to ease the weight of this new burden. Her body demands sleep and sustenance, but first she must appease her god.

She's too busy thinking of how to pin the demon to the oversized cross to notice the disturbance. It's far off at first, riding the wind, but the din builds into a deafening rumble that shakes the earth. The sound reminds her of a fleet of semis strafing the highway. She turns to see an unbroken line of leather, chrome and black paint, approaching from the south. A black-and-orange Harley-Davidson with a passenger in its sidecar leads the procession into the lot.

Edna's feet remain firmly in place. Her acolytes make subtle moves to hide behind their peers, edging toward the safety of the office building. Officer Pierce takes a reluctant step forward and perches his hands on his belt buckle.

The lead Harley rumbles to a stop a mere fifteen feet from Officer Pierce. A crush of Harleys file in behind the leader, clogging the lot—no coming or going for anyone. Two motorcycles brush past Pierce and ride the sidewalk to its end at the building's main entrance. They park in front of the doorway, a makeshift barricade. Across the lot, four more motorcycles skip the curb and chew up the grass, presumably taking up residence at the building's two other entrances. The motorcycles—thirty of them in all, by Edna's best guess—kill their engines in unison, more or less.

"I want three of you at every exit," the man on the lead Harley barks to the rest of the pack. His voice, friendly and calm, carries a hint of Georgia or Texas or Tennessee—some red state far below the Mason-Dixon Line. He removes a pair of black leather gloves and tosses them into the lap of the helmeted skeleton sitting in the sidecar. Unlike his ghastly passenger, the man wears no helmet: only mirrored aviator sunglasses, scuffed black boots, a short-sleeved black T-shirt, tattered blue jeans and a road-weary denim vest with the word FANG patched onto one breast and the word CLAW patched onto the other. He steps off the bike and approaches Officer Pierce.

"You can't park here, not like that," Pierce says, a bit sheepishly. He shuffles his feet, trying to stand tall, likely because the biker has at least six inches on him.

"Sure thing, Officer. We'll be out of your hair just as soon as we tend to some private business."

He steps toward Pierce, arm outstretched and palm open. Pierce moves to accept the gesture.

In one swift stroke, the man in the Fang and Claw vest pulls a Buck knife from his belt and thrusts the glinting tip into the soft space beneath Pierce's chin. Pierce goes rigid, eyes wide, as the man advances the eight-inch blade through the soft palate, the septum, the brain and, finally, the crown of the eggshell-soft skull. Pierce's lifeless body falls to the ground, the blade still in place, dug in up to the hilt.

Nearly a dozen bikers stride past Pierce's body, past the klatch of shocked Methodists, showing no emotion. The bikers encircle the building. Some stop at points of ingress, while others venture inside.

Edna, unfazed by Pierce's murder, stands by her oversized cross, arms folded under her well-hidden breasts.

"I don't know why you had to go and do a silly thing like that," she says to the man in the denim vest.

"No one's going to get hurt who doesn't deserve it," he tells her. "You all right with that?"

"That all depends," she says.

"We're here for the demon."

Manna from Heaven, she thinks. Manna from Heaven.

"Get in line," she tells him.

He smiles and bows courteously. He extends a callused hand for her to shake.

"I'm Ronald," he offers. "My brothers and I have come to collect a debt."

"I hope you take his head and leave the rest to burn."

The Lord has answered her prayers, though she expected God's messengers to look different than these hooligans. Then again, why should she care how they look if they're able to slay the damned critter or at least send it hobbling back to Hell, preferably in small pieces?

"Ronald," she says, tasting the word on her tongue. "I thought you'd have a Biblical name."

"Well, honey," he says, pausing to light a Camel and suck smoke through its marbled filter, "I'm no angel."

"I like your sidecar skeleton. What's the significance?"

He leans in and whispers, "I like to tell the boys that death rides with me, and they like it when I say things like 'at. But to tell it right, I just like the way it looks." He nods toward the building. "He in there?"

"The beast? It might be, but I haven't seen it today. Sneaky bugger. If not, you'll find plenty of coconspirators inside who carouse with it, enable it, help to spread its poison. Subhumans, if you ask me. Let them sleep in the beds they made, as far as I'm concerned. Start with the hussy attorney on the first floor."

"We'll see what happens."

"A favor, Ronald," she says. "Make the bastard suffer."

"Count on it."

"And once you've beaten it to a pulp, I'd be honored if you'd permit me an indulgence: Drag it out here so I can spike it through the heart, if it has one."

Ronald drops the Camel to the asphalt and extinguishes the butt beneath the toe of his boot. He strides toward the building and steps inside, five or six of his Fang and Claw brothers filing in behind him.

Edna looks to a cloudbank sailing in from the east, the only break in an otherwise all-blue sky. She sinks to her knees and clasps her hands together, grateful for the gift delivered by her bloodthirsty god.

\* \* \*

When the telephone's obnoxious ring stirs Basil from his meditation, he's surprised to see the clock has advanced the time to nearly nine thirty. He can count on one hand how many times the phone has voiced its raucous rings since he moved in, and every one of them had been a wrong number. He holds the receiver to his ear and hears labored breaths, followed by whispers. A few seconds pass before he realizes the man on the other end of the line is Herbert.

"I was just thinking about you," Basil tells him.

"You have to get here now," Herbert says. His voice is unsteady.

"Bulcavage riding your ass for the new Devil Smoke copy?"

"They have the place surrounded. They might have a bomb. They're looking for you."

"More Edna nonsense?"

"Not Edna. Bikers. Dozens of them, by my count. They call themselves 'Fang and Claw,' or something like that. Basil, they have guns. Hurry."

"Is Melody all right?"

"I don't know, but—"

The phone goes dead in Basil's ear.

His thick fingers dial the office number, but the call does not go through.

*The number you have dialed has been changed, disconnected or—*

He hangs up.

Was this Herbert's idea of a joke? A ploy to get him to delay his return to Our Fiery Home, to make him stay in Beak? If so, he considers how harsh of a punishment his well-meaning friend deserves. But ... what if? He scours his memory for proof that he told Herbert about his run-in with the bikers at Beak Tavern. No, not to his recollection. So, what if the Fang and Claw Motorcycle Club had tracked him down and come to exact vengeance?

He clops into the kitchen and steps in a curled-up pile of shit left by his impish houseguest, mashing the feces into dimples in the linoleum. He rifles through some loose papers on the counter until he finds a piece of paper bearing a poem he wrote, with Melody's business card stapled to the upper left corner. He takes the phone in his hand, wavering over whether to call, just to be safe. If he dials and Audrey Pernie picks up, he can just hang up—mystery solved, crisis averted.

He punches the digits into the keypad and hears the same ominous refrain: *The number you have dialed has been changed, disconnected or—*

"Just forget it," the voice tells Basil. "Just forget them. You have enough wars to fight."

The voice is right. He has a kingdom to reclaim. He'll never see Herbert or Melody or Bulcavage again, so why should he care? He could drive out to Patriot Rock, crash his noisemaker into the nearest ditch and wander across the golden field until he finds the mouth of the cave that will lead him back to Our Fiery Home.

The voice reminds him: "Whatever problems the humans have manufactured are theirs to solve."

After all, Herbert thinks his copywriter is an asshole.

Melody couldn't care if he lives or dies.

Bulcavage is scum.

Leaving them all behind is the *only* choice.

At least, it should be.

Sense retakes him. He panics, not for himself but for the humans—*his* humans. If the Fang and Claw has tracked him to his place of business, they likely know where he calls home too. He scoops up Boothe and rushes from the apartment to the next door down, banging frantically on the cheap wood. He scans the parking lot for signs of an ambush. Finally he hears the lock being undone, and the door opens to reveal his neighbor, the bleary-eyed, messy-haired Chester, still in his sleeping clothes: a sleeveless white T-shirt, plaid pajama bottoms, a single argyle sock.

"To what displeasure do I owe this great insult?"

"You're in danger, Chester. On my account, I'm afraid. Put on your shoes and come with me."

"The apocalypse isn't scheduled for another twenty years, give or take. Wake me when we get to critical mass."

Chester closes the door.

Basil's hurled fist separates the door from its hinges. Chester sprawls to the carpet. Basil grabs Chester by the ankle and drags him toward the exit.

"Okay, dickhead, I'm awake now," says Chester, calmly. Boothe finds a perch on Chester's gut, chirping with glee. "What the fuck is this little maggot?"

"His name is Boothe. Unimportant. We must go. Now."

"I assume you think you have a good reason for this intrusion, so I'll refrain from trouncing you, but please don't drag me across the concrete. I have two working legs, you know."

Basil lifts Chester off the floor and leads him to the parking lot.

"There may be bad men coming here, looking for me," Basil says. "I don't pretend to know what they might do. Tell me someplace safe I can take you."

"The tavern opens at ten."

"Climb on."

Basil mounts his noisemaker, and Chester gets on behind him. Boothe inserts himself between the two. They speed off, Chester barking in Basil's ear—"Turn right, turn left, another left, I have to throw up"—until they arrive at a single-story all-brick building with three pickup trucks in the parking lot. A gray-haired man as squat as the building itself keys open the front door, and four men in ball caps line up behind him.

"You can drop me here," Chester says.

Basil pulls up to the front door and lets Chester off the bike. Basil eyes his friend—stained white shirt, threadbare pajama bottoms, shoeless—and smiles.

"I'm taking leave of you, my friend," he says. "Time for me to go home and see what's left of the place. I'll miss our talks. Please do take care of yourself."

Chester inhales deeply, offering a smile of his own.

"I'll drink to that," he says. "May the gods, or whatever power compels you, assist you in your journey into the cold fires of Hades."

He claps Basil on the back. He then yanks off the sole argyle sock and hands it to Boothe. The imp promptly shreds the fabric.

As Chester disappears into the darkened doorway of the public house, Basil angles the noisemaker onto the road and speeds toward the office. His mind races between worlds, imagining the fights that await him in each. First things first: the Fang and Claw. He knows he can best a hundred men, maybe a thousand, but not their weapons—their cherished firearms. He recalls his wounded horn, where the bullet bit him. Even now he can feel pieces of the bullet lodged within him, something unnatural that has been working to poison his blood and deaden his flesh.

His thoughts take him back to Our Fiery Home, back to Kamala. He knows Lubos would not have been kind to her.

Something lies in the road ahead, right on the faded yellow line dividing northbound from southbound. As the noisemaker slows, he studies the smashed carcass of a redbird—a northern cardinal. Its fleshy parts fill every crevice, its broken feathers pointing up at perverted angles. The sight recalls a conversation he had with Chester during one of their wine- and whiskey-soaked evenings on the patio. Twenty minutes into one of his drunken rants, Chester recounted the alleged origins of Beak.

"This was the Eighteen Twenties, maybe the early Eighteen Thirties," Chester said. "Back then there wasn't much to do here but work in the fields, pray in the churches and hunt the shit out of any living thing that came within blasting distance. Back then, Beak ... well, it wasn't Beak just yet, but regardless of the name the town went by at that point in history, the place was overrun with birds of every sort: robin, cardinal, jay, bittern, thrush, bunting, woodpecker, hawk, egret, owl—you name it. Something about the wind patterns and migratory routes and the copious vegetation on the edge of the Sand Hills. Flocks of every feather, with so many birds taking wing, the sky looked black rather than blue. The embarrassment of avian riches didn't last too long, of course.

"The morons killed everything, as morons tend to do. Farmers poisoned anything they suspected of spreading disease or harming a hair on the head of a single steer. Hat makers issued bounties for birds with the brightest, most intricate plumage, which, of course, the birds didn't give freely.

"One day a man named Osmond Ricketts walked into a public house at the edge of town. Word has it he got into a dustup with the barkeep, the barkeep telling Mister Ricketts he wasn't welcome back until he could settle his considerable debts. Imagine. So the next morning the barkeep comes in to open up the pub and finds a dead goshawk nailed to the front door, its wings outstretched and the dollar amount Mister Ricketts owed—let's call it ten bucks, which would have been a fortune at the time—stuffed right into the bird's bloody kisser. And that's how Beak became Beak, or at least that's how it got its name."

Basil can't help but wonder if he should look for meaning in the smashed redbird—a lone wanderer, a casualty of being in the wrong place at the wrong time, its corpse left to rot on the sheet of warm, black rock. If he is to meet his end, either at the hands of gun-toting bikers or at the talons of demons on the eve of all-out war, he hopes to do what the poor little smashed redbird could not: take as many of his enemies along with him, to share his fate.

The landscape changes, from cornfields and lonesome tractors tilling earth to lightly crowded storefronts. He enters downtown, or what passes for downtown in Beak, and estimates he's less than a mile from the office. He decides to leave the noisemaker behind and go the rest of the way on hoof, surreptitiously, to avoid getting torn up in a hail of bullets. He pulls the noisemaker into an unused spot in front of the feed-and-tack store and lets the front tire glance the curb. As he kills the engine, a massive vehicle pulls up alongside him, horn blaring. He nearly shits himself.

"It *is* you!" the driver yells in a shrill voice. "My God, Basil!"

He recognizes the woman's voice, knows her face, but he can't quite place her.

"Mary Jane!" she reminds him. "Mary Jane Pix, from the unemployment office! It's been an age!"

"Of course, Miss. Pix," Basil says, calming. "How nice to see you."

"Who's your little friend?"

"Oh, him," he says. He motions to Boothe, prancing on the leather seat behind him, a strip of argyle dangling from its mouth. "Just an imp."

"You've been on my mind. When I heard you got the job at Savage, I was so happy. How's everything going?"

"Oh, you know. Keeping me busy."

"Wonderful. I'm so pleased I was able to help in some small way."

"Immensely."

"Listen, you look busy, so I'll let you get to wherever you've got to get to. Don't be a stranger."

She prepares to back out of the spot.

"Miss. Pix!"

She presses the brake, and the brake pads squeal against the rotors.

"Do you know the way to the office building where I work?"

"Of course."

"I don't suppose you would mind giving me a ride."

## Chapter 29

# Counting

Basil leans into Mary Jane Pix's ear and explains his theory: Heavily armed bikers have overrun the office building and taken hostages in an attempt to lure him to his death. Some of Beak's finest citizens are likely in grave danger, "including the woman I love," he adds, mostly for effect.

Mary Jane Pix replies, simply, "Get in."

Basil has a willing accomplice.

He climbs into the back of her cloud-blue Chevy Suburban and asks if they should contact the police. She answers, "Those loaves of dog shit? The sheriff couldn't hit the side of a barn with a shot bullet if the wall was ten feet in front of him. The only thing he'd shoot without aiming is his own foot, which I think he's done twice now. You're better off on your own."

Mary Jane suggests a drive-by to scope out the situation, rather than going in "all willy-nilly," and Basil agrees. She pulls up to the mouth of the parking lot and rolls by slow enough for a look but fast enough to not draw attention, or gunfire. Basil peers over the seat cushion and sees as many as thirty motorcycles crowding the lot. Six or seven bikers mill about with some of Edna's basket-case klatch, though he can't quite get a sense of the dynamic. Two or three more bikers stand guard at the nearest entrance. A heap lies motionless on the ground—another smashed redbird, by the looks of it, this one human.

"Weird," Mary Jane says. "Want me to circle back for another pass?"

For a Midwestern woman with no experience in combat or professional subterfuge, she has surprisingly keen instincts.

"I think I've seen what I need to see," Basil says. "Tell you what: Let me out on the other side of those woods."

She makes a left down the first gravel-strewn road past the parking lot entrance—Echo Glen Lane, according to Mary Jane, in homage to a shuttered quarry nearby—and they gain a vantage point of the building's other two entrances. A pair of bikers stands guard at each doorway. The building disappears behind a wall of bark and leaves. Mary Jane makes another left and then parks the Suburban on a residential street, a row of modest colonials on one side and a stand of chokecherries, buckeyes and towering silver maples on the other. He climbs out of the Suburban and stretches his legs. Boothe follows, doing figure eights around the vehicle's rear tires.

"Thank you, Miss. Pix," Basil says. "Again, you have proven yourself to be indispensible. I won't forget you."

"Wait," she says, reaching behind her, into the back seat. "You'll want this."

She hands him a shiny nickel-plated revolver.

"It's fully loaded," she says. "Twenty-two long rifle. You can take out six of those bastards if luck goes your way."

She places the gun in his palm and shows him how to hold it, how to fire it and, more or less, how to kill a man without being close enough to see the color of his irises.

His index finger is too thick to squeeze into the space between the trigger and the trigger guard, so he hands the gun back. He doesn't want the weapon anyway—much too crude and imprecise for the task at hand. He rounds the front of the Suburban and, with a friendly wave, steps into the woods. Boothe trails him, chirping absentmindedly. As Mary Jane pulls away, birdsong and the soft, slow whispers of wind-brushed foliage replace the grumbling of the Suburban's engine.

An odd feeling sweeps through him—a mix of calmness and gratitude. He knows he should be strategizing, but he can't help but feel thankful for having met humans such as Mary Jane Pix. He compares the saint in Mary Jane with the devil in Edna Babych, wondering how two members of the same species could differ so greatly. This, in turn, makes him wonder if he can salvage Our Fiery Home. He always assumed every demon wanted to either lead or be led, to dominate or be dominated, with no room in between. Living here, among the humans, has taught him otherwise. If he wants something else from a life underground, something more than pain and punishment, perhaps so do the others. Many of his fellow demons would follow Lubos to their doom for a chance at something better, while others would follow purely because they see an opportunity to plunder, set ablaze or otherwise annihilate everything their eyes show them.

This, he decides, is a problem for tomorrow.

For now he must contend with the Fang and Claw.

For a hundred yards he sees only fallen leaves, moss-coated rock and columns of gray-brown bark. The trees thin to reveal glimpses of the stucco and tinted glass of his office building. He sneaks behind a tall silver maple at the tree line and leans into the trunk. As he digs his talons into the peeling bark and feels the rough skin against his own, he whispers, "Remember this." He eyes the building's northwest corner—the only one without an entrance, meaning the only one without guards—and mulls his plan of attack. Mary Jane Pix probably would have known how to proceed, he figures, wishing her back by his side.

Evergreen shrubs encircle the building, each one two or three feet taller than him. The shrubs will make fine cover. He nods, takes a deep breath and steels himself against the silver maple.

"You stay here," he commands Boothe. "You stay."

The imp takes a break from gnawing an exposed root and eyes its master quizzically, and then returns to the root with a newfound hunger.

Basil bolts toward the building, the earth soft and hollow beneath his thunderous hooves. He slams into the stucco behind the nearest shrub.

No shots fired. First step completed without carnage. Now all he has to do is slip inside the building without detection, infiltrate the hive, and kill every well-armed intruder along the way—all without causing the deaths of Herbert or Melody, or incurring any mortal wounds of his own.

"Details," he whispers. He hugs the side of the building as he moves, feeling the stucco nip at his bare back.

A smoker's cough breaks the silence, and Basil embraces the nearest evergreen. He breathes deeply, hoping the piney scent will settle his nerves. Cigarette smoke fills his nostrils, and anger replaces his fear. He peeks through the fronds of the evergreen and sees two bikers jawing. As he prepares to lunge, a mourning dove takes flight, cooing as it goes. The two bikers turn and approach, each with a shiny black pistol drawn. As the first one turns the corner, Basil steps out from behind the shrub. He grabs the man by his denim vest and hurls him against the side of the building. Bones snap and pop, shattered stucco falls to the ground in a heap.

*One down, twenty more to go. More or less. Hopefully less.*

The second biker, shocked, watches a Fang and Claw brother in his final convulsing throes. Basil thrusts his right hoof into the man's face. The head detaches from the body and sails into a patch of grass fifteen yards away. It rolls to a stop at the gravelly edge of Echo Glen Lane.

*Two.*

Basil drags the headless corpse into the shrub line.

"You two useless fucks all right?"

The throaty yell comes from the entrance at the building's southeast corner. Basil squats by the evergreen and waits. The metal of a dropped pistol glints in the sunlight, and Basil curses himself for his fat fingers. Three more bikers approach—two with pistols, the other with a hunting knife nearly as long as a machete. Basil grabs two by the throat and slams them together, repeatedly, until their faces turn to red pulp. Their pistols tumble to the ground. One of the guns sheds a bullet.

*Three and four.*

The third rushes forward, eager to plunge the knife into Basil's soft middle. Basil drops the dead man in his left hand and uses the one in his right as a weapon. He swings the corpse like a club, and one skull cracks against another. The unused knife falls noiselessly to the dirt.

*Five.*

"There!"

Basil looks up to see Edna Babych with her arm extended, her index finger pointing the way for those who wish to end his life. She stands stone still, but the cross-less Christ dangling from her neck seems to rattle against her breastbone.

Basil turns toward the entrance and slips inside. As he locks the door behind him, shots fire. Glass shatters to the floor. Priorities: First, make sure Melody is safe, and then get Herbert and anyone else who needs his help. He creeps down the hall toward Melody's first-floor office and sees at least seven bikers moving toward him. Change of plans. As he enters the nearest stairwell, he catches two bikers by surprise—*six and seven*—and climbs to the landing on the second floor. He peers around the corner to see two more bikers standing guard outside the door to Savage Communications. Each holds a long, black assault rifle.

Time to change tactics.

"I'm here," he says as he steps into the open.

They train their rifles on him.

"Holy Christ," one of them says. "Hunter wasn't shitting. Look at that fucker!"

"I'm not here to fight," Basil says.

"We got him," the other says into a walkie-talkie.

"Peachy," crackles a voice on the walkie-talkie's other end. "Bring him in."

The men with the heavy artillery open the door to Savage Communications. One of them uses the rifle's muzzle to nudge Basil inside. Basil complies, and he plants his hooves squarely on the carpet of the reception area.

"Well? Where we going?"

"The meetin' room," says one of the bikers.

Basil nods and follows the hallway toward the conference room. He imagines Herbert and Bulcavage lying dead on the floor, pooled in gore, Karen bent over a chair with her ass in the air and panties around her ankles. He shakes the image from his head as he creaks open the door to the conference room. He's relieved to see all three of his co-workers alive. Bulcavage sits at the head of the table, stoic as ever. Karen sits next to him, trembling, with her face buried in her cupped hands. Herbert sits by himself on the edge of a credenza, trying to look like he's not about to shit his pants.

Basil's attention turns to another man in the room, emerging from the corner over Bulcavage's left shoulder. He's tall—almost seven feet, by Basil's best guess—thin and muscular, skin dark from the sun. Salt-and-pepper whiskers stubble his chiseled face. He wears a black T-shirt emblazoned with a coiled silver cobra, a long knife dangling from his belt. Bluish-black tattoos color the skin of both forearms: a row of serrated shark's teeth encircling his right wrist; a viper biting its tail constricting the left; a flaming black billiard ball with the number sixty-nine in its center; the caricature of the devil astride a motorcycle, the handlebars made of bone, the wheels more like circles of flame, complete with a banner that reads, "Chew the Road"; and a young girl's cherubic face, with feathered wings on either side, and the name "Laura" scrawled beneath. The man gives a shrill whistle and says, "My, my, my. You are quite a specimen, ain't you?"

More bikers file into the conference room behind Basil, including the one from Beak Tavern so many weeks ago—the one who got away.

"All of you should leave now," Basil replies.

"We just got here, and we're enjoying the hospitality of our gracious host," the tall man says. "Ain't that right, Robert?"

"You two know each other?" Basil asks.

"We're just starting to become acquainted," the man says. "I'm Ronald, and it's a pleasure to meet someone of your … stature. Wouldn't have guessed someone like you existed, to be frank. When Hunter here told me about the misunderstanding at the bar a while back, I figured he just lost his mind somewhere along the way. But I'd say he's right on the money. You are a beauty. Have a seat."

Basil stays put.

"As long as you're comfortable," Ronald says. "So. We find ourselves in a bit of a pickle, don't we? You left two of my brothers dead and bleeding on the floor of that shitty roadside bar. True?"

"They're dead."

"Good of you to admit it," Ronald says. "I respect a man who owns up to the things he's done. Now, shit happens from time to time. I'll grant you that. But you took something that doesn't belong to you. One of our bikes, I mean. True?"

Basil nods.

"See. Now that I just can't abide. The way I see it, you owe me a debt."

"Consider it paid. Get up, Herbert."

Herbert leans off the edge of the credenza.

"Sit down, Herbert," Ronald says, his eyes not leaving Basil's. He pulls a revolver from the small of his back. He cocks the hammer.

"I don't doubt my boys were being pricks as usual. In fact, I expect it. So you did what you thought you had to do. No foul there. My issue is with the bike."

"You can have it," Basil says. "I no longer need it."

"I'm afraid it's not that simple, amigo."

"Just take it and go. You've made your point."

One of the bikers approaches Ronald and whispers in his ear.

"Looks like the body count just keeps on growing," Ronald

says. "My boys just informed me of your handiwork downstairs. I'm impressed. But I can't let you walk out of here. It would make me look bad. And that's a damned shame, because you and me? I bet we'd get along famously under different circumstances. But you always have to consider the circumstances." He pauses. "Robert?"

"Yes?" Bulcavage lifts his eyes.

"You're first."

"To do what?"

Ronald holds the revolver to Bulcavage's head and pulls the trigger. Tangles of Bulcavage's brain paint the wall. Bulcavage falls forward. His face slams into the table, the chair kicks backward, and the body flops onto the floor. Karen screams and bolts from her chair. She runs straight into a thick glass pane and knocks herself unconscious.

"Sort of figured she wouldn't get far," Ronald says, laughing.

The two bikers with rifles flank Basil.

"Yeah, it's a damned shame we didn't meet sooner, amigo," Ronald says. He steps toward Basil and again cocks the hammer. "Open wide."

"His rack of antlers will dress up your trophy wall real nice, boss," says one of the bikers at Basil's side.

"Shut up, moron," Ronald says. "Respect the process."

Basil does as instructed and opens his mouth.

Ronald moves the revolver into Basil's maw until the muzzle touches the tip of the sandpaper tongue, the front sight an inch below the enamel of Basil's front teeth.

"I'll be gentle," Ronald says.

Basil closes his mouth around the pistol and wrenches it from Ronald's hand, taking the index finger up to the first knuckle. Ronald drops to his knees, eyes wide at the spurting stump. Basil swats the rifle away from the biker standing closest to him and then sends the man face first into the drywall. He kicks the other one between the legs, feels the man's genitals pop against the keratin of his hoof. He then turns to collect Herbert and runs straight through the thick glass pane, into the hallway, toward the exit. He deftly slits the throats of two bikers standing just outside the office door. They crumple to the floor and watch their carotids run dry.

*Eight, nine.*

Shots fire as Basil turns the corner, and an ember bores into his side. He enters the staircase and meets a waiting muzzle. Basil brushes the gun aside and thrusts two fingers—index and middle—into the gun bearer's eyes, fishing around until they find the brain.

*Ten.*

Basil hears a door open downstairs, followed by the clamor of more men eager to meet their doom. The smells of fear and tobacco smoke find his nostrils. Basil studies the panic on Herbert's face, calculates the chances of his friend surviving a firefight in the close quarters of a stairwell—far too slim for his liking—so he chooses the only other option: flee.

"Don't you worry," he whispers. "We'll get out of this yet."

He tightens his grip around Herbert's waist and bounds up the staircase. He turns the corner, wincing from the red-hot slag of metal that has ripped his side wide open, and sees the exit door, mercifully unguarded.

\* \* \*

"Just calm down and be quiet," Melody says.

"I don't want to die in here," says Audrey Pernie, her voice piercing, her words rapid. "I want to go home."

"If you shut up and calm the fuck down, you will," Melody responds. "Now stay away from the goddamned door."

The door rattles, and Audrey peeks over the desk to see two silhouettes through the frosted glass. The handle shakes, and then a second time with more intent. Something hard and metallic taps against the glass—the muzzle of a gun, Melody assumes, or maybe the butt of a knife.

"We see you in there," says a hardened voice. "Now open up and say *ahhhh*."

Metal hits glass once more, hard and loud. Audrey gets up and runs away screaming.

"Damn it to Christ, Audrey!" Melody seethes. She backs away from the reception desk and crawls on all fours to find a suitable weapon.

A series of hollow thuds echoes through the office, and Melody follows the sound to the conference room, where Audrey slaps her palms against a tinted window, pleading for help from the outside world. Melody hurries to her office and rummages through the drawers of her desk for a letter opener, a screwdriver, a stapler with some heft—anything to fend off an attacker. Her fingertips brush the cold marble of a paperweight with sharp edges.

The glass entryway shatters and falls to the floor in a sheet.

And just like that, Audrey has new justification for her shrieking.

* * *

The biker named Hunter slicks his finger against the trigger as he leads seven would-be assassins up the dimly lit stairwell. His left hand cradles the barrel of the Remington pump-action shotgun, ready to blow a hole the size of a bowling ball through the demon's chest—just as Ronald instructed before Hunter left the conference room.

"No more fucking around with this shit-heel," Ronald barked, swaddling his newly four-fingered hand in a T-shirt cut from the back of a slain Fang and Claw brother. "Take no chances. When you see the fucker, blast him. And put a bullet in that faggot friend of his too."

Other than the motionless bodies of more of his fallen brothers, Hunter sees no trace of the demon on the second floor or the abandoned third. Then, he finds the first breadcrumb: a thick bead of nearly black blood, congealing in the gritty treads of a concrete stair. He turns the corner slowly, sees more blood—small puddles rather than discrete drops—and eyeballs the exit door leading to the roof. A bloody handprint browns on the silvery finish of the door's push bar.

"Fucker's on the roof," Hunter says into a walkie-talkie. "And he's hurt."

"Slaughter the son of a bitch," Ronald hisses from the other end, his voice laced with static.

"Aye-aye," Hunter replies. "Nowhere for him to go but down."

He motions his band of killers forward, and creeps up the last eight steps. He inhales deeply and heaves on the push bar. The door flies open, and air and sunlight flood the stairwell. As his eyes adjust, Hunter sees the demon standing in the center of the rooftop—an all-black silhouette, featureless, against the all-blue sky. The demon drops slowly to his knees. Gravel crunches beneath the immense weight.

"I'm yours," the demon growls. "Come and get me."

No sign of the demon's human friend, the one Ronald had deemed a queer in need of culling.

"Surround him," Hunter says to his brothers, and they cautiously obey, muzzles trained on their target. "I'll find the pansy."

Hunter zeroes in on a low-profile Rheem HVAC unit near the roof's far corner. It's the only place for the pansy to hide, unless he already jumped. Either way, problem solved. Hunter tramps the rooftop gravel, taking note of the spectacular view and the strong wind as he approaches the HVAC unit. The unit makes a loud, mechanical hum. He turns the corner to see the demon's human friend crouched in a ball, his back to the HVAC unit, staring at the roof's raised lip only ten to twelve feet away.

"I should make you jump," Hunter says to him. "You probably wouldn't die right away, likely break every bone you got. But I'm going to do it quick and painless, even though it ain't what you deserve."

Hunter grasps the shotgun's forend, braces the stock against his shoulder and raises the barrel until the muzzle tells him there's no chance of missing his target.

"Say good night, fuck-face."

As his finger touches the trigger, he hears the din of footfall grinding on gravel. He turns to see a black blur speeding toward him. He takes an instinctive step backward, raising the gun as he retreats. He pulls the trigger as the demon hurtles into him, driving the breath from his lungs, and the two tumble off the edge of the roof.

## Chapter 30

# What It Means to Suffer

Melody wonders if she can succeed where Audrey failed. Huddled beneath the conference room table, she eyes the tinted glass separating her from the freedom of escape. The window would probably withstand a bullet, let alone a hurled chair.

As Audrey squeals, Melody sees her receptionist's yellow locks in the grip of a beefy biker wearing a sleeveless denim jacket, arms painted with ink. A second biker in the same uniform, this one squat and balding, follows close behind. He eggs his friend on, adjusts his crotch with his free hand.

"Stop playing around and get to it already," says the shorter of the two.

"Let me go, let me go, let me go," Audrey begs, mewling like a trapped cat.

"Don't worry, sweetheart," says the biker with a handful of her hair. "As soon as I have a taste of that peach fuzz you got down below, you'll be free as a dirty bird."

Melody clenches her teeth as the bikers drag Audrey out of the office, into the hallway. Another door opens, and Audrey's squealing ends abruptly as the door comes to a muffled close. Although she's more terrified now than when the bikers broke through the door and started taunting, "Here, piggy-piggy," Melody decides to wait. A new sound chills her blood: the door to the conference room hissing open. A pair of big, black, cowboy boots, overlapped by worn blue jeans, eases past. She hears the strike of a match as the man lights a cigarette. The door opens and closes again, but Melody can't see around the end of the table to know if she's alone again, if she's safe. She crouches low to the floor and looks into the hallway, seeing no one. She peers around the edge of the table, exposing herself, and that's when she realizes she's caught.

A tall man with stubble and sunglasses sits in a cushioned chair by the door. A blood-soaked cloth swathes his right hand.

"You must be Melody," he says. "Come on out here and say hello, why don't you? Seems I could use a good attorney. I'm Ronald."

She finds her feet and brushes the wrinkles out of her skirt.

"Are you and your thugs just about finished here?" she asks calmly. "I have deadlines to meet. Besides, the cops should be here any minute."

"The more the merrier, I always say."

Ronald takes a long, deep drag on his cigarette. He removes his sunglasses and tosses them onto the sheer tabletop. They slide along the smooth surface and tumble off the edge, snapping at the bridge as they hit the floor.

"I should tell you," he says. "People are talking about you."

"And what are these people saying?"

"So glad you asked. They say you and the demon are two peas in a pod."

"You've been misinformed."

"Aw. That's not what my friend Robert Bulcavage told me. His last words, in fact, right before I varnished the walls with his gray matter. He had quite a lot to say about the pretty little thing downstairs, meaning you. He didn't use quite those words exactly, but I'll spare you his crassness."

"How kind of you."

"Now, we got a little problem. We came here to reclaim what's ours—a bike that some goat-footed son of a bitch stole from one of my fallen brothers, to be precise. I'm pretty sure you have a good idea who I mean."

"Ask Basil. It's his mess."

"Well, I could've done that, but chances are he's deader than a flattened armadillo by now, or damn near close to it. Do you believe that fucker bit off my finger?" He holds up the bloody stub for Melody to see. "I'm hoping you can tell me where it is."

"Your severed finger?"

"The fucking *bike!*" he barks.

"Sorry to disappoint you."

"I can't tell you how happy I am to hear that."

She refuses to show any emotion, but his words terrify her.

"Oh?"

"It means I can take my recompense in other ways."

He mashes his cigarette into the glass tabletop and undoes his belt buckle.

"I going to bend you over that table, and you're going to thank me while I'm giving you what you got coming. Now get that Armani ass of yours over here."

"You can go fuck yourself," she hisses. She backs into the far corner and grabs a bust of Abraham Lincoln off the cherry-wood credenza.

"Good," he says. "I like it when they fight."

She moves to her right, keeping the table between her and her attacker. His long strides help him cover ground quickly. He steps around the corner, surprising her, and nabs a fistful of her skirt. She bashes his good hand with the Lincoln bust. He yelps.

"I'm going to make you sorry you did that," he says.

She runs to the other side, toward the door, only to be thwarted by a chair that's been jammed beneath the handle.

"Enough playtime, little mouse," he says. "This cat's hungry."

He heaves the conference room table onto its side.

She has nowhere to go.

As he steps toward her, she realizes she will have to endure yet another assault. She hopes not to survive this one.

The light changes suddenly. Then comes the explosion. Glass shatters as a huge, shiny projectile sails through the window. The object slams into the half-wall, taking Ronald with it. Beads of glass spray the room, cutting Melody's face, hands and calves. As she turns, the softness of wind brushes her cheek. In the glassless window frame stands Basil, haloed by sunlight. To her left lies a broken and bloodied Ronald, a mangled motorcycle atop him. She smells gasoline.

As Basil steps into the room, glass crunching under his hooves, he looks no better than Ronald. Blood seeps from deep wounds in his head, chest and abdomen. One of his horns spears a clump of grass, with a pound of dirt held together by a web of roots.

"You all right?" he asks her.

"Splendid," she says, dropping Lincoln's bust to the floor. "Good timing."

He exhales.

Two bikers—the same two who had taken Audrey away—fill the space where the conference room door had been. Their mouths drop as they see their leader, Ronald, crushed on the floor.

Basil roars, and the denim-clad pair stumbles away.

"How many more of these pricks are there?" she asks.

"I estimated twenty to twenty-five total," Basil says. "I took care of"—he rushes through a tally—"ten or so on the perimeter and inside, another seven or eight on the roof. Let's see if this one can tell us anything."

Basil blankets Ronald in his shadow. He places his right hoof on the motorcycle and leans into it with most of his weight. Ronald winces and chokes on his own blood.

"Fuck you," Ronald says, groaning. He slaps the fuselage with his good hand, which, like the one missing the finger Basil removed with his teeth, is sticky with blood.

"On the contrary, fuck *you*," Basil says. "Tell me of your numbers."

"I can't feel my legs."

"Like I give a shit."

"I can't feel anything."

"Probably because you broke something important. How

many of these leather-bound sons of bitches came with you? Don't make me ask again."

"Twenty-two," Ronald groans. "We brought twenty-two."

"I wish you would have left like a gentleman, when I asked like a gentleman."

"If you think I'm going to beg for my life, you've got shit for brains," Ronald gurgles.

"Of course not," Basil says. "You'll live, but only because I'm not ready for you yet." He pauses for effect. "You know who I am, what I'm meant to do in this world." Another pause. "I want you to listen closely, and I want you to remember what I'm about to tell you, and to ruminate on it every day for the rest of your meaningless life: Your skinny little ass belongs to me."

Ronald wrinkles his chewed-up forehead. Blood dribbles from the soft space of his right temple, a shard of glass jutting from the wound.

"Where exactly do you think you're going when your heart stops?" Basil asks. "You'll come right to me. Sooner or later, your body will fail—and you'll come right to me."

Basil bends closer, his face contorted.

"The day your broken body ends up in one of my boiling cauldrons, you'll gain a new understanding of what it means to suffer. First goes your flesh, peeled from your body for you to eat, strip by salty strip. Then I'll take your other nine fingers, up to the knuckle, followed by each toe. Those will find a way into your belly too. Any internal organs you can do without, those will be the next to go. Your bottom jaw—consider that gone too. And that's where the real fun begins."

He slices Ronald's lower lip with a shaky talon.

"A hundred demons a day will slide their jagged cocks down your throat until you choke on their cum. Through it all, your eyes will stay firmly in their sockets, because I want you to see the approach of each hungry blade, each herpetic cock, each fang-filled mouth eager for a taste of whichever part of you will be the next casualty. I promise you this: You will beg for death, but the great thing about where you're headed—great for me, anyway—is that you cannot die without my permission."

"Go fuck yourself," Ronald utters, halfway between a whisper and a cry.

"You had your chance, amigo. I'm afraid your only option now is to muddle through the remainder of your mortal life, a cripple with a colostomy bag. There's no way out of this trap you've made for yourself, I'm afraid, not even if you take your own life. You'll simply make your way to me that much sooner. So, for you and me, this isn't goodbye. It's TTFN."

He turns his back to Ronald and bends toward Melody.

"Ta-ta for now," he whispers to her.

"Smooth," she says. She wipes pinpricks of blood from her sweaty brow. "Basil, you look like you've been through the wringer."

"I've had better days," he says. As if on cue, he drops to one knee. He leans forward with his palm flat to the floor. Reddish-black blood slicks the torn carpet, leaking from holes in his punctured abdomen.

Chapter 31

# A Better Dragon to Slay

Melody exits the building first, at Basil's insistence. He pauses at the door. The shattered glass resembles a spider's web. The pattern reminds him of the world's better places, the ones not yet fouled by men. Tears wet his eyes as he realizes he will never again see these sights. Worse, his eyes will never again see any parts of the human world, not after today.

*Minutes and hours and days*
*The ticking hands that mete them out*
*Bid farewell, begging, "Forget me"*
*The stillness of ponds, the roving lust of meadows*
*The faithful stink of mud*
*Setting suns and burbling brooks, babbling*
*A language all their own*
*Insect wings, humming, thrumming like plucked strings*
*All gone, but maybe*
*Never were*
*Melody losing sharpness with each verse*
*A grasped thread slipping through the arthritic twigs of ancient*
  *fingers*
*Mirror lakes, delicate waifs, wagging tails on brick-dumb dogs*
*Too fragile, too soft for such a hard place*
*Let it all die, and me along with it*

He takes three deep breaths before stepping outside. The sunlight blinds him, makes him squint, and even this smallest of exertions steals more life from his sapped body. Despite his best efforts to look strong, his hooves clop unevenly on the sidewalk. Blood trails each step. The drops shine black against the sun-bleached concrete.

"Thank Christ!" Herbert yells from the parking lot. Boothe, the diminutive imp, leaps excitedly at Herbert's feet.

Another response starts small and builds in intensity with each syllable.

"No! No, no, no, no, no!"

It's Edna Babych, haggard and incredulous.

"Damn you!" she screams.

These, it seems, are the only words she can manage. She yanks the cross-less Christ from her neck and hurls it across the parking lot. The figurine strikes the fuselage of an abandoned Harley and breaks into three pieces. The part containing the head and limbless torso ends up beneath the back tire of a burgundy sedan flecked with road dust. Edna moves in circles, struggling to make up her mind, and strides toward the cross at the edge of the parking lot. She leans into the wood, all her weight behind it. The cross moves inch by inch, until momentum takes control, and the oversized T topples forward. The left edge of the horizontal beam stabs the hood of Herbert's car. It lingers there for a second before the beam turns and the cross's right edge slaps the windshield, splintering the glass.

Herbert can merely look on as it happens. His shoulders droop.

The remaining protestors abandon their signs, the villain victorious in his fight to the death with the leather-clad saviors. The crowd parts as Melody leads Basil toward Herbert. Horrified facial expressions tell Basil he must look perilously close to death.

"The cops and the fire department are on the way, apparently," Herbert says. "Bomb squad, too, someone said."

"Don't know what good they'd do at this point," Melody says. "Maybe send a demolition team in their place. A bomb would only help at this point. The whole structure is shot to shit."

Basil sees the motionless body of Officer Pierce, silhouetted in a pool of brownish red. Karen sits on the curb, a purple knob on her forehead, looking sullen and trying not to hyperventilate. Other familiar faces amble around the lot, looking lost. There's no sign of Audrey Pernie.

"You saved my life—twice," Herbert tells Basil. "I owe you everything."

"You can return the favor by giving me a ride," Basil replies. "You said you know the way to the cave entrance."

"Patriot Rock. Sure. Just let me"—Herbert inhales sharply— "settle myself."

"Take all the time you need," Basil says as he counts his many wounds.

"Wait," Herbert says. "Can I leave? I mean, should I? Isn't this a crime scene?"

Basil tilts his head and says, "Did you commit a crime?"

"I guess not."

"Then get in the fucking car."

Basil sees Edna stomping on a patch of dry grass. He stumbles toward her. No hard feelings, he'll say. As he extends an open hand, she slashes at him with a pocketknife. The blade slices the flesh of his palm. She then jabs at him, trying to add to the holes in his war-torn abdomen.

Through blurred vision, he catches her hand in his. He squeezes her grip until bones crack. Her lips tremble, but she refuses to drop the blade. Basil shakes the knife to the ground and kicks it across the lot.

He should kill her, because she deserves it, but he has no more fight in him.

"I swear," he tells her, "I'm going to miss you in a strange way."

"Good riddance," she hisses. "I hope you rot from the inside out."

"You'll miss me when I'm no longer here. You'll have to find some new target for all of that hate you've got in your heart."

"It's all for you," she tells him. "Every last drop."

He can tell she doesn't mean it. She's angry at the life she's lived.

"You'll never find a better dragon to slay," he says.

He backs away from her, half-expecting her to pounce on him and start clawing at his eyes and other vulnerable parts. He ambles over to Herbert, who struggles to remove the toppled cross from the hood of his car.

Melody waits by the passenger-side door.

She motions with her index finger, inviting Basil to come to her. He limps over, and the agony in his abdomen makes him want to scream.

"So you're going home," she says.

"It's time."

"Be safe. Will you make it a better place than it was when you left it?"

"No more rape, you mean."

"I was trying not to say it."

"I will remake my home in Beak's image."

"Well, then everyone's fucked," she says with a wink.

"I've enjoyed my time here. Half of me would rather stay."

"Clearly, you have a traumatic brain injury." She gives a halfhearted smile. "Listen, Basil. I'm glad I met you. I'd say you're more human than most of the people I've met. A better human, to tell it right. I'll miss you."

He nods, saving his strength.

"I'm sorry if I was mean to you," she adds. "Even if you deserved it."

"I wish we had met at a different time, under different circumstances, but I suppose everyone says those words at least once in a lifetime. I'll miss seeing you, hearing your voice, smelling you ..."

She slips her hands over his bloody, fang-filled mouth.

"Inappropriate," she tells him. "Now get out of here before I start hating you again."

Basil eases into the passenger seat of Herbert's car. Boothe finds an open space too. Herbert fires up the engine and turns to his injured friend.

"You've got a long way to go," Herbert says. "You going to make it?"

"I'll be fine."

As Herbert pulls away, Basil scans the area for his nemesis, Edna Babych. There's no sign of her, save her spangled denim jacket, left unceremoniously in the middle of the parking lot.

"What do you expect to find when you get back home?" Herbert asks.

"Bedlam. But I've seen worse."

He's not so sure.

Herbert turns on the radio. The announcer drones on about dropping corn prices in light of higher yield and falling demand for U.S. exports.

"Herbert, what the hell are you listening to?"

"The IA-NE Farm Report," he says.

"I know what it is. But why?"

"It calms my nerves. I don't even listen, really. I just like the fact that it's always there."

"So is cholera. Can you please put on something soft, soothing? Classical music, jazz—something civilized. I'd rather not have my last moments above ground filled with prattle about corn futures."

The car speeds past a small sign that reads: YOU ARE NOW LEAVING BEAK. COME BACK SOON.

*Not likely.*

"Your vehicle has seen better days," Basil says. "I'm afraid I'm not helping matters any. The upholstery's ruined. Please forgive the carnage."

"Let's call it incentive to upgrade this ancient hunk of junk."

Basil wants only to sleep the dreamless sleep. Every limb

hurts. His skin feels hot and sticky. He's lost so much blood. Too much. Nausea overtakes him. He breathes deeply through his nose, out through his mouth, until the feeling passes.

"Herbert," Basil says. "I expect great things from you."

"Likewise. Will I see you again?"

"It's difficult to say. I suppose Lubos will have something to say about that. Boothe should stay with you. Here in Beak, or wherever you end up. He likes you. He'll make a good companion."

"Based on how tightly he's clutching your leg, doesn't look like he intends to stay here. Besides, I know nothing about housebreaking minor fiends."

"Forgive me, Herbert, but I need to rest."

Basil's limp body moves in sync with the car, forehead smacking the cracked windshield each time Herbert steers into a pothole. His horns scrape the fabric-stripped ceiling as a tire clips the caved-in carapace of a snapping turtle lying dead in the road.

Basil closes his eyes. The engine whines, working harder than it should have to. Boothe voices its inquisitive chirps. Then, everything goes silent.

## Chapter 32

# The Fall

My eyes scan the exodus for someone who might help me in my darkest hour. Filthy ditch diggers and pickmen shamble along the clay-lined channel dimpled with hoof prints. Coal dust and dirt coat the bare shoulders of men and boys alike, the patina broken only by rivulets of their own sweat.

My eyes dart from one face to another, searching for the only man who might show me some kindness. Henry. I wish I knew his last name.

My spirit rises as I see him bring up the rear. A fresh scab has browned on the side of his face. He eyes me as he climbs out of the channel, scurrying up a mud-caked timber like a man much younger than his years.

"Where you been?" he asks me. "We ain't worked alongside each other in half a week."

"Trying to keep the whole ball of yarn from unraveling. Listen, Henry—"

"Can't do it."

Although he barely knows me, he knows me well enough to know what's coming.

"I'm not asking for money," I insist.

"Whatever it is, I don't have."

"A place to room. An overnight."

"You'd rather wander, you said."

"Not for me. For my wife."

"Didn't realize you were hitched up."

I have erred again, for he knows not a whit about me, or I about him.

"Put her to work," he tells me. "Have her take up a trade. There's money to be had for people who ain't afraid to work."

I let the insult pass, the insinuation that I would not suffer such troubles if I had been digging in the dirt beside him all this time. He knows I can outwork him. To his mind, a man's no longer a man if a day passes without a pick in his hand.

"She ran an apiary before," I tell him. "She kept bees."

"Bloody lot of good that'll do here. Can she whore?"

"She's my wife!"

"So what."

"She's pregnant."

"From whoring?"

"Say that again and I'll brain you."

"Calm down, lad, before you hurt yourself. I'd help if I could, but I don't have the room to give."

"She's with child!"

"We can't very well put that in a pot and cook it, can we? What would you have me do?"

"Show mercy."

"I told you: We're full up."

"I'll pay you."

Henry pauses to consider my offer.

"How much?"

"I don't have much to give."

"Everything."

"Pardon?"

"All your wages. Day's pay for each night you take up the wee bit of space in my home somebody else ain't already claimed as theirs. That's just for the floor to lie on and the roof to keep the wet out."

"Be sensible."

"Hitch it back to Berwick."

"She's just come from there. She'll never forgive me."

"We all got our ditches to dig."

Henry looks past me and extends one of the three remaining fingers of his gnarled right hand. As I turn, my eyes settle on the spire of a church near the entrance to London Bridge.

Henry tells me this: "You want mercy? Get it from God."

He passes me, nearly clips me with the mud-caked pick slung over his shoulder.

The sky darkens.

And that is when the lightning bolt hits. I know what I must do.

\* \* \*

The sun sets as I arrive at the stone steps of Saint Botolph's Church. No sign of Old Billy. Parishioners come and go through the massive oak door. They seek the same thing I seek—aid, relief, sanctuary from the storm—though our similarities end there. I have come not to give but to take.

I stand in shadow, an eye out for anyone who might suspect my treachery. The cellar windows are dark. I expect to see Old Billy slither through the unbarred window and blend into the night. No sign of him, after nearly an hour. Either he has long gone or he remains dead to the world, asleep in the cellar wall.

Given my predicament, I have no choice but to risk an encounter with him. My fate hangs in the balance either way. Still, his warning lingers in my thoughts.

I wonder what she's doing now, my bride. Alone in a city she does not know, the darkness climbing around her.

I must hurry.

My feet slide along slippery cobblestones and lead me down the alley toward the church's rear. I hesitate at the window well and test the glass with my foot. The window yawns open. I wait for claws to latch onto an ankle and yank me to my gory demise. I then crouch down and slip inside, careful not to end up face first on the floor this time. The cellar looks the same. The same musty smell surrounds me. My eyes instinctively move to the hole in the wall, and for the briefest of moments I imagine two yellow eyes peering out.

I make haste for the exit and push through the door, entering the church proper. Every room is quiet and still, so I must be the same. I remove my boots to muffle my footsteps. My bare feet clap against dusty wood as I slink down the corridor. I stop at a half-open door and poke my head through, pleased to find the room empty.

I place my boots just inside the doorway. My hands overturn the contents of every unlocked drawer. I find only papers and nicely folded pieces of cloth and ampoules of sacred oil. Important to someone, worthless to me.

The sound of a clicking lock echoes from somewhere close by, followed by the approach of footsteps. I sprawl behind a large wooden desk and wait for the footsteps to pass. I peer out from my hiding spot.

A priest enters the room, struggling with a wicker basket. We have met once before, he and I. The same priest accused me of trying to rob the church and then drove me away with his bronze staff. Turns out he was right about me all along—prescient, in fact—a devil in a man's body.

The priest moves to the far end of the room, past the drawers I already raided, and kneels before a waist-high cabinet. He swings open the door to reveal an ancient strongbox. He works the lock, opens the latch and pours in the contents of his basket. Coins join a deep sea of others, based on the ruckus they make. The plume of coins slows to a trickle as the priest diverts his attention. He leaves the empty basket by the strongbox and moves toward the exit. He sees something.

*My boots.*

He stops at an open drawer and notices the dangling cloths— the effect of my sloppy rummaging. He then picks up one boot, studies it. He tests the sopping fabric between his fingers. His gaze falls to the floor, no doubt seeing my wet footprints, drawing a line straight toward the desk. Toward me.

"Hello?" he says. "Someone there?"

My boot falls to the floor. The priest takes a few cautious steps toward the desk.

I eye the open lid of the strongbox.

"I said: Is someone there?"

I am had.

My bride needs me, and I need every penny in the strongbox to make things right. I rise from my hiding spot. The priest's eyes grow wide.

"You again," he says.

"I want no trouble, Father."

I step toward him, and he darts from the room.

"Coward," I whisper, thankfully.

Before I know it, I am kneeling by the strongbox, taking shillings and pennies by the handful and dropping them into the priest's wicker basket. I am rich. A few loose coins bounce off the lip of the basket and skitter onto the plank floor.

A heavy blow to my back drives me forward, onto the basket. The woven fibers crunch beneath my weight. I turn to see the priest, wielding his bronze staff as if it were a truncheon.

"You devil," he says.

"I'll take only what I need," I tell him. My back burns from his assault.

"God decides what we need. Leave now and repent while you still can."

"I want no trouble from you, Father."

"And yet you've found it," he gasps. "Return every coin and you'll be forgiven. God hasn't damned you yet."

The bronze staff looks heavy in his weathered hands. He is an old man, weak and tired, though I am a young man, weak and tired. I remind myself he deserves no ill will from the likes of me, but I did not ask for my troubles either.

He is a man of God, allegedly, but to me he is an obstacle to be overcome. I return to the strongbox and clutch another handful of coins.

A fist strikes my cheek. The blow deadens the side of my face, from my temple down to my chin. I turn and see the pain on the priest's face, horrified by what he has done. His outstretched hand quakes—with fear, with rage, with regret, all the same feelings that consume me.

"God has a plan for you, son," he tells me. "This thievery cannot be part of it."

Without thinking, I cuff the priest on the side of the head. He drops like a dead horse. His staff clanks to the floor. I kick him once in the gut and move to deliver a second, but I stop myself. I have more important battles to fight.

Yet the priest refuses to go peacefully.

He grabs onto my leg, swatting at my shins with his feeble fists. I bend to teach him a lesson, and his fist connects with my chin. The blow stuns me, knocks me on my arse. The priest straddles me, his knees trying to pin my arms to the floor. His fingers grind away at my Adam's apple.

"You ... animal!" he says. "You ... fiend!"

His hands tighten around my throat.

I reach up and return the favor, squeezing with all the strength in my ruined hands. His grip loosens, though he quickly finds a new target. Fingernails claw at my wrists, and this invasion— this penetration, of his flesh into mine—enrages me. I thrust my hips forward and pull the priest by the collar. His face smacks into the plank floor, and he goes still. I turn him over. He is conscious but dazed. A feeble moan escapes his lips.

"Leave here, you damned devil," he whispers.

The command is too much for me to bear. The beast within me takes over. I cannot imagine I am beating him as my fists rain blows upon his head—five, six, seven times—until his blood tints my knuckles. His moans cease. Supine, arms at his side, his face a crimson mess, he must be dead.

My chest heaves. The outcome of this cocked-up scheme

brings tears to my eyes. Yet I must finish what I have begun. To have spilled his blood for no reason, this shame would haunt me forever.

*The strongbox.*

I shovel more shillings and pennies into the ruined basket— more money than my eyes have ever seen. The priest remains motionless on the cold floor. His blood colors the wood grain, fills the empty spaces between planks.

I drag the basket toward the door so I can collect my soggy boots. I toss them into the basket and hoist my take, surprised by the weight. My hands fail to do their job right—fingers broken, knuckles bruised and bloody. Coins spill through gaps between snapped wicker branches and drop to the floor.

The half-dead priest lifts his head. He spits out a tooth.

I exit the room with my take and move down the corridor, past open doorways, an eye out for the exit. I take a left through an open door and find three men huddled around a table, their mouths full of porridge. They are appalled to see me, as I am to see them. I back away and keep moving, knowing they will surely follow.

Panic grips my chest. Coins spill from the basket in a steady stream. I find my way into the main hall of the church and sprint past the altar. My foot slips on the smooth marble and I sprawl to the hard floor. The basket crashes to the ground and comes undone. Coins scatter like spilled gin. I clamor to collect as many as I can. Pennies and shillings fill my pockets.

"Stop!"

Three men stand by the altar. The priests I am robbing, I suppose.

A dozen or so parishioners watch from the pews. I feel the weight of their revulsion.

Coins trickle from my pockets as I race down the center aisle. My shoulder slams into the oak door, and the night chill seeps through the widening crack. I then spill down the slick stone steps. More coins jangle from my pockets. More coins, lost. My left ankle turns. The kneecap of my right leg shatters.

"Thief!"

I try to run, but my crippled legs reduce my gait to a stagger.

The rains have stopped, the skies clear. The streets have gone empty.

There may still be hope. If I can drag myself into the shadows, I can hobble back to my lonely bride with enough for a few nights off the streets.

I can buy time, if nothing else.

Something hard as stone cracks the back of my skull. My vision goes white, and I collapse. More coins roll away and settle in the unseen cracks between sunken stones. Time passes, but I have no good way of knowing how much. I feel poisoned. All too slowly, the haze clears to show me the constable and his eager truncheon, well equipped to brain me. It seems he already has.

"That's him," says a fat, gray-haired man, likely one of the priests from Saint Botolph's. "That's the bugger."

"His crime?" the constable asks.

"He's killed and burgled," the priest says.

"Murdered, did he?"

"Close enough to it," the priest insists. "Father Edward has a hole in his head he didn't ask for, thanks to this dirty bugger. This one here, he burgled his way in and swiped every blessed coin from God's coffers. Every penny. Likely this one's the same godless reprobate who's been defacing the church grounds, streaking the windows with his waste."

A crowd surrounds me.

"Let him dangle from the gallows," someone shouts.

"Dice him up and feed him to the dogs," says another, the voice female.

A boot connects with my gut. Then comes another, taking my wind. I shield my head and curl myself into a ball, but the blows keep coming, too many for my body to know which parts hurt and which do not.

The constable tries to quell the crowd. There are too many, their thirst for my blood too intense. Finally, he gives up and lets the crowd have its way.

They tear at my clothes, making sure not a single coin remains. "Pitch him into the Thames!"

Cheers of assent fill the night air.

My body passes from grip to grip. A fist clubs my testicles. Fingers pinch the skin of every extremity. Hands yank tufts of hair from my tender scalp. My pleas for clemency go unanswered.

I do not dare ask God to intervene.

They drag me toward the balustrade, punching and kicking along the way. An inky mist shrouds the Thames, but I can hear the river passing below. Its wretchedness fills my nostrils. As I look up, toward the silhouette of Saint Botolph's Church at Owlsditch, my eyes serve only to deceive. Old Billy, the so-called Beast of London Bridge, dangles playfully from the church spire, an audience to my demise. One hideous hand and snakelike tail hold fast to the Christian cross, supposedly pointing the way toward Heaven. The light of the moon outlines his fur-slicked body. He raises a hand to offer the slightest wave, as if to say, "Fare thee well."

My hands fight for purchase on coat sleeves, hat brims and the ears of these goons — anything to keep me rooted to the earth. A blow to the jaw dazes me.

*And a good night to you, Old Billy.*

The crowd heaves me. I am aloft, tumbling through the blackness. In the seconds before I hit, I picture my pregnant bride, sitting alone in a cold and hopeless part of the world, wondering when I will return.

My shoulders land first. My head snaps against the stone-hard surface.

Slowly I sink toward a lightless bottom, somewhere on the plane between consciousness and oblivion.

Frigid water numbs my flesh.
Darkness blinds me.
My lungs burn.
Then, all at once, everything goes silent.

## Chapter 33

# Blind, Bloodied and a Long Way from Home

Basil snaps awake at the sound of his name.

"We're here," Herbert says.

Basil looks to his left, through the driver's window. A pile of rock lies at the top of a hill across an untended plain of wildflowers. Old Glory flaps in the stiff breeze.

Patriot Rock.

"Thank you, my friend," he says.

Boothe leaps out the passenger-side window and wanders into the dry grass. Basil opens the door and unfolds himself onto the gravelly shoulder. He limps to the front of the car, where Herbert stands, looking forlorn.

"A quarter mile across that field you'll find the cave entrance," Herbert says. "Then I guess it's down, down, down."

"Forgive me if I ruined everything."

"Don't worry about the car."

"I don't mean just the car. I feel like I left a big mess for someone to clean up."

"You opened a lot of eyes. We were sleepwalking before you showed up."

"I suppose we part ways here."

"You've lost a lot of blood. Sure you'll be all right?"

"I'm not going to kiss you goodbye, Herbert."

"Fuck you."

Man and demon hug.

Basil claps Herbert's back because it hurts too much to bend.

"I don't suppose you have a torch," Basil asks.

"A flashlight, sure. You're welcome to it. *If* it still works."

Herbert breaks their embrace to dig around in his trunk. He

returns with an oversized, metallic-red flashlight. He shakes the cylinder twice, batteries knocking, before pressing the ON button.

"Consider it a gift," he says. "For your friendship."

"Be happy with your life. Forget your father. Go be gay with someone."

"I really wish you knew when to shut up."

"I didn't get to give Chester a proper so long."

"I'm sure he'll understand."

"Perhaps you can be gay with him."

"Just go. Please."

A horn blazes, a semi rumbling past. The wind of the passing freight nearly knocks Basil over. He waits for a break in the traffic and clops unsteadily across the asphalt. Boothe has made it halfway across the field by the time Basil steps into the waist-high wildflowers.

He will miss humans, and he will miss the world: the cruelty of sunlight, the vastness of sky, the way leaves dance on the branches of an elm, the hardness of pebbles in the creek bed, the ideas he will leave behind—this new breed of poetry, advertising. Even the experiences he wishes to forget: mornings after the all-too-brief pleasures of scotch, the taste of raccoon and its ginger-ale chaser, his noisemaker, most human men.

His eyes settle on a bank of clouds moving slowly to the west. He recalls the night beneath an ash tree in a puddled field, the night the heavens sent jagged bolts of current down to destroy him. He thinks of his uneven marriage to the clock that ticks off the hours, to the rising and setting of the sun, realizing how he at once treasures and abhors the way time passes above ground, cataloging every breath.

The wildflowers thin toward the field's far edge, where green stems and orange and red petals give way to beige-colored crags. As the incline steepens, Basil struggles. He coughs, and out comes a ball of blood that pops against the rock. He turns to see Herbert offer one final wave and then climb into his car.

The light is different now, at August's end—softer, dying. It seems to be at once holding on and letting go. He enters the cave entrance with the light at his back. The temperature drops ten degrees within one step. He turns back one last time, sees Herbert's car pull away, make a U-turn and then head back toward Beak. The car shrinks to a speck until Basil can no longer see it.

"Let's just stay here, just lie down and sleep the dreamless sleep," he tells Boothe. "Between worlds—a fine place for a misfit who belongs nowhere."

He tamps down the urge to weep, and then realizes there's no reason he shouldn't, as his eyes will never again see such wonders. He eases his rear into the groove of a rock and mourns the inevitable loss of everything beautiful, just sitting here, waiting to die. The tears flow freely, and each sob seems to crack him open and leave lacerations for new parasites to fill.

*They don't know how good they have it.*

He feels warmth against his leg, and he looks down to see Boothe cuddling his calf, trying to soothe its master. He studies the undulating grasses, brushed by the wind. Cars and trucks zip by on the seam of asphalt beyond the field. They're so far off they might as well be ants, so he imagines that's exactly what they are.

Finally, the setting sun tells him it's time to go.

"Enough of this childish musing," he says to Boothe. He wipes away the tears spilling from the corner of each eye. He will mourn later.

The imp scampers ahead and disappears into the mouth of the cave, as if swallowed by the darkness that bore him. Basil follows, ready to reclaim his throne, if it will have him.

* * *

Basil steps gingerly through the cool passageway, though his aim fails him. Each time he attempts to avoid a jagged rock, he either trips over it or gashes the skin beneath the thin pelt of fur on his calves. The beam of the flashlight bounces off the tunnel walls. When he closes his eyes to rest, he has Boothe's insistent chirping as a guide. At least one of them seems eager to return to Our Fiery Home.

When the route forks, he aims the flashlight toward the ceiling to seek out the three-dotted directional marking the path, the one leading him home. With each step he realizes the world below will look different, smell different, be different, given everything he has seen on the surface. Though he left the world of men in his wake only hours ago, the surface now seems like part of a long-lost dream, remote and unlikely.

A new verse:

*The world broke me open, split me into threes and fives*
*My right arm, torn free just outside of Lincoln*
*And now the anthropologists fight for custody, ranting*
*"It belongs where it belongs"*
*My left foot, toeless and useless and writhing with happy maggots*
*On a weedy roadside somewhere between Des Moines and Chicago*
*My spleen and liver pulverized*
*Their dust clotting the air above Minneapolis*
*Organ smog*
*My heart a ghost, too, though I applaud its absence*
*Turned to liquid silver and spilled*
*Through the scaffolding of my ribs*
*To pool at her feet*
*She tramped my heart puddle, taking vengeance*
*A few drops hitching a ride on each sole*
*To dry and return to stardust*
*My liquid heart, or ninety-seven percent of it, remains there still*
*A throbbing, burping mess, hopeful*

*For the return of her shadow*
*The shade that quickens the pulse*
*Of this lonely, lowly muscle*

Despites mankind's challenges, and all his horrors, most of the humans he met managed to retain their kindness and love of beauty. He just hopes he can find a way to bring out the same in his own people. If he cannot, why go back?

Several hours have likely passed, an entire day gone, as he ponders the mechanics of time. He has taken three forks, and lost too much blood to wager, when a distant pranging pricks his ears. He crouches and listens beyond the echo of water dripping, each drop finding a new home in a shallow puddle. Then the sound comes again: the clang of metal against rock.

His return is imminent. As he clops forward, his ears detect another sound.

*Voices.*

He beckons Boothe and whispers, "Make yourself scarce." He then flicks off the flashlight and presses on, into the darkness. Soon his eyes catch the first glare of firelight, his nostrils pulling in the skunk-like stink of demon sweat. He hugs the side of the tunnel, inching closer, and sees a troupe of demons taking axes and burs to the ceiling, the walls, bringing down massive boulders.

*Widening the route to the surface. More elbow room for an army of demons and the kraken, Cthaal.*

He has no more time to waste. He steps into the firelight and calls out—no words, just a resonant bellow.

Every demon in the tunnel turns toward Basil. One of them drops his ax, and the blade rattles against the rock. Three of them pounce, their makeshift weapons raised, and Basil deflects them with one mighty swipe. He mashes their bodies into the wall until bits of flesh fill the pores of the metamorphic rock. The rest of the demons—a band of eight to ten, Basil guesses—hang back, waiting.

"Why do you assault me?" he asks. "I am your ruler, returned."

"Your reign has ended," says one of the demons, the one-eyed male Basil knows as Gideon.

"I'd like to meet the fool who has taken my place," he responds.

"Lord Lubos would like to see you as well," Gideon seethes.

Basil stumbles forward, and the demons give him passage. He trips over a rock torn from the ceiling, and he tumbles. His chin breaks his fall. Demons cackle in delight.

"Get up, you stinking rotter," Gideon says. "Get up and meet your ruin."

Basil's arms strain to lift his girth from the cave floor. The desire to simply roll over and die burns strong, but he refuses to meet his end here, so far from anywhere that matters.

"Pick him up and drag him," Gideon directs, and the other demons hoist Basil by the armpits until he finds his hooves.

Basil clops unsteadily toward the blur in front of him. Soon he senses a shift in the air: a slight rise in temperature. Then his eyes show him a sight that stops him, shocks him: The gate to Our Fiery Home yawns open, flames burning hot beneath the cauldrons he once stirred. He steps through the doorway and discovers a world transformed: the charred corpses of demons, piled thirty to forty high; stacks of freshly cast iron weapons, and, everywhere, frantic demons and imps and troglodytes pacing in circles, eager to do their worst.

The denizens of Our Fiery Home halt when they see him—a leader who abandoned them, a traitor wearing a coat of his own gore.

Lubos slithers out from between two cauldrons. An oversized ax dangles from his good hand.

"Welcome home," he says.

"Where's Kamala?" Basil replies.

"I'm delighted to see you. You've never looked better."

"Where's Kamala?"

"Doing penance, as you soon will. The humans were unkind to you—such a surprise—but I will be even less forgiving." He turns his back to Basil and utters a command: "Bring him to his knees."

The demons hesitate at first. Then one pounces, followed by another and another still, until Basil has no fight left in him. He feels the sting of a blade pierce his thigh, digging so deep the iron tastes bone. A net of flesh covers his nose and mouth, suffocating. The weight drives the wind from his lungs, and then ... the weight eases. Basil lies motionless on the cavern floor, chest heaving, his lungs hungry for air. He watches the ceiling, where giant vampire bats claw from one rookery to another.

"Haul him to the Room of Contrition," Lubos commands.

Basil closes his eyes and feels himself being dragged away. The tips of his hooves carve ruts in the soft, gray earth.

# Chapter 34

# Wasted Breath

Kamala stirs at the commotion. Her cheek cools against the smooth, damp stone. The door to the Room of Contrition scrapes open, and two hulking troglodytes drag in a bloody, black mess. They toss the heap onto the floor, and a moment passes before Kamala realizes what she's seeing. She thinks she has gone mad.

*Basil.*

Instinct compels her to go to him, to help her former master and commander. A jolt of pain stings the space between her legs as a jagged shard bites the rubbed-raw skin. A column of hardened semen runs from the mouth of her vagina to the floor, forming a congealed puddle around her hooves.

Basil lifts his head. As his eyes connect with Kamala's, he utters, "Forgive me. I should not have left."

"You had to," she whispers.

Lubos slithers into the Room of Contrition.

"Wrap him up good and tight," he blusters.

"He half-dead already," grunts one of the trogs.

"Well, make sure nothing keeps me from taking what's left."

The trogs twine leathers around Basil's throat, around each of his horns, around each wrist and pastern. They then hoist him so he's upright, on his knees, though he lacks the strength to stiffen his spine. When the trogs snap the leathers taut, the veins in Basil's neck dance to the surface. He gasps. Blood pools beneath him.

"I will succeed where the humans failed," Lubos says. "Today, you become nothing. I'll grant you the dignity of a private death, but my kindness ends there. Quite a shame you'll miss the public dismemberment and the roast to follow. All of Our Fiery Home will gnaw every last morsel from your bones—a fitting meal before battle, I'd say. I should pluck your eyes from their sockets, pry your horns from skull and snip your shriveled genitals from the dead space between your legs, keep them as reminders of my triumph. What fine talismans they would make."

Basil gurgles.

"Yes, a pity you won't be here to see our new world take shape," Lubos continues. "You deserve much of the credit, after all. If not for your nomadic longing, I may not have found the inspiration to lead every cur out of this place and savage all corners of the civilized world."

Lubos moves to a metal rack affixed to the near wall and studies the arsenal, the many implements of torture. He steps to the left, letting his fingertips graze the warm metal of each weapon, and then turns on his right hoof and does the same, left to right, with his other hand. He settles on a crudely made ax: heavy, dull, the blade dingy from ash and time, nicked from overuse.

"Say goodbye to all things," Lubos says as he plucks the ax from the wall.

"Even the simplest beast craves the sweet pain of life," Basil starts, the words strained by the leathers closing around his throat.

Lubos tests the ax's weight.

"To have the winds of time fill his lungs with their breath ..."

Lubos brings the weapon to his face and lets his finger ride the blade.

"As the last puff of air passes through his lips, what will consume his thoughts?"

Lubos raises the ax overhead.

"The sticks and bricks of the structures he has built ..."

Lubos inhales, flexes his arms, his three-fingered hand struggling to grip the gnarled handle.

"Or the blueprints of things his hands will never touch?"

Lubos heaves the ax toward the floor, and the blade finds

its juicy target. The ax parts Basil's forehead. Blood splatters Lubos's eyelids and lips. A chipped piece of Basil's right horn skims off the wall and spirals to a stop at the base of a burnished guillotine. As the trogs release the leathers, Basil falls forward. His left shoulder slams to the floor. The ax blade digs deeper into the cleft in Basil's skull, grinding against the stone with every twitch. The right leg kicks wildly every few seconds, and then the body goes still.

Lubos stands above the fallen demon king. His jaw hangs open, stunned at his achievement. Slowly, he comes around, as if realizing he now has serious work to do.

"You'll never have what you think you want," Kamala says. Her words trail off as a horrid taste builds in the back of her throat. "You will fail."

"Shame you won't live long enough to prove me wrong," Lubos tells her. He turns to one of the trogs and orders the hulk to seal the door closed. "You'll choke on the stench of your own decay."

\* \* \*

Kamala stares into the lifeless eyes of her former king. The muscles of his face have relaxed. He looks peaceful, a far cry from the bruising bastard at his worst. Now, though, she can remember his better days, the tenderness he showed only when all others had their backs to him.

Her arms dangle loosely, her body parallel with the floor. She tests her bonds again, but they do not give. The flesh of her wrists has torn away to expose the moist, pink layer beneath. The knots will hold no matter how much she struggles. Only then does she permit herself to weep.

She stops when she realizes she's not alone.

Something chirps in the shadows by the room's closed door.

A dark, squat shape moves with the curvature of the

shadows. Then, the shape bumps into the hilt of a pike, and the lanky weapon knocks into a blood-blackened chopping block and brushes the links of a long, rusted chain. The chain unfurls noisily, link by link, and coils onto the floor. The commotion spurs the creature to panic and, in its panic, reveal its form.

A reddish-black imp leaps onto a table heaped with whips, bone saws and crocodile shears, then ping-pongs off the near wall and dithers in the middle of the room, looking for a place to hide. It then weaves its fat body into the bony prongs of a candelabra fashioned from the antlers of an unknown beast. A toppled shield spirals to a stop in the center of the room, its ruckus melding with the cries of the screaming imp.

"Calm, little one!" Kamala yells, and then realizes she should lower her voice. "*Calm.*"

She hums to the imp and, slowly, it quiets. The imp then squeezes its girth through a gap in the candelabra and inches toward Basil's slack body. It nuzzles him, and when he doesn't respond, the imp pokes him in his open eye, urging its master to show life. The body refuses. So the imp stands there, arms at its sides, sighing and staring at the floor. It curls into the space beneath Basil's scabbed chin.

"He's gone, little one," she tells the imp. "He's gone."

Or is he? Only then does she consider the possibility: the *Locuri* reanimation grammar. She heard Basil whisper it a hundred times—to reanimate a bat that had fallen from the ceiling or, just for kicks, to give life to a turd—and it almost always worked. She then stops to consider whether she *should* bring him back—and if she even can, considering the viciousness and precision of the blow that felled him—or if he should remain dead, as punishment for his cruelty, including the miseries she had to endure, either under his thumb or because of his absence. Her memory returns to glimpses of the kinder soul within him.

This, somehow, is enough.

"Come to me, little one," she tells the imp. "Come quickly."

The imp doesn't move from its bed beneath Basil's chin.

"There may be time," she insists. "Come. Release me."

Instead the imp laps at the dried blood on Basil's chin. It sobs after each flicker of its bifurcated tongue.

"Little one," she says calmly. "You can save him. Now come to me."

The imp finds its three-toed feet and waddles over.

"Break my bonds."

The imp eyes her tethered wrists and goes to work, gnawing the toughened leather. For an imp, brainless as most imps tend to be, it has a delicate touch, careful not to take any flesh. Soon her left wrist breaks free. She peels herself off the stone, leaving some of her belly's flesh on the clammy surface. Her lower half still numb, she topples to the floor. The column of hardened semen collapses, and it shatters against the floor in greenish-white chunks. Her legs useless, she drags herself to Basil's side. Now, up so close, she sees the extent of the wounds marring his body.

"You were dead before Lubos's ax fell," she tells Basil's corpse. "What kind of trouble did you get into up there?"

Her fingertips touch the cold skin of his cheek, tacky with fresh blood. She grasps the ax handle and gives a yank. Basil's head jerks forward, and something in his neck voices a distressing creak, but the blade stays put. She gets to her knees and, taking the handle firmly in both hands, pulls upward. Iron grates against bone until the blade releases its grip with a moist *pop*. She eases the ax to the floor and moves in close, her lips millimeters from Basil's right ear.

She takes a moment to recall the *Locuri* grammar needed to reanimate him. It comes to her in pieces, syllables, until she believes she has pieced the puzzle together. The first few whispers come slowly, until she finds her confidence. She pauses after the last wisp of a syllable, and presses her lips to his, inflating his lungs with the air from her own. Nothing happens. Again, she repeats the cycle, each word hissing from the space between her fangs. Again, she presses her lips to his, biting this time to taste his blood, and air spills down his throat. She pulls back at the slightest movement, the subtlest noise—only to realize it's her own breath passing over his lips, her efforts fruitless.

His body remains an inert heap. His skin seems to have lost some of its sheen, like the dusty gray of charcoal rather than its usual tar black.

"Once more," she tells the imp.

Then the thought occurs to her: Even if she works the grammar a third time and it somehow takes hold, will Basil return as a shadow of his former self, a crippled and mindless gimp drooling into his own lap, suitable only for sitting in a corner and waiting for death to find him again? Perhaps she should let his pulse remain still so she can wander as a solitary figure for as long as Our Fiery Home's fires burn.

Rage boils in her gut. *Lubos.* The mere thought of him conjures the all-too-recent memory of the torture and gang rape—her sentence for opposing him, for wanting to remake Our Fiery Home. She grabs Basil by the horns, one of them missing its curved tip, and pulls him toward her.

"Come back, you useless sack of waste," she yells. "Come back before it's too late."

She screams the grammar a third time, directly into his face, and slams his head to the floor. His body flops over, from stacked on its side to supine, and his massive back slaps flatly to the dusty stone floor. She blows air into the tunnel behind his icy lips, seemingly to no effect. She lies on top of the body and sobs as she realizes he is gone, the grammar having failed.

Our Fiery Home is lost, and she along with it.

Again, the breath leaks from his mouth, but this time she feels air being pulled past her cheek, into his nostrils. His chest rises and then falls, rises and then falls.

"He breathes again," she says, astonished, as she backs away from him.

She has never before used the grammar with effect, so she knows not what to expect of her leader, brought back from the dead. Basil breathes deeply, his exhalations fuller, and she can smell death leaving his body. She kneads the muscle of his left shoulder so he can feel the warmth of another as he rouses.

"Am I dead?" he says, eyes still closed. "If I am, blind my eyes so I cannot see what's come to greet me."

"No, you fool. I brought you back."

The imp emerges from behind the stone slab. It chirps in Basil's ear.

"You should thank this little one," she says.

Basil opens one eye and sees the imp waddling toward him.

"Boothe." He coughs as the imp nuzzles. "His name is Boothe."

He sits up, wincing.

"Does it hurt?"

"I'm sore," he says. "And stiff. And I have a splitting headache."

He reaches up and touches the crease in his forehead, still tacky with blood.

"Lubos," he says, as if remembering. "Am I too late?"

"His departure is imminent, and he aims to lead Cthaal before him. Toward the surface."

"How many have joined his army?"

"Nearly all in Our Fiery Home, from what I gather—a bottomless sea. And Cthaal, of course."

"We must act."

"The Elders are gone. Slaughtered."

"Of course. I would have done the same."

Her eyes become glassy. She shifts her weight, the ache in her belly another reminder of the trauma Lubos inflicted on her. Her insides feel hollow. Tears streak her cheeks as she sobs.

"Where do we go now?" she asks.

"Go?"

"We can't stay here—not now. Lubos will make Our Fiery Home uninhabitable. We'll be nomads roaming the ashes left in his wake. We'll wander in darkness forever."

"No. We stay and fight. This is our home, and we have pledged to defend it."

He moves to her, cradles her in his arms, soothes her. She slaps his chest with an open palm, and the sound echoes in the close chamber.

"So what must we do?" she asks. "Lubos would be shocked to find you alive. So would every other demon following him."

"Surprise fades quickly. Lubos is cunning, adaptable."

"Those loyal to you, those who would obey you, no doubt they remain among his ranks."

"They have no reason to do so now," he says. "He'll have poisoned their minds with promises of glory and plunder, of conquering sunlit lands their hooves were not meant to touch."

"How was it? Up there, I mean."

"Indescribable. I saw beauties my eyes could not grasp, and horrors my mind still struggles to parse. I drank from unpolluted streams, befriended humans and indulged in a new breed of art, called adver—"

He pauses as his mind grasps for the edges of an impossible idea.

"I know what we must do."

He gets to his hooves, unstable, working the stiffness from his body. He clops around the room, searching. He feels along the walls with his flattened palms until his fingertips find what they seek: the edges of a doorway, well camouflaged.

"I must get to the Hall of Ignoble and Prodigious Elders," he says. "It's the only way to save Our Fiery Home from destruction."

"I told you, the Elders are gone. Dead. Decapitated. Digested at this point. They can't help you now."

The hidden doorway groans open. Stone grinds against stone.

"It's not the Elders I seek. I seek what lies beneath their chamber."

"Tell me," she insists.

"We must free *him*," he says.

And then it occurs to her. The secret — the horrible, wonderful, unfathomable secret Basil shared before leaving Our Fiery Home in her care. Her eyes grow wide.

"Basil, you can't — "

"Consider it our only hope. We must unleash Lucifer."

## Chapter 35

# Meat to Tempt a Starved God

Fire-licked walls light Basil's path. He inches through the passage connecting the Room of Contrition to the Hall of Ignoble and Prodigious Elders, made tight by boulders liberated from the ceiling. At the passage's slimmest junctures, he must squeeze through fissures in the fallen rock. Prior to his resurrection, the movement would have sent waves of agony through his bullet- and blade-shredded body. Now, he's the same demon in virgin form—whole, healed, strong enough to overwhelm death itself.

He owes Kamala his beating heart, and he hopes he has the opportunity to show his gratitude when the time is right—when Our Fiery Home has been saved or, he realizes, completely upended. In either outcome, he will have time to spare.

His mind races, his eyes tracing every corner and every moving shadow. Soon enough he reaches the passage's end in the form of a massive stone. As his talons find the edges, he heaves the stone to the left, and the stone moves easily along the arc of a primitive wheel, sunken into the rock. Besides Kamala, he owes a debt to whichever of his predecessors had the forethought to create these covert passageways.

Basil steps into the dimly lit Hall of Ignoble and Prodigious Elders. Stains darken the floor. The smell of offal hangs in the dead air. He moves to the center of the room and rests his knuckles on the stone table where the Elders once sat. He permits himself a moment to mourn their absence. How many times had he stood behind them, looking over their frail shoulders, seeking their measured counsel?

The dulled chink of clashing iron, the thump of flesh pounding flesh, filters through the thick rock. He recognizes the clamor as demons in the main cavern preparing for war, just beyond the hall's sealed door. He'll have to keep quiet.

Basil sweeps his palm across the table and wipes away the sheen of chalk. The table measures more than thirty feet long, must weigh far more than a ton. He tests the stone slab, trying to pry it off its legs, but it doesn't budge. Death stole much from him, and his strength has not yet fully returned. He knows he can move the slab with some doing, but it won't be quiet work. He prays the demons on the other side of the door are too focused on spilling blood to notice the ruckus he's about to make.

He crouches and grips the table's edge. Talons bite into stone. He steadies himself, each thigh flexing, and counts down from three. As he arrives at one, he jerks upward, and the stone peels away from its legs. Particles of stone dust fill the air. The muscles in his upper body bulge, forcing every vein to the surface. Teeth grind, jaws clench. Something tears as his abdominal muscles strain. His legs tremble, approaching the point of failure.

Slowly, the slab slides off its moorings and thunders to the floor. The slab lands on its side and cracks in two. Each half falls flat with a deafening *boom*.

The dust cloud dissipates all too slowly. Basil struggles to catch his breath, tasting stone dust on his tongue. He winces, in part from the spent energy, but more so from the uproar. One eye open, fixed on the closed door, he half-expects the walls to come down under the weight of a thousand heavily armed demons.

No one comes.

He wastes no time. He studies the floor, searching for the edges of the hidden door, then drops to his knees and blows dust from the edges to fully expose the frame. He digs the talon of his index finger into the seam to claw out years of grime. He's found the lock. Now he just needs the key. More than a dozen weapons line a rack on the far wall: a spear, a few swords, a cudgel, a trio of thorny clubs. He finds a flat iron bar and sinks one end into the inch-wide seam between the hidden door and its frame. He pries up the door, drags the slab out of the way and braces for what's to come.

The foul stink assaults his nostrils, turns his stomach—the stench of decay and death and wickedness. He fights the urge to vomit. A faint greenish light reflects up from below.

He steps onto the stone staircase winding down.

A distant memory charms his mind. He has tramped these steps before, at the beginning of his tenure as liege of Our Fiery Home, after Calvin the Elder gave an oral history of Basil's kingdom. For reasons they never articulated, the Elders forbade writing down anything of significance, though Basil now knows it was likely out of fear that history could somehow be used against them.

"It is your right to know," Calvin told him, "but no one else must."

Calvin told the story of a mystical being named Lucifer from a time when man and demon walked the same earth, side by side. Lucifer's lust and appetite led to his expulsion from a great kingdom, since gone extinct. If he had chosen to walk into the horizon alone, Lucifer's punishment would have ended there. Instead, he abducted a number of humans to take along with him—a dozen fecund females for breeding, a few males for amusement—so he became a target, the enemy, hunted. His only option was to leave the sunlight at his back and crawl through a seam in the earth, doomed to live in darkness.

"And so began the kingdom we know as Our Fiery Home," Calvin said. "Lucifer always intended to return to the surface some day, to reclaim his place in a world ruled by men, these sheep who worship something they cannot see, who kill and die for an idea. Until that day, he would devote each breath to haunting and taunting the creatures he blamed for casting him out. Humans."

Impossibly cruel and wickedly inventive, Lucifer created the lake of blood by emptying the arteries of those who opposed him into a crevasse. His cruelty spawned an epoch of endless rebellion until the moment he was beaten and chained and dragged away to live out his days, feebly, in a hole beneath the floor of Our Fiery Home.

"He is singular, this Lucifer, different than you and me," Calvin told Basil. "His hatred will keep him alive until the world reaches its end, and even then, I believe he will find a way to live on."

With Lucifer deposed, the strongest demons vied for power. Some reigns lasted an age, while others ended in a blink. Each successor earned a nickname, posthumously, to characterize his rule—to honor, to vilify or to mock. First came Jakob the Butcher, named for the blood he spilled in his quest to tranquilize Our Fiery Home after the vanquishing of its founder. Then came Frederick the Cruel, though the epithet dripped with irony; his mild manner led to his swift evisceration and beheading, well before he had the chance to claim any notable accomplishment. Then came Panzu the Explorer, a demon plagued by an intense wanderlust that drew him to the farthest reaches of the underworld. His urge to expand Our Fiery Home's borders hastened his demise, when a two-ton boulder dropped from the ceiling of a new tunnel he had commissioned, remaking him as a paste of blood and shattered bone. Then came Tor the Weary and Khan the Suicide, whose respective reigns began and ended in the time it takes to move one's bowels. After Khan bested Tor in a duel of axes, he purposefully impaled himself on a pike—no one professed to know why, exactly, but Basil has some inkling— Byron stepped in to fill the void. The Elders gushed over Byron and his rule, allegedly the longest and most fruitful of Lucifer's successors, in part because of his remarkable threshold for pain. Byron earned his sobriquet—the Scarred Back—for a peculiar fetish: encouraging his minions to whip him with a thorn-tipped cudgel, suggesting to anyone who dared to grip the cudgel's handle that he would forfeit the crown if the lashings drew a single tear from his eye. Byron remained in power until the last revolt, when chaos once again gripped Our Fiery Home and he stood hoof to hoof with a young and foolish brute named Basil.

As the tale goes, Basil outmuscled Byron, pried the sacred spear from the ruler's hands and ran him through. Even now Basil has no memory of the skirmish, or of the decapitation that formally ended his predecessor's reign. Without knowing, without trying, Basil became the seventh successor of Lucifer the Eternal One.

After Basil cycles through the list of Our Fiery Home's deposed rulers, he considers the lore of humans—demons, devils and the tiresome list of aliases for the individual who supposedly spawned them all: Abaddon, Apophis, Apollyon, Azazel, Beelzebub, Belial, Diabolos, Iblis, Lucifer, Mephistopheles, Nidhogg, Satan, The Enemy. Did all of these individuals once exist, or were they merely mankind's fabrications to explain the world, giving names to the monsters man could not see or touch? If each name did have a basis in reality, did each one refer to the same principal being? Had the Eternal One, the creature Basil is about to set free, once belonged to a race of supernatural beings known as angels, only to be cast out and relegated to a subterranean existence? Had Lucifer once tempted and taunted a holy man rumored to be the Son of God? Had he laid waste to ancient civilizations? Is he responsible for every evil impulse and every tragedy that has ever befallen humanity?

Likely not, Basil knows, because humans, despite their many endearing attributes, have a fondness for exaggerations in their storytelling.

He has no good way of distinguishing truth from fiction, in part because of Our Fiery Home's undocumented history. Even if his people had taken the time to etch words in stone or put them down on a page to mark past events, who can say what is "truth"? History, after all, bears the fingerprints of the historian.

He wonders: How will the underworld remember him when his final day comes? What sort of epithet will he earn based on his triumphs, misdeeds and missteps?

His hooves leave the last stone step and travel the flat terrain of a cavernous chamber, strangely familiar. Flashes of neon green and orange paint the walls. The colors dance and leap. The pattern reminds Basil of moving water, of the cool creeks bordering Nebraska's Sand Hills. As he walks, a distant rumbling finds his ears. The sound reminds him of his worldly noisemaker, the all-black Harley he both loved and hated. He turns a corner and enters a wide expanse. There he discovers the source of the rumbling: the air escaping the lungs of Lucifer himself.

Lucifer crouches with his elbows resting on his knees, but even in this cramped position he easily towers over Basil. His ancient flesh the color of buttermilk, his body glows in halos of orange and green. Strands of long, gray hair flow over well-muscled shoulders. His left hand lacks two fingers, ring and index, just smoothed-over stumps in their place. Two gnarled horns twist toward the ceiling.

"Stop cowering in the shadows and step toward me, son of mine," Lucifer commands. "Show me that you look as dreadful as you smell."

Basil gulps as he emerges from a veil of shadow. His voice cracks as he speaks Lucifer's name. The syllables echo.

The Eternal One stands upright. Shackles clatter. Bones and tendons pop. The earth trembles beneath him.

"Come to me," Lucifer says, like air hissing from a gently pricked balloon.

Basil obeys. He genuflects before the Eternal One.

"I remember your face, though you smell different," Lucifer says. "Speak."

"Call me Basil, the caretaker of your kingdom—the seventh to succeed you," he says. "Hear me: A pretender to our throne seeks to destroy all we have built. He wishes to abandon the warmth of the fire and ascend to the surface. If he succeeds, all your children will follow, and the flames of Our Fiery Home will go out forever. All shall perish on the sun-kissed earth. The world will reach its end."

Lucifer wheezes, seems to contemplate Basil's warning.

"I demand your aid," Basil adds. "With your brawn and cunning on my side, I may be able to prevent this possibility from becoming fate."

"Let it all crumble, beneath your hooves and mine."

Basil's jaw hangs slackly. "You, more than anyone, know the consequences of inaction."

"Don't pretend to know my mind," Lucifer says. "You're nothing but a wart on my belly."

"If saving what you've built is not enough, do it for the sake of vengeance. You will walk freely once you have fulfilled your debt. I give you my word."

"I'll take what I want, starting with the marrow sucked from your bones!"

"Respect me," Basil says. "I could turn on my heel and leave you here to rot."

"But you won't." Lucifer laughs.

"The world has gone on spinning just fine without you."

Lucifer sneers, adding, "So the Nameless have risen up."

"Aye. Led by an agitator named Lubos. He wishes to undo time."

"He has the right idea, though I'd hate for him to beat me to it. The world wants to die. It begs and pleads for a merciful end, to rid itself of the curse of man."

"You remember wrong, Eternal One. I have been to the surface. The human world deserves to go on living."

"What a pitiful ruler you must be."

"No more pitiful than you. Only one of us wears chains."

"Why not let our worst devils run free? What is there left to save, either above or below?"

The question stops Basil. His thoughts return to days

beneath blue skies and hot sun, beneath dark heavens pricked with far-off stars, pregnant with the swollen moon. Synapses in his brain explode as he envisions meadows alive with the blushes of black-eyed Susan, beardtongue and prairie phlox; the far-reaching shade of towering silver maples; cold, clear creeks lined with mossy stone; cottontail rabbits and mule deer, timber rattlesnakes and sharp-shinned hawks. And humans— yes, even humans. The worst of them aside, even they deserve preservation.

"I have seen the good in man," he says. "Let him settle his own discord."

"Good? What purpose does *good* serve?"

"The world is not lost. Our people belong below. Let them stay here."

He eyes his surroundings, this lifeless pit reserved for a forgotten god who starves for fresh meat. Even here, in this hole, he has no doubt: The flames of Our Fiery Home must continue to burn. Given a fresh canvas, he can reimagine this place and then reinvent it.

First it must survive this tribulation.

"Release," Lucifer whispers.

Lucifer rolls his head from one shoulder to another. A line of black spittle spills from his lips, painting his chest. Basil does not compare to this magnificent beast. If and when Lucifer roams freely again, Basil wonders about his own place in Our Fiery Home. Assuming Lubos can be deposed with Lucifer's aid, what then if Lucifer attempts to reassert his hold on power?

This, he thinks, is tomorrow's problem.

"I want to trust you," he says, "but give me assurance. Tell me you will not ascend to the human world. It's far too precious."

"My blood flows through your veins," Lucifer wheezes. "My mind is your mind. We are different but the same—a father and his child. I, too, am meant to return."

Lucifer stretches each hircine leg, flexes the muscles in each arm until blood-thickened veins riddle his skin like highways on a roadmap.

"Release," the Eternal One pleads.

"If I agree, you are bound to me."

"We shall see."

Loose rock falls from the ceiling and shatters against the cavern floor. Basil eyes the massive shackles adorning each of Lucifer's wrists and pasterns. A pale yellow crust discolors the runes on the face of the silvery metal. Basil steps forward to utter the words that will free this demon-king-turned-prisoner. With the emancipation grammar on his tongue, he measures the odds of meeting his doom beneath the Eternal One's massive hoof.

*"Release!"*

The venom in Lucifer's voice freezes Basil where he stands. Only then does he feel the weight of Lucifer's request. Only then does he realize the horrors he could set in motion by unleashing this ancient monster. But he has no choice.

# Chapter 36

# Butchery

"Volunteers?" Lubos asks.

Not a soul steps forward.

Lubos claws the shoulder of the demon nearest to him, Gideon.

"You'll do fine," Lubos says.

Dozens of demons catch Gideon in a net of flesh and bone—the lamb chosen. They force Gideon onto his back, bind his wrists and pasterns, and tether a leather cord to his neck.

"Your brothers and sisters appreciate your sacrifice," Lubos utters. "Let this knowledge numb your pain."

Lubos heaves Gideon onto his shoulder and scales an outcropping at the edge of the Pool of Infinite Perdition. He presses Gideon over his head and tosses him into the lake of blood. Gideon lands with an awkward splash. Thick droplets of blood splatter the shore. Gideon's head dips beneath the surface and then bobs up a moment later. He gasps. Blood, as viscous as melted candlewax, slicks his bald skull and paints the whites of his eyes red.

"Please," he gasps. This is all he can manage before his chin dips below the surface and blood fills his mouth. He thrashes as best he can.

"Good," Lubos says. "Let the dim-witted fiend know exactly where you are."

A line of ripples moves toward Gideon's bobbing head. The telltale hump crests the surface. Cthaal.

"Please! Lubos!"

Lubos smiles. He hands the tether to the nearest troglodyte so he can climb to a better vantage point. In return, the trog hands him a sleek iron rod with a sharpened tip. There, perched on a boulder, Lubos waits.

A massive tentacle rises above the surface, poised like a cobra, and slams down onto Gideon's skull. Tentacle and demon disappear. A second later the surface boils as the kraken reveals itself: bulbous black mantle, each slit-like eyeball larger than the head of the largest troglodyte, venom-barbed tentacles slicing the air, including the one bearing Gideon's limp body. Three tentacles lash out and grip the boulder-strewn shore, and the monstrous cephalopod pulls its girth free of the muck. The tentacle bearing Gideon's corpse curls under to feed the parrot-like beak on Cthaal's marbled underside.

Lubos hurls his harpoon. The iron barb pierces the kraken's rubbery mantle, and the beast screeches. Lubos waves his arm, ordering two other demons to release their harpoons. Both irons find their meaty targets. Three muscle-bound troglodytes hold the tethers taut, awaiting Lubos's command. Cthaal thrashes in retreat, dragging the trio of trogs toward the lake's edge.

"Hold your ground," Lubos bellows from his roost. "A slow disemboweling for anyone who loses his line!"

Cthaal slips beneath the surface, but the trogs hold tight. The lines stretch to their breaking point, each fiber voicing its distress. Then the lines go limp.

The kraken bursts from the muck and flops onto the shore, whipping the trogs toward their respective ends. One smacks into the cavern's back wall and becomes a rose-red starburst. Another clips a stalagmite, which frees his head, and the rest of him helicopters into a waiting thatch of irons. The third rockets toward the ceiling to be impaled by a stalactite.

Demons scatter, but Cthaal has no shortage of targets. Its barbed tentacles effortlessly shred bodies into strips and residue. As its enormity emerges fully from the lake, the kraken reveals a long, prehensile tail.

Lubos abandons his perch and fetches an ax. Intent on taming this beast, he strides toward Cthaal and raises the ax over his head. He singles out one of its more than a dozen undulant tentacles. As he prepares to swing, another tentacle wallops his gut and sends him sprawling to the ground. His ax skitters into the shadows.

He stands, dazed. The kraken scales the walls of the cavern. While two tentacles rake the cavern floor, sweeping up fleeing demons, two more tentacles scrape a rookery of vampire bats from the ceiling. Leathery wings flap like flags as the bats' dead bodies hurtle toward the cavern floor.

Lubos smiles at the kraken's sheer size, its overwhelming ferocity and, above all, his gift for unleashing such a catastrophe. Even if he cannot cajole Cthaal into laying waste to the human world, at least he will have succeeded in reducing Our Fiery Home to rubble. Either way, he will have his vengeance on a place that deserves to meet its end.

An odd sensation pulls Lubos from his reverie. The ground trembles beneath his hooves. His ears home in on a distant grumbling, a murmur distinct from the high-pitched squeals of his people succumbing to the barbs and beak of his irascible new pet.

With a deafening roar, the outer wall to the Hall of Ignoble and Prodigious Elders splinters. A curtain of rock cascades to the cavern floor. With a second boom, the wall crumbles. Massive boulders topple, crushing everything in their path. As the dust clears, Lubos sees the silhouette of a massive bipedal figure. Its yellow-white flesh seems to glow. With outstretched arms, the figure unleashes a roar that loosens Lubos's bowels.

The legends are true: The Eternal One has awoken. Lucifer has returned to reclaim his throne.

Lucifer wags his head from side to side, as if struggling to choose a path. As the Eternal One clops away, another figure, though much smaller by comparison, steps into the void.

*Impossible.*

Basil steps across the shards of collapsed boulders. His

wounds healed, he looks strong, capable, whole. The gash in his forehead has scabbed over.

Lubos scours the earth for his ax. His weapon of choice nowhere in sight, he bends to retrieve a sturdy spear. He sneers as he slips into the cover of shadow, seeking a route to higher ground.

* * *

Warm blood slicks the cavern floor. Motionless bodies and severed limbs make for gory litter. The carnage reminds Basil of the turmoil that led to his crowning so long ago, the revolution that ended when Basil struck down his predecessor, Byron the Scarred Back.

Though the demons have done their best to flee Cthaal's roving tentacles, dozens appear to have fallen. For now the beast busies itself on the ceiling, making meals of juvenile vampire bats that haven't yet learned to take flight.

Basil watches Lucifer skulk, ape-like, through the cavern. A demon missing its legs drags its torso toward the safety of the shadows, painting the pane of rock black with its blood. The Eternal One stomps the halved demon. Lucifer twists his hoof and grinds the creature—bones and all—into the red rock.

As if a switch has been flipped, the demons stop their flight. A shared knowing, or perhaps a cloud of pheromones, tells them they now have a new enemy. Dozens emerge from the shadowed perimeter to form a ring around Lucifer. The Eternal One drops to a knee and tilts his head toward the floor, as if in submission. The demons pounce. They claw, bite, carve ruts in Lucifer's exposed flesh, tangle their limbs in his stringy hair.

Lucifer's restraint confounds Basil. Then Lucifer rears up and extends every limb, shaking off the demons as if they are flakes of dead skin. One flails from Lucifer's flank, talons lodged deep in the flesh. Lucifer doesn't seem to mind. He takes joy in butchering every demon within reach—playing—and then pursues any demon trying to escape his wrath. His yellowed flesh shines black with blood.

Basil's skin grows hot. His pulse quickens.

"Basil!" a voice booms. "This scourge is Basil's doing!"

He lifts his chin to see Lubos dangling from a ledge by an outstretched arm.

Two troglodytes step in front of Basil. Although huge and heavily built, the troglodytes are dumb and slow, made even slower by thick armor. Basil kicks the first in the groin, and as it drops, he thrusts his talons into the cushion of its throat. The second trog takes a wild swing with a scimitar-like blade. Basil ducks the assault, leaps up and stabs out the trog's eyes. The trog does not acknowledge the injury, just keeps swinging and hoping to land a deathblow. Basil gives the blinded trog a wide berth and waits for his moment. As the trog sinks the blade into rock, Basil scales the trog's back and grasps both of its gnarled horns. With one sharp jerk, he crushes to bits the vertebrae in the trog's neck, and the trog falls violently to the floor.

As the paralyzed trog takes its final breath, Basil raises his head and realizes he is being handed a gift: an unpolluted view of two cataclysms coming together.

Cthaal descends from the ceiling, a twitching vampire bat dangling from its beak. The tentacled beast writhes before Lucifer, who makes a show of licking fresh blood from his thin lips. The kraken shrieks as it slides down the wall, seeming to respect the might of a worthy foe. With the quickness of a viper, Cthaal lashes Lucifer with a tentacle, trailed by a second and a third. Venomous barbs sink into Lucifer's left arm. He howls and drops to a knee, and three other tentacles snake around Lucifer's limbs, hundreds of venom-tipped barbs biting into the buttermilk-tinted flesh. The tentacles yank Lucifer forward and drag him along the ground, then lift him up and use his mass to pulverize a boulder. The kraken repeats the action three more times and, with a triumphant shriek, hurls its foe into the far wall.

Lucifer drops in a heap and lays still. As Cthaal moves closer, Lucifer turns onto his side and dashes toward the beast. He swiftly detaches a tentacle with his fangs and spits out the arm as if bitter. The disembodied limb wriggles away like the body of a decapitated snake. Lucifer grabs two more tentacles, one in each hand, and pulls without mercy. Ink sprays Lucifer's face and chest, floods his mouth. Cthaal's rubbery skin stretches until the tentacles snap.

Basil winces at the rout, having expected more fight from the flagging kraken.

Lucifer sinks his talons into two more of Cthaal's tentacles and whips the mammoth cephalopod over his head, clipping rocky outcroppings, and then bashes its mantle into the cavern floor. Air dribbles from Cthaal's tube-like siphon. The sound reminds Basil of a wet fart.

Lucifer lifts the kraken into a bear hug and squeezes until the mantle seems ready to pop. Inky fluid spills from the pores of its skin, like water from a sponge. Lucifer then hurls the beast toward the field of cauldrons. The kraken's mantle bowls over more than a dozen cauldrons, spilling their bubbling contents. Soft flesh melts against hot metal. Cthaal screeches as it twists its scalded tentacles free.

Basil smiles, his plan playing out—*his* monster getting the better of Lubos's.

An electric pain sizzles inside his head. A warm sensation builds behind his right ear. He suddenly finds himself on his knees, staring at a severed ear—his ear—glowing black against the red rock.

Lubos stands in front of him with spear in hand. Basil's blood drips from the spear's blackened tip.

"This time I'll leave nothing intact," Lubos says.

Basil regains his hooves, shaking the fog from his head. He

snatches the tip of the spear and thrusts a fist into Lubos's face. Lubos sails backward, sliding along a bed of dust and pebbles. Basil twirls the spear and moves in on Lubos, now weaponless. He stabs at the earth, but Lubos rolls out of the way and gets to his hooves. Lubos limps away, his talons teasing the cavern wall, hiding the pale scar that runs the length of his torso.

"Nothing can stop what I've set in motion," Lubos says. "Our Fiery Home has already fallen."

Basil hurls the spear. It catches Lubos in the left shoulder and pins him to the wall. Basil steps forward, ready to tear Lubos apart. He then feels a blade enter his back, just to the right of his spine.

Demons loyal to Lubos rush in to overwhelm him. An immense weight—a troglodyte's three-toed foot—presses him to the floor.

"Let him up," Lubos commands, still pinned to the wall. "One of you wretches, fetch my ax."

The troglodyte drives its foot deeper into the center of Basil's back. Two demons work to free Lubos, breaking the spear off at the shoulder. Another places the ax in Lubos's hand, kneeling and then extending an open palm to receive his earned praise. Lubos knees the demon out of the way.

"I think I'll take your head," Lubos says to Basil. "Bow."

In a blur, a massive object falls from above.

The tentacle mashes the troglodyte into the wall. Basil turns onto his back to see Lucifer dragging the kraken by one of its remaining tentacles—no more than five, whereas its body once sprouted a dozen or more. Lucifer tightens his grip and whirls the kraken over his head, three full rotations, and then hurls the beast toward the ceiling. It smacks into the rock and stays there for just a moment, either because of its suction-cup tentacles or because of the tackiness of the blood leaking from its many wounds. Slowly, the cephalopod peels away from the ceiling and free falls, smacking into the center of the lake of blood.

Waves drench the shoreline. The kraken lingers on the surface for a moment and then sinks into the depths.

Having witnessed his precious kraken defeated, Lubos stands in silent awe, so he seems surprised when the tip of a spear pokes through his belly. He drops to his knees, and behind him stands an unsteady Kamala, holding the other end of the spear. Basil bolts forward and grabs Lubos by the throat.

"Your false reign has met its end," he says.

He places his right hoof on the spear tip and kicks down. The blade tears Lubos, from the belly down through the pelvis. Intestines snake onto the floor. The breath leaves Lubos's lungs. Basil then takes Lubos by each hoof and holds him upside down. He pulls one hoof east, the other west. The flesh along the big white scar rips, a zipper coming undone, until Lubos once again finds his body halved.

His voice strained, Lubos uses his remaining strength to curse Basil's name.

"I promise you a long and painful demise," Lubos utters.

"Some day my heart will beat its last hollow thump," Basil says, "but not at the hands of a callow fool like you."

Basil takes Lubos's head between both hands. He squeezes until bone cracks and the skull collapses. The body goes limp, and dark liquid leaks from the sores of Lubos's eye sockets, now eyeless. His palms slick with blood, Basil drops the body to the floor, where it settles in a pile, like an obscene rug.

Basil feels the floor shake beneath him, and he turns to see Lucifer clopping toward the nursery, the Hardened Womb, where Our Fiery Home's youngest demons and their mothers reside. Lucifer bends toward the opening and reaches inside, seeking easy victims.

"No more," Basil says.

He picks up the spear, takes careful aim and lets the weapon sail. The spear arcs across the cavern and pierces the tender flesh of Lucifer's wrist. The monster yelps and backs away from the nursery. As he studies the new wound, he seems fascinated that something so primitive might have caused such pain. Lucifer brings his wrist to his mouth and yanks the spear free with his teeth, spits it toward the floor. The spear snaps against the red rock.

Lucifer turns toward Basil.

"Reclaim," Lucifer says.

"You have no claim here," Basil says.

Kamala steps behind him. Others fall in line behind her.

"Then I shall start over," Lucifer wheezes.

Lucifer brings his massive claws together and whispers a *Locuri* grammar Basil does not recognize. Vapors of sapphire rise from cracks in the cavern floor and form an electric-blue orb between Lucifer's palms.

Basil feels his skin cool as the temperature drops. He does not know the grammar Lucifer speaks, but he can guess at its destructive power—energy pulled from Earth's core, to be used as a nuclear blast to wipe the slate clean. He must act. He sees an ax nestled in the rigid hand of a fallen demon.

In one fluid motion, he dives for the ax, wrenches it free from the dead demon's grip and hurls the weapon toward Lucifer. The blade strikes the glowing blue orb and turns to metallic dust.

Basil exhales in defeat. He takes a step toward Lucifer.

"This kingdom is ours," he tells the Eternal One.

Lucifer cackles as the orb gains strength, his torso glowing blue. His expression changes abruptly and, for a second, Basil thinks he sees fear in the Eternal One's eyes. A thick black cord snakes around Lucifer's throat and pulls him backward, taking him off his hooves. The glowing blue orb falls to the ground, and its energy disperses, harmlessly, like spilled water.

Lucifer glides backward across the cavern floor, the revitalized kraken dragging him toward the Pool of Infinite Perdition. He fails to grip the tentacle's slimy flesh. Instead, he digs his claws into the hardened earth. There the twin behemoths remain, locked in a standstill—Cthaal at the edge of the lake of blood, its hard-as-steel tentacle straining to hold on to its prize, and Lucifer, strangled and wheezing, the muscles in his arms taut, claws fastened to the rock.

Basil approaches the Eternal One. He eyes the kraken's tentacle, the barbs biting deep into the flesh of Lucifer's throat. An uncommon prickling stirs in Basil's belly. Despite the threat Lucifer poses, despite the horrors this ancient beast has committed, Basil pities the monstrous brute—a god, beaten and deposed, then revived and set free. He feels a sense of profound debt, of thankfulness, for what the Eternal One created far below the surface, and for his role in unseating Lubos.

He wonders, for a moment, if Lucifer can have a place here.

The tentacle tightens around Lucifer's throat.

"You have my gratitude," Basil says.

He eyes a young demon standing near Kamala, a too-heavy ax clutched in its hands. Basil extends his arm and shows an open palm. He utters one word: "Please." The young demon scurries to Basil's side and hands over the ax. Basil nods to the young demon and offers an appreciative smile.

Basil tests the ax's weight as he eyes his target. He then hoists the weapon above his head and brings down the blade. The blade bites through two of the three fingers on Lucifer's left hand on its way to striking rock. Lucifer's eyes bulge. The marred hand loses its hold, and Cthaal does the rest.

Lucifer slides across the pane of rock toward the shoreline, where the rest of Cthaal's hungry tentacles coil around Lucifer's torso, arms and throat. One tentacle blankets his eyes, its barbs blinding him, and pulls him into the sludge of the shallows.

A moment later the two titans disappear beneath the surface.

The lake roils and ripples. Then, after rising bubbles pop in the humid air, the surface goes still.

Basil shifts his weight, trying to excise the adrenaline from his body. His right hoof nudges one of Lucifer's detached fingers. Best to leave no trace, he knows, so no parts of Lucifer can take root and grow into something else. He bends to collect both fingers, each nearly as long as his forearm, and tosses them into the Pool of Infinite Perdition. One of the fingers twitches as it sinks. The rational part of Basil knows it's merely the nerves in their death throes, but the rest of him believes every molecule in Lucifer's body will keep fighting, even though the fight has reached its undeniable end.

Basil feels a soft hand on his right shoulder.

"Welcome home, Basil."

He turns to see Kamala.

A ragtag army surrounds him, the demons warming to their leader, newly reborn.

He embraces Kamala and rests his chin atop her scabbed head.

"I beg your forgiveness," he tells her.

"I've missed you, believe it or not," she says. "I'm glad for your return."

"I will be better. *We* will be better, from now until eternity."

"The walls still stand," she adds. "Everything else we can rebuild."

They have nothing else to say, so they survey the carnage in silence, the quiet broken only by the faint crackle and hiss of so many bodies smoldering in the fire.

## Chapter 37

# Redemption in the Dreamless Sleep

The modest horde gathers at the access to Basil's chamber. The young demons fail in their attempts at stealth, as Basil, supine on the slab, lifts an eyelid. He could stop this nonsense before it goes any further, but he pretends the ruckus has not disturbed his sleep. He will let the children have their fun.

*"Poor old King Basil, sleepless on his bed,"* they sing. *"Toothless King Basil, curse his ugly head."*

Basil roars as he chases the juvenile demons from the chamber lobby. They halt their teasing and scurry off, laughing from the safety of the shadows, singing the same tune as they scatter.

He's happy to hear the laughter of youth, to see the most vulnerable of his people playing in the open. The constant threat of death in Our Fiery Home has vanished.

*Basil the Toothless*, he considers. When his life reaches its end and his people choose a sobriquet to commemorate their fallen king, Basil the Toothless would be just fine with him.

He stretches the sleep from his body. He scans the walls, scrawled with lines from newly borne poems. He settles on a short poem he once loved, taking in every word of every line.

*The villains come to plunder*
*The innocent come to bruise and bleed*
*The beautiful souls come to be set free*

The words somehow feel different on his tongue. Part of him wishes to paint over these words and replace them with new ones, but they serve a purpose: to remind him of a once vile place he abandoned and then remade. He decides to keep the lines in place, though he adds three more beneath the last.

*Should their hearts find calm*
*Amid ash and war and the crack of broken bone*
*Let them find redemption in the warmth of the fire*

There's no way for him to know how much time has passed since his return—six months, a year, perhaps longer. Regardless of the number of Earth days that have ticked by, a new era has dawned in Our Fiery Home. With Lubos gone, and with Kamala's vision of peace having taken hold, the underworld remains tranquil, more or less. He can recall no killings in recent memory—none pointless or undeserved, anyway.

Almost as if to spark memories of his tribulations, Boothe appears at Basil's hooves. The imp looks tired, its skin scuffed and scabbed. Boothe bears a package of human origin: something rectangular wrapped in brown paper, the edges seared.

"Bring it here, little one," Basil says.

Boothe skirts the perimeter, hesitant to part with its prize.

"What have you brought me?"

Boothe zigzags toward Basil and then holds up the package for Basil to take, but the imp won't relinquish. Basil gives a firm tug and lifts the imp off the ground. He holds his open palm beneath the imp's feet. The imp relaxes its grip and falls into Basil's palm, then skitters off to find some other way to be useful. It crouches in the corner and defecates noisily, and then darts away like a frightened cat. Intestinal fumes linger.

"Thank you kindly, little one," Basil says to the empty chamber.

Basil considers the new covenant he formed with Boothe, shortly after the demise of Lubos and the disappearance of Lucifer: to serve as Basil's link between worlds, above and below. For Boothe's first mission, the imp would return to the surface with a note of thanks etched into a slab, to be delivered to his friend, Herbert Teak. Although Boothe had been gone for what seemed an age, the resourceful imp succeeded in its quest.

Basil drags a talon across the corner of the package's brown paper and gingerly peels back the lacerated edge. He finds a cherry-wood plaque beneath, so he abandons any restraint. Tatters soon litter the floor of his chamber. The plaque bears a logo for something called the Midwest Advertising Impact Association. Five uneven lines of copy beneath the logo read: "'Devil Smoke' by Teak Demon Communications, Chicago, winner of the 1998 Gold Award for Most Impactful Print Campaign – Consumer."

A postcard flutters to the floor. As Basil bends to retrieve the card, he recognizes Herbert's familiar scrawl. Herbert's note explains his move to Chicago, where he founded his own advertising and public-relations agency, taking with him a handful of paying clients poached from the now-defunct Savage Communications. He thanks Basil for his work on Devil Smoke— and, again, for saving his hide more than once. He says he hopes to see his old friend again someday, jokes about how difficult it is to find a good copywriter. And, he writes on the last line, he's seeing someone.

The note does not mention Herbert's ailing father or Melody K. Mulroney, Esquire.

The sound of hooves against loose rock pulls Basil away. He looks up to see Kamala lurking in the doorway.

"What do you have there?" she asks.

Instinct compels him to conceal the plaque, which he holds behind his back.

"Doesn't anyone knock?" he says. "No one knocks."

"Perhaps if you had a suitable door," she replies. "Listen: The exploration team is just about ready to set off. I thought you'd like to come along, at least for part of the way."

"I'm sure you have everything under control, my dear," he tells her. "It's your vision, after all—'Expand out and not up,' you said. Our people should see you out front. Besides, I have work of my own to do here."

Everything must be written down—the history of Our Fiery Home, as he sees it, as much as he can remember, or at least as much as he can piece together. The prohibition on the past has reached its end. With the deaths of the Elders so much of Our Fiery Home's history has been lost, so he considers it his burden to explain all that has happened, from the kingdom's beginnings, when Lucifer carved a path toward Earth's core, to the triumphs and tragedies of each of the seven successors, to Lucifer's return and supposed demise in the bloody depths of the Pool of Infinite Perdition. Basil will line his walls with these stories, among others, for the enlightenment, horror and entertainment of his people—his peers.

"I shall return only when I have suitable news to share," Kamala says. "You'll manage without me?"

"Of course. Be careful."

She smiles and backs away from the entrance, leaving him alone in his chamber.

Basil waits a moment, anticipating further interruption. When none comes, he returns his attention to the plaque—the award that he and Herbert earned, or, better put, the award Herbert earned with a little help from Basil's pen. He admires the plaque's glossy surface, how it catches the firelight. He steps toward the wall and places the award on an outcropping at eye level. He backs up a pace, then another, to study the shiny black face. He's done it. He's made his mark on the world.

More importantly, his friend has found his way.

A wave of sadness dulls Basil's mood, so he tries to lighten his grief by envisioning Herbert sitting by a sunlit window, massive computer on his desk, the picture of a smiling couple framed on an unused sliver of space next to his telephone. Basil knows his time in Herbert's life has concluded. Each will die without seeing the other's face again, except in memory.

Heaviness builds in the center of Basil's barrel chest. A sigh parts his lips. To stem his loneliness, he beckons his newfound companion.

"Harmony," he calls.

In reply, something stirs.

The bipedal creature, seemingly feminine, emerges from the shadows. She stands before him, swaying. She does not utter a word, because she cannot.

He has only himself to blame.

Not long ago, he used a *Locuri* grammar to animate this creature—this golem—her body shaped from ash, the maggot of a dung beetle and a drop of his own blood. He did his best to make her resemble Melody Mulroney, and the golem does bear a slight resemblance in terms of body shape, but she's poor company. All she does is shamble about and follow him around like a brainless puppy. She cannot disagree, cannot challenge him and certainly cannot inform his view of the world.

Prior to his time on the surface, Harmony's silence would have pleased him. Now, her shortcomings serve only to remind him of her flesh-and-blood better, Melody.

He decides his memories of Melody are more than enough.

"Come to me, Harmony," he mutters. His voice cracks.

She stumbles toward him in short, jerky steps. Her right foot trips over air, and she falls on her face. As she gets up, he sees the damage from the impact of the fall, her nose flattened, absent. She feels no pain, he knows, but he cannot help but pity her. He takes her ashen chin between his thumb and index finger.

"It's time," he tells her. "Thank you for your companionship."

He whispers the *Locuri* grammar for disintegration, and she collapses into a column of ash and slag.

He pokes through the ash pile with the tip of his hoof, just to make sure. Rather than try to distract himself with remembrances of the things he has let go, he will focus on maintaining peace in Our Fiery Home, on promoting civilization and, per Kamala's vision, on broadening his kingdom's loose borders. He recalls the recent exchange with Kamala, who now shares his duties as ruler.

"We can expand, not to the surface but beyond our walls," she told him. "The promise of a wider kingdom is all around us, far beneath the crust. We can branch out, build down, toward the core. We can carve new tunnels and have more room to rove."

"Then let it be so," he said in assent.

Another decision: Every newborn demon shall receive a name—liberty as a birthright. Every demon will have the freedom to explore, to do as Basil once did, if he or she wishes. But their first priority is to fortify, to improve upon the world in which they belong. Any demons already on the surface can stay there, as additions to humankind's ever-growing list of problems to solve.

Although he knows he has seen the last of Melody, Herbert and Chester—his humans—he will permit his mind to return to them and the moments they shared. His spare minutes will pass foolishly, fondly, imagining how to import the wonders of wind and moving water and the feathery branches of willow trees, even though the realist in him knows he cannot recreate any of those miracles here, so far from the fertile crust. No, he can never go back. If he did, he would find a changed world, and changed people, so there would be no point in attempting to duplicate the experience. He can only abide, savor the small joys each moment brings.

Although remade, Our Fiery Home has its troubles. An eyeless corpse appears every now and then, and no one seems to have a clue of its origin. Sometimes a shrill scream disturbs his sleep, and when he goes to investigate he finds only remnants of wrongdoing: a detached hand, a few droplets of blood, luminous pearls of spilled demon seed.

"Baby steps," he tells himself.

If Shakespeare words of "what's past is prologue" hold any truth, he knows everything could come undone all too easily. His gaze often wanders to the Pool of Infinite Perdition. The surface has remained still since the kraken's barbed tentacles dragged Lucifer into the fathoms. He imagines Cthaal recessed into a tube-like cave, tentacles reaching into the darkness and plucking a slab of buttermilk flesh from Lucifer's lifeless body. Unlikely, he figures. He half-expects to wake one day and see the Eternal One lumber ashore, eager to murder any demon standing in his path. But Basil doesn't linger on the thought. If Lucifer does gain the strength to return, then Basil will react.

But until then …

As he runs his fingers along the smooth edges of the fissure creasing his forehead, Basil ponders the minutiae of his long, strange trip to Beak and back. He feels rested, the result of the stretches of deep sleep he now feels safe enough to take. He no longer worries of assassins lurking outside his doorway. He no longer imagines the teeth of a hot blade against his throat. And he no longer dreams of the human named Emmitt Wells and the struggle to make a life in a cold, hard part of the world that did its best to swallow him and spit out his acid-bleached bones.

Or, if he does dream of such things, he no longer remembers.

Maybe his good friend Chester had tapped into something profound that late August night on Basil's patio as the three of them—Chester, Herbert and Basil—chatted beneath a sky abloom with stars after a bacchanalia of pork ribs, whiskey and beer. Maybe, as Chester drunkenly hypothesized, Basil had in fact once walked the earth as a human, a luckless Englishman, and after his mortal death been reborn as a demon, as penance for his theft and his adultery, his pride and his rage—all the horrible acts he committed in his foolish quest to tame an untamable London. And maybe, just *maybe*, the slate was wiped clean after Lubos's ax opened Basil's skull and stopped his heart.

Implausible? Certainly. Unlikely? Absolutely. But given the absurdity of Basil's adventures, nothing seems impossible anymore. He trusts his gut.

*So,* he thinks, *this is Hell.*

"Maybe so," the voice tells him, "but that doesn't mean you can't enjoy it."

# Acknowledgments

I likely would not have finished (or perhaps even started) this novel without the support and encouragement of several people: Donna Schoener Donahue, my wife, partner and best friend, for thoughtful critiques of early drafts and too many other things to adequately mention here; Don Swaim and the past and present members of the esteemed Bucks County Writers Workshop (Lindsey Allingham, Candace Barrett, Chris Bauer, Beverly Black, Kevin Callaghan, Bob Cohen, Daniel Dorian, Natalie Zellat Dyen, Tracy Grammer, Cathy Hilliard, Martha Holland, Jim Kempner, Wil Kirk, Kevin Knabe, George MacMillan, Fran Nadel, Jacqueline Nash, Bill O'Toole, John Schoffstall, Alan Shils, David Updike, Sharyl Volpe and John Wirebach); Gregory Pas Jr., for introducing me to Nebraska's charms; and Krystina Kellingley of Cosmic Egg Books, for her thoughtful treatment of the manuscript. Each of these individuals has my sincerest gratitude.

I'm also indebted to the nonhumans in my life—Marbles, Crash and Baxter—for providing the best possible kind of disruption when I was trying to write or edit pages.

# About the Author

William J. Donahue's earliest career aspirations included, in order, a Catholic priest, an American ninja, a professional wrestler, a horror-punk icon and a goon for a minor-league ice hockey team. Although he failed miserably in each of these pursuits, the experience he gained in the process provided ample material for his fiction.

In addition to *Burn, Beautiful Soul*, Donahue has authored three short-story collections: *Too Much Poison*, *Filthy Beast* and *Brain Cradle*, one of which (*Filthy Beast*) was a finalist for *Foreword Magazine*'s Book of the Year Award.

When he's not writing fiction, entertaining his cats or wandering quietly in the woods, Donahue works as a magazine editor and features writer. His writing and on-camera reporting have earned multiple regional and national awards for excellence in business journalism. He currently oversees three monthly lifestyle publications serving the Greater Philadelphia Area, and he is also on the editorial staff of a literary journal focused on the remarkable people, places and history of Bucks County, Pa.

He lives in a small but well-guarded fortress somewhere on the map between Philadelphia and Bethlehem, Pa. There's no moat, but it has plenty of snakes.

# FANTASY, SCI-FI, HORROR & PARANORMAL

If you prefer to spend your nights with Vampires and Werewolves rather than the mundane then we publish the books for you. If your preference is for Dragons and Faeries or Angels and Demons – we should be your first stop. Perhaps your perfect partner has artificial skin or comes from another planet – step right this way. If your passion is Fantasy (including magical realism and spiritual fantasy), Metaphysical Cosmology, Horror or Science Fiction (including Steampunk), Cosmic Egg books will feed your hunger. Our curiosity shop contains treasures you will enjoy unearthing. If you have enjoyed this book, why not tell other readers by posting a review on your preferred book site.

# Recent bestsellers from Cosmic Egg Books are:

## The Zombie Rule Book
A Zombie Apocalypse Survival Guide
Tony Newton
The book the living-dead don't want you to have!
Paperback: 978-1-78279-334-2 ebook: 978-1-78279-333-5

## Cryptogram
Because the Past is Never Past
Michael Tobert
Welcome to the dystopian world of 2050, where three lovers are
haunted by echoes from eight-hundred years ago.
Paperback: 978-1-78279-681-7 ebook: 978-1-78279-680-0

## Purefinder
Ben Gwalchmai
London, 1858. A child is dead; a man is blamed and dragged
through hell in this Dantean tale of loss, mystery and fraternity.
Paperback: 978-1-78279-098-3 ebook: 978-1-78279-097-6

## 600ppm
A Novel of Climate Change
Clarke W. Owens
Nature is collapsing. The government doesn't want you to know
why. Welcome to 2051 and 600ppm.
Paperback: 978-1-78279-992-4 ebook: 978-1-78279-993-1

## Creations
William Mitchell
Earth 2040 is on the brink of disaster. Can Max Lowrie stop the
self-replicating machines before it's too late?
Paperback: 978-1-78279-186-7 ebook: 978-1-78279-161-4

**The Gawain Legacy**
Jon Mackley
If you try to control every secret, secrets may end up controlling
you.
Paperback: 978-1-78279-485-1 ebook: 978-1-78279-484-4


Readers of ebooks can buy or view any of these bestsellers by
clicking on the live link in the title. Most titles are published
in paperback and as an ebook. Paperbacks are available in
traditional bookshops. Both print and ebook formats are
available online.
Find more titles and sign up to our readers' newsletter at
http://www.johnhuntpublishing.com/fiction
Follow us on Facebook at https://www.facebook.com/JHPfiction
and Twitter at https://twitter.com/JHPFiction